Flawed Hearts

Celeste Night

Playlist

Some songs that inspired me while I was working on this book!

Today - Smashing Pumpkins
Lifestyles of the Rich & Famous - Good Charlotte
Love-Hate-Sex-Pain – Godsmack
Lovesong – Snake River Conspiracy
Brand New Numb – Motionless In White
like u – Rosenfeld
I Can't Decide - Scissor Sisters
Mount Everest – Labrinth
Cemeterysexxx – Doyle
Hurt Me Harder – Zolita
Venom – Eminem
Words As Weapons – Seether

To all of the people that thought the guys in my books were too nice. This one is for you.

I have learned things in the dark that I could never have learned in the light, things that have saved my life over and over again, so that there is really only one logical conclusion. I need darkness as much as I need light. - Barbara Brown Taylor

Author's Note

If you have read any of my previous books before, I need to make a note. This is NOT like those. This is a dark college bully romance, emphasis on bullying. The guys are not nice guys, even to our FMC.

I would put in my typical disclaimer of if you are my family don't read it, but that hasn't worked in the past. I will never be able to make eye contact with you at family dinner again. *It's fine.*

A fictional experimental drug is contained within these pages. The term tea and tease will be used interchangeably for its name.

This is an MMFM why choose romance, meaning that our leading lady will have multiple love interests and will not choose between them. There is a cliffhanger at the end of this book. I promise that there is a happily ever after at the end of the series. Trust the process. For warnings about what this material contains, please visit my website, www.celestenight.com.

Character Guide

Welcome to Clearhaven

Ivy Spencer – Our Main Character

The Forsaken

Vincent – Boss

Angel - Underboss

Rhyker – Enforcer

Camden Barrett

Nikolai Stone

Trey Harrison

The Order of The Exalted

Fletcher Vance

???

Other Notables:

Rosalyn Jensen – Ivy's BFF

Thomas Spencer - Ivy's Father

Abraham Wells - Dean of the local college

Caleb Vance – Fletcher's Grandson

Luthor – Caleb's Cousin

Arabella – Caleb's Cousin

Violet and Emmaline - Arabella's Friends

Prologue

The burn of the alcohol sliding down my throat made me wince as I watched the ripples glide across the top of the water. A cool breeze caressed my skin as I deeply inhaled, the scent of muddy lake water invading my nostrils. My toes dug into the cool silt of the shoreline and I allowed my mind to wander, moonlight reflecting off of the crystalline surface.

Music drifted down the hill from the house that belonged to someone's grandfather. It was where all the people I once called friends were hanging out, no doubt laughing or dancing. Couples would be sneaking off into corners to lose themselves in each other, fueled by hormones and liquor.

And here I was, sitting by myself. When I slipped away earlier, no one noticed, or even gave a fuck.

This was supposed to be a celebration, the first party marking not only the beginning of summer but also our transition between high school and college. I just couldn't find it inside myself to get excited. After the events of the past month, all that existed was a deep-seated sense of numbness.

First, there were the nightmares that had been plaguing me. Phantom images of men surrounding me, touching my body and ripping at my clothes. The dreams were fuzzy around the edges and didn't quite make sense. I could never recognize who tormented me, but it was all too familiar.

Before the sun rose every morning, I woke up screaming with sweat covering my skin and my body shaking, wondering what in the hell that was about. It had been happening for months on end, and there was no reprieve in sight. No matter how much I drank or how high I got, there was no relief from the terror. When I asked my father, he simply shrugged it off and told me he was sure it was something my brain had conjured up. "Lay off the horror movies late at night, Ivy."

That was when my father was still around to talk to. Less than a month later, my world came crashing down around me after a simple knock at the door. Our housekeeper Maggie answered and was met with federal agents who swarmed the house with a warrant.

"Mr. Spencer, we need you to come with us. If you could place your hands behind your back," a dark-haired officer calmly told him as he pulled cuffs from his waist.

I watched in shock as my father silently complied with his requests. At some point, I'd fallen to my knees, and the men milling around in the foyer looked at me with sympathy. Maggie, the closest thing I'd ever known to a mother figure, pulled on my arm to get me to stand and pressed a cold bottle of water into my hands. "Get yourself together," she commanded. "He has one of the best legal teams in the state. I don't know what this is about, but he'll post bail by tomorrow. Mark my words."

And after that, I stood by unmoving as my entire house was trashed by men I'd never met who unceremoniously deposited my father into the back of a black SUV. Initially, my reaction was that there was no way my father was guilty of the crimes the government had charged him with. Sex trafficking? After all, this was the man who raised me. Surely I would know if he had done something wrong. I'd been his biggest defender for a few weeks, proclaiming his innocence to anyone who would listen.

Then the evidence was leaked to the press. There was no more denying the charges. The lingering glances painted with disgust and hushed words were too much to take. The last few weeks of my senior year were miserable.

My father's lawyer called me shortly after that to tell me the government would seek to seize assets and that included my college fund. It was the nail in the coffin and finally, I broke, shattering into a million pieces. Being poor didn't bother me, but losing my future did. Well, that and the fact that Maggie had to find new employment. She was one of the last things I had left.

Everyone that I once counted as my friend avoided me. I was certain that pity was the only reason I'd received an invitation to the party happening less than a hundred yards away.

My head floated and my vision blurred as the alcohol swam through my veins, giving me a sense of relief that nothing else had been able to lately. Heavy footsteps sounded behind me, and I turned my head to look at the person approaching.

Micha and I had gone to school together for as long as I could remember and was one of the few people who would still speak to me in passing. He shifted uncomfortably on his feet, rubbing the back of his neck. "Hey, umm, Ivy." His voice wavered as he faced me. "My dad just called. Someone set fire to your house and…"

Time stopped while I allowed his words to sink in. I hadn't moved out yet. It was one of the things the legal team had bargained for. I was supposed to have until the end of June to find somewhere new to stay. Tipping my cup back, I emptied the rest of the contents before speaking. "How bad is it?"

Hesitantly, he laid a hand on my shoulder. "Nothing's left."

My eyes burned and my throat was tight, almost like it was difficult to breathe. Just count to ten. *Don't let him see you cry. You've cried enough this month.* "Can you take me?" I just needed to see for myself.

He nodded and helped me stand. The world spun a bit as I tried to find my balance, though if it was from the beverages or the news that my childhood home was gone, I wasn't certain. We shuffled to his car, and he opened the door for me, ensuring that I slid inside safely. After I was buckled in, he drove silently, occasionally glancing at me with his mouth pressed into a thin line.

Did the drive take twenty minutes or twenty years? It was too long and yet not long enough to prepare me for the riptide of emotions. Fire trucks still sat on the curb outside of where my home once stood. The place I had lived my entire life was gone, and the only thing that remained were charred boards and smoldering embers. I tried to walk onto the property, but Micha caught me, holding onto me tight around the waist as I struggled against him. Hot tears stained my cheeks and it felt like something was lying on my chest.

That was when I knew nothing would be the same. I just didn't know what would happen next.

Ivy

How the mighty have fallen, I thought as I looked out the car window trying to ignore whatever my aunt was discussing. She was probably saying for the millionth time that she was sorry about everything, and it wasn't my fault. I already knew it wasn't, but I couldn't believe I was such an idiot.

My favorite was when she professed my father's innocence, claiming it was all just a mistake, and soon everything would be cleared up. I'd seen the evidence and knew beyond a shadow of a doubt he was guilty. Even if he wasn't guilty of the charges stacked against him, he needed to pay for the sins he'd committed.

Or maybe she was letting me know yet again that "everything happens for a reason; we've just got to trust God's plan." I rolled my eyes at the absurdity of that statement given the situation. I wasn't raised in the church, but there was no way in hell any deity or cosmic force had planned for any of this to happen. If they did, they weren't someone I wanted to talk to anyway.

I kept my mouth shut, though. My aunt cherished her faith and who was I to dismiss something that brought her comfort? She was the only family I had left, even though I didn't know her well.

The late August heat clung to the car's interior and the air conditioning did nothing to ease it. I rolled the window down a few inches, praying that the wind would be cooler than what was blowing from the dash's vents.

"You know that it's all going to be okay, right?" Regina asked, giving me a worried look from the driver's seat.

I scoffed to myself. She was my father's sister, but we looked nothing alike. She was wiry and thin with heavy makeup coating her face. Somehow her short bleach-blond hair was teased in the front with enough hairspray that the humidity didn't touch it. If I stared really hard, I could tell my father and her shared the same nose, but that was where the resemblance ended.

I had no actual relationship with her. The entire time I was growing up, no one had mentioned her, not even once. Maybe if my mother was around, she would have, but I had no memories of her either.

The only family I'd ever known was my father, little good that had done me. In the course of a summer, I'd lost him, all of my friends, and my home, and now I was moving across the state. Sure, I could have tried to get a job and maybe move in with one of my so-called friends, but after they discovered what my dad had done, I'd been shunned even though I wasn't the guilty one. I guess it was the whole sins of the father thing.

"Yeah, I know it isn't my fault," I mumbled, more to myself than her, clutching the door tightly. "It's just a lot of changes and stuff."

It was better this way, I reminded myself. Moving to Clearhaven from Strathmore meant I got to start over and no one knew who I was or that I was related to Thomas Spencer.

Thoughts of how I ended up here continued to flit through my head and I shoved them down. *Not right now*, I reminded myself. *You can think about everything tonight after you make it through the day.*

We pulled into my aunt's neighborhood, and I stared at the small houses lining the street. It was a far cry from the life I'd grown accustomed to.

Clearhaven was a coastal town of a few thousand people. Most residents worked at either the local steel plant, which was going under, or the paper mill on the outskirts of town. Everyone knew everyone here. It was like a modern-day Mayberry, except they also knew everybody else's business and gossip spread like wildfire. That part didn't bode well for me. No one could ever find out about my past or what had brought me here.

Other than my aunt offering me a place to live, Clearhaven offered me one other advantage. The local college. It was the only good thing my father had ever done: arrange a scholarship that covered all the tuition and fees, even if I had to pay for my textbooks. After my college funds were seized, he contacted one of his friends to see if could help arrange something and Abraham Wells agreed.

I remembered Dean Wells vaguely from the parties that my father threw, but that was the extent of it. Clearhaven University was a far cry from the Ivy League schools I had applied to, but I was still grateful. It was better than nothing, which was what I expected in May.

The plan was to keep my head down, attend classes, and try to find a job. The next four years would fly by and I could get the hell out of here. Maybe get a fresh start somewhere else. Somewhere no one knew who my father was. Somewhere no one knew who I was.

We pulled up in front of a small white shotgun house, and Regina parked the car near the curb. I hesitantly opened the door, knowing that once I stepped out of the vehicle, that was it–the beginning of my new life. It was both exhilarating and nerve-wracking. The clean slate I'd been looking for.

Sweat rolled down my skin from the humidity, and I hoisted my backpack over my shoulder, everything I owned inside of the bag. Exiting the vehicle, I approached the house and ascended the cracked concrete stairs, noting the gray peeling paint. *Home sweet home, I guess.* Regina slid her key into the red front door lock and it swung open.

A warm gust of stale air hit me in the face. Walking into the house felt foreign. Scarred hardwood floors lay under my feet and a worn sofa from a different decade sat in the living room. My aunt hurried away, muttering about turning on the window unit "real quick". I brushed back the tears forming in my eyes as I ambled into the small hallway in front of me and spotted three doorways.

Cautiously, I pushed open one and found a small bath-room. It contained powder pink tile, a matching tub, and a toilet. I raised my eyebrows in shock, unsure of what to think. Prior to this moment, I'd been unaware that pink toilets ever existed.

I closed the wooden door and opened the next one, finding it empty except for a small twin bed sitting near the window. A gray tub with a lid sat at the end of the bed and a threadbare quilt was laid on top with a plaid fleece blanket folded at the foot. An old alarm clock sat on the windowsill.

My old bedroom consisted of dark wood furniture and carpet so plush your toes sank on impact. It was such a drastic departure from the life I'd left behind. One full of parties where you plastered a polite smile on your face, new dresses, fruity cocktails, powerful men with wandering hands, and secrets that you didn't dare utter to anyone else. This would be safer.

"I'm glad you found your room," my aunt stated happily behind me. "Remember, we can paint it any way you decide."

I gave her a small nod despite the tears in my eyes. She really was trying, and we had both been thrust into an unfair situation. "So where do I put clothes?" I asked, completely overwhelmed.

She gave me a pat on the back and gestured toward the gray tub. "Here for right now. We'll find a dresser soon at the thrift store. I know this is a tremendous change for you, but we can make it work." She fidgeted with her fingers, obviously nervous. "I was thinking we should make a trip there before your classes start. You'll need new clothes."

And she wasn't wrong. Earlier this summer, everything that was mine had burned in the fire. Two pairs of jeans, three t-shirts, a nearly empty bank account, and a scholarship were all I had to my name, but I couldn't help but feel guilty. From looking around the house, my aunt didn't have anything either, and I couldn't allow her to purchase my clothing. I would simply have to search for a job.

"I'll leave you to settle in tonight and tomorrow we'll get started. I'm sure you want to rest." The last thing I wanted to do was rest or relax. It just gave me time to think about things better left alone.

Dropping my backpack in the corner, I sat on the bed, mattress squeaking under me, and let the weight of the world crush me as tears streamed down my face. The temperature inside the house was suffocating, but it wasn't as heavy as the emotions churning inside of me. I dug my nails into my palms, focusing on the sting and wishing it were just a little more. The temptation to dig through my backpack for something to dull my feelings was there, but I knew I'd turn up empty-handed. Just one more reason to get a job.

Instead, I closed my eyes and laid back, allowing the sharp bite of pain to ground me while my memories and the heat swallowed me whole. I tried to not think of the night my father was arrested–the night my entire life was turned upside down–or the night that my childhood home had burned to the ground. Just a few short months ago, I'd had it all, riding on the coattails of my father's success–no matter how ill-gotten.

Now all that was left behind was ash.

Ivy

Men wearing three-piece suits sipped bourbon, murmuring in low voices and leering at the young woman strapped to the poker table in front of them. Her facial features were cloudy, but she looked vaguely familiar, like I had seen her before. I tried to get up to help her because I knew what would happen next, but my body refused to cooperate. Trying to move my arms and legs took more strength than I had. I opened my mouth to scream for her to move, but my tongue was caught like it was made of lead. I'd been here before and I was trapped in my skin.

Panic engulfed me and ice flooded my veins as one man stood, skating his fingers along the inner thigh of the woman dressed in her pretty blue cocktail dress. Her mascara ran down her face in black streaks and there was nothing I could do as he unceremoniously lifted the hem of her skirt. I tried to close my eyes, but it was as if they were glued open.

"Just sit back and enjoy, little lamb," a deep voice whispered, his breath making my stomach churn. "Soon it will be your turn. I can't wait to see what you'll look like pinned down and at our mercy."

The woman's panties were ripped from her body, expos-
ing her to everyone in the room, and yet she still lay there
silently. The whispering man's hands brushed along my
arms and fear crept up my spine. I tried to turn my face
to look at him, but I couldn't.

Why couldn't I move? Why couldn't I fucking breathe?

The alarm clock blared from across the room, pulling
me from the nightmare I'd been having. All night, memories of the past blended together with scenarios pulled
from the recesses of my mind, things that could have never possibly happened. Dreams like this had been occurring since the beginning of summer, haunting me every
time I closed my eyes. I would often wake up breathless
and shaking, asking myself what in the fuck was that
about. When I was still partying back home, I chalked
it up to too much alcohol or too many drugs. Silently I
hoped that once I moved here, they would disappear.

I wasn't that lucky.

Shifting on the squeaky bed, I threw my blanket off and
rubbed the sleep from my eyes before stumbling toward
the source of the noise, trying to figure out how to turn
it off. Every muscle in my body ached from tossing and
turning all night long, but I ignored it. I didn't have time
to think about nightmares, crappy mattresses, or the fact
that I felt like a ninety-year-old woman. According to the
bright red numbers, it was already nine and I had a full
day of job hunting ahead of me.

The house was thankfully cooler this morning, and the
sound of my aunt chattering with someone reverberated
down the hallway. Another quieter voice, slightly lower

but no less enthusiastic, chimed in. Not quite ready to deal with whatever was happening, I stepped into the bathroom to splash cold water on my face and twist my hair into a messy bun on top of my head. Once I'd delayed as long as possible, I finally strolled into the outdated kitchen.

My aunt and someone approximately my age with short brown hair and smoky umber skin were seated around the small round table. The stranger was wearing a blue floral sundress and flip-flops. "Ivy, you're awake! We've received the best news this morning! Truly a blessing."

The other person grimaced a little at my aunt's words and caught my gaze. I plastered a polite smile to my face, one that had been practiced over the years, and replied, "Oh really?" while opening the cabinet near my aunt's ancient coffee maker.

While looking for cups, she rambled on, her entire face lit up with excitement. "Well, I had mentioned during Sunday school last weekend how you were coming to stay with me for a while and how difficult it was going to be trying to balance transportation between the two of us. And Mrs. Jensen told me that her son had a car he wasn't using anymore. It needs a lot of work but…"

My aunt continued filling me in on the details of her discussion, waving her hands in the air for emphasis, while I poured coffee into a mug that said "love is kind." I added sugar and powdered creamer, trying to focus on everything she said. It wasn't exactly high-end coffee, but it would have to do. By this point, her guest looked like she was ready to crawl under the table or escape through one of the curtained windows, but Regina didn't notice. "Mr. Jensen's willing to part with it for a hundred dollars a month! Isn't that great? Then you won't have to worry about riding the bus everywhere!" She folded her hands in her lap and waited for my reply.

I didn't want to seem ungrateful and needed to muster an equal amount of enthusiasm, which with a lack of caffeine, was difficult. This was a big conversation to have first thing in the morning, especially after not sleeping well. The extremely uncomfortable young woman sitting at the table saved me. "Ms. Spencer, give her a chance to wake up first. Can't you see she's half asleep on her feet?" Her voice was deep and sultry, her thick southern accent music to my ears. "Forgive me for speaking out of turn, Ivy, but I know this is a lot this early in the morning. Come sit down and drink your coffee. My name's Rosalyn."

I arched an eyebrow at her, but followed her advice and joined them at the table. "Thank you," I mouthed to her and she gave me a subtle wink.

"Rosalyn is Mr. Jensen's granddaughter and you couldn't find a better friend. She was raised in the church and can help you meet the right kind of people," Regina beamed.

"Now, now, Ms. Spencer. Who are we to say who the right and wrong type of people are? You know, Jesus himself hung out with tax collectors and lepers. If we aren't bringing the good word to everyone, then are we really doing our duty?" Rosalyn shot back with a smile.

My eyebrows had climbed into my hairline by this point and I kept my eyes cast down, hoping to hide my expression. "You've got a good point, dear. I just want to make sure Ivy meets good people." My aunt glanced up at the clock on the wall and was startled. "Oh, the time got away from me. I've got to get ready for work. Now, the two of you behave today. Ivy, Rosalyn's going to show you around town and take you to pick up the car this afternoon." She wrapped her arms around my shoulders. "Be sure to thank Mr. Jensen for me."

"Don't worry, I will."

Once my aunt was out of earshot, Rosalyn shot me a serious look and lowered her voice. "Go throw on some clothes and brush your hair. If I have to spend another minute in this house, I might scream. Don't get me wrong, I love your aunt, but some days she makes me want to steal the communion wine."

I snorted at her as I stood, trying to figure her out. "Yeah, I'm learning she can be a little intense."

After getting dressed in record time, my aunt handed me sixty dollars to spend on clothes at the local thrift shop and for lunch. Gone were the days of eating overpriced salads and shopping at boutiques, which was fine. I was quickly learning that I would take Rosalyn's company over that of my ex-frenemies any day. "So, you and my aunt..." I prodded while sitting in the passenger seat of the gigantic truck she fondly called Black Betty.

Rosalyn grinned at me and pulled a pair of rose-tinted aviators from the dash. "Your aunt's a nice lady. I've known her since before I was born. She goes to church with my whole family down at First Community. I mean, she can get a bit zealous, but she means well. The good news for you is that she thinks I'm a saint, and that's going to work to your advantage."

She turned up the radio, drowning out any attempts at awkward conversation with hip-hop music. I laid my head back against the leather seat and let the bass vibrate through my body as I looked out the window. Soon we pulled into a small parking lot that contained a chain budget store, a grocery store, and the local thrift shop named Mustard Seeds. I jumped out of the truck and brushed the wrinkles from my clothes while I waited on Rosalyn.

She pushed her sunglasses to the top of her head and gave me a big smile. "Don't be alarmed, but the thrift shop is also run by First Community," she said as she linked arms with me. We drew closer and the small print on the bottom of the banner suddenly made sense. "Just like in the book of Matthew, we're moving mountains!" This town might be the death of me. "You'll get used to it, I promise. Now to find you some clothes," she whispered as we entered the shop, icy air hitting my skin.

I scoured the racks of clothing and Rosalyn held up items she thought would look good on my short, curvy frame, wiggling her eyebrows at a few of the more suggestive tops. Once we hit the dress section, her excitement ratcheted up to an eleven. "You need at least one of these!"

She held up a short black body con dress with cutouts around the midriff and my eyes grew wide. "No! What would I need something like this for? Remember, these are clothes for class," I hissed under my breath. The thought of crawling beneath the rack of clothing occurred to me briefly.

Her hearty chuckle filled the room, and she shook her head. "There is no way I'm letting you leave here without at least one dress for a night out. Did you seriously think I would let you hide in your bedroom every weekend? As your self-appointed best friend, I would be failing."

"Fine." I took the dress from her hands, pondering how in the world I would even fit in the thing, and added it to the top of the pile of clothes in my arms. So far, I had five t-shirts, two pairs of jeans, and one extremely small dress. It nearly doubled my wardrobe and would have to do with the budget I was on. "Hey, after this is there anyway–"

Rosalyn cut me off by waving her hand in the air. "Already taken care of. After this, we're going to lunch–my treat. Later this afternoon we can stop by my grandfather's house to pick up the car. Don't worry so much, girl!"

I paid at the small cash register and thought about how it was good that my newfound, self-proclaimed best friend was paying for lunch considering the clothing total came up to $56.45. Despite being worried over money, and the stark differences between Clearhaven and Strathmore, things were shaping up. So far, no one knew

who I was and shopping, even if it was at a store named
Mustard Seeds, was a break from the chaos of the past
several months.

Camden

Every muscle in my body ached as I stood beneath the lukewarm spray of water in the locker room. Practice this afternoon had been brutal with the midday sun beating down on us. We were getting ready for the first game of the season in two weeks, and Coach was determined to use every moment to torture us.

As I lathered the soap onto my body, I did a mental checklist of what needed to be done this afternoon. The guys were supposed to be waiting for me in the parking lot because our presence was being requested by Vincent at his house on the east side. After that, as long as orders didn't interfere, we were going to grab a bite to eat and hang out. Rinsing off, I tried to focus on letting my muscles relax while I thought about what Vincent wanted. He was the head of the local chapter of the Forsaken and in his eyes, we were nothing. Just three college guys who could push his product or shake down people who owed him.

Turning off the tepid jets, I grabbed my towel and quickly dressed, ready to get things over with. I had more important things to focus on, specifically the party we were throwing on Friday night. Football was great, a way to uncage my inner demons, but I lived for the nights we got together and let loose. It wasn't necessarily about the drinking or the drugs, though those were a plus. It was all about finding a toy to use that night, and women lined up in droves. They'd heard the rumors and knew what was in store for them at our hands.

Just the very thought had my pulse quickening and my cock getting hard, but I ignored it. Business came first, then I could let my monsters out to play.

Exiting the school into the parking lot, sweat immediately formed on my skin again, and I swore under my breath while looking for Trey and Niko. I glanced down at my phone, questioning where in the hell they were. Vincent didn't enjoy being left waiting, and they'd promised that for just once in their lives, they would be on time this afternoon.

Tires squealed and the twenty-five-year-old black Mustang Cobra sped down the empty drag of asphalt with the top down, stopping abruptly next to me. "Get in, loser," Trey yelled over the thrum of the bass from inside the car.

I glared at Niko, who sat in the driver's seat with sunglasses on staring forward, looking completely unbothered. "Why do we never take Trey's car? It actually has a back seat I can fit in comfortably."

Niko shrugged one shoulder, his black shirt straining under his muscles, and didn't bother glancing in my direction. *Fucker.* Trey laughed at me and hitched his thumb toward the tiny backseat. "Just get in. We don't take my car ever because it would break down on the side of the road and you know it." He had a good point, but I would never let him know that. Instead, I grumbled as I folded myself into the car and set my bag next to me.

Niko had spent time and energy completely rebuilding this car. Every weekend for months, he poured all of his sweat and frustration into the project that he now proudly called his baby. Somehow, he'd even scrounged up enough money to get a new paint job and tinted windows.

Trey... He was too busy with other projects. Even though he technically had a car, it needed repairs more often than not. I'd offered to help him, but he waved me off, telling me we both had more important things to worry about.

"If you're so worried about legroom, go buy yourself a car instead of complaining all the time," Niko mumbled as he adjusted the rearview mirror.

I stayed silent and stared up at the sky as we pulled away from the college, knowing he was just looking for a fight. Ever since that night, the two of us had been on rocky ground, but neither of us wanted to bring it up. Choosing to ignore the tension, I let the wind whip around my face while I thought about everything.

Reliable transportation was in my near future, it just hadn't been my main priority yet. Finding a way to leave my house and ensure my sister's safety was. That was what led me to the Forsaken in the first place. It was a way to become financially independent in a town with few opportunities, at least legal ones.

The landscape close to the college slowly fell away. The polished building exteriors and well-manicured lawns slowly morphed into dilapidated houses that had seen better years and sidewalks where dandelions sprouted in the cracks. Old men sat on one of the porches invested in a game of cards, cans of beer scattered around a makeshift table. A toddler in nothing but a diaper roamed inside one of the fenced-in yards, no parents in sight, and I turned my head. This was why so many children turned up missing here; mom was probably too high to even realize the kid had escaped outside.

Niko cut the engine in front of a creamy yellow house with a white awning and grass-green shutters that hadn't been updated since at least the eighties. A rusted chain link fence surrounded the perimeter of the building and cars were parked against the street curb. Guys we'd grown up with stood around the carport, smoking whatever was available and watching two of the neighborhood girls dance with one another. *Home sweet home.*

It was no wonder that we had all fallen for Vincent's speech about how he had an easy way for us to make a little quick cash. Now that I was older, it was easy to see through his bullshit, but when you're a fourteen-year-old kid with nothing? We had thought he was a god among men. There was always food and weed, parties every night, plenty of liquor, and lots of free pussy. In the beginning, he had a way of making us feel special, but as time went on, things changed. Now he was nothing but a means to an end.

I sighed as I unfolded myself from the car and stretched, dreading what he would have us do this time. Last time it was to shake down one of the elderly shop owners near the Strip who refused to continue to pay for his protection. The time before that, it was to threaten a drug dealer who had encroached a little too close to Forsaken territory.

"Let's get this over with. We have plans that have nothing to do with this hellhole," Trey said under his breath as he pushed his glasses up his nose.

Strolling toward the house, Vincent's right-hand man clutched my shoulder roughly, catching my attention. "How's practice going? Are we going to beat Holden next week?" Angel asked as he tipped back his drink.

Angel was probably my favorite one of Vincent's underlings. His calm demeanor made him easy to get along with. It was ironic that despite everything going on, and all the things there were to worry about, he was asking about the opening game of the season.

I gave him a quick smile. "You know we're going to win... as long as Coach doesn't kill us first."

"That's the spirit." He patted my back and let me go. "Be careful with V today. Something has crawled up his ass, and he's been in a bad mood." Great. That was the last thing I wanted to face, but I couldn't help but be thankful for Angel's heads-up. Niko shook his head and turned on his heel, headed for the house with Trey tagging along behind him.

After delaying as long as I could, I finally followed them. As expected, Vincent sat in the living room rapidly typing on his phone while other people hung around on the remaining furniture vying for his attention. Despite our arrival, he acted like we weren't there while he finished whatever conversation he was holding. Niko leaned against the wall, his dark eyes observing the scene unfolding before us, and Trey shoved his hands in his pockets while staring into space. Not nearly as patient as either of them, I pulled one of the chairs in front of him and sat down, crossing my arms over my chest.

Vincent's icy gaze finally lifted, and he paused for a moment like he could see into my soul. If he thought intimidating me would work, he was wrong. After nearly eight years, very little scared me. "Who said you could move my furniture?"

The tension permeating the room ratcheted up to a ten. Vincent wasn't exactly the type of man you messed with and no one dared to cross him, at least on this side of town. I studied him carefully, taking in his platinum blond hair and the scar running down the left side of his face near his eye. Whereas everyone else here dressed like they were headed to the beach or just getting off work at one of the plants, Vincent always looked like he was ready to step into a boardroom. Just another thing that was an illusion.

Trey shifted uncomfortably, messing with the edge of his t-shirt. I gave him a confident smirk and leaned back. "Me, but don't worry. I'll put it back before I leave. I was just getting comfortable waiting to see when you would address your loyal subjects. After all, you asked us to be here ten minutes ago. Something about it being really important and you couldn't trust anyone else."

Vincent's usually serious expression cracked and he let out a chuckle, his eyes crinkling around the corners. "You have some serious balls, Cam. You come into my house, move my furniture, and then act like a little shit. I guess I'll give you a pass today since, as you mentioned, we have something important to talk about. Everyone but you three needs to get the hell out of here. Go have a drink or something."

We waited while people shuffled from the room and Vincent leaned forward, his elbows on his knees. Once we were alone, he finally spoke. "I know I ask a lot of you, but I have a special favor. Someone very important approached me with an experimental drug named tease and I need to offload some of it. It's going to be very lucrative, and I wanted to approach all of you first. I know you could use the money given your personal situations and your positions at the college."

My eyebrows raised slightly. "Experimental drug? What are the side effects?"

Vincent lifted a hand in the air flippantly, dismissing me. "Not your concern. The only thing I need from you is the distribution of the product. Maybe at one of those after-game parties?"

Niko inhaled deeply, the muscle in his jaw flexing from whatever he refused to say, and Trey's nervous movements stopped completely. Both of them were waiting for my reply. "How long do we have before we need to give you an answer?"

Vincent rolled his eyes at me. "Cam, I'm not really asking. Just because I phrased it that way doesn't mean it was a request. Even though this is your last year of college, you're still Forsaken until I say so. Remember your oath. *Blood in and blood out.*"

Niko

Anger simmered beneath my veins the longer Vincent talked. *Blood in and blood out.* Yeah, I remembered every word of that stupid fucking oath we took before our balls had even dropped and how easily he'd persuaded us to take it. He knew the position that each of us was in and how desperate we were to get out of Clearhaven. I flexed my fingers at my side and watched Cam's reaction to Vincent's words.

Cam talked a big game, but the only reason he was mixed up in this shit was Maya. It was the same way that Vincent had trapped me with Katya and Sergei. Trey was an entirely different story. Between the three of us, our parents weren't exactly winning awards. Two were completely absent. One was an addict, one was an alcoholic, another was in prison, and the last one was dead.

"Let's go," I barked. "We have his orders and there's nothing else to discuss."

Vincent's eyes grew wide and the corner of his lips twitched. "So you do speak." He shoved an envelope in my hand. "You know what to do."

I simply pulled my shades from the top of my head and walked out, never bothering to respond. He wasn't worth it. The guys knew my opinion of the entire situation and I had other things to worry about. If he wanted us to sell his drugs, there was nothing I could do to stop him.

In the past, when I'd refused to follow his orders, he'd threatened my father, but when he saw that didn't work, he switched tactics. The day my brother came home from a friend's house telling me that Vincent had visited him, I knew I was cornered. My siblings' lives were more important to me than fighting against the inevitable. If he wanted this new drug to be at every party for the next month and we refused, he'd just use someone else to push them.

I started the car and waited for Trey and Cam to say their goodbyes to everyone, turning up the music playing on the radio as loud as it would go without busting my speakers. I didn't have the money to replace them right now. Rent was due next week and Katya's cheerleading fees were supposed to be paid yesterday.

Was my father remotely worried about any of that? No, he was more concerned about where he was going to get his next fix. The only reason he hadn't tried to sell my car was that the title was in my name. I'd waited until I was eighteen to purchase it for that reason.

I started growing impatient as I watched one of the neighborhood girls lean close to Cam and whisper some-thing in his ear. His hand wrapped around her waist. He could come back by here later tonight without me. I laid on the horn, hoping to get his attention. Trey raced to the car, hopping into the front seat before Cam let go of whoever he was touching and waltzed in our direction.

He jumped into the back, this time not complaining about the amount of space. "You're being extra grumpy today, Niko baby. I think you need to have your dick—"

"Shut your fucking mouth unless you're offering," I interrupted as I pulled away and headed to the Strip, not wanting to hear what he would say next. I wouldn't exactly turn down a blowjob, but what I really needed was a night away from everyone else and a willing participant who shared some of the same interests I did. Friday was thankfully a few short days away—I just had to wait until then.

Trey grinned and put his hand under his chin, eyes darting between the two of us. "Now, boys, I think you need food and then to kiss and makeup. I hate it when Mommy and Daddy fight. What would your mothers say?"

"Well, considering that my mother is dead," I mumbled under my breath, "nothing." Trey and Camden snickered at my words, knowing that dark humor was my way of coping with things.

Turning onto the Strip, I noticed Rosalyn's gigantic black truck parked near Master Pieces, a pizza place that was frequented by students from Clearhaven. Every weekend, live bands played on their back patio and they had the cheapest beer prices in town. I pulled into the spot next to hers.

"Woah, are we really not going to discuss where we're getting food?" Cam asked.

As they got out, I ground my molars together and scanned the skyline noticing some ominous clouds on the horizon. Securing the top of the car into place, I took a deep breath, trying to find a sense of calm. "No, we aren't discussing what we're eating. Whenever I ask, the two of you claim you don't care. Besides," I gestured at Rosalyn's truck, "I need to make sure she's still okay picking Sergei up on Tuesdays from tutoring."

Rosalyn and I had known each other since kindergarten. Hell, we all had. Despite my best efforts at scheduling my classes so that I could be around for both of my siblings, this year hadn't quite panned out as I'd planned. To graduate from high school, my brother desperately needed tutoring in calculus and it was the one subject I wasn't great at.

We strolled into the restaurant and I kept my eyes peeled for Rosalyn, who was sitting at a booth in the back corner. Opposite her was someone with long auburn hair thrown into a messy bun. As I ordered my food, I tried to get a peek at her companion, but from that angle, the only thing I could see was the pale skin covering her neck.

"Who's that with her?" Trey whispered as we paid.

Cam grinned at him, grabbing his cup to fill at the soda fountain. "I have no idea, but how long has it been since someone new moved into town?"

I quietly made my way to the booth and sat beside Rosalyn. Camden slid in beside the new girl, essentially caging her in, and Trey pulled a chair up to the end of the booth from a nearby table. Rosalyn ignored us, continuing to chew her food as I gave the new girl a once-over.

Her skin was the color of porcelain, and a smattering of freckles accentuated her nose. Before I could begin fantasizing about what she would look like at my mercy, with scuffed knees and covered in bite marks, her jade eyes met mine. I shifted in my seat, my breath catching in my throat. She was stunning, and I was curious about what her body looked like beneath the baggy shirt hiding her curves.

Rosalyn cleared her throat and glared at me. "Don't get any ideas. Ivy doesn't need the trouble the three of you bring."

Trey feigned innocence and held his hand to his chest. "Us? What kind of trouble would we start?"

Cam wrapped his arm over the object of my attention and a pang of jealousy ran through me, though whether it was for the girl or him, I wasn't sure. Definitely the girl. "Ros, you know she's in excellent hands with us. We wouldn't let anything happen to her."

"Mm hmm. You wouldn't let anyone else hurt her, but I know how y'all work and so does everyone else in Clearhaven. Ivy, are you ready to go? We still need to pick up your car."

I stood up to let Rosalyn out of the booth. "We're still good for Tuesdays?" I asked in a low voice, the music from the speakers nearly drowning out my question.

She gave me a small nod. "You know I've always got you. Now these other two..."

The redhead pushed at Cam's body, hoping he'd take the hint. Instead, he gave her a smirk. "Ask nicely, and I'll consider moving, or maybe you'll be trapped here while I finish my food."

Ivy puffed out her cheeks and blew a breath upward toward the tendrils of hair that had escaped into her face. "Can you move? Please?"

Cam shoved a bite of pizza into his mouth and stood. When she scooted out of her seat, he caught her by the waist and held her there, leaning close to her ear. "We're having a party Friday night. Rosalyn, make sure she comes with you."

I tapped on my knee under the table. This was definitely not the way to the new girl's heart, or into her panties. From the look of shock on her face, she wasn't used to taking orders from anyone. "Cam–"

Rosalyn shot me a look, and I closed my mouth. "Don't worry, your majesty. We'll be there," she said as she raised one eyebrow at us. "But only because of the free beer."

I hid my face behind a napkin as I watched Cam's jaw drop. After all of these years, he'd never figured out how to take Rosalyn's sass. She was one of the few women at the college that didn't literally fall to her knees over his golden boy façade.

Unfortunately for us, she was going to warn Ivy away from us before we had a chance to play. Rosalyn knew all of our secrets and had heard the rumors. She knew all about the gang, drugs, and what we did after the parties on Friday nights.

Both the women left without a backward glance and for the first time in a while I felt alive. The thrill of the hunt tended to do that.

Later that night, my phone buzzed in my pocket and I pulled it out to see who would text me at that time of the night. All the kids were in bed and Cam was chilling on the couch next to me. Neither of us was in the mood to talk or really do anything else.

Arabella: I need a hit.

Me: Sucks to suck, I guess.

Arabella: Please. I'll pay double. Plus, I can give you what you want.

Me: And what would that be?

Me: Nevermind. Don't answer that and I'll let you surprise me. I'll be there in fifteen.

I didn't know why she was so obsessed with the guys and me. She'd wasted the night that I'd chosen her, running out of the room in tears as soon as Trey pulled out his knife after Cam put her on her knees. Her grandfather would drop dead if he knew that his perfect grandchild who came from a perfect home wanted to be used by three "thugs," as he'd called us.

I sighed and grabbed my keys just as Cam caught my wrist. "Where are you going?"

His gaze was dark and flames danced under my skin at his touch, but I shrugged at him. "Just need to deliver something. I'll be back soon."

He looked down at where his hand gripped my arm and then dropped it before running a hand through his sandy colored hair. "Want me to go with you? I can pay for a six-pack on the way back?"

He chewed on his bottom lip, and I turned away from him. "Nah. It shouldn't take long. I'll pick up some for us for later."

He said nothing as I exited the house, not looking over my shoulder. I needed to escape for a little while and clear my head. I needed to get away from him and chase away some of the demons that were crawling in my chest. The last thing I wanted to be was bound by some of Cam's ridiculous rules tonight, especially after hearing that we were pushing some new shit from Vincent.

I didn't really want to see Arabella, but I needed the money. Using her mouth would just be a bonus and if it was stuffed full of cock, then she wouldn't be able to talk. I could put all the lip fillers that her grandfather paid for to good use. As long as I didn't touch her pussy, Cam wouldn't say a word and what he didn't know wouldn't hurt him.

The ride to the other side of Clearhaven wasn't long enough as I watched the run-down houses give way and poverty fade. The divide between the rich and the poor was stark. I pulled up in front of her house—well, it was closer to a mansion—noting that no one else was home.

I'd been here before, usually to sell drugs to the rich kids that wanted a fix, but every time it astounded me. The sheer size combined with the fact it had a private beachfront screamed wealth, power, and decadence—things that I wasn't used to. At home, I was just happy if Katya wasn't hogging the bathroom in the morning to do her makeup.

Shoving some weed, coke, and the new shit in my pockets, I strolled through the yard slowly. Before I even made it down the walkway, the door swung open and Arabella leaned against the frame, giving me what I assumed was supposed to be a seductive look. "I knew you would come through for me, Niko."

Not that Arabella was unattractive–if you liked women who were made of plastic. She had long black hair that hung straight down her back and a perfect hour-glass figure that had been honed by hours in a gym and underneath a surgeon's scalpel. Yet as she stood in front of me wearing nothing but a tiny bikini top that threatened to expose her nipples and bottoms that were a size too small, I felt nothing.

I managed to smirk at her. "Yeah, and I brought some new product to try."

She reached out and grabbed my hand, leading me inside. I didn't bother looking around at the art hanging on the walls or the crystal chandeliers that adorned the ceiling while she dragged me through the space to exterior doors that overlooked the ocean. On the small patio sat a cafe table with two tumblers and a bottle of whiskey that cost more than my rent. She poured two fingers into each glass and offered me one. "So tell me more about the new product."

"I don't know. I got it this afternoon." Pulling out the contents of my pockets, I watched as her eyes lit up with excitement. She picked up the small baggie that contained the experimental drug and ran her tongue over her bottom lip. I took a small sip of the liquid while watching her dump the contents onto the tabletop and sniff some before cleaning her face with the back of her hand.

She picked up her glass and leaned back in her chair, pressing her thighs together. "Fuck, Niko. I need more of whatever that is." I suppressed an eye roll as she arched her back toward me, pushing her breasts together. "The only thing that would make it better would be your cock inside of me."

I wanted a distraction from my life, but wasn't willing to fuck her. Not the way she wanted me to. I tossed back the contents of the glass and poured another two inches into the glass. "That wasn't part of the deal."

Her face fell a little before she dropped to her knees and crawled over to where I was sitting. Her hands traveled up my thighs and unzipped my pants. "Oh, Niko. Why did you show up then? You must be stressed out to turn me down. You know I can make you feel good."

I sat unmoving as she wrapped her hand around my cock and pumped. Blood rushed to the area as she moved her hand up and down over the row of barbells. I drank more of the whiskey while I closed my eyes, envisioning that it was someone else. The grip would be stronger and more calloused as ocean blue eyes peered up with me, begging me to return the favor. I thrust my hips upward into the hand covering my cock.

And then a whiny voice pulled me from my fantasy. "I've never been with a guy with piercings before. I read an article about Jacob's—"

I cut off whatever she was going to say by fisting a handful of her and forcing myself into her mouth. If she really wanted to make me feel good, then she would shut the hell up. "Less talk, Arabella. If you're so desperate for my dick, then suck it like the slut you are."

She moaned as I moved her head up and down my length, her hand disappearing inside her bathing suit bottoms. I closed my eyes, trying to get back into the fantasy that I had conjured moments ago, and zoned out her slurping noises. I tangled my fingers further into her hair, trying to imagine that it was someone else's tongue swirling around the head of my cock. Another moan slipped out of Arabella's mouth and I pushed her head further down so that her nose was flush with my skin. She gagged, but that was fine by me as I imagined the scent of the ocean enveloping me and larger hands tugging at my balls. I pistoned my hips against her face, wishing that she would suck harder or graze her teeth against me. *God, even her throat was loose.*

Every noise she made set me back further from coming, but finally I could feel a tingle near my spine. I clenched her hair in my fist and held her down, not giving her a warning. She sputtered and choked as I pulled her off. Cum spilled from the sides of her bruised lips and her eyes were glassy.

Tucking myself away, I zipped my pants. "I need to get the fuck out of here." I didn't make eye contact with the girl who was still on her knees, choosing to hold my hand out. "You know the deal, Arabella."

She sighed and reached into her bathing suit top, pulling out a wad of cash and slapping it into my palm. "You don't want to hang out longer or go for a swim?"

I narrowed my eyes and turned my head to her, sneering. "Why the fuck would I do that?"

Her face turned red, and she brushed through her mussed up hair with her hands. "You're an asshole, Niko."

I didn't respond to her as I left and headed to my car. I was an asshole.

The worst blowjob in the history of blowjobs didn't result in taking my mind off of anything. In fact, it only aggravated me further. The one person I was trying to forget about was who I ended up coming to.

Rosalyn stayed silent as we left the restaurant, unlocking her car without a word and leaving me to think of the three men who invited themselves to sit at the table in front of us. In one word, they were intense. Gorgeous with dark eyes that seemed to dissect my every thought. The only person whose name I had managed to catch was Cam, the one with tattoos that peaked out of his collar. Who had wrapped his large hands around my waist, holding me in place and stealing my breath.

It was unexpected. Part of me wanted to bask in his warmth and the hard muscles pressing at my back. The rational part of me screamed I should run and hide. Something about the way he looked at me was unsettling.

The way all three of them had.

"So, who were they?" I broached as Rosalyn pulled into a small neighborhood near the Strip. The area was nice with small colorful houses that dotted the street. Somehow, the plants that lined the yards flourished rather than withered despite the heat.

Rosalyn's lips curled up with amusement. "Those three? Well, it seems like you're acquainted with Camden now. Trey is the one with glasses, and the one whispering in my ear was Niko. I see the stars in your eyes from here and don't get me wrong, those three are fine as hell, but don't think that any of them are relationship material. I wasn't joking when I said that they are trouble with a capital T." That was fine because I wasn't looking for a relationship with anyone right now, much less men who looked at me like they already owned me or could see into my soul.

She slowed the truck and parked in front of the most adorable coral cottage I'd ever seen with bushes blooming bright pink and ferns hanging from the front porch. All the houses where I was from were painted in "respectable colors" like white or beige, and all the shrubberies were well-tended evergreens. This neighborhood was unexpected, but I loved it.

I unbuckled my seat belt and followed behind her to the front door, but her words piqued my interest. "What makes them trouble? Just so I have a clear understanding of why I should avoid them."

She quirked her lips and a small laugh slipped out. She held up a finger. "Well, for one, they're members of the Forsaken. Your aunt would have a field day with that. And two," a second finger joined her first, "let's just say the tales of their sexcapades are legendary and they have very specific tastes."

Curiosity bubbled up inside of me at her words and my cheeks flushed as the thought of Cam pressed against me fluttered through my brain. "Such as?" She cut me off with a look as she knocked on the door, plastering a grin on her face.

An older man with short silver hair and pale skin opened the door. "Well, I was wondering when you would get here, Ros. How's my favorite granddaughter doing today?" he asked as he wrapped her in a tight hug.

"Good now that I'm here. This is Ivy, Regina's niece she told you about. We came to see the car," she said as she squeezed him back.

He let her go, and his face lit up with recognition. "That's right! Ivy, it's great to meet you." He extended his hand, and I took it awkwardly, unsure of what to say. Thankfully, he didn't wait for a response. "Now, I'm sure your aunt told you it's a hundred a month, but don't worry about that. You need to focus on getting a job and starting your classes first."

He moved aside, letting us into the house. The faint scent of old paper filled my nose as I entered. It was a cozy space filled with a leather armchair and a matching loveseat. The walls were covered with bookshelves overflowing with antique hardbacks and my fingers longed to trail along their spines and see what secrets hid inside the pages.

He cleared his throat, drawing my attention back to the present. "Rosalyn's grandmother isn't here right now, or she'd probably be the one to show you. In the afternoons, she meets up with some of the other ladies from town to plan events. The car used to belong to our son Marcus, but these days he doesn't drive."

The carefully painted expression on Rosalyn's face fell for a fraction of a second, but she was quick to fix it. "It's alright, Pops. She's busy, and Ivy doesn't need our entire family history. You know how she can get." She threw in a strained chuckle and straightened her dress.

He patted her back again and then turned on his heel, walking through the house. "Let me grab the keys. It's not a lot to look at, but it will get you from point A to point B. It needs a little bodywork, but I might be able to ask around town."

Filing away Rosalyn's reaction to ask about it later, we followed her grandfather out the back door to a small cinder block garage sitting off an alleyway. He lifted the door and dust flew into the air, the contents of the building obviously not disturbed for a while. We coughed before inching into the dark space. "Sorry about that. I don't spend as much time out here as I once did."

The older man grabbed the corner of the cloth covering the car and yanked it away, uncovering a small red sedan. It was still in good condition, except for the driver's side door which was caved in. He had mentioned that it needed a little work, but what he said didn't exactly prepare me for this moment. It was fine, though. I just needed a car to get to school and work.

Mr. Jensen pressed the key into my palm. "It's a 2003 Honda Civic. It runs pretty well. The automatic locks don't work right, so you'll have to manually unlock the doors and the driver's side won't open. I'll start asking around to see who I know that can help you."

I swallowed the lump in my throat and gave him a small smile to show him gratitude. It was nothing like the BMW that I had my senior year of high school, but none of that mattered. Prior to this morning, I'd resolved to either walk or ride the bus for my freshman year of college. "It's perfect, sir. Thank you so much for everything."

He gave me a small nod of his head and patted my back. "Now, until we can get everything fixed, you'll have to open the passenger side and crawl through, but hopefully that will be short term. The window on that side might not roll down either." If I was a betting person, I'd say it didn't. With the extent of the damage, I would be surprised if it did. "You girls better get going. Ros, carry her by Frankie's place to put in an application. I overheard she needs a cashier."

I wasn't sure who Frankie was, but at this point, it didn't matter. Any job would be welcome. Between textbooks and now a car payment, I would take nearly anything.

Rosalyn gave her grandfather one last hug and glanced at me. "I'll wait for you to start the car, we'll drop it off at your aunt's, and then I'll take you over to Frankie's. You're going to love it."

After unlocking the passenger side door and heaving myself across the bucket seats, I put the key into the ignition and started the car with only a little trouble. Despite the sputtering, I was happy. After I paid the $1000, it was mine. It gave me a small sense of freedom and independence for the first time in a while.

My aunt was gone when I parked the small red car in front of her house and, in some ways, I was grateful. I needed to figure out how to respond to her eternal optimism despite everything feeling so bleak. We hadn't discussed what her hours were at work yet, but that was something I needed to find out sometime soon.

Rosalyn drove us back toward the Strip and continued several minutes down the road until the buildings thinned out. A small turquoise building sat on the left-hand side of the road with several parking spots in front of it. We turned in and I stared for several moments at the mural painted on the side of the building, trying to find the courage to get out of the truck.

Rosalyn threw open my door and placed her hands on her hips. "Come on, let's get this over with. The sooner you have a job, the sooner we get to chill out. As your new self-appointed best friend, we have parties to go to and things to do."

My eyes widened at her words. I wasn't exactly accustomed to having friends anymore. "I wasn't aware you were my friend. I mean, we just met this morning. We're taking things kind of fast, but I'll accept it," I joked as I jumped out of the truck. "I can use all the allies I can get right now. Besides, I guess I don't want the next four years to be boring."

She chuckled at my words and turned to the shop. "Oh, I would never let that happen."

She opened the heavy glass door and strode into the establishment with me directly behind her. Inside was a variety of surfboards, shell necklaces, and swimwear in a kaleidoscope of colors that bombarded my senses. An older woman with purple hair and leathery tan skin sat behind a cash register toward the entrance wearing denim shorts and a tie-dye tank top. She eyed me warily before grinning at my new friend. "Rosalyn, no one told me you were coming in today. How's your grandfather?"

Roslyn gave her a hug. "Actually, he's the one who asked me to come down here. Frankie, she's looking for a job and I heard you need help. Ivy is Ms. Spencer's niece, and she just got into town yesterday."

I didn't know what I had expected from someone named Frankie, but it certainly wasn't a woman my grandmother's age with eggplant-colored hair. The older woman's mouth turned down slightly into a frown. "Well, do you know anything about running a cash register?"

I gave her the most confident smile I could and straightened my shoulders. "No, but I'm a fast learner and I really need a job. I was hoping to find something that would work with my schedule. I'm starting classes next week at the college."

She curtly thrust her hand toward me. "How about we do a trial tomorrow afternoon? Be here around noon and we'll see how well we work together."

I cautiously took her hand, excitement bubbling up inside of me. Was it really that easy? As long as I passed her test, I could be working before the weekend. I would have money to pay for my car note and my books.

Perhaps everything would be okay after all.

Ivy

The rest of the week quickly passed by and thankfully gave me little time to think except at night when I was by myself. Days were filled with working at Frankie's shop and the evening was spent with Rosalyn gossiping, drinking, or both.

I discovered that I really enjoyed working with Frankie. She was foul-mouthed and loud, but everyone that walked into the shop loved her. It didn't matter if they were fifteen or sixty-five. Somehow, I managed to pass her tests with flying colors. How, I still wasn't sure.

On Fridays, the shop closed at six and by the time I was done counting down the register and sweeping the sand from the floor, I was exhausted. I was ready to crawl over the seat of my car and drive home, but fate had other plans.

Rosalyn strolled in wearing a short denim skirt that showed off a decent amount of leg, a tight teal crop top, and a pair of flip-flops. In her hands was the tiny black dress she convinced me to purchase at the thrift store. I grimaced at her. "No, absolutely not. I'm tired and just want to go to sleep, not try to squeeze into that."

Frankie snorted behind me at my commentary, but continued straightening a rack of swimsuits nearby, acting like she wasn't listening to every word that slipped out of my mouth. Rosalyn simply grinned and pushed the dress toward me. "We have a party to go to and your presence is being requested." She leveled her eyes at me. "Besides, you don't exactly say no to the members of the Forsaken. Cam will never let me live it down if you aren't there."

My mouth went dry at her words. I hadn't really thought of the three guys from lunch this week. Well, except a few stray passing thoughts, but I'd been busy. *I'm here for a fresh start and to go to college, not some entanglement with members of a gang.* Rosalyn's words about me steering clear of them and whatever their specific tastes in the bedroom echoed in my head. But so did the intensity of Cam's blue eyes and the black ink trailing up Niko's arms. What harm would a few drinks and some light flirting do?

Shaking my head, I sighed and logic won out. "I really am tired. Plus, I thought you told me to avoid them."

Frankie cleared her throat and looked at the ceiling. "Girl, you still have a lot to learn about Clearhaven. Your friend is right. You can't ignore an invitation from the Forsaken. They can either make your life heaven or hell." She ushered me back to a room in the back corner of the small building. "Get changed. I don't know how you're going to fit into that thing," she muttered mainly to herself.

Slipping into the dress was surprisingly easy as the fabric stretched across every curve I had. The air conditioning of the shop hit every exposed piece of skin, chilling me. My nerves ratcheted up to a ten, and I tugged at the hem, willing it to grow longer. When I stepped out into Frankie's line of vision, she clicked her tongue and pulled a pair of sandals from a rack near her. "You can't wear sneakers with that."

"But I can't take–"

She cut off my argument. "You can and you will. Go have a good time tonight before classes start on Monday." I slipped the sandals on and fastened the thin straps around my ankles while they silently watched me. Rosalyn glanced at her phone several times while I folded the clothes I wore earlier and placed them neatly into my bag. Once I was ready to go, she gave Frankie a hug.

"Make sure she's safe tonight," Frankie whispered to her. "Is it at the beach or the house?"

Rosalyn's mouth curled upward, and the air was thick with unspoken tension. "The beach. I'll do what I can. It will be fine, I'm sure."

I puffed out a small breath, blowing a stray hair out of my face. "We'll be fine. It's just a party. What could possibly happen in one night? We'll have some drinks and dance, then go home. Alone," I stated with more bravado than I felt. In reality, my boss' words made me nervous.

I carefully hoisted myself into Rosalyn's truck, desperately trying not to show my underwear, but it was useless. I threw my bag into the back seat as she turned the key in the ignition and off we went, driving silently down the road until she turned off into a small parking area near the ocean. The moon was high in the sky, reflecting off of every surface, and the scent of salt water filled the air. A light breeze ruffled through my hair and I inhaled deeply.

Tonight wouldn't be that bad. I could simply grab a drink, sit near the water's edge, and be home before midnight.

Rosalyn linked arms with me as we made our way down the sandy embankment closer to where the bass reverberated from a nearby speaker. A fire roared in the middle of the beach and shadows danced around the flames in time to the beat. Bodies melted against one another, limbs twisting and moving. Rosalyn ducked her head close to mine so that I could hear what she said. "Let's grab a drink."

My feet sank into the silty ground, sand filling my new sandals. The last party I had been to was months ago, and the chaos of everything around me clouded my senses. A drink right now would be amazing. I stopped briefly to pull off my sandals while Rosalyn sauntered up to a guy in his mid-twenties standing at a folding table with bottles lining the top and held up two fingers to him. I couldn't hear their exchange, but he grinned at her and gave her a quick wink while he poured something into red plastic cups. She threw her head back and laughed at whatever he said before taking the cups from his hands.

I tossed my sandy shoes to the left of the table. "Who's he?" I asked as I took the drink and took a large sip, letting the fruity pink beverage mix coat my tongue.

Rosalyn shrugged a little as she tipped her cup back. "Rhyker. He's just one of Vincent's henchmen, but he's gorgeous isn't he?"

I glanced at the man in question with his black waves that swept over his face and broad shoulders covered by the dark cotton of his dark t-shirt. Fine indeed.

The alcohol warmed my stomach. It was deceptive—smooth and sweet, camouflaging the bitterness of whatever it had been mixed with. I made an internal note to pace myself because I hadn't really eaten anything other than a sandwich hours before my shift.

Those thoughts were soon forgotten, though. The more we drank and talked about nothing, the more all the demons that continually played at the back of my mind faded. Their constant uttering went from the usual shouts to a dull mutter before being completely silenced. The first cup quickly turned to a second and then a third.

My body was light and warm, buzzing with electricity. Rosalyn led us into the crowd of bodies, saying something that I couldn't quite make out. How many people were here tonight? It didn't matter. I was free finally. No one knew who I was.

Her hands grabbed my waist as our hips moved, sweat beading on my body from the humidity and the nearby fire. No one paid attention as we twisted to the tempo. I giggled to myself for some reason I couldn't quite place. Suddenly I was glad that I'd come here instead of heading back to the empty house across town.

All the fatigue from earlier was replaced by movement. The music itself vibrated through my body and every touch against my skin felt like fire licked paths along it. Alcohol had never affected me like this, but I chalked it up to the atmosphere, music, and the flames dancing beside me.

Strong hands grabbed my waist from behind, trailing along the cut outs at my midriff. Whoever it was smelled like musk and the ocean. I wanted to turn my face to bury it in their chest, breathe deeply, and commit the scent to memory, but I managed to stop myself. Rosalyn wiggled her eyebrows at me and giggled, stumbling slightly on her feet.

"Having a good time, little ghost?" The deep baritone caressed my ear, breath feathering along my neck. The fire beneath my skin turned into an inferno. I wanted to get lost in the hard body pressed into my back, moving seamlessly with the rhythm.

The only reply I could think of was, "I really like the music." It sounded so juvenile and didn't encompass how I was feeling. A rumble of laughter came from behind and all I could think was that the timbre was beautiful, melding perfectly with the music wrapping around my body. One hand gently circled my throat and a soft whimper escaped my mouth. The fire spreading through my veins traveled between my thighs.

I didn't even know who it was, but I'd never felt a connection like this with anyone. All throughout high school, boys had chased me, but I played it safe. I questioned their motives and what they really wanted from me, especially after the news of my father's crimes was announced. The handful of dates and kisses I shared was lackluster, yet here I was with a complete stranger, anticipating what his next move was. Would his touches drift up along my skin? Would the hand wrapped around my throat squeeze tighter?

Would I like that?

Warm, soft lips brushed along my shoulder, and my eyes briefly fluttered shut, relishing the sensation. When I opened them, Rosalyn's eyes were wide, but she chuckled to herself. Bending close, she whispered, "Seems like the Forsaken have made their choice tonight, and so have you. Be careful." She was telling me something important, but I couldn't focus enough to figure it out. "I'm going to find a new dance partner. Find me before you leave."

I nodded before losing myself to the tempest raging inside of me. I wasn't me at that moment, simply a vessel for the fire that burned brightly, crackling against the dark sky. There was nothing else even when a second set of hands, this time slightly smaller, found my skin. One drifted along my ribs and the other traced my jaw. Familiar whiskey-colored eyes from lunch earlier in the week peered at me.

Trey had seemed like the nicest of the three, the safest. His laid-back mannerisms put me at ease. Tonight I questioned that assumption while he looked at me like he was ready to devour me.

Somehow, every golden brown hair was perfectly in place, even with the movements of our bodies. The black-rimmed glasses from earlier were gone and embers reflected in his irises as the fire popped. If Trey was in front of me, who was behind me? I tried to remind myself yet again about the warnings Rosalyn had given me, but at that moment, they didn't matter while I stared at the flecks of amber and gold swirling in his eyes. Instead, I chose to lean further into his touch.

Trey pulled his bottom lip between his teeth, his grip on me tightening. "Stop looking at him like that, little ghost. If you don't, he'll strip you down in front of everyone here and make you choke on his cock," the man behind me murmured into my ear.

My thoughts raced as moisture slicked the inside of my thighs. Would I let him do that? The answer unequivocally was that I would be willing to give the two men surrounding me my virginity without a second thought, even if there were people watching our every action.

I shook my head trying to clear it, and pulled away from them, needing a moment to myself. I turned to face them and was met with the bluest eyes I'd ever seen. Cam. He was the one who had caged me in at the pizza place and more importantly the one who smelled like the ocean. "More drink," I told them, shaking my cup for emphasis.

As I walked back toward Rhyker to get more alcohol that I certainly didn't need, I laughed to myself and decided to throw caution to the wind.

Here's to bad decisions.

Cam

Seeing Ivy creep through the crowd of bodies, silently moving between the masses unnoticed, reminded me of a specter. It was almost like she was used to making herself as small as possible, and it piqued my curiosity. Why would someone as beautiful as the new girl want to be unseen? Her auburn hair reflected the color of the flames, contrasting with the paleness of her skin in the moonlight.

I stood to the side with Trey and Niko for a while, sipping whatever beverages we'd chosen for the evening. Tonight, everyone's drinks were spiked with the shit Vincent demanded I distribute. Well, everyone's except ours.

After what happened last year, I needed to know what the side effects were to prevent another incident. The night before, we had all sampled the experimental drug and nothing bad had happened to us. The best way to describe it was almost like it was a mixture of ecstasy and marijuana. Everything was a little brighter, and every touch was heightened. It was like being on a cloud from how light you felt and the way all of your problems just faded into the background.

I could see the appeal of wanting to distribute it, but wasn't sure about any of the details. Who was making this and why? I needed to see what happened on a larger scale. Trey, ever cautious, tried arguing with me that spiking everyone's drinks was a dangerous move, and Niko didn't exactly agree with my plan either, but in the end, both backed down. I had told Rhyker just to mix in a little, and so far things were going smoothly. No obvious overdoses, no aggression. Just people dancing and drinking.

The pull toward Ivy was magnetic and as much as I wanted to fight it and stay away, after a while I laid my bottle down and drifted toward her, mesmerized by the way her hips moved to the music. I imagined how she would look beneath me and writhing to a different tempo with her cheeks flushed and lips parted.

The decision about who we played with at the end of the night was typically a group discussion, but Ivy was an exception even though I knew nothing about her. Well, except that I wanted to mark her as mine for more than just tonight.

That wasn't how we did things, though. One girl per night with no repeats. It was a rule we didn't break. None of us wanted anyone getting attached or assuming that there was more to the arrangement than there was. None of us had the time and with our lives, women would bring nothing but complications. We couldn't ensure our own safety, much less theirs, from other members of the Forsaken or organizations they associated with. Yet as

I was lured in closer to the mystery girl dancing in the sand, I contemplated if it could be different.

I molded my body behind hers and allowed my hands to travel along her soft skin, enjoying the way she responded to me. Every touch and whisper she devoured, begging for more as she ground against me, never questioning who was wrapped around her. Every whimper that fell from her lips made me harder.

Surprise lined Rosalyn's face but said nothing as the three of us danced, fueled by alcohol and hormones. Despite the decree that she was off limits, I was half tempted to see if she wanted to join us tonight, but quickly shot the idea down. I didn't want to deal with the fallout from our leader or her grandfather and the people associated with him. The temptation was completely extinguished when she drifted away without a second glance, no doubt looking for a hookup of her own. My bet was on Rhyker, but I had been proven wrong before.

Trey had been watching us from the edges of the crowd and took the opportunity to move in where Rosalyn once stood, gliding his hands along her torso. Ivy's skin felt like heaven beneath my palms, and her neck fit easily into my hand. I squeezed lightly, testing to see what she would do, and she melted further into me gasping.

Trey smirked when she suddenly pulled away from us, stating quietly she needed more drink. "Out of anyone here tonight, you had to choose the new girl. Does she know the rules?"

Everyone thought that out of the three of us, Trey was the gentle one. They were wrong. He hid behind his computer screen and studies with his mask carefully in place. "I think that she'll be a fast learner."

We exited the sea of bodies and followed behind her to the drink table, giving her space, but not enough to truly escape. Rhyker winked as he handed off another plastic cup filled with alcohol and she sipped on it while tugging at her clothes due to either being overheated or how sensitive her skin was from the substances coursing through her body.

Trey approached her like he would prey, slowly and with soft words that lulled her into a false sense of security. "Hey, new girl. Want to get away from everyone for a while?" His fingers trailed up her arms, and she nodded at him, not knowing what he was really asking. He took her free hand and cradled it in his as he led her away from the crowd.

I caught Niko's eyes and jerked my head in the direction they were walking. The music faded, and the light fell away as we headed to the small grove of trees further down the beach. We came here sometimes to drink alone, but it was the best place for what we had planned. At the edge of the trees, two huge logs formed an L-shaped bench, and we stood there silently for a moment, simply watching the gorgeous girl as she took a seat, her dress riding up her legs.

Trey was the first to make a move. He sat so that he was straddling the wood and wrapped his arms around her from behind, allowing his fingers to caress her skin as he kissed along her neck beneath her ear. Niko deposited himself on the other side and grasped her chin before leisurely running his tongue along her bottom lip. Her eyes closed and mouth parted, granting him entrance to delve inside. I watched for just a moment, my cock painfully hard at the sight and rubbing against the zipper of my jeans, before stalking toward her.

Kneeling in front of her, my fingers brushed up her calves slowly, inching to where I wanted them to be. Once they reached her knees, I nuzzled them apart and hooked them over the other men's legs, exposing her to me. My mouth found the sensitive flesh on the inside of her thighs and her legs widened further. I nipped a place inches from the black cotton strip that I knew would be drenched and sucked the skin, trailing my tongue across it to soothe the sting. I kept my eyes on the scene happening in front of me, not wanting to miss a single thing that happened or how Ivy reacted to the three of us.

Niko's fingers tangled into her hair and grasped the elastic tying it back. Roughly, he jerked, her hair cascading down around her body. Trey cupped one of her breasts through the black dress, squeezing it as his mouth assaulted the exposed portion of her shoulder. I continued to move slowly upward, and she pulled away from Niko's kisses, her breath ragged. Her cheeks were rosy and her eyes hooded. It took everything in me not to yank down her underwear and plunge inside of her. *Patience*, I tried to remind myself.

She bit her bottom lip, hesitating for a moment. "I've never done anything like this. What if..."

Was she saying what I thought she was saying? Was Ivy a sweet little virgin ready for us to corrupt her? Niko handled the situation, running his thumb over her pouty lip, freeing it from her teeth. "Trust us, pretty girl. We'll be careful with you."

There was no way in hell he would keep his word, but she didn't know that. I ran a finger along the cloth covering her pussy, gauging her reaction. I'd been right that she was already soaked and ready for us to do whatever we wanted. She gasped and dropped her drink, the sweet alcohol splashing on me as she bucked against me. I ignored the cold liquid as I pulled the wet cloth to the side and gingerly ran my tongue through her folds. Focusing on her clit, I swirled my tongue around the nub. She completely lost herself in the moment and grabbed at my hair, holding me against her.

Trey's hand disappeared beneath the top of her dress and Niko captured her mouth, stealing all of her moans from me. Pressing two fingers inside of her, her walls squeezed around them, and I curled them upward. As I worked them in and out of her, I continued to assault her with my mouth. Her chest heaved, and she arched her back, nearly on the cusp of falling over. When I sucked the sensitive bundle of nerves between my lips, she pulsed around my fingers and wetness coated my face. Watching her body thrash against my friends and hearing the noises coming from her was a thing of magic. I prolonged her orgasm as long as I could before finally pulling my fingers from her when her hands untangled from my hair.

I held my hand up to her mouth and gave her a smirk. "Little ghost, I think you need to clean up the mess you made." She looked hesitant at first, but when I pressed my fingers between her lips, her tongue swirled around them, licking and sucking them.

Fuck. I stood and leaned over her, pressing my mouth to hers. She was perfect. Right now I was willing to forget every rule I'd ever made for myself and I hadn't even had my cock in her yet.

When I pulled back, Niko smirked at me like he could read my thoughts. He grasped her face between both of his hands, holding her attention. His lips skated over hers and he ran his thumb along her cheek. "Do you want to play a game with us?"

She giggled a little from nerves. "What kind of game?"

It took everything in me not to laugh out loud and tell her the kind of game that she wasn't ready for, but I simply shook my head. Trey righted her clothes while he whispered to her, coaxing her into doing what we wanted. "When we tell you to run, you run. You try to hide in the trees behind us. If we catch you, then we do whatever we want." His fingers traced the neckline of her dress. "But we can make you feel good again. How would you like that?"

She was apprehensive and swallowed hard, her throat bobbing with the motion. I wanted to wrap my fingers around the column of her throat again to feel the muscles work beneath them. And then she stood, messing with the hem of her dress. "You'll be careful?"

"We promise," Niko told her, the lying bastard. "I'll even give you a head start this time."

I leaned close to her and smiled. "Run."

Niko

I vy tasted like spun sugar and as I swallowed her moans, I committed the way her body shuddered against me when she got off to memory. The way her face twisted with pleasure and she arched her body toward us, twining her fingers in Cam's hair, would be a fantasy I played on repeat when I was alone.

When she finally came down from the high of getting off, her eyes were glassy and she looked dazed. I never expected her to agree so quickly to the game I wanted to play. My pulse thrummed in my chest when Cam told her a single word.

Run.

This would be the only time that I would chase after her like this, all because of Cam's stupid rules. He didn't want any of us getting attached and I'd never questioned it before tonight, but seeing Ivy's pale legs pumping as she sprinted with wide eyes toward the thicket of trees made me regret our agreement.

Cam smirked at me while we waited, giving her a head start. "Her pussy is mine."

I rolled my eyes at his statement. That was fine by me. I was more interested in pursuing her while her heart beat erratically. Seeing the pulse in her throat pounding away from fear and adrenaline while she tried to calm her breathing. Maybe she would try to hide from me in the shadows with her hand covering her mouth.

Trey looked down at his watch and jerked his head in my direction, letting me know it was time. My feet padded softly along the sand toward the small grove, moving as silently as possible. The leaves from the trees blocked the moonlight and darkness shrouded me while I listened, trying to make out any movements. Thirty feet in, something rustled nearby.

The pretty girl isn't very good at hiding yet.

My motions stilled while I listened, intentionally treading loudly to spook her. Fallen leaves from a storm several weeks ago were scattered along the ground and I kicked at them carefully to see what Ivy would do. A whimper echoed in the night and my pulse quickened, roaring in my ears. Prowling toward the noise, she stood and darted out, running blindly in the opposite direction. I took off behind her at an easy pace, my cock hard in my pants while I listened to Ivy drag in harsh breaths.

She was wearing down, that much was clear. Her movements were growing sluggish, and I didn't want her completely spent. Not yet. Closing the distance between us, I grabbed her around the waist and pulled her tight against my chest, my arms banding around her like a vise. Her soft body struggled against mine for a moment, fingernails digging into my forearms. Trey and Cam were several feet away, the sound of their footsteps slowly approaching.

"Caught you," I murmured against her skin, noting her scent. Beneath the sweat, she smelled like oranges and vanilla. I ran my tongue along the column of the neck, licking the salt from her flesh as her body shuddered beneath my grasp. Her chest heaved, and she sniffled.

Hmm. She's crying and probably doesn't even know why. Perhaps subconsciously she could see beneath our masks at the monsters she agreed to play with. Her tears excited me, the sense of helplessness she felt being at our mercy.

Trey gave her a cruel smile when he stepped in front of her and reached out, brushing his fingers along the tears that tracked down both cheeks. His other hand descended into his pocket and he pulled out a small knife, flicking it open with ease. "Ready for round two, new girl?"

Ivy's breath caught in her throat and she sniffled again before biting her lower lip. Her next words surprised me. "Yes."

My grip on her loosened, and I allowed one hand to travel to her hip, clutching it tightly. "You like this, don't you? You enjoyed being chased and not knowing what we'll do next. If I checked right now, I bet your pretty little pussy is soaking for me, begging for my cock."

The whimper she let out was enough verification that everything I said was true. Cam leaned against a nearby tree, his hand slowly rubbing himself through his pants while he patiently waited for his turn. The blade in Trey's palm gently glided across Ivy's skin, never leaving a mark, trailing down her neck and then across her collarbones.

"I think we need to see what's underneath this dress," Trey stated, holding Ivy's gaze as the knife ripped through the thin fabric clinging to her body. Letting go of her for a moment, I jerked the cloth from her shoulders allowing my hands to linger on her arms, leaving her in nothing but the black cotton underwear that hugged her round ass.

Even in the dim lighting, she was perfection with thick thighs and a belly with a slight curve. And her tits. Pale globes of flesh that were made for worship. Pulling her flush against my body, I palmed one of her breasts, her nipple hard beneath my hand. I traced my other hand down her torso, snaking it beneath her panties and cupping her. "Tell me who this belongs to tonight."

The tip of the blade traveled across her other nipple, the peak growing harder as Trey circled it, teasing her. "You," she replied.

I clicked my tongue and pinched her nipple roughly and pressed the heel of my hand against her clit. She cried out and pushed her ass back against me, seeking more pressure. "Wrong answer. Who do you belong to tonight?" My fingers didn't move as I waited for her answer.

Trey chuckled as his blade continued downward, brushing along the planes of her stomach. I glanced toward Cam, his eyes hooded and dark. His hand had disappeared beneath the waist of his pants and my pulse quickened in my chest further. I watched him stroke himself, the fabric moving in a slow rhythm before I tore my gaze away. "All of you," Ivy whispered, laying her head back against my chest.

Those words were enough to break the small amount of restraint that I had. Spinning her around, I feathered my lips against hers for a moment as a reward before placing my hands on her shoulders. Bearing down on them gently with just enough force to encourage her I said, "Then show me."

She sank to her knees in front of me, and Trey followed behind her to the hard ground. With shaking hands, her fingers fumbled with my zipper. Trey rolled her nipple between his fingers while the edge of the knife skimmed her thighs in circles. She gasped and her eyes widened when she released my cock from where it was confined. "I've never done this before and... it's pierced."

Trey chuckled, the dark sound forming goosebumps on Ivy's skin. He sliced through the thin strings holding up her underwear, the fabric falling away completely exposing her to us and the night air. The handle of the knife dipped between her legs hidden from sight. Her eyes closed, and I caressed her cheek, allowing her a moment to just feel before I eased her into what I wanted. "It's okay. I'll teach you what I like. Open your mouth."

Her lips parted, and I waited, my thumb never leaving her face. Tentatively, her tongue brushed along my dick, running up the length and tracing along the path of metal barbells with uncertainty. "Fuck, this is hot," Trey mumbled to himself, pulling his dick out of his pants. I watched as he positioned the knife on the ground near

Ivy's knees and plunged his fingers inside of her while he slowly stroked himself.

Whatever he was doing caused her to lose the unsureness she'd had moments before. She closed her eyes and took my crown in her mouth, swirling her tongue along the bottom ridge. My fingers wound their way through her silky flame-colored locks, tightening as she took me deeper and partially enveloped me in hot, wet heat. Her head bobbed up and down my shaft, never taking its full length. When her cheeks hollowed out around me, it took everything not to slam the rest of the way inside.

There was no way she'd never sucked a dick before, no matter what she said. I reminded myself to focus and drag this out as long as possible.

Trey's motions quickened, and she moaned, the vibrations from her mouth coursing through my body. Pushing her head down my length by her hair, I forced her to take more of me until her nose grazed my pelvis. When she gagged, I let up briefly, allowing her a moment to recover. "Just relax, baby," Trey told her in a soft tone, reassuring the girl who was willing to let us use her. "And breathe through your nose."

After she caught her breath, I thrust in again easing into the back of her throat, and held her there for a moment, relishing the warm heat. Her eyes sparkled with unshed tears as I began slowly rocking my hips back and forth, chasing my pleasure. Even when she shuddered against Trey, an orgasm ripping through her body, I didn't slow my rhythm. "Fucking beautiful," he murmured and stood beside me, jerking himself faster. I watched as his grip tightened and his jaw tensed. When he groaned, jets of cum landed on Ivy's pretty flawless skin, dirtying her up and marking her as ours.

I slowed my motions as Cam moved in behind her and pressed down on her shoulder blades, forcing her to bend onto her elbows. Like the good toy she was, my cock never left her mouth. She claimed she was a virgin and Cam had promised her he would be gentle with her, but I had my doubts. He enjoyed being cruel and rough. Add in the size of his dick, and I didn't envy Ivy's pussy at that moment. Cam pushed his pants down his thighs and he held my gaze as he stroked himself twice before driving into her in one motion. She moaned and gripped the knife beside her in her fist.

My eyes were still locked with Cam's and I watched as he pounded into her. His assault was unrelenting as his face contorted in pleasure. A sharp sting of pain bit my hip and I glanced down to see that the pretty girl had cut me. *That's unexpected.*

She was ballsy to try to match our level of crazy. It wasn't deep, barely a nick, and yet watching the scarlet drops fall down my skin pushed me closer to my destination. It wasn't the sight of the blood that excited me. It was the fact that out of all the women we shared, none would have had the balls to do what Ivy just had.

I wrapped my fingers around the hilt of the knife and pressed it further in. Tingles started at the base of my spine as I focused on the sensation of her mouth and Cam's tempo, his cock sliding in and out of her as the sting sharpened. My muscles clenched and reality faded when I finally came, holding Ivy's hair tightly and forcing her to swallow every drop. When I was done, I fell to my knees and grabbed her jaw. Sweat beaded along her brow and her hair clung to her face. *One more kiss as a reward.* "Such a good girl for us tonight, Ivy," I whispered against her lips.

My hand slipped between her legs to her already sensitive clit. Slowly circling it at first, I pinched and she came apart again. The look on his face as he brutally used her was one of pure ecstasy, and soon she careened over the edge with her body shaking. His grip on her hips loosened as he came inside of her and I could see the bruises forming on her skin from his fingers.

Ivy crumpled to the ground, muscles worn from fatigue, and I ran my fingers down her spine, basking in the feeling of her skin. I leaned close to whisper to her while Cam adjusted his clothes, nuzzling my cheek against her hair.

Trey held out his shirt to me for her, and I growled at him, pushing it away. If she was going to be wearing anyone's shirt, it would be mine. Instead, I tugged my shirt over my head and helped Ivy into a sitting position. As I gently pulled the fabric over her head and threaded her arms through it, her eyes fluttered closed and she sighed. I cradled her against me and she relaxed into my chest, seemingly completely trusting us despite what we had just done. Trey raised one eyebrow at me in question and I simply lifted one shoulder in answer. *Hell if I knew.*

Despite the savageness that we'd shone while we fucked her, I wanted more. Even just one more night.

One more night to see Trey allow his demons out to play. One more night to see Cam's face lose its hard edges and soften as he forgot everything around him. Another time to swallow her moans and have her body pressed against mine. One last chance to see the girl who lay in my lap match my viciousness. They didn't know it yet, but she was perfect for us.

A while later, we pulled up in front of the house Ivy had been staying at. We'd known Regina Spencer since we were kids forced to attend Vacation Bible School each summer. She didn't exactly approve of us, but the feeling was mutual. She would get the fuck over it. How was she going to react to seeing her sweet, innocent niece being carried inside by us?

The front door was unlocked and Cam pushed it open for me. Regina sat at the table in the kitchen with a sour look on her face while I held Ivy to my chest, sound asleep. "Evening, ma'am," Cam said with his voice barely above a whisper, waltzing into the kitchen toward her while I continued through the house.

Trey opened every door before finding a small, bare room with a twin bed. He pulled back her blankets, and I tucked her in, taking my time to press my lips to her forehead and breathe in her citrusy scent one last time.

I shut the door quietly behind me and headed back to the kitchen to rescue Cam. Regina and he were in a heated argument about something, voices drowned out by the roar of the air conditioner in the window. "Just stay away from her," she spat out, her face ruddy from anger.

We'd see about that.

Ivy

Soft morning light filtered through the window, pulling me from my sleep. I'd somehow slept through the night. Last night, for the first time in forever, my nightmares didn't haunt me causing me to wake up tangled in my sheets with a scream caught in my throat. There were no apparitions clawing at my skin and no faceless girls being tortured.

I rolled over and my body ached, pieces of the night before drifting back to me. My hand drifted between my thighs at the memory, wondering if my brain had conjured it up from some subconscious fantasy. *Definitely not.* The sensitive skin was sticky and tender from being used so roughly.

My cheeks burned at the thought I had lost my virginity in such a way, and yet remembering the actions of the three men made me shiver. The intensity of Niko's eyes while he thrust into my mouth while Trey touched me. The silver barbells that lined his length and the way he shuddered as my tongue ran over them. The set of Camden's jaw while he gripped my hips. A part of me wanted to deny that it had ever happened, but the way

I felt between my legs told me it was all true. What was I even thinking last night?

My eyes slowly fluttered open, and my vision was hazy. I wasn't prepared for the pounding in my head or my surroundings. Confusion and the remnants of sleep clouded my thoughts, and it took several moments for me to realize that I was where I was supposed to be. This was my home now, not the 3500-square-foot estate I'd grown up in.

I glanced at the alarm clock and noticed that it was only eight. Deciding that medicine for my headache and a shower were top priorities, I rolled out from underneath my blankets and noted that the shirt I was wearing definitely wasn't mine. Despite my curves, it hung to my knees, and I lifted a corner to inhale it. Beneath the musky scent, sandalwood clung to the fabric making my heart speed up.

The house was silent as I walked to the bathroom, and my muscles protested the entire way. The first thing I did was pop open the medicine cabinet in search of something that would ease the pain in my head. After swallowing two of the off-brand pills, I stripped off the shirt and folded it, placing it on the edge of the sink.

I looked at myself in the mirror, questioning if outwardly I looked different. Dirt marred my skin and bruises littered my body. Tiny marks covered my shoulders and neck. Other than that, everything was exactly the same.

The spray of warm water stung the scrapes on my knees and elbows that I hadn't noticed before now, bits of rock from the night before still clinging to the abrasions.

Soaping up my body, I gently washed and noticed the lack of blood on my thighs. It was confusing, especially as roughly as they treated me.

But then again, some women didn't bleed when they lost their virginity. Maybe I was just lucky.

I lathered my hair with the orange-scented shampoo and allowed myself to enjoy the feeling of the water cascading over me, relieving the aches in my body. While I scrubbed, I was completely on autopilot, lost in my thoughts of the night before. A lot of things didn't make sense in the light of day. Why did I react the way I did? Was the sex so good that my nightmares vanished? And out of everyone there, why did they choose me?

After toweling off and putting on clean clothes, I gathered the shirt folded on the sink and tucked it under my arm. Padding quietly to my room, I held it to my face and inhaled it one last time, wondering which of the guys had tucked me in and how I had gotten home. Placing it inside the small gray container, I prayed my aunt had been asleep or gone.

Soon I learned I wasn't that lucky. Of course, I wasn't. As soon as I entered the kitchen, my aunt was waiting for me with a cup of coffee in her hand. She raised her eyebrows and said nothing as I scoured the cabinets for a clean mug, hoping that caffeine would help the pounding behind my eyes.

The coffee cup she was holding clattered onto the wooden tabletop and she turned to me as I was pouring the steaming liquid. "I want you to stay away from those three, Ivy. No niece of mine is going to be involved with them."

I closed my eyes and took a deep breath, reminding myself that I shouldn't lose my temper. My aunt simply wanted what was best for me, even if she didn't really know me. I took a sip of the bitter, hot liquid before speaking. "We're just friends."

Were we even friends? I somehow doubted that. One night of hormone-fueled sexual activities hardly started a friendship of any type, but telling that to the woman who spent every Sunday morning in the front pew wouldn't do me any favors. I knew nothing about any of them except they were a part of the Forsaken and everyone kept telling me to stay away from.

She huffed and wryly chuckled. "I doubt that. I've known them since they first started school and I've heard the rumors. Plus, if you were just friends, why were they carrying you inside at two in the morning? Nothing good happens after midnight. There are rules in this house and one of them is that from now on, unless you are with Rosalyn, you are to be in before ten."

My mouth fell open at her statement. The past several months, I had dealt with things no one else my age could fathom. I was starting college in two days, and yet I was standing here with someone I barely knew telling me I had a curfew. In another life, I would have argued and told her she couldn't tell me what to do, but I stopped myself. The words would fall on deaf ears and I didn't know how far I could push her.

If she kicked me out, I had nowhere to go. I mean, sure, I could pack my clothes back in my bag and sleep in the car I'd acquired, but how long could I do that for? Would it be safe?

"And one more thing. I want you to go to church with me starting tomorrow morning. Services start at 10:45 a.m. I'll pick you up something appropriate to wear this evening. If you aren't at work, then you'll be learning about God's love." Her eyes narrowed as she picked up the mug off the table and she shifted in her seat. "Or at least maybe how to keep your legs closed. Even good girls make mistakes," she mumbled under her breath.

My cheeks heated at her words, and anger flooded my system, making my hands shake. There was so much to unpack in what she had just said, and I didn't have time for that. Instead, I poured more coffee and turned away from her, stalking to my room to look for my shoes. I needed to get the hell out of here.

I didn't mind going to church with her, and I could live with a curfew even though I was starting college. Staying away from Cam, Niko, and Trey would be easy. After classes started, I wouldn't have a lot of free time, anyway. But the phrase "keep your legs closed." It made my blood boil. She was assuming things about what happened last night, and even though she was correct, I hated it. And what did "good girls make mistakes" even mean?

It didn't take long for me to realize my bag from yesterday was still in Rosalyn's truck, and my new sandals were all but forgotten in the sand last night. My car was still parked outside of Frankie's from the night before. I leaned against the wall and ran my hands over my face. The first thing I needed to buy with my money was a cell phone. If I had Rosalyn's number, I could simply text her I needed my shoes and ask for a ride.

I was a mess and had an hour to spare before work. Rather than letting the tears that were burning my eyes fall, I set my jaw and finished getting ready. I brushed my hair and straightened my shoulders. The distance to the bus stop was only ten blocks away, and once I got to Frankie's, I could use the shop's phone to call Rosalyn. Well, if Frankie had her number. Right now, I wasn't in the mood to speak to my aunt or ask for her help. I couldn't deal with what would come out of her mouth next or the judgment in her eyes.

I slipped out the front door, carefully closing it behind me so that it would make as little noise as possible. It wasn't hot yet, but my feet weren't used to the heat of the concrete being warmed by the sun. I stared at the ground as I walked, diligent to avoid any large gravel or the shards of glass I could see.

Five blocks into my journey, I wanted to give up. With every step, tiny rocks dug in and the sidewalk scorched my soles. Sweat rolled down my back and the late summer sun beat down on my skin. If Hell was truly a place where you were tortured for all of eternity, then my punishment would be to relive this journey repeatedly. All of this while nursing the worst hangover of my life. *I am never drinking again,* I thought as I continued my trek.

Stubbornness won out in the end, driving me closer to my destination. Five blocks was my halfway point, and there was no way I was going to turn around and ask my aunt for anything. Not after what she had said. Instead, I staggered off the concrete into the grass at the edge of the yards lining the street. It wasn't great still, but the dry, crunchy lawn was better than the burning cement that blistered my feet.

Two blocks from the bus stop, a car pulled up beside me. Niko sat in the driver's seat with sunglasses on, and Cam sat opposite him, casually observing me. I continued forward, ignoring the fact that they were following me. "What are you doing, little ghost?" he said loud enough to hear over the sound of the engine.

I rolled my eyes at him even as goosebumps formed on my skin from the bass of his voice. "What does it look like I'm doing?"

His lips twisted with amusement and I stopped beneath the shade of a tree for a moment, grateful for a reprieve from the sun. Niko stopped the car and allowed it to idle, turning his face to look at me. "Where the hell are your shoes?"

I stared at him for a moment, deliberating how much to say. "Look, I left my bag in Rosalyn's truck and I forgot my only other shoes at the beach last night. I have work today and–"

I stopped speaking when Niko reached underneath his seat and pulled out the sandals from the night before. "I forgot to bring them in last night. Get in the car. It's ninety degrees outside."

I eyed him warily before stumbling toward the car, my feet screaming every inch of the way. I was ready to settle into the back seat, but Cam opened the door and pulled me into his lap, banding his arms around my waist. "Pretty sure this is illegal. I can sit in the back."

His grip on me tightened and he rested his chin on my shoulder. "Nah, you're sitting here. Besides, lots of things we do are illegal. The cops around here won't pull us over. Trust me."

Niko handed me the shoes, and I fastened them as he pulled away, trying to ignore the hard body beneath mine. "You're working at Frankie's now, right?" Cam asked as he pressed his lips against my salty neck, and I nodded. Most of the drive was spent in silence with me trying to move as little as possible and trying to ignore Cam's hands and mouth. I jumped when Niko's hand grabbed my thigh and squeezed, allowing his fingers to linger there. At least the wind cooled the sweat on my skin, but by the time Niko parked in front of the surf shop, my entire body felt like it was on fire.

I reached for the car door, signaling that I needed to get out, but Cam's voice stopped me in my tracks. "Where do you think you're going? You didn't thank us or tell us goodbye yet." I turned my head to look at him and his mouth crashed into mine. It wasn't a tender kiss meant to convey affection. It was all-consuming and fevered, like he was staking a claim on me. I pulled away dazed and breathless, gingerly touching my fingers to my lips. He smirked at me and opened the door, gesturing that I was free to go.

I hopped out and gave Niko a wave before disappearing inside the small building, willing my heart to slow down.

Frankie simply shook her head from the stool next to the large windows but didn't comment.

That was good because I didn't know what to tell her if she asked questions.

Trey

The code on the screen in front of me blurred together, and I rubbed my eyes, trying to stay focused. The work was tedious, but in the end, it would be worth it. After last night's play session, I couldn't sleep. Visions of Ivy picking up the knife beside her and cutting open Niko's skin played in my mind on repeat. I ignored how painfully hard I was knowing that it would be foolish to jerk off to her memory. Our rules were in place for a reason, part of what cemented us together in this shitty town. The last thing I needed was to obsess over someone who was now off limits.

So I tried to preoccupy myself and started working on a new string of code. I wasn't sure what I was going to use it for yet, but I knew it would come in handy. It wasn't nearly as satisfying as getting off or fantasizing about marking Ivy's pale skin, but it distracted me. The basic idea behind the new "program" was to have access to private information on a user's cellphone. Text messages, web history, emails. People did everything on their phones now and knowledge was power. Especially if you were trying to get the hell out of Clearhaven. I didn't have all the details worked out just yet, but I had some ideas floating around.

When the sun rose, I stood up and stretched. The small desk I worked at was nestled in the corner of the living room, a few feet away from a tiny kitchen. I sauntered over, desperate for a caffeine fix, and celebrated when I discovered Cam had left a pack of energy drinks in the back of the refrigerator. Grabbing one, I popped it open and took a gulp before shuddering. The taste wasn't why anyone drank these. It was purely for the energy to either cram for exams or to avoid sleep.

Moving into this apartment was the best decision I'd ever made. Escaping from my family had been my top priority after high school. I'd never known my father–he got a life sentence before I was born–and my mother… that was a completely different story.

The best way to describe her was absent. She was more concerned with partying and looking for her next ex-husband than raising a kid. I scratched at my wrist as I thought of the last man she'd brought home and tried to push away the memories that threatened to claw their way to the surface.

By the time my sophomore year of high school rolled around, I knew I had to get out of that house, and the only way I could do that was money. The errands we ran for the Forsaken weren't enough, so I taught myself how to repair computers. I spent every waking moment hustling or studying, hiding my hard earned cash in a hole in the underside of my mattress. The day I turned eighteen, I walked out of the trailer my mother lived in at the time and never looked back.

Despite that, sometimes it was lonely. Holidays and birthdays were the worst. I spent most of them with a bottle of vodka in front of my computer, trying to forget I existed. Cam and Niko had both promised that as soon as they could, they'd move in with me and help pay the rent, but right now, they were busy raising younger siblings that their parents seemed to forget existed. They crashed here some nights, especially now that the kids were getting older, but it didn't fill the emptiness inside of me.

One day, everything would be different. I wandered back to the computer that I'd built from parts scavenged out of old systems that were beyond repair and ignored the quiet of the house, fixating instead on the project in front of me. Hours later, the front door opening pulled me from what I was working on. Looking up from my desk, Cam leaned against the wall next to my desk. "You look like shit. Have you even slept yet?"

I blinked to clear my vision and ran my hands through my hair, debating if I should be honest or not. Niko strode in balancing pizza in one hand and beer in the other. He placed everything on the counter and looked me over before shaking his head. "Another all nighter I see."

Cam motioned for me to get up. "Come get some food, asshole. If you haven't slept, I know you haven't eaten all day."

The scent of sausage and onions filled the air, and my stomach chose that exact moment to rumble. We opened the boxes sitting on the cabinet and I reached for a beer, but Cam's hand wrapped around my wrist, stopping me in my tracks. "Water first. You can't live off alcohol and energy drinks." I glared at him briefly when he added, "And after this, you need a shower."

"Fine, Dad," I grumbled before shoving a piece of pizza into my mouth while grabbing a bottle of water. My aggravation fell away as I ate, the pit inside of me disappearing. Cam was just trying to show me he cared, even if he was overbearing. I finished the bottle of water and grabbed a beer while we ate in silence.

Once we'd finished, Niko glanced between me and Cam before tipping his bottle back. His gaze lingered on Cam for a few moments before he spoke. "So last night..."

I cocked an eyebrow up, waiting to see where this went. Not that we didn't sometimes discuss our conquests, but last night was different. Usually, by the end of being used, the girl was in tears or ready to run from us. A few had tried coming back for more, but we turned them away.

And then there was Ivy. She took everything we gave her and then curled up in Niko's lap with her eyes closed.

"What about it?" Cam asked as he peeled up the edge of the label on his bottle.

Niko's lips pressed into a thin line, and he crossed his arms over his chest. "I want her again."

A thread of hope formed in my chest for some reason, and I couldn't quite place the feeling. "I do too," I admitted quietly, more to myself than anyone else.

Cam sighed and rubbed the back of his neck. "You guys know the rules and–"

"Fuck the rules," Niko barked, taking a step closer to him. "She's different. We want her and so do you. Don't deny it, especially after that car ride."

"What are you talking about?" I asked, curious about what I had obviously missed.

Niko looked in my direction for a moment. "Nothing, other than the fact that we found *little ghost* wandering around barefoot and gave her a ride to work." He leaned close to Cam, their faces inches apart. "You wouldn't even let her sit in her own seat. Insisted she sit in your lap."

Cam shoved at his chest. "You're just jealous because it wasn't you."

The tension in the room mounted the longer the two of them stared at each other. Niko was the first to look away, his eyes focused on something near the ceiling. "Classes start on Monday. We aren't the only ones who noticed her at the party the other night. Are you telling me you'll be okay with other people touching her? Sticking their dick—"

Cam balled his fists at his side and clenched his jaw. "Shut the fuck up."

I cleared my throat to gain both of their attention. "He has a point. If you don't want her, that's fine, but someone else is going to snatch her up. Is that something you can live with? Especially after you took her virginity?"

"Well, there's some debate about that," Cam muttered. I wasn't sure what he was talking about, but I would ask him later. He bit his cheek before putting his hands in the air. "Fine. I'll consider putting our rule aside for Ivy on one condition. Trey, I want to know everything about her. Tonight."

He wouldn't hear any arguments from me. A different girl each night was getting old, and I wanted to know more about Ivy. I grabbed another beer to put beside me on my desk and strode to my computer, closing out the program I was working on. Tapping out a quick text message to Rosalyn, I asked what Ivy's last name was. When she responded, a lump formed in my throat. Spencer. *It had to be a coincidence.*

I pulled up my search engine and typed in her name. My heart fell into my stomach because Niko and I had already lost.

Most college girls have a huge internet footprint. Photos from every social media site, YouConnect updates, Chirp statuses. Those are the first things you see. Pictures of their dogs or summer vacation photographs. Not Cam's little ghost. He was going to be pissed once I told him.

I tipped my beer back, finishing the rest of the bottle in one drink, and began loudly reading from the news article in front of me. "Ivy Spencer, the only child of Thomas Spencer, was seen leaving the Crimson Cove Correctional Facility earlier today. Mr. Spencer was recently accused of sex trafficking and conspiracy to traffic minors. He is being held without bail and is considered a flight risk."

The silence was suffocating once I finished. The only sound you could hear was the drip of the leaky faucet in the bathroom. Niko's eyes had gone wide, but Cam... he was pissed. His face was ruddy and the vein in his neck pulsed. Suddenly he turned around and punched the wall hard enough that the plaster underneath caved. *Just fucking great. One more thing to fix.*

I knew he was going to react this way. His younger sister Maya was one of Thomas Spencer's victims. He hadn't told us all the details still, and I didn't know if he ever would. The courts decided to drop the charges regarding Maya, claiming there wasn't enough evidence to pursue the case. A week later, Cam found her on the bathroom floor attempting to overdose.

He shook his hand out as his chest heaved with every breath. "I want her gone. Gone from Clearhaven and the university. Fuck that bitch," he managed to grit out. "We're going to make her life hell."

I didn't agree with the idea of torturing Ivy for something that her father had done, but I wouldn't go against Cam's wishes. Maya deserved justice, however warped that was. The three of us intimately knew that sometimes you paid for the sins of your parents and that life wasn't fair.

After I got to work on Saturday, Frankie asked me to watch the shop around lunchtime and disappeared for an hour. When she came back, she shoved a prepaid phone at me and told me I "didn't need to be driving around town without a way to call someone, especially not in my car." My mouth opened to argue, but she dismissed me and said that she'd already programmed her and Rosalyn's number in it. I texted Ros the bag that had my keys in it was still in Black Betty. Within fifteen minutes she showed up with not only my belongings but also a soda. I was grateful for the caffeine and sugar after the morning I had.

The rest of my shift was quiet, my hangover slowly fading into the background. When I got home, I chose not to speak to my aunt, the fight from the morning still fresh in my mind. Instead, I undressed and crawled beneath the covers on my bed, hoping that my dreams would be empty like they were the night before.

It wasn't meant to be.

I spent the night tossing and turning, waiting for oblivion to pull and under. When I finally fell, it was the same thing that had been happening for months and then I woke up, clawing at my throat, a scream bubbling up in my chest. The phantom hands that clutched at me still ghosted against my skin and sweat covered every inch of my body while I tried to catch my breath.

The real horror wasn't even the dreams that haunted me every night. Sunday morning, my aunt barged into my room holding an ankle length navy blue dress covered in white flowers, complete with shoulder pads and elbow-length sleeves. While she hung it on the back of my door, I stared in shock at the clothing that was ripped straight from the early nineties. She demanded that I get up and shower because we needed to leave early for church service.

I made a note to myself to beg Frankie for Sunday shifts while I quickly showered. In an act of defiance, I ripped the shoulder pads out of the dress before yanking it over my head. My hair still dripping, I twisted it into a messy bun and threw on the sneakers I wore with every outfit. In the back of my mind, I wished I owned makeup because if I did, my finishing touch would be heavy black eyeliner.

Sunday church services weren't actually that bad, just a long-winded discussion of what was considered a sin, damnation, and, of course, a small mention of Hell. As the preacher droned on, my eyes grew heavy and I pinched the skin on my hand to stay awake. The last thing I needed was to fall asleep here and wake up screaming. My aunt would be mortified and I would definitely be chastised for that.

As soon as I was home, I changed clothes and headed out, foregoing lunch with my aunt and her friends.

I checked my phone, noticing a missed message.

Ros: I just want to see how you are after everything.

I mulled over a way to respond before finally settling on, "I'm fine," and hit send, throwing it into the center console. There was no point in pouring out my frustrations on the one friend I had.

I drove aimlessly, wasting precious gas while I thought about everything I needed to do and how much my life had changed. Monday was the beginning of the next four years of my life.

A clap of thunder made me jump, and my heart skipped a beat as I shimmied into fresh clothes the next morning. The nightmares that plagued me hadn't slowed since my move to Clearhaven. If anything, they had become more vivid except for my one night with the Forsaken. My stomach rolled from nervousness and excitement.

Briefly, I wondered if I would see any of them on campus later in the day, and a different type of anticipation built inside of me. I had assumed that Friday night's party was just a one off, a stupid decision that was fueled by alcohol. Then Niko and Cam rescued me on Saturday. That kiss. *It meant something, right?*

I threw my bag over my shoulder, shoved my new phone in my pocket, and grabbed my keys off of the cabinet. Suddenly, I wished I had a hoodie to protect my hair from the rain that was coming down in sheets outside. That would be the next thing I purchased from the thrift store in town. After I locked the door, I turned around and my heart fell.

What in the fuck? The Honda Civic that I hadn't even made a payment on was covered in spray paint. Words like whore and bitch covered every inch. My personal favorite that made me want to vomit was "we know." Someone had discovered my secret, and I hadn't been in town for a month.

My body pulled me forward into the rain against my will. Lightning flashed through the sky as my fingers trailed over the car's body, taking in every inch of what had been done sometime during the night. To make matters worse, three of the four tires were flat, huge gouges cut into them.

I froze and allowed myself to live in the moment. Tears mingled with the rain falling from the sky. For the first time in forever, everything had been going right. Well, mostly. I had made a friend, found a job, and was starting classes today. This was my fresh start and now that was over.

I sank to my knees as the gravity of the situation hit me, allowing my clothes to be saturated by the water pelting me from the heavens. Even the sound of the thunder faded away and a small part of me wished that the ground consumed me. Who had done this? How would I be able to afford three new tires to get back and forth to school? My hands shook as I pulled my phone out, calling the one person I could think of.

Rosalyn answered after two rings, sounding happy despite the hour and the storm raging over us. "What's up?"

I sniffled, and the words tumbled out of my mouth before I could stop them. "Can you come pick me up?"

"Ivy, what's going on? Have you been crying?"

A sob caught in my throat. "Someone slashed my tires–"

Even over the phone, anger laced her tone. "I'll be right there."

Standing up, I went back inside the house on autopilot, knowing that I needed to change into dry clothes. I tucked my emotions back inside, determined to not let anyone see me fall apart and dried off. Just as I was putting on the sandals Frankie had given me, Rosalyn pulled up. I ran out the door to jump into her car with my bag that was soaked from the rain.

Her jaw was clenched and her lips were pursed as she narrowed her eyes at my car. She peeled away as soon as my seat belt was fastened. "Do you know who did that?"

I shook my head at her. "No idea. How am I going to pay for new tires? They're so damn expensive and even working at the surf shop... I mean, I still need to buy books for my classes..." I was fumbling with my words and my throat felt thick from all the emotions.

She tightened her grip on the steering wheel. "I've got some ideas. Number one. I saw an ad online the other day on one of the campus forums. The football team is looking for a tutor for one of their players. They didn't say who it is but there's no harm in applying. And number two." She hesitated for a moment and then gave me a soft smile. "The tires won't be that bad. We can go to the takeoff place across town. Most of the time they're less than forty a piece."

I laid my head back against the seat and allowed relief to wash over me. Rosalyn's speech had put me more at ease. Forty dollars wouldn't be nearly as bad as the $150 I was expecting and tutoring sounded like a good way to make a little extra cash. I would simply have to fit the sessions in between my classes and work. "So, what am I going to do about the spray paint?"

She rolled her bottom lip between her teeth, thinking. "Leave that up to me. I have a trick I can show you this afternoon."

Soon we pulled up on campus and she parked the truck in a lot close to several academic buildings. Rosalyn grabbed her bag from the back seat and gestured for me to do the same. "Today is going to be an amazing day. Don't let this morning get you down. It's just a minor setback. What time is your last class over?"

I gripped the set strap in my hand, embarrassed by my theatrics earlier. "Three. I tried to schedule everything for Monday, Wednesday, and Friday. I wanted to have more time to work."

She tilted her head up in acknowledgment and pulled the hood of her jacket over her hair. "I'll wait in the dining hall for you." She lingered beside me for just a moment and then grabbed my hand, gently squeezing it. "Don't worry. Everything is going to be fine, I promise."

I gave her a cautious smile and threw my bag over my shoulder, preparing myself to run through the rain to my first class. "Yeah. It's all going to be okay."

It had to be. I jumped out of the truck and shut the door behind me before jogging to a nearby building. I'd studied the campus map some last night and most of my classes were thankfully nearby. Rain pelted my skin, drenching my clothes once more. Entering the lecture hall where my first college class was held, I looked like a drowned rat. I really needed to invest in a jacket. Half of my day would be spent in damp clothes.

Every class that day went the same way. The professor handed out a syllabus and then discussed expectations for the semester. Afterward, they reminded us it was important to have our textbooks by the end of the week and that this was no longer high school. Even if we were honor students then, we would have to study now. I wasn't worried about it but made a mental note to see how much my textbooks were this afternoon. My first paycheck from Frankie was being deposited Thursday and there was no way it would cover everything. I had only been working there a few days.

It was just one more thing to worry about.

That afternoon, the rain finally let up. After hours of listening to professors drone on and struggling to stay awake, I quickly stopped by the bookstore. My stomach rumbled, reminding me I hadn't eaten anything since the day before and it was now lunch. I ignored it knowing that I only had three dollars to my name and there was something to eat at home, even if my aunt was the one who purchased it. I was still angry about what she had said Saturday morning, but I also wasn't foolish enough to rock the boat too much yet. Right now, I needed her, even if her support came with judgment.

Pulling the sheets from my nearly dry backpack, I perused the shelves and tried to keep my eyes from popping out of my head. All the books were expensive, but calculus might have been the worst. Nearly $300 for one book? Even if Frankie was extremely generous with my pay, I would need to sell a kidney to make it through this semester.

Sighing deeply, I glanced through, trying to see if there were any used copies of the textbooks I needed for my classes, and then at the small bulletin board near the entrance where people posted books they were attempting to sell. Of course, the ones I was looking for weren't available.

Howard Athletic Complex sat across campus and I decided to make the trek there to apply for the tutoring position before meeting Rosalyn. I would need every penny this semester between classes, gas money, books, and now tires. Students laughed and talked with each other as they sauntered to their next destination and a hint of longing struck me. I wanted that kind of easy companionship again. I hadn't seen any of the guys from Friday night on campus yet, but part of me wanted to catch at least a glimpse of them.

Looking down at my feet, I lost myself in my head, worrying about what I was going to do. Not paying attention to where I was going, I suddenly stepped into something solid. The breath was knocked out of me and I looked up, my face instantly heating. Standing in front of me was

Camden. His jaw was clenched and his eyes narrowed as he glared at me. I had hoped to run into them today, but this wasn't what I had in mind. "I'm sorry," I blurted out.

Trey and Niko stood nearby, casually watching our interaction with bored expressions. Cam gave me a cold smile and slowly prowled closer. He tucked a piece of hair behind my ear that had fallen out of my bun at some point and leaned close to my face. Whatever softness I had seen from him on Saturday morning had vanished, and a look that could only be described as malice had replaced it. His breath caressed my skin and goosebumps formed along my arms. "No apologies are necessary, little ghost. In fact, I was wondering if you would show up today after what happened to your car."

His fingers trailed down my neck and wrapped around my throat in a warning. The realization that they were responsible for what happened to my car floored me. *What in the fuck did I do to them? What possibly happened in the past forty-eight hours?* My heart sped up as I tried to jerk out of his grip, but he was faster than I was. His other arm banded around my waist, drawing me flush against his body.

"I need you to listen closely to what I'm going to say. You should leave Clearhaven, withdraw from all of your classes, and purchase a ticket to somewhere else. Seeing you makes me sick."

I looked over to the other two men that I'd spent the night with and neither moved a muscle. Niko stared down at his nails while Trey fished a knife out of his pocket, twirling it between his fingers.

Steeling my spine, I met his stony gaze. His blue eyes looked like the sea on a stormy day, dark and wild. "No," I gritted out from between my teeth, my embarrassment from earlier gone. I fisted my hands in his shirt, my cheeks on fire from anger. "Get fucked, Camden."

Our lips were a fraction of an inch from one another and from the edges of my vision, I could see a crowd forming around us. He lowered his voice so that only I could hear. "Oh, but I already have, little ghost. Here's a helpful hint. The next time you decide to fuck around, don't play the innocent, coy girl. It doesn't suit you. There's no way in hell you were a virgin as tight as your sweet cunt is, and as rough as I was while I plowed into you. Imagine my surprise when I discovered there was no blood coating my cock after you acted so timid about sucking Niko's dick."

Rage and hurt dueled inside me. This self-absorbed prick. I wasn't pretending to be *anything*, but his words brought back the questions I'd had in the shower the morning after. Choosing not to address that for the moment, I turned off all of my emotions, willing the burning behind my eyes to go away. "I don't know what in the hell this is about, but if you were worried about me becoming clingy or getting attached, don't bother."

He let out a loud laugh and then squeezed tighter, leaving me to struggle for my breath. "You didn't think anyone would discover your dirty little secret, did you?" I clawed at his hand that branded my throat, but it did no good. "If you don't leave, I'll make your life a living hell.

I'll make sure that your pathetic existence is lonely and everyone knows exactly who your daddy is."

The edges of my vision darkened. Sucking in a deep breath, desperate for precious air, I plotted out my next move. It was unfair that I was going to be punished yet again for my father's actions. Any logical person would realize I had no knowledge of my father's crimes. When the evidence was leaked to the media, I was as shocked as everyone else. "I'm not going anywhere," I somehow managed to rasp out. "There's nowhere else for me to go."

I lifted my knee quickly in one last desperate attempt to escape his grasp and missed my mark. Instead of kneeing him in the dick, all I managed to do was hit his rock hard thigh, injuring myself in the process. He squeezed once more before pushing me away like I was trash. I stumbled back a few feet and landed on the concrete. Pain shot through my body but my hands drifted to my throat as I quickly sucked in several breaths, trying to calm my racing heart.

Niko stalked toward Cam and laid a hand on his forearm, shaking his head at him. Cam ignored him and ran his tongue over his bottom lip. He raised his voice so that the onlookers could hear him."No one speaks to Ivy Spencer. She's dead to everyone in Clearhaven. Spread the word. If you go against us, there will be consequences."

I glanced around at the crowd of people. A few had looks of pity on their faces, and some were bored. A group of girls dressed in athletic wear had their phones pointed in my direction. Great, just what I needed–for my face to be all over social media again. Trey moved closer to the others and cleared his throat. "Alright, the show's over, guys. Get the hell out of here."

The three of them turned their backs to me without another word and sauntered off like they didn't have a care in the world as the onlookers slowly dispersed. I sat on the ground for several moments, stunned by how quickly my day had gone to shit.

Nothing was going according to plan at this point. Clearhaven was supposed to be my fresh start.

If Cam thought he could break me by turning me into a social pariah, he was wrong. I'd already lived through that back home. It hurt a lot worse to be cast aside by people I'd known my entire life than by people I had just met.

Even though, deep down inside, it still hurt—just a little.

Ivy

Trudging inside of the athletic's building, I first darted inside of the women's restroom to clean myself up. One look in the mirror told me everything that I needed to know. My cheeks were still ruddy from the confrontation I'd had with Cam and my hair poked out from the haphazard bun I'd thrown it into this morning.

Turning the water on, I stuck my hands under the cold liquid and noticed a sting on my palms. They were scraped from my fall earlier, but I hadn't noticed until that moment. My pride was more wounded than my body at this point. I splashed cold water on my cheeks and carefully blotted my face with paper towels before trying to dust my clothes off.

When I was leaving the bathroom, a dark haired woman in a crop top sneered at me while flipping her hair over her shoulder. *Whatever.* Her attitude could have nothing to do with Camden's royal decree and everything to do with the fact I looked like a hot mess. My phone buzzed in my pocket, but I ignored it. I would check it after I applied for the tutoring position. I was going to prove that no one, even the Forsaken, would run me off.

Down a small corridor, I finally found an administrative office tucked into a corner, hidden away from the rest of the world. Behind a wooden desk, an ancient woman with horn-rimmed glasses typed on a keyboard. When I walked in, she held up one finger, asking me to give her a moment. I awkwardly stood there listening to the sound of keys clicking and the tick of the clock hanging on the wall. Finally, she looked up at me and sighed, her face drawn. "How can I help you?" Her tone told me she would rather not be bothered now or at any time in the future.

"Yeah, I'm here about the tutoring position," I managed to stammer out.

She sniffed and stood, handing me a piece of paper from the top of the desk. "Fill this out, but the position is yours. No one wanted it because of this student's... attitude."

I raised my eyebrow as she shoved the pen and paper in front of me. Whoever it was couldn't possibly be as bad as Cam. I could put up with nearly anything. I found it odd that she didn't ask how I was qualified to tutor the student or even mention which subject it was.

On the form, there was a line asking if I was comfortable reading and discussing literary works. *Piece of cake.* I filled in the blanks on the sheet quickly and handed it back to the older woman. She nodded and shoved it into a folder. "The hours are Tuesday from noon to two. He's requesting that you meet him at the campus library on the third floor near the archives. Pay is one hundred dollars a week with a bonus payout at midterm and the end of the semester–if he passes. Well, and if you make it that long."

I gave her a tight smile. "Thank you for your time. I'll be there."

When I exited the building, I pulled my phone from my pocket. I had been ignoring it while I was pulling myself together and applying for the tutoring position. There were twenty notifications, all from Rosalyn.

Ros: Where are you?

Ros: We were supposed to meet after classes.

Ros: I'm worried about you. I'm sending a message to Trey.

My heart sank. Was she included in the whole "no one can speak to me" thing? Even though we hadn't been friends long, I really liked her.

Ros: I'm going to kill them

Ros: Just tell me you're okay.

Ros: Fucking assholes.

Ros: I'm waiting for you in the dining hall still.

Ros: After we take care of your car, a bottle of vodka is calling our names

Ros: I can't believe they are the ones responsible for your car. I'm so pissed right now.

I shut off my phone and picked up my pace, headed to meet her. At least I knew she wouldn't abandon me based on the decree of one gigantic douchebag. A bottle of vodka sounded fantastic right about now.

Stepping into the dining hall, I spotted Rosalyn instantly. Her jacket from earlier was gone and in her hands was a bag of food. She jogged toward me and handed me a soda. "I picked up food for us to eat on the way. We have shit to do. "

If I thought I was determined earlier, she was on a whole other level. Her shoulders were pulled back and her head held high as she pulled us through the people milling about on campus. Every time someone so much as looked our way, she held up her middle finger in their direction.

"Ivy, you will not allow those three thugs to run your life here," she stated as we approached her car. "I love them all. Grew up with them." She swung the door open and met my eyes. "But this time, they're wrong." She hoisted herself into the driver's seat and motioned impatiently for me to get in.

As I fastened my seat belt, she dug through the brown bag and passed me something wrapped in paper. The scent of onions filled the car and my stomach growled again. "Eat," she commanded.

She didn't have to tell me twice. It was just a hamburger, but the first bite was heaven. In less than three minutes, the entire sandwich was gone. Placing the paper crumpled into the bottom of the bag, I opened the cap on the cherry soda and took a deep drink, hoping that the caffeine and sugar would make me feel more alive.

For some reason, I had assumed we were headed back to my aunt's house. Instead, Rosalyn pulled her truck into the parking lot of a blue cinder block building with two garage doors. The side had the words "Mack's Tires and Oil" painted in spray paint. The logo was pulled straight out of the 1960s and reminded me of the old-school DC Comics' 'pow' or 'bam'.

I took another sip of my drink and Rosalyn jumped out of the car. An attractive tall, broad man with sleeve tattoos stalked out of the building and caught her around the waist. *What did they put in the water here? Why were all of the men insanely gorgeous?* She scowled at him and pushed him away, placing her hands on her hips.

One day I hoped to convey the same level of sass. Finally, I exited the truck, curious about why we were there. "Baby girl, your car's almost ready. If you two want to help, then this can be done in less than an hour."

My eyes widened at his words, confused by what he was talking about. My car was ready? I'd left it in front of Regina's house this morning.

Ros bumped my hip with hers, grinning. "I asked for a few favors this morning and picked up the spare key to the car from my grandfather. Surprise."

My heart beat faster. She had helped me despite everything today. "Ros, I don't have the money to pay you back..." I stalled, unsure of what to call the bronzed god standing nearby. "Or your friend."

He offered me his hand and chuckled. "Mack, but don't worry. She doesn't owe me cash. I'll take my payment out of her—"

Ros' cheeks turned bright red as she shoved an elbow into his ribs, stopping his sentence in its tracks. "Enough from you," she muttered. "Now, what do you need us to do?"

Mack laughed harder, throwing his head back at her reaction. He handed us rags when we entered the shop and a bottle of nail polish remover. Sitting in the bay was my Honda with four new to me tires and half of the spray paint missing from the body. "I was in the middle of taking the graffiti off when you texted me to say you were on the way. I didn't have time to fix the door today, but the two of you should be able to finish this up in the next hour while I make some calls."

He pressed a quick kiss to the top of her head while she glared at him. Once he was safely out of earshot, the corner of my mouth lifted. "So you're...?" I poured a small amount of acetone onto the rag and gingerly rubbed at the graffiti while waiting for an answer.

She pursed her lips while she thought of what to say. "Aren't together. We have an arrangement. He wants more than I'll give him. Plus, I can't exactly bring him to meet my family. I can just imagine what my grandfather would say. 'Boys like that are nothing but trouble.'" She mimicked an old man, and I snorted.

"Okay, so you and Mack aren't a thing... yet." I peered up at her over the hood and lowered my voice. "You didn't have to help me. I'll never be able to repay you."

She rolled her eyes as she scrubbed at the spray paint. "I didn't have to do anything, but I wanted to."

My emotions were creeping right below the surface of my skin, and I swallowed hard. "What if the guys find out? They said there will be consequences if anyone defies them."

The corner of her mouth tipped up with amusement. "Yeah, for most people, but I'm not like most people, am I? Besides, Niko needs me too much and they won't do shit. Some things are bigger than the Forsaken."

We spent the next hour in comfortable silence, listening to the music playing over the shop's speakers. When everything was done, my car looked like it had when I picked it up from Ros' grandfather's last week.

Later that evening, we drove to a cemetery on the outskirts of town and parked. Rosalyn pulled a bottle of vodka out from underneath her seat and grabbed my hand. "Let's go."

Shivers of excitement traveled down my spine. I wasn't sure what we were doing, but I loved ancient places like this. They held secrets no one dared utter, not even in the middle of the night. We crept past the broken iron gate, the chain that had locked it long since gone. We walked for a while, an owl hooting overhead. The clouds from earlier had dissipated and now the moon shined down, casting everything in its glow. Some tombstones were crumbled and a tall mausoleum lay on the right side of the property.

"Why are we here?" I whispered.

She chuckled at me as she opened the glass bottle and tilted it up, taking a drink. "It was here or the beach and

I thought after the day you had, you'd prefer not to run into anyone else." A stone bench from decades gone past sat on the left-hand side and she took a seat. "Besides, I like to come here at night and think. It's quiet. The dead don't bother me. It's the living you have to worry about."

I grabbed the vodka from her hand, not knowing how to respond, and let the alcohol burn my throat. I winced a little, trying to suppress the cough I knew was coming. We passed the bottle back and forth for a while, the owl still calling out overhead and the cicadas screaming. "The only time that the graveyard isn't quiet is around Halloween. The Forsaken throw an enormous party here."

I picked at the hem of my shirt where a thread was coming loose. "I'll be sure to stay home that night," I mumbled under my breath before taking another swig and allowing the warmth to spread through my veins.

"Absolutely not." She took the bottle from my hands and stared up at the sky. "They'll be over it by then, hope-fully." She sniffed and then coughed lightly, clearing her throat. "I know why they reacted the way they did. Well, Camden anyway. He's got a younger sister and well…" She rubbed her eyes before tipping the bottle back. "They dropped her case. Your dad… She's doing better now, but for a while it was hit-and-miss. I don't agree with how he's acting, but they won't stand up to him. Niko might once he gets fed up."

What a hell of a way to end the day: drinking cheap vodka in an abandoned graveyard and discovering that your father hadn't just ruined your life, but also the life of a girl you'd never met. "I get it, but it still sucks," I said, peering at the weathered stone in front of me. "I just wish things were different."

She clutched my arm and laid her head on my shoulder. "So do I."

There was an entire list of things I wished were different and regrets I had. As we passed the bottle back and forth, I thought of Cam's sister, a girl I didn't know but that my heart hurt for. There was more to the story that wasn't said, but I was quickly learning that whatever was done in the dark would be brought to light, eventually.

Cam

By the time Niko and I got home that evening, all of our siblings were bustling around the kitchen preparing dinner. Maya ignored me as she cut potatoes into chunks. Niko ruffled Sergei's hair as he passed by, looking for a glass in the dish rack. Only his younger sister, Katya, greeted us. "Why are you guys late? We had to figure out what to cook without you!"

Katya was the exact opposite of her brother, with bright green eyes and white-blond hair. She'd formed a fast friendship with my sister when they were in preschool. Niko and I had raised all of them given both of our home situations. Between absentee parents, alcoholic mothers, addict fathers, and poverty, we had managed to win the lottery.

"Squirt, we had something to take care of. Besides, it looks like the three of you managed all on your own." I winked at her, keeping my mask in place. Really, the rage from earlier still simmered under my façade and I didn't know what to do with it. Even practice hadn't helped to displace the darkness swirling inside of me. Out of every person in the world, Ivy had to be related to him.

"We shouldn't have to, Camden," she sassed back.

I rubbed the back of my neck and closed my eyes. "Kat, all three of you are in high school now. It isn't fair, but you're going to have to pick up the slack."

By the time Niko was her age, he and I had started the weekday dinner tradition and we all spent the night at his house afterward. It was safer here than at home. His mom had overdosed when we were younger leaving behind everything, and his dad was never home, off looking for his next fix, but it was still better than my mother.

For years, we made sure that all of their homework was complete, everyone brushed their teeth, and they were tucked in. Maya slept on a bunk bed in Katya's room, oblivious to everything happening around her, thinking that every night was a slumber party. We would sneak out once they were sound asleep to do whatever needed to be done, and afterward we crashed in Niko's bed.

Katya interrupted my bitter stroll down memory lane. "I get it. You have business," she used air quotes and I rolled my eyes, "to take care of. Just a little warning would be nice."

Maya hummed in agreement while she tossed seasoning onto the potatoes and Sergei - well he watched them while leaning against the wall.

After everyone's homework was finished and the dishes were washed, our siblings disappeared into the neighborhood while Niko and I pulled our textbooks out. He passed me a bottle of beer from the refrigerator. Our fingers met for a moment too long causing sparks to ignite beneath my skin. "We need to talk," he mumbled as he pulled a stool beside mine.

I cocked an eyebrow up and opened my drink. "What about? If it's about Ivy—"

He put his hand over my mouth, silencing me. He leaned closer, and I wasn't sure what he would say next. His eyes were dark with anger and something else I didn't want to think about right now—or remember. "Cam, shut the fuck up. This isn't about Ivy. It's about Sergei, but if you want to fight about this afternoon, we can. You acted like a complete dick." I stayed silent and he removed his hand. "He wants to join the Forsaken, and I need you to convince him otherwise. We joined so they wouldn't have to. It was supposed to be our ticket out of this place, but now it's basically anchoring us here. I don't want that for him or the girls."

I narrowed my eyes at him. "Over my dead body will either of the girls join. You know what that means for both of them." I looked away to break the intensity of the moment. "I'll talk to Sergei. He's smart and his grades are good. Right now, he could make it out of here." I almost added "unlike us," but kept my mouth shut. I knew better than to feed into Niko's current mood. The last thing I wanted tonight was a fight between the two of us or where it might lead. Coach would ream my ass tomorrow at practice if I showed up with a black eye.

Opening up the literature anthology, I sighed. The words jumbled together, and I pressed my fingertips into my eyes, allowing spots to form beneath my lids. It had always been like this for as long as I could remember. In high school, I'd skated by convincing other people to write my papers and sweet talking my teachers.

College had proven to be more difficult, and I needed to get it together. American literature was one of the last classes I needed to graduate. Sure, I could pay someone to write my papers–the quiet girls in class were more than happy to help me however I needed, basking in the little attention I gave them–but if I didn't understand the material, I would never pass the exams.

Niko placed his hand on my shoulder, all the fire from moments ago gone from his expression. "You know I'll help you, right?"

I just bobbed my head at him, completely exhausted. Between running drugs for the gang, practice for football, taking care of Maya, and now Ivy, I just wanted to sleep. I gave him a cheeky grin that I didn't feel to reassure him. "Hey but C's get degrees. And C's keep me playing on Saturdays."

He rolled his eyes at me. "Did they find a new tutor yet?"

"Yeah, I checked my email earlier and I get to meet the new person tomorrow at noon."

He gently squeezed my shoulder, and I pulled away. He frowned at the loss of contact, but I ignored it. Even something as small as physical comfort was a luxury I couldn't allow myself. "Don't run this one off, man. I know it pisses you off, but keep your temper. You need them."

"I know. Besides, if I can just make it through this one class, I'll be good." I pulled out the blue reading ruler from my bag. "Your next race is Thursday night? Have you told Trey that he has to leave his hole to make an appearance yet?" We all did things on the side to make a little cash. Niko's was street racing, and I had never seen him lose.

He tapped a pencil on the piece of paper in front of him. "I'll call him in a little while. We probably need to make sure he has food again. I don't understand why he won't just eat dinner with us every night."

I looked down at my book and pretended to focus on the words in front of me. Niko didn't understand, but I did.

Trey didn't want to burden us any more than he felt like he already did. Living on his own, he knew all about financial struggles, but he didn't understand that one more person wouldn't matter. We would do anything for him. The three of us were brothers, not by blood, but by choice. We were stronger when we were all taken care of.

Around lunch the next day, Niko and Trey dropped me off on campus before they headed to Vincent's house. He wasn't pleased that I wouldn't be there, but I had politely told him to fuck off. Between meeting my new tutor and practice, I didn't have time for his shit. I would deal with him on Thursday.

Phillips-Thompson Library was nestled next to a greenway. All the main buildings were scattered around a fountain, and students gathered on the grass to study and talk in the sunlight. For a fleeting moment, I questioned if all of their lives were as complicated as mine.

After stalling for as long as I could, I stepped inside the tall brick building and turned left to climb the stairs to the third floor. No one really came up here and I liked the privacy that it offered. A table sat in the corner near the large windows that overlooked the campus and was hidden from sight by tall bookshelves piled with dusty books that no one had checked out in years.

I dropped my bag beside the table and sat down in a chair, staring out the window and wondering who the athletic department would send this time. All the previous tutors had lasted less than a month, frustrated over my progress or scared off by my outbursts. I was only doing this to continue playing on the team.

Really, I wanted nothing more than to disappear inside the darkroom on campus and develop the photos I'd taken. Trey helped me sell some prints online and the money I made went to groceries and Maya's therapy bills. In a town like Clearhaven, becoming a full-time photographer was a pipe dream. No one had the money for photography sessions here. Every penny went to either making ends meet or drugs. Still, I held onto the hope that one day we would all escape. It was one of the few things holding me together.

I tapped on the wooden table in front of me impatiently and glanced at the time. 12:05. Punctuality was obviously not in my new tutor's vocabulary, and I found myself getting annoyed. These two hours a week were the time I had carved out in my schedule to make sure I could pass this class–especially since I failed it over the summer. At any moment, some lanky guy wearing glasses would come sauntering up the steps holding an overpriced cup of coffee from some chain off campus. The longer I sat there, the more aggravated I got by the situation. By 12:10, I was livid.

And then she walked in.

My lips curled into a cruel smile as she scanned the room, looking for whoever she was supposed to be meeting. She hadn't noticed me yet. If Ivy was my new tutor, fate had a fucked up sense of humor. It would work out perfectly for me. Two hours a week to torment her and convince her that she needed to disappear from Clearhaven for good.

Finally, her eyes met mine, and realization dawned on her. Her face paled and her eyes grew wide. I winked as she shuffled slowly to the table and took a deep breath. This semester had just taken an interesting turn.

Ivy

I'd been running slow all morning. My nightmares were back with a vengeance and the lack of sleep was getting to me. When I saw it was already 11:40, I left the house, breaking every traffic law that I thought I could get away with. It looked bad to show up late to my first tutoring session, and I really needed the job.

The parking lot near the library was full when I arrived on campus. I knew it would be busier than it was at eight in the morning but this was ridiculous. I followed the signs to the overflow lot across campus near the athletic complex and grimaced realizing I was going to be late even if I jogged the entire way. It wasn't exactly a great first impression, but perhaps they would understand.

There wasn't a cloud in sight as I locked the door for my car and took off, practically sprinting. The sun beat down on me and sweat trickled down my back. The bag slung across my shoulders felt like it weighed a million pounds although it only held a notebook and some pens. *Only two days until I can buy part of my books,* I reminded myself.

Entering the air-conditioned library, I breathed a sigh of relief and then realized I would need to climb two flights of stairs. *Fuck my life.* Looking down at my phone I saw it was already 12:09, and I prayed that whoever was waiting for me had some degree of patience. My thigh muscles screamed when I finally arrived on the third floor. I scanned the nearly empty space, looking for any sign of life. I quietly wandered, peaking around bookcases for any student that might be waiting.

And then I saw him. *You have got to be fucking kidding me.* Out of everyone on campus, it would have to be Camden. My heart skipped a beat as I made my way to the table he was sitting at. *It would be okay. What was the worst thing that would happen?* He needed help with his lit class; I needed the cash. Surely everything from yesterday would be forgotten, right?

Wrong. As soon as he saw me, his lips turned up into a malicious smile and I knew things wouldn't go according to plan. When he stood, I took a step back away from him, hoping to gain some much-needed distance. Despite his coarse words from yesterday, my traitorous body still reacted to his presence.

"Hey, little ghost. You're looking pale, even for you."

He prowled closer, and soon I was trapped. My back hit one of the metal bookcases lining the room and I held my breath, waiting to see what he would do. His proximity and the scent of the ocean clouded my senses. He picked up a lock of hair that had fallen from my bun and rubbed it between two fingers. "So, I guess you aren't going to drop your classes and leave town like I suggested yesterday." He dropped the strands and edged closer, placing both hands beside my body and caging me in.

The heat from his skin and the smell of the ocean enveloped me, giving me a false sense of security. Logic told me not to let my guard down despite his calm demeanor. I swallowed hard and tilted my head up to look him in the eyes. "No. I told you yesterday that I wouldn't. I'm stuck here just like you are," I said, my voice wavering a bit.

Cam dropped his face closer, his mouth hovering near mine. His breath feathered against my lips and his left hand suddenly gripped my hip. He stalked forward, eating away at the little bit of distance that was between us. "Is that so?"

Like an idiot, I froze. My brain screamed at me that I was in danger, but my body was a traitor. Between his proximity and the breath caressing my face, my heart sped up and my nipples hardened. I could only pray that the baggy t-shirt I was wearing helped hide the effect he was having on me. The last thing I needed was for him to know and hold it over my head. I gritted my teeth together, trying to think of what to say or do. "What makes you think that you're the only one trapped here, Cam?"

His fingers brushed up my torso from my hip to below my breast and my mouth suddenly felt dry. "It must be so hard for you, Ivy, to go from having everything that kids around here could only dream of to having nothing. Tell me," his thumb brushed over my nipple, sending sparks of arousal shooting straight between my thighs and he raised an eyebrow. "How badly do you need this tutoring position? Being stuck with me once a week for two hours will be your own personal hell."

I bit down on my lip and stalled, trying to think of how to get out of the position I was in. Telling him I needed the tutoring gig seemed like a misstep, but the reality was that I wasn't leaving the library. An extra $400 right now would help me buy my books, a jacket before cooler weather set in, and gas to get to work. "You don't scare me. I need the money and you need to pass this class to keep playing sports for the university."

His thumb continued to circle my hardened peak. Voices echoed softly from somewhere across the room behind the massive shelf I was trapped behind. I grabbed his wrist, coming to my senses. "Stop. Someone might see us and we're wasting time. I'm here to help you with literature, not suck your dick," I told him, my voice coming out louder than I intended. "We have less than an hour and a half to get started."

He smirked and moved his mouth close to my ear. "Shh. I need you to be quiet or I'll find something to shove into your mouth." His teeth grazed my earlobe, and I bit down on my lip. "Here's the thing. The reason we only have an hour and a half is that you were late. You wasted my time and now we have to come to some type of agreement. Since I can't convince you to quit and save us both the heartache, I think we should have a little fun. Turn around."

My eyes widened at his words. His audacity knew no bounds. "Absolutely not," I hissed, careful to keep my voice lowered. "Let go of me so that we can get started."

He gripped my shoulders and turned me quickly like I was nothing more than a feather, pressing my front into the shelf behind us. I tried to struggle, but he banded one arm tightly around my mid. "Here's what I think is going to happen. I could have had any person on campus show up today, but it had to be you. Since you need this job so desperately and you don't want your secret about daddy getting out, I think we need to come to an understanding. You'll do everything that I say without an argument."

One of his massive hands cupped my breast and squeezed as he sucked the skin below my ear into his mouth. My cheeks flushed at his words and I clenched my thighs together, praying that this moment would be over soon. "And if I don't?"

His hand snaked below the hem of my top and the feeling of his fingers against my bare skin caused my breath to hitch. Leisurely, he trailed up my torso until he caressed the edge of my bra. "I'll make sure that the pictures of you and your father end up plastered all over social media, including the university groups."

Cam's words were a punch to the gut. The last thing I wanted was for anyone to know about my past. Right now, I was only a social outcast because he had commanded no one to speak to me. If word got out, I would either be hated or pitied.

I tried to throw an elbow backward–anything to stop him and show my displeasure–but he easily dodged it and chuckled before rolling his hips against my ass. He was hard. Really hard. His fingers dipped beneath the cup of my bra and he rolled my nipple between his thumb and forefinger. "Tell me something, little ghost. As much as you want to hate me at this exact moment, how wet would you be if I were to check right now?"

My cheeks were on fire and I was embarrassed knowing that although he was essentially blackmailing me into what he wanted, my underwear was damp. How was it possible to be angry, ashamed, and turned on all at the same time? "Go fuck yourself, Cam," I whispered.

He laughed again as the arm that was banded around my waist loosened and his hand splayed across my stomach. He bit down hard on the side of my neck causing me to wince before his tongue lapped along the sensitive skin. Goosebumps erupted on my arms and I leaned my head back, my body acting without my permission.

What the fuck was he doing to me? He quickly undid the top button of my jeans before pushing beneath the fabric. He knew exactly the effect he was having on me, no matter how unwelcome it was, as he slowly slid his fingers through my wet folds.

"Fuck, you really do like this, don't you?" he murmured. "Me caging you and trapping you like you're nothing more than prey." He rubbed against my clit and a whimper escaped from beneath my throat. It felt good even though I didn't want it to. He quickly yanked the hand that was clutching my breast from beneath my shirt and covered my mouth, his fingers gripping my face. "None of that now. There is someone on the other side of this bookshelf and I know that the last thing you want is for someone to hear us. You have to be quiet for me."

I fought against the waves of arousal as they coursed through me, driving me higher and higher as he drew circles around the sensitive nub. Suddenly, he plunged two fingers inside of me, grinding the heel of his palm against my clit. I gripped his arm, trying to steady myself, digging my nails into his flesh until it broke the skin.

I could fight this. He could use me however he wanted, but I wouldn't give in. Cam sucked along the column of my neck hard enough to leave marks as his fingers thrust in and out of me, every pass grazing my clit. My walls tightened around him and I tried to think of anything else but the sensations that had overtaken my body.

"Just give in, ghost. I feel how tightly your pussy is wrapped around my fingers. Your body is begging for you to let go. Let me see you lose control." Behind my eyes stung at his words. He knew what I was doing. He moved his hand from my mouth and turned my face to his. His mouth met mine, and he forced his tongue inside, tasting like mint. At the same time, the fingers inside of me curled upward, hitting a spot that made me groan, and that was all it took.

My traitorous body gave him what he wanted.

Cam's hold on me tightened and my body trembled as the edges of reality faded. Arousal dripped down my thighs and my walls pulsed around his fingers. It was both heaven and hell wrapped in one neat package. The person who wanted to destroy me swallowed my cries as I came and a tear fell down my cheek.

My breathing slowed and reality crashed back in. What in the fuck had I just done? I turned my head, and he removed his fingers from inside me, moisture glistening on them. I glared and pushed at his hard body, willing my heart rate to slow. He took a step back and gave me a lazy smirk as I adjusted my clothes and fastened the button on my pants.

"Freshly fucked is a good look on you," he said as he pulled some money from his wallet and threw it on the table. "Here's your pay for this week."

My jaw dropped at his statement, and a mixture of anger and hurt suddenly struck me. He was dismissing me and treating me like I was a whore. Not his tutor. We hadn't even cracked open a book. Without realizing what I was doing, my hand raised and swung toward his face. He caught my wrist and squeezed, a tinge of pain running up my arm. His grin widened at the action. "Don't you dare. I like your spirit, but if you hit me, I'll put you on your knees and shove my cock in your mouth. Next week I expect you to show up on time or I'll change where we meet to somewhere much more private."

Completely ashamed of myself and livid at his words, I grabbed the money and my bag. I couldn't deal with his shit right now and I had to work at the surf shop. If he thought he could somehow break me or treat me however he wanted, he was wrong—no matter how pretty his stupid face was. He didn't deserve any of my tears. He could fail for all I cared.

As I raced out of the library, people looked up from their books and stared at me. Whatever. They could fuck themselves, too. I had other things to worry about, like figuring out how to exist.

Ivy

I t was Wednesday, and I was struggling to keep my eyes open as the professor at the front of the room discussed the development of society. World civilization was a mandatory general education class for graduation, but most of the information that was being relayed had already been covered in my AP classes in high school. And middle school. It didn't help that sleep the night before was restless and fevered. The memory of the dream was still fresh in my mind and I rubbed my hands down my cheeks.

"*Little lamb,*" *a deep voice said as I stared at the golden light fixture hanging from the ceiling. My vision was blurred, and the object was hazy. I was always immobile, unable to use my legs or arms. I wanted to scream as his hot breath scorched my cheek and bile rose in my throat. My body was stiff, and I wasn't sure where my clothes were as his fingers touched me in places that I didn't want. His hands were harsh, like blades of ice as they dug into my hip. Out of the corner of my eye, I glimpsed a shadow move to my other side. Hot trails of tears streaked my cheeks from fear, and I was certain that I was suffocating.*

"We've all waited so long for this moment." the man stated with reverence as someone parted my thighs. Which was worse, that I couldn't scream or that I couldn't fight them off while I was stuck in my head? Between my legs burned at the intrusion of something, and pain lanced through my body.

No, no no! This couldn't be happening.

I managed to make a muffled noise, but someone tsked at me. "I thought you said you gave her enough. She shouldn't be able to say anything," someone grumbled.

Another of the shadows spoke, black eyes standing out in the haze. "Don't worry, I'll take care of this. Next time, we'll give her more." Rough hands grasped my jaw, painfully forcing my mouth wide as they shoved something inside.

The deep voice next to me whispered, almost like he was consoling a child. "Hush, little lamb. If you relax, it will be easier. You knew your turn was coming."

Even in the light of day, sweat formed on my brow, and panic clawed at my throat. I knew they were only dreams, but sometimes they felt so real. I inhaled sharply and focused on the blank paper in front of me, drawing shapes on the corner of the page.

Finally, the professor stopped her lecture, and I sat up straight, trying to pay attention to whatever homework she might decide to dole out. "This week I want everyone to read chapters one through five. Remember to check your university email! I'll be sending out a document outlining a project that is worth thirty percent of your final grade. You need to find a partner before next week."

Great.

After the Forsaken's declaration last week, finding someone who was willing to openly defy them was going to be difficult. Maybe if I spoke to the professor, she would let me work alone. I rubbed my eyes and shoved my notebook into my backpack, waiting for the class to trickle out so I could speak to her alone.

I walked down the stairs in the large auditorium and waited to the side while she spoke with a tall guy. He had broad shoulders that pulled at the seams of his polo while he moved and hair that reminded me of wheat. Overall, he was classically handsome with a sharp jaw. When he caught me watching them, he gave me a friendly smile and a wink. I rolled my eyes and continued to wait. Once he finally shifted and moved out of the way, I approached the older woman who was packing her things away.

"Umm, excuse me, Professor," I racked my brain trying to remember her last name. "Hurst. I was wondering if I could talk to you about the project. Is there anyway that I can work on it solo? I just moved here and I don't really know anyone. Add in work and–"

She cut me off and gave me a sympathetic look. "Miss, I'm sure you have good reasons for wanting to complete your project on your own, but part of the college experience is participating with others in an academic setting and fostering a sense of community. I'm sure that you will find someone willing to work with you." Her lips flattened as she picked up her bag and she turned her back to me. "Besides, Mr. Vance needs a partner, so you're in luck."

The conversation didn't go the way I hoped it would, and there was no way that I could explain that no one on campus was supposed to have any contact with me. I seriously doubted that Mr. Vance, who looked like he was pulled straight out of an American Eagle ad, would want to stand up to gang members. I sighed as I shuffled to the door, not intending on speaking to him. *How much would she dock my grade if I just completed it on my own?*

The guy, whose first name I still didn't know, caught up to me as I exited the building. "Hey, wait up!" he called out from behind me, but I pretended not to hear him, keeping my head ducked low. His hand landed on my shoulder, stopping me in my tracks. "Listen, I need a partner for the project, too. I overheard what you said to Hurst."

I narrowed my eyes at him. "That's not a good idea. You seem nice enough, but surely you've overheard that you're not supposed to speak to me."

He rolled his eyes and gave me an easygoing grin. "Oh, you mean the whole 'no one can speak or touch' thing I saw plastered all over the internet last night because of Camden Barrett? Yeah, I'm not worried about him. They won't bother me."

I raised my eyebrows at him, curious about what that meant. "I can just work by myself, but I appreciate the offer."

He ignored me as he grabbed my hand and pulled me along toward the computer science building. Several girls stared as we passed by, and I knew that word was going to make it back to my tormentors. "So, it's decided. We're partners and we can get started on the project this week-end. Let's go check our email and print the guidelines out."

I was shocked by his brazenness and shook my head. It was his funeral.

"My name is Caleb, just in case you were wondering." He opened the door to a small computer lab and ushered me inside. "Looks like one of your friends is here."

Sure enough, sitting across the room Trey stared at something on the screen in front of him. I stared for a moment, drinking in the set of his jaw while he concentrated and how he brushed his hair from his eyes, causing it to wave across his forehead. I loathed the fact that I still found him attractive, especially after he hadn't stood up to Cam. He was completely oblivious to my attention while he worked, occasionally typing something on the keyboard.

Hopefully, I could keep it that way. I sat at one of the computers nestled toward the edge of the room and logged into my university email. I hadn't checked it yet and as soon as it popped up, I learned I had missed twenty emails. Sorting through them, I quickly found out that most were pointless advertisements for clubs and groups. One was information regarding Greek rush, and I quickly deleted it.

I didn't have the time or money for something like that right now. Besides, being forced to wear dresses and plaster on a fake smile no longer appealed to me. I'd left that life behind when I moved here.

One email held my attention, and I quickly clicked on it. It was a personal note from the dean and I was nervous, wondering what the contents would hold.

Dear Ivy,

I am requesting for you to stop by my office at your earliest convenience. As you may be aware, I am close friends with your father and promised that I would look after you during your stay at Clearhaven University. No appointment is necessary.

Sincerely,

Abraham Wells

Well crap. The email was sent on Monday and I knew I needed to stop by before I headed to Frankie's this evening. The email was odd, but given that he knew my father, perhaps it was nothing. Just him trying to check up and make sure I was settling in.

I quickly printed off the assignment the civ professor mailed to us while Caleb stood by patiently waiting and gave him an apologetic smile. "We should exchange numbers. I hate to run, but I have something I need to take care of."

"I understand. Give me your phone," he said, holding out his hand. I did as he asked and in my periphery, I caught movement. Trey had finally caught sight of me and stalked toward us. Caleb was unaware of the confrontation that was about to occur, and I held my breath, bracing for impact.

Trey leaned against the wall near us and watched silently for a moment twirling a knife. When Caleb finally looked up to hand me back my phone, amusement glinted in his eyes. The atmosphere was stifling, and part of me wanted to hide from the awkwardness. Caleb didn't seem concerned as he crossed his arms over his chest. "Hey, Trey. How's it going?"

Trey looked at Caleb with indifference. "It would be better if you would listen for once. You heard the rule. New girl is off limits."

The situation made me nervous. *Who just pulls out a knife in the middle of a computer lab?* Caleb tilted his head to the side and looked Trey up and down, completely unfazed. "Nah. I don't think so. Besides, she needs a partner for Hurst's project. You had her last semester, so you know how that goes." He broke eye contact and grabbed my hand. "Come on, Ivy. You just mentioned you have things to do today. Trey will be fine, won't you?"

My eyes widened when Trey nodded. "Sure, but you know I have to tell Cam and Niko."

Caleb scoffed at him and pulled me toward the door. "Do whatever you need to. I'm not worried about it."

Once we were outside, I pulled my hand back, unsure of what I had just seen transpire. Was it some type of dick measuring contest or was Caleb genuinely not concerned? I cleared my throat. "Hey, I'll catch you in class on Friday. I've got to go." I hooked my thumb toward the administrative building.

He simply hefted his backpack higher. "Saturday we should figure out our project. You have my number if you need me."

I gave him a thumbs up, unsure of what to say before turning and jogging across the academic quad toward the building I knew the Dean's office was in while making a mental note to ask Ros about Caleb. I had less than an hour before my next class, but curiosity, with a hint of trepidation, pushed me to discover what he wanted.

Abraham Wells was someone I vaguely remembered from some of the parties my father held in the past. They were always stuffy affairs where men in suits smoked cigars and drank scotch while women in cocktail dresses chatted quietly in corners. For an older man, he was attractive with dark hair that silvered at the temples and even darker eyes, but there was nothing that stood out in my mind about our previous interactions other than sometimes he stared a little too long. All of my father's friends did.

The administrative building was a massive brick structure that called back to a different period. Flowers still somehow bloomed in front of it despite the scorching late summer heat and concrete stairs with wrought-iron railings lead to its entrance. I stepped inside the air conditioning, immediately grateful for the cooler air, and noted how quiet it was. The ring of the phone echoed off of the tile floors and as the heavy door shut behind me, I startled.

"Can I help you?" a woman wearing a red blouse asked from the information desk.

I strode closer so that I could ask her which office was the Dean's without raising my voice. "Can you direct me to Abraham Wells' office?"

She frowned at me with distaste and sniffed. "Do you have an appointment?"

"Umm. No, I received an email from him that said—"

She waved her hand in the air, dismissing me. *Rude.* "The dean only sees students when they set up an appointment. He's extremely busy. Perhaps your academic advisor could handle whatever issue you're having."

A door opened across the large space, and someone cleared their voice. "Miss Juliet, that's enough. I told Ivy to stop by at her earliest convenience." His lips curled up into something that resembled a smile, but it didn't reach his eyes. As he gazed up and down my body, I twisted my hands into the hem of my t-shirt from discomfort. I forgot that Abraham Wells made my skin crawl. All of my father's friends did. "Come on, Ivy. I'm sure we have a lot to catch up on."

As soon as I was close enough, he placed his hand on my lower back, pushing me inside of the dark enclosure he called his office. His touch made my blood turn to ice, and I wasn't sure why terror clawed at my throat. The door closed behind us and he motioned to the chairs in front of the desk. "Take a seat and get comfortable, Ms. Spencer." He sat on the corner of the oak desk and I knew I wanted to put as much space between us as possible.

"No thank you, sir. I would rather stand. My next class is in a few minutes and I really need to make sure I'm there on time," I replied, looking for a polite way to turn him down.

"Nonsense. You don't have another class for at least thirty minutes. I took it upon myself to look at your schedule." I shifted on my feet before choosing the seat furthest from him. A dark look passed over his face, but it was gone so quickly that I could have sworn that it was just my imagination. My nightmares were probably messing with my head.

"Tell me how you're settling in, Ivy. I know you've had a lot of changes happen in such a short period of time."

I folded my hands in my lap and pressed my thumb into the skin of my index finger until a crescent moon shape formed, allowing the pain to distract me from the anxiety tumbling through my brain. "Everything is fine. Classes are great and I found a job at a local shop. Clearhaven is wonderful."

The weak smile I gave him apparently wasn't very re-assuring. "I see. Well, if you need anything at all, please let me know. I want to ensure that your college years are a success in every sense of the word. It's really a shame about your father. He's a good man."

My first thought was that my father was not a good man. The façade he presented to society was good, but underneath it all he was evil. The evidence presented to the court showed that.

My second thought was that it was weird. Within the past half hour, I had two different people offer their help. One offer I wasn't sure about, but this one unnerved me. Perhaps it was because of his proximity to my past, but I knew I wouldn't be letting him know anything anytime soon.

He leaned closer and grabbed my hand not unlike what Caleb had done earlier. My breath caught in my throat, and nausea churned in my stomach at his touch. He ran his thumb along my wrist and my eyes widened. "Perhaps you can come by my house sometime soon for dinner? For old time's sake."

I stood quickly and darted to the door, my heart racing in my chest. "Thank you for the invitation, but I'm pretty busy right now. Some other time?" I managed to say as I pulled open the door and escaped as quickly as possible.

I wasn't sure what that was about, but I really didn't want to find out. Ever.

Sunlight blinded me as I took a deep breath, inhaling as much oxygen as my lungs would allow. Off to the side, Niko sat on the stairs next to a pretty girl with black hair, the same one that sneered at me from the athletic's building. A feeling that I didn't want to name reared its ugly head as he smirked at her. Suddenly, he grabbed her hand and I caught what was happening. She passed him an unknown amount of cash and he handed her a baggie of something discreetly.

They weren't flirting. Well, not necessarily. I had just witnessed a drug deal in front of the campus administrative building. For some reason, the three of them peddling drugs didn't surprise me, but I filed the information away for later. Not that I was interested in drugs exactly, but some weed might silence my nightmares, or at least my racing thoughts.

Cash was tight, but I could potentially scrounge up enough money soon. I knew there was no way in hell Cam would sell to me, but maybe I could convince one of the other guys.

Niko

I'd been stalking Ivy all day, but she didn't know that. Trey had pulled up her schedule for me, assuming it was part of the plan to run her off, but it couldn't be further from the truth. I understood Cam wanted to punish her for the crimes that her father committed, but I wasn't behind his plan. I couldn't be.

Ivy haunted every dream and waking moment I had, even if I wasn't allowed to touch her.

Calculus, world civilization, sociology, and American literature. It seemed easy enough to track her movements across campus and ensure that no one other than us spoke to her, but then Caleb Vance appeared, holding her hand. Anger and jealousy ripped through me as I watched him lead her across campus to the computer labs. I clung to the shadows observing him. If he thought he could defy us, or worse, move in on Ivy to offer her some comfort, he was wrong.

I didn't care who he was connected to.

I leaned against the side of the building and waited, scrolling through my phone to kill time. When Ivy came out of the building, Caleb was holding her hand again, touching what wasn't his. I saw her give him an awkward look as she pulled away and gave him a thumbs-up before racing across the campus green toward some of the administrative buildings.

Standing up straight, I tucked my phone away and approached Caleb, intending on intimidating him some. I stepped behind him wordlessly and he sighed. "I know you're there, Stone. It must be my lucky day because I just spoke to your friend inside."

He was talking about Trey. Most of his waking hours were spent inside of a computer lab or in front of a screen. This time of the day, Cam was probably holed up inside of the art building processing film between classes and practice.

"Oh, and what did he say? That you should stay away from Ivy? I know that you've heard what happened the other day." I crossed my arms over my chest when he turned to face me.

The corner of his mouth lifted in amusement, and he rolled his eyes. "Sure, I heard just like the rest of campus. Half of the cheerleading squad took pictures of Ivy and put it on YouConnect with the hashtag trash. But you know as well as I do that your rules don't apply to me."

My scowl deepened at his words. *Fucker.* "I don't care who you're related to or the fact that you think you're untouchable, Caleb. Ivy is off limits."

"That's up to her, isn't it?" He shrugged at me and glanced over his shoulder in the direction Ivy had disappeared in. When he looked back at me, his smug smile widened. "Look, I have somewhere to be, but tell Cam I said hello. He's got to be pretty busy right now with the first game of the season happening in a few days. Some-times I question how he juggles it all. I mean between taking care of his sister because of a drunk mom, and dealing drugs–"

I couldn't stop myself and before I knew it, my fist slammed into the side of his face, knocking him back and throwing him off balance. No one talked about fucking Cam like that. Caleb couldn't understand the things he had gone through or the choices he'd been forced to make. I grabbed the collar of his polo and glared at him, blood trickling from his nose. "Keep his name out of your mouth, Vance. You don't know shit."

I shoved him back hard, and he wiped his nose with the back of his hand, smearing a streak of blood across his cheek before grinning again, and cocked his head to the left. "I mean this with the utmost disrespect, Nikolai. Get fucked."

His uncaring attitude pissed me off worse and I balled my hands into fists at my side, reminding myself that now wasn't the time and I couldn't face disciplinary action right now. He hiked up his bag higher on his shoulder and gave me a wave before sauntering off without a care in the world.

I would talk to Trey and Cam about him later, but right now, I wanted to see where Ivy was going. According to her schedule, she was supposed to be headed to sociolo-gy soon, which was definitely not in the direction of the administrative building.

Strolling in the general direction I had seen her disap-pear in, part of me hoped perhaps she was just going to see her advisor. My stomach sank at the thought the dean had requested a meeting with her. Rumors had floated around campus about him, and while there was no evidence about his alleged indiscretions, I believed them. After all, I knew how he worked on a personal level.

As I approached the concrete stairs, someone tugged on my arm, trying to get my attention. My focus was solely on marching inside of the building and seeing what Ivy was doing, so I attempted to ignore them. I continued to the door, vaguely aware of the person following me, persistent in their attempt to get my attention. The glass cutout out of the heavy doors was in front of me and I had time to glance inside, my hand reaching for the knob.

Dean Wells' hand was firmly planted on Ivy's lower back, ushering them inside his office. The door closed and before I could react, a feminine voice pulled me from my haze. "Niko, are you ignoring me? I'm trying to talk to you."

Arabella glared at me, still holding onto the sleeve of my shirt. Why was she touching me again? Arabella was attractive enough, but I wasn't interested in her or whatever she had to say.

I raised an eyebrow and let a mask of indifference slip over my features. "What do you want now?"

She huffed out a breath and sat on the top step, motioning for me to join her. I settled down next to her and she leaned close to whisper. "I need some of the new product that you're pushing. Lambda Pi is having a party this weekend and Jenny told me you have more tea."

I closed my eyes, hating that this is what my life had become—that people knew I was the campus drug dealer and the person to go to when you wanted something. Instead of saying any of that or telling her to fuck off because I was busy, I went with, "How much?" I needed to push the new product and get Vincent off of our backs.

"Whatever you have on you. If it's a hit, then I'll need more next week." I managed to hold in my sigh and told her my new price before digging into my pocket. Mid exchange, the door behind me opened. If it was Ivy, I didn't want her seeing me sitting next to Arabella because to the untrained eye it would look like more than it was.

Without counting, I shoved the money in my pocket and announced that I would see her next week. Her face fell, but I didn't give a shit. Arabella was a stage five clinger and I couldn't deal with her today.

I rushed down the stairs and grabbed my obsession's shoulder gently. "What did the dean want?" I asked, my voice coming out in a growl.

She spun around, her fiery locks blazing at me in the sunlight, and narrowed her eyes. "The better question is, what do you want, Niko? After everything that happened the other day. You didn't step in or tell Cam to fuck himself! You acted like you were bored and now suddenly you're concerned about what I'm doing in my free time? Get over yourself. I don't owe you answers."

I clenched my jaw and leaned close to her ear, allowing my breath to fan across her skin. Her cheeks flushed, and it crept down her neck at my nearness. Images from Friday night with her on her hands and knees flashed through my mind, and I absentmindedly touched the cut on my hip she'd given me. "I like it when you're angry; it's hot. And I already told you what I want. What did the dean say to you?"

"Nothing," she muttered, not meeting my gaze. "He just wanted to know how I was adjusting to Clearhaven." She wrung her hands together while she stared at the ground, and it clicked.

She was hiding something. I didn't know what it was, but I would let her keep her secrets for now. Eventually, I would find out. I always did.

I inhaled deeply, taking in the scent of citrus that had been haunting me before I pulled away. "Stay away from Caleb. If you don't, Cam will make your life hell."

She finally looked up and rolled her eyes. "He already is. Besides it's for a project, Niko. There's nothing else happening there. If we're done, I have class and then work." She walked by, checking her shoulder into the side of my body, and I grinned.

Cam didn't realize the fire blazing beneath Ivy's skin, but I could see it. She was angry, and she didn't even know it. One day, she was going to explode and I couldn't wait to see the havoc it caused.

My phone vibrated in my pocket, and I suppressed a sigh, wondering who it was this time. Putting in my passcode, I glanced and bit the inside of my cheek until I tasted copper flood my mouth. It was like he knew I had been watching him and wanted to know what he was up to. The text from Abraham Wells was short and to the point. *Tomorrow at noon. We need to talk.*

Later that evening, after everything was settled, Cam and
I convinced Trey to come over so we could talk. Between
classes and Cam's football schedule, we spent less time
together during the fall semester, and there were things
we needed to figure out. The first one was what to do
about Caleb. Trey also had a run-in with him, although
he somehow had less blood involved.

We sat wedged together on the tiny back porch of
the house, drinking lukewarm cheap beers and swatting
away the mosquitoes that landed on our bare skin. "We
should teach him a lesson about defying us. Hypothetically scare him a bit," Trey offered.

Cam mulled it over for a moment and rubbed his hand
across his chin in thought. "Yeah, that's a good idea. We
can't take it too far, though. If his grandfather finds out–"

I cut him off between sips. "He won't tell anyone. Trust
me."

Trey eyed me warily before reaching into his pocket
and pulling out his knife, opening it with a flick of his
wrist. "How can you be so sure?"

I examined the bottle in my hands and peeled back the
edge of the label. "Because we have something that he
wants." Cam raised an eyebrow at me in question, urging
me to continue. "Little ghost. He won't dare to bring any
more attention to her than he already has. Besides, I'm

sure he'll lose interest in her as soon as the newness wears off."

Or at least that was what I hoped. I would share her with my brothers, but Caleb was a wealthy dickhead I'd never gotten along with. He and Ivy had no future together. Caleb was too much of a coward to introduce her to his family. He would openly defy us, but he wouldn't go against the command of his grandfather and risk his inheritance.

Ivy deserved to be more than someone's dirty little secret.

"One more thing," I added. "We have a meeting with the dean."

Trey's knife slipped when the words registered in his brain, creating a shallow slice on the palm of his hand. Crimson droplets trailed his hand but he ignored it. "What does he want?"

Cam closed his eyes and answered for me. "The same thing he always wants. To remind us about what we owe him."

Ivy

Thursday morning, I woke up to a notification on my phone that my first paycheck from Frankie had been deposited into my account. When I logged into online banking, my breath caught. There had to be a mistake. *There was absolutely no way I had earned this at the surf shop.*

My hands trembled as I pressed call to talk to my boss and I nearly dropped the phone several times. Frankie sounded amused when she answered. I could practically hear the laughter in her voice. "What do you need, Ivy?"

"There's been a mistake." My voice was shaky and the tremor in my hands hadn't stopped. "I checked my account just now and I can give the money back."

Frankie cackled at me. "Ivy, calm down. You need to get a cup of coffee and then head to the bookstore. There's no mistake. Think of it as a sign-on bonus." A *sign-on bonus?* They offered those for important positions. Doctors, lawyers, nurses. Not someone who helped to fold clothes or run a cash register. "And before you argue with me, don't worry. You'll earn every penny. I think Sunday we should wax the floors."

Working on Sunday would get me out of another church service with my aunt, so it sounded perfect to me. "Better than the alternative," I joked quietly.

Frankie simply chuckled again and told me she would see me later in the day. I showered quickly and threw on whatever clothes were clean before getting a cup of coffee.

A *thousand dollars*. That was how much I had in my account. It was enough to pay for my books and stop by the thrift store for another pair of jeans and a jacket.

It was still early and the campus bookstore would be open at eight for me to grab what I needed. I sent a text to Ros to see if she wanted to meet up at Mustard Seeds before I needed to clock in at work. I felt lighter than I had in a while. While nothing had changed on the social front and I would still have to deal with the guys from the Forsaken harassing me, but at least the money situation was looking up for now.

Right when I pulled up on campus, Ros sent me a text letting me know she would wait for me. I entered the bookstore and grabbed a basket and the list from my back pocket. Scouring the shelves, I found everything that I needed easily. My arms ached as I toted the books to the front toward the cash register and I wasn't looking forward to lugging them around campus, but at least I would have them. I waited with bated breath on the total while the cashier scanned things looking bored and half asleep.

The total damage for the books came up to nearly $800, and I tried not to vomit as I slid my debit card to pay.

There was a time not too long ago when the total wouldn't have impacted me. Since May, I had been trying to live as cheaply as possible and spending that much at one time made me nervous. As the employee placed my books in the bag, I clutched the receipt they'd handed me like it was a life preserver anchoring me to reality.

Black Betty was parked in front of Mustard Seeds when I finally arrived, and as soon as I pulled the key from the ignition, Rosalyn was already rushing toward my car. "They don't open for another fifteen minutes so we have time to catch up," she told me as she pulled me into a tight hug. "Plus, it gives me time to convince you to go to the game on Saturday. And the after party."

I patted her arm, signaling that she was squeezing the breath out of me, and she giggled while she loosened her grip. It was hard not to give in to her enthusiasm, but attending a football game sounded like hell, and going to the after-party was a terrible idea. "Umm, do you re-member that whole 'no one can talk to me' thing? Pretty sure that includes parties."

She waved me off and dragged me closer to the door. "They'll be fine, especially since Clearhaven is slated to win. Cam will be so busy drinking and drowning in girls that he won't even notice you're there." She lowered her voice and looked around to make sure that no one could hear her. "Besides, you know the rules, right?"

I shook my head in confusion. Rules? This was the first time I heard anything about them. "What do you mean?"

Her eyes lit up with mischief. "The Forsaken have this set of guidelines they came up with in high school. It's a one-and-done thing. Because they chose you at the beach party, you're safe. They won't mess with you again."

I should have been ecstatic. After all, this week Cam had made it a point to humiliate me in front of the school. And then there was the library incident, where he gave me one of the best orgasms of my life after blackmailing me. For some reason, my emotions were jumbled and a pang of emotion cut through my chest. *Was I jealous or sad? Both?*

Whatever it was didn't matter because they were assholes.

I cleared my throat even though my chest was tight. "Yeah, that's probably for the best. I had one crazy night that I can tell my grandkids about and it happened before they turned on me." The words tasted bitter on my tongue as I recalled the things Cam had uttered this week.

Rosalyn grabbed my hand and squeezed. "I'm going to say this with my whole chest, Ivy. Fuck them. They don't know what they are missing. Come to the party and we can dance, drink, and since they are preoccupied, find you someone to flirt with." She wiggled her eyebrows and I couldn't help the laugh that spilled from my mouth.

Begrudgingly, I agreed. "Fine, but I need to find a really cute top to wear." If I was being forced to attend a party and see women crawl over the guys, then I wanted them to at least realize what they were losing out on. An older woman whose silver hair was neatly styled into a bun unlocked the thrift store's doors, pausing the conversation. I gave her a small smile and nodded in acknowledgment as I made my way to the rack of jeans.

Ros gave me a questioning look, her eyebrows furrowed and her hands on her hips. "I'm not saying no to shopping because I'm sure we can find you something that looks amazing, but what happened to your dress?"

I groaned, dreading her response, and my cheeks heated. There was no way I could lie about the reason my dress was no longer an acceptable choice for anything. "So... Trey kind of cut it off."

Her mouth gaped open and then closed. And then opened. "What do you mean cut?" she whispered, looking over her shoulder toward the elderly woman straightening racks.

I pulled out a pair of jeans and hung them over my arm. "With a knife. It's exactly what it sounds like."

Ros' eyes grew comically wide. "I've heard rumors, but I never knew—"

I smiled as I shuffled to a rack with hoodies on it. "Whatever you heard about them is probably true."

The door chimed as someone else entered the small shop and a familiar face with golden brown hair stood in the doorway, scanning the small space. His nose looked slightly swollen and under his eye was lightly bruised.

What had happened? We just saw each other yesterday. He tucked his hands in his pockets and strolled through the haphazard piles of clothes like he owned the place. Once he was close, he gave Ros a one-armed hug and leaned against her.

She glared at him, but her mouth twitched at the corners, giving away the fact that she wasn't really annoyed. "What are you doing here, Caleb?"

I tried to ignore their exchange, my heart beating faster in my chest. "Well," he drawled, "I saw your truck and Ivy's car out front and decided to say hi." *He knew what my car looked like?* We had only spoken because of the project yesterday and partners were apparently mandatory.

Rosalyn untangled herself from his hold and drifted to the tops a few feet away. "Ivy needs some clothes, and I'm trying to convince her to go to the football game this weekend."

Caleb stalked closer to me, the woodsy scent of his soap filling the air. He stepped directly behind me, not touching me but close enough that the heat radiating off of his body warmed my skin. "And what did she say?" he asked as his fingertips traced a path down my biceps.

Rosalyn's hands stalled for a moment when she looked up and saw how close he stood to me. "Well, I think I convinced her to go. And to the party. She might need a little more convincing."

Caleb slowly trailed his hands down my arms, leaving goosebumps in their wake and I swallowed roughly. "Do you really need convincing, princess?"

I didn't respond, instead focusing on the black hoodie in front of me. My voice came out low, and I almost didn't recognize it. "What happened to your face?"

His hand caught my wrist and his thumb slowly caressed the pulse point as my heart hammered inside of my chest. "Don't worry about that. Your boyfriend thought he could run me off. He doesn't realize I can be very persistent when it comes to something I want."

I froze as his words hit me. I tried to turn to face him, and he wrapped his free arm around my waist, enveloping me in his warmth. His body was hard behind mine and my mouth went dry. *What was wrong with me? Spend one crazy night with three hot guys and all of a sudden, my libido didn't listen to common sense.*

"Who?" I croaked.

His hand splayed across my abdomen. "Don't worry about it. What you need to be concerned about is the fact that we're going to the football game. While we're there, we can even discuss this project." He let go of me and moved back, shooting me an arrogant smirk, almost like he knew the effect he had on me. "I'll see you at the game."

I watched as he exited the building, leaving me even more confused than I was mere minutes ago. Rosalyn's voice brought me back to the present. "What was that about? Are you just collecting men?" she asked with a sly grin.

"I have no idea."

And I didn't. Not really. I had three men who claimed they wanted to make my life hell and another who didn't care what they wanted. I could tell Rosalyn that he simply wanted to work on our paper but that would be a lie. Only one thing was certain. Saturday night's party was bound to be interesting.

Cam

On Thursday morning, I woke up irritated with good reason. I was stuck going to a bullshit meeting with Abraham Wells. We didn't need a check-in to remind us that he could ruin the rest of our lives with a single word. I had practice this afternoon, homework to complete, a game on Saturday, and obligations to the Forsaken. It was almost time for Vincent to give us another "assignment" and my stomach churned at what it might be. Add in Maya, Katya, and Sergei, along with Niko's race tonight, and my schedule was full.

It didn't help that thoughts of Ivy had been preoccupying my mind since I saw her, distracting me from what was important. What happened Tuesday in the library had been playing on repeat every time I was alone. Even when I tried breaking her, she still managed to tell me to fuck myself. Even though I hated her and what she represented, somehow she still got me hard. I craved her, yet I still wanted her gone.

It was exhausting.

Beside me, Niko still dozed peacefully, completely unbothered by the fact that he'd slept through not one, not two, but three alarms. Midnight waves fell across his forehead, nearly falling into his eyes. My fingers twitched, nearly reaching out to brush them away but thinking better of it. The covers had fallen during the night, showing off the ink that swirled in patterns at the top of his chest. My eyes traveled down his body, noticing the blankets pitching below his waist. My heart rate picked up, and I averted my eyes, blowing out a steady breath while a memory from a different time crept into my thoughts.

The wind was like blades of ice cutting through our skin as we stalked silently up to the house just outside of Clearhaven. That was the thing that no one realized about living near the ocean. In the summer the breeze coming off the water cooled your skin and filled the air with the scent of salt, but in the winter it just felt bitter. I hunched my shoulders up further around my face and shoved my hands in my pockets, cold metal caressing my fingertips. Tonight, I was taking care of unfinished business and no one else could ever know that we were here.

My mother had failed to protect me from the men that stumbled into the house late at night. She had failed to protect me from herself. Now that I was older, I intended to protect myself.

He deserved what was going to happen to him.

After prying open a window, we crawled inside the dilapidated house and caught our breath. The air was still chilled, but at least we were protected from the wind. The darkness helped to shroud us as we took in the interior. A loveseat and recliner were pushed against the far wall and a hallway sat to the right. Given the time of night, Patrick would be asleep, which was unfortunate. He might need a wake up call so that he got the full experience.

A door at the end of the hallway was open, and loud snores filtered toward us. The only light in the house came from the window behind the bed casting the room in a blue glow. Sitting on the bedside table was an open bottle of whiskey with only an inch in the bottom and a half-smoked joint. He was passed out. That was why he didn't hear us.

Other people would probably feel something at that moment. Anxiety. Adrenaline. Terror. Happiness. Relief. Remorse. And yet all that existed was a black void as I stared at his sleeping form.

Patrick had changed little since the night he shoved his hand over my mouth to muffle my cries. I was smaller then and the memory of his hot stale breath that smelled of tequila and chewing tobacco had haunted me for years. He had a few more gray hairs and a few more lines around his face, but he was the same that he had always been. He got off on hurting children. The bruises had faded, but the memories would always be there.

Niko and Trey stood by waiting to see what I would do. I winked at Niko and straddled Patrick's chest, covering his mouth and nose with the palm of my hand. His eyes shot open, first in confusion and then in panic as he realized who it was that was depriving him of air. He struggled to push me off, but he couldn't—not now that I was older. I outweighed him by at least fifty pounds.

"Hey, Patrick. I know it's been a few years, but it's nice to know you still recognize me." The man beneath me shook his head, trying to convey some sort of message, but I wasn't interested in talking. I had tried to tell my mother about it after the first time, but she waved me off and told me I must have had a nightmare. Patrick would never do something like that.

Honestly, she was the one I should have killed that night. I hadn't– yet–but there was still time and I had an entire list of people that deserved everything that they got.

I pulled the piece from my pocket, a sliver of moonlight glinting off the metal. Patrick tried to scream beneath my palm, but I laughed at him. No amount of begging would stop me. I pressed the muzzle against his temple and pulled the trigger; the pop echoed through the silent house. Liquid splattered onto my hands as gunpowder and sulfur filled the air.

I kneeled on top of him, staring down at his face and watching as any remnants of life left his eyes. Inky stains marred my skin and the sheets as blood pooled beneath Patrick.

I still felt nothing. A part of me had thought I would feel something afterward. Happiness or closure. Perhaps regret. The only thing that existed was satisfaction at the fact his chest was no longer moving.

Niko grabbed my bicep and tugged at me. "Come on, Cam. We need to go in case the neighbors call the cops."

"We've got to get the fuck out of here," Trey hissed as he pushed past us.

I sauntered out of Patrick's home, trying to fight the hysteria that was bubbling up inside of my chest. By the time I crawled into Niko's backseat, laughter slipped out of my mouth. My body shook as I pulled a pack of cigarettes from my pocket and both of my friends stared at me.

"What the fuck?" Niko muttered. "Why are you laughing?"

Good question. Who the fuck laughed after murdering someone? I wiped my hand over my eyes and shook my head. "It's nothing."

The ride home was silent after that as Niko dropped Trey off at his small apartment. I sat in the back and rolled my window down. Niko growled from the front seat and swung open his door roughly before gripping my arm and dragging me from where I was sitting.

"Get the fuck up, Cam. We need to burn your clothes before someone sees them," he muttered at me. "The last thing we need is Maya or Katya asking questions about why you're covered in blood." He pulled me along to the front door and through the house before forcing me into the bathroom.

"You need to chill out," I hissed. "No one will ever know." Our siblings were all nestled into their beds hours ago, safe and warm. Completely unaware of what had transpired across town.

Steam filled the bathroom as the shower ran in the background and Niko tugged at my shirt insistently, mumbling under his breath about how sloppy my kill was. It wasn't the first for any of us, but it was the first one that was personal.

It was also the first one that wasn't sanctioned by Vincent.

I stood and stripped before stepping under the warm spray, staring at the tiles in front of me, not bothering to

respond. Niko gathered my clothes and disappeared for a
while, leaving me to stare at the occasional streak of pink
water in the bottom of the tub. I grabbed the soap and
scrubbed my skin, washing away whatever evidence was
left.

Finally, Niko came back and threw open the thin plastic
shower liner, turned off the stream of water, and held a
towel out to me. His voice was still lined with anger when
he spoke, and he stared at the bathroom wall. "I've got the
fire going outside already. Get dressed so you don't freeze."

After I shrugged on the clothes he'd laid out, we trudged
through the house silently, careful not to wake anyone. A
fire was started at the edge of the yard and two camp chairs
were set up in front of it. I settled into my seat, allowing the
heat from the flames to lick at my skin. It was better than
the numbness that permeated every ounce of my being.

For a while we passed a bottle of cheap vodka back and
forth, letting it burn our throats, and just watched as embers danced in the air. There was tension between the two
of us and had been for a while. The alcohol blurred my
vision and crushed my barriers. I leaned closer and grabbed
the collar of his shirt. He tried to pull away, but I clutched
him tighter, not willing to let go just yet.

"What the fuck is your problem tonight? Everything
went according to plan."

He swallowed and I watched as his Adam's apple bobbed,
wondering what it would feel like under my fingers. Eventually, I let him break free and he held my gaze for a
moment before clearing his throat. "I think we need to–"

Acting on impulse, I cut him off, pressing my lips to his roughly and silencing whatever he was going to say. I wasn't sure what I was doing, and I would deal with the consequences of my actions later. Niko thought I had missed how sometimes his gaze would linger or how his touch would last a few seconds longer than necessary. I hadn't, but feelings weren't something I was willing to explore with anyone right now.

Potentially ever.

He sat stock still, his body a statue as my tongue glided into his mouth and my hands bunched into his shirt. Everything felt right as I slowly coaxed him into relaxing while I explored his mouth.

And then he finally responded. His body came to life under my touch, one hand grasping my jaw and the other wrapping around my neck, squeezing gently. We were lost in each other as the fire crackled in front of us. He nipped at my bottom lip, first tentatively and then harder, drawing blood. The taste of metal and salt flooded my tongue, and I gingerly licked at my lip. He pulled at my hair, jerking my head back and yanking me back to reality. His eyes were dark and he frowned. "We should stop. Between the alcohol and earlier tonight..."

I grabbed his dick through his pants and it was hard, just like I knew it would be. I squeezed and his eyes fluttered closed. "You want this as much as I do right now. Tell me you don't want me."

When he opened them, the grip on my hair tightened and he leaned close to me, his breath scorching my skin. He squeezed my throat again, this time leaving me struggling

for air. "I didn't say I didn't want you. Tonight is a bad idea."
He let go of me, shoving me away.

Fuck him for being logical. Fuck him for making me feel
something.

I pushed the memory aside, unwilling to deal with it for now. Secret touches and whispered words hidden by the darkness of night were more dangerous to me than even my preoccupation with Ivy.

I took in a deep breath again and reached for Niko's shoulder, shaking it roughly. He let out a groan and reached for my wrist, wrapping his fingers around it. "Five more minutes." His voice sounded like gravel and I swallowed roughly, choosing to start coffee instead of fighting with him.

Throwing back the covers so that they landed on him, I padded down to the kitchen and pulled the canister from the cabinet making a mental note about what I needed to accomplish. Once the pot brewed, Niko stumbled into the kitchen looking bleary-eyed and half asleep. I poured him a cup of the bitter liquid and handed it to him, our fingertips grazing briefly. He tipped his head to the side and eyed me with a question, but I cleared my throat as I pulled away. "Are you ready for tonight?"

He brushed his hair out of his face and grinned. "I always am."

An hour later, we were standing outside Clearhaven First Community Church. The building looked like it had been plucked from the pages of history with stone columns that wrapped around the exterior. Thick clouds covered the sun lending to the already somber mood I was in. A weeping willow grew at the side of the building and I frowned. Before my grandmother passed away, she used to tell me they symbolized nothing good. She had lots of superstitions that she believed to be true and an unspoken set of rules that she lived by.

At that moment, I wondered if they were all accurate.

Leaning against the car, the three of us said nothing, choosing to wait in silence. The hairs on the back of my neck stood on end when I heard the car pull into the empty parking lot. They were finally here.

The black Mercedes whipped into the parking space next to us and knots formed in my stomach. The car cost more than the house we lived in, and the demonstration of wealth and power caused rage to swim in my veins. Here we were peddling drugs and doing whatever else they told us to do just to put food on the table every evening, but these assholes got to keep their hands clean while living in the lap of luxury.

The driver's side door swung open and Abraham Wells exited the vehicle, carefully straightening his clothes. A serious expression was painted across his features while he waited for his passenger to make his appearance. Time dragged on until finally Vincent unfolded himself. He gave me a bitter smile, and I realized that this wasn't just another meeting to threaten us.

They knew something that we didn't.

"Boys, it's been a while," Dean Wells stated. "Hopefully you're doing well. How are Maya and Katya?"

I flared my nostrils at him, but Niko was the one who answered. He leaned further back against the car and stared at him. "That's none of your fucking business."

Vincent clicked his tongue and his grin widened. "That's not true. You three know they are most definitely our business. The well-being of the youth of the city is something we take great interest in." Wells laughed at the joke and I flexed my fingers, trying not to give them the satisfaction of a response.

"What the fuck do you want?" I gritted out. "We've done everything that you've asked, and a text message should have been sufficient."

Wells snorted and exchanged a quick look with Vincent. "You would do well to remember who's in charge here, Mr. Barrett. The same goes for Mr. Harrison and Stone. After all, it would be a shame for the police to find out about that incident last summer. If that information were to slip out and someone knew exactly where that young man's body was hidden... well, let's just say all three of you would take the fall. Who would take care of poor Katya and Maya then? There are several men in the community who I am sure would open up their homes for young women during desperate times for just a small fee."

The thought of going to prison was terrifying, but the idea that these monsters would get their hands on either of the girls? Maya had barely lived through it the first time and she wouldn't survive it again.

I wasn't sure how the Forsaken and the Order of the Exalted were interconnected, but I knew that girls from the wrong side of the tracks went missing in Clearhaven all the time. No one knew who all the members of the order were—they operated in whispers—but every position of power in the city was held by someone who was rumored to be associated with them.

The only person who I could guarantee was a member was Dean Wells. After the incident, as he so eloquently put it, I had seen a brand of a serpent swallowing his tail on his forearm—an ouroboros. I knew.

Trey rolled his eyes beside me as he shoved his hands into his pockets. "Gentlemen, if we could stop posturing and get back to the matter at hand. Why are we here? Dean, you usually insist on sending commands through text message and Vincent... we're distributing the tea just like you asked. Everything is in order and I have better things to do."

Dean Wells' laughter cut through the air. "Not so fast, Mr. Harrison. We need two favors. The new girl on campus, Ivy Spencer, I need you to make sure she's getting this new drug. Do whatever you have to, but make it happen."

As much as I told myself that I hated Ivy, something about the situation was off. Niko gritted his teeth so hard beside me, I could hear him. I put my hand on his arm to tell him to keep his cool, but the muscles in his forearms strained beneath my touch. "Why?" I asked. "What do you want with her?"

Vincent snorted. "Calm down, boys. We won't hurt your pretty little plaything. At least not yet. Don't think that we haven't all noticed the three of you sniffing after her. I'm sure you noticed that tease helps people relax a little. That's all." He avoided my question completely, brushing me off like usual. "Tomorrow night, I need the three of you to pay a little visit to Ashton Haney. I'll send you the address, but there's a rumor that he's been talking to the new detective at Clearhaven PD. Detective Ross is a pain in my ass and has been digging things up about the Forsaken. I think we need to shut Haney up. You know what to do."

T he meeting from earlier replayed in my mind over and over while I forced my way through the crowd. The idea that my sister, or Cam's, was trapped in the sight of Abraham Wells made my blood boil. I clenched my jaw at the thought as I pushed through the sea of bodies.

I wouldn't give Ivy tea just because they asked me to. Something about the situation unsettled me. Why was the dean insistent that she needed it?

There were more people hanging around Hangman's Alley tonight than there usually were on a race night. Women wearing tiny shorts and barely there tops hung around the cars that were parked hoping to catch the eye of someone. They knew that when the dust settled at the end of the evening, people would look to funnel their leftover adrenaline into pussy and liquor. Someone with dark hair grabbed at my shirt as I tried to find Tyler. I jerked away and glanced down to see who was trying to get my attention.

Arabella. Lately, she had been showing up at races and trailing me on campus. Ignoring her wasn't getting the message across. Tonight she was wearing a hot pink halter top that barely contained her tits and a skirt so short that if she bent over, I would see what color her underwear was–if she was wearing any.

"Not now," I gritted out as I spotted Tyler.

"Niko, we need to talk. Please?" She pouted at me and fluttered her eyelashes, looking like she was having some type of seizure as she pressed her breasts together. At any moment, a nipple would slip out of her top. I struggled not to roll my eyes as I inhaled sharply. *Did she think that made her look sexy?*

She placed her hand on the edge of my shirt and I brushed it off, focusing on the older man in front of me. "Unless this deals with business, no."

Arabella scowled and stomped away, probably back to where her sorority sisters were drinking. I crossed my arms over my chest and waited as Tyler took people's money and scrawled on his clipboard. He looked more like an accountant with his silver-rimmed glasses and button-up shirts than someone who helped organize illegal races and street fights, but what did I know?

His eyes twinkled when he saw me waiting and ushered me close. I pulled the entry fee out of my pocket and handed it to him. "You going to win tonight?" he asked in a thick New York accent.

I bowed my head. "I always do."

And I did. I had too much on the line to lose. The rent needed to be paid, the lights had to stay on, my siblings needed food, the leak under the bathroom sink needed to be fixed, and Sergei probably needed new shoes again. While my father was busy snorting, smoking, and injecting whatever he could get his hands on, I was handling shit the best I could. Winning one race brought in more money than I could in an entire week working at one of the crappy tourist shops near the beach.

The older man shoved his glasses up on his nose and peered over his clipboard at me. "Have you given any more thought to what I asked?"

Tyler had been on me to sign up for one of the underground fights he organized because he knew I was desperate for money, but Saturdays were busy for me. I tried to attend Cam's home games with Trey. Add in homework and everything else... It wasn't exactly a no, but it definitely wasn't a yes either. I rubbed the back of my neck. "Give me more time." He simply tipped his head in acknowledgment of my answer before beckoning the next person forward.

I slowly fought my way back through the crowd, ignoring the looks from people as I shoved through the bodies. Settling into the front seat, I leaned my head back and closed my eyes. Anticipation for the events of the evening made me feel jittery, and I drummed my fingers along my pants as the sound of the crowd turned into a dull roar. I let everything fade away as I focused on the rise and fall of my chest, knowing that I needed to be focused when it was time. The twists and turns of the road we used were challenging, and I had a lot riding on tonight.

Someone's engine revved beside me and I opened my eyes to glance out my window, wondering who had pulled me from my thoughts. I huffed out a breath when I saw the obnoxious yellow Aston Martin sitting beside me. *Of course, he would fucking show up tonight.*

Caleb Vance didn't belong on this side of town. Between his perfect family, his perfect life, the car that screamed look at me, and a mansion that sat near the ocean, I'd never understood why he didn't go away to some Ivy League school and escape Clearhaven. Sure, his grandfather tied him here, but he had a trust fund he'd inherited at twenty-one.

We had raced against each other a few times before and I'd always left him in the dust despite his expensive car. I was just a better driver, plain and simple.

And then he hopped out, leaving his car running and ran off to the sidelines, wrapping his arms around a girl's waist and spinning her around. It wasn't just any girl; it was the girl I'd been obsessing over all week. I bit the inside of my cheek and grabbed the bottle of water sitting in the center console.

Why was she here, and why was he touching her again? Why couldn't she just listen and stay home instead of openly defying Cam? Instead of her becoming the social pariah he'd hoped, she simply ignored what he said and did what she wanted.

All focus I'd had previously was gone as I watched her tilt her head back and laugh at something Rosalyn or Caleb said. He brushed her hair behind her ears and smiled like she was the most perfect thing in the world. The longer I sat there watching that dickhead touching her, the angrier I got.

I glanced into the crowd and caught Cam staring in their direction, his entire body tense. He started to walk in that direction, but Trey stopped him. The look on both of their faces said everything I needed to know. Neither of them liked him touching her.

The flag girl of the night took her position in front of the cars in my periphery, but all of my attention was back on Caleb. He grabbed Ivy's hand and brushed his lips against it like he was some knight seeking favor before a tournament. *Who even does that?* If she were mine, I would press my body against her and sear her soul, ensuring everyone knew who she belonged to. I was half tempted to jump out and do just that when I heard the engines revving around me, signaling that it was almost time.

I drank a sip of the water and placed it back in the cup holder, trying to regain some semblance of concentration. Gripping the steering wheel, I stared out the windshield at the girl holding the flag wearing a short black dress, but my mind still wandered to the girl standing on the sidelines who should be cheering for me instead of the douchebag driving a yellow car. *Who drives a yellow car?*

I turned my music up to deafening levels, letting the bass vibrate my body and drown out everything else. If Ivy thought I wouldn't talk to her about this later, she was wrong.

The flag went down and then we were off. Muscle memory took over as I shifted gears and let adrenaline pump through my veins. I wound around the asphalt and relished the darkness that covered the landscape, choosing to focus on the curves of the road rather than the other drivers around me. My hands sweated and my heart pounded in my ears.

Soon, I'd left everyone far behind. Everyone except Caleb. Up ahead, the road narrowed into two lanes before sharply twisting to the left and if I could put some distance between us there, then victory was mine. Out of nowhere, the Aston Martin pulled up beside me, hovering there for several yards. I gave the car more gas and pushed it thinking that it would give me the space I needed, but instead, he easily coasted, drifting in front of me right before the twist.

This time of the night, no one traveled these roads, and I was confident enough to change lanes to try to pass him after we were out of that curve. I gritted my teeth and readied myself, the road opening up in front of us. Changing lanes, I pushed the car once again, the wind shaking the exterior from the speed and the roughness of the untended road. Trees were on either side of us, a thin metal guardrail the only protection from the ravine on both sides.

Suddenly, headlights appeared in front of me and the sound of a horn cut through my music. I cursed under my breath as I debated my best course of action and realized I couldn't pass him. I slowed to drift back behind Caleb as the headlights grew nearer. The final sharp curve closed in on us and his lead grew.

My hands clutched the steering wheel as the finish line came back into sight, the road opening back up to four lanes. And despite my best efforts, it was over as quickly as it began.

Caleb jumped out of the Aston Martin and ran over to Ivy as I was throwing the car into park. As I slammed my door behind me, the only thing I could see was him pressing his lips to her mouth. I stalked close to them, watching both get caught up in the celebration. Someone caught me by the shoulder and jerked me back. My fist balled up on instinct, ready to swing at whoever was touching me. "Chill the fuck out," Trey hissed at me. "We're taking care of him, but not today. Not in front of so many people."

Cam glared at me as he held his hand out. "Give me your keys. We're getting the fuck out of here."

Both of them knew why I was here tonight—how important it was to win. I threw the keys at Cam and allowed Trey to drag me back so that I could lick my wounds in private.

This was just one more reason to show Caleb that he wasn't the boss around here. One more reason to punish Ivy. If she hadn't shown up, I would have won. Just like every other time.

Trey and Cam sat on my front stairs passing a bottle of whiskey between them. No one had said anything on the ride home, all of us too trapped in our heads. The evening hadn't gone the way any of us expected.

To make matters worse, once I got back, my father was passed out at the kitchen table with a lit cigarette hanging from his mouth. It took everything inside of me not to lose it as I dragged him to his room and threw him on his bed where he could sleep off whatever he had taken earlier in the evening. I wasn't even sure why he came home at this point.

If he could get his shit together, I wouldn't have to win any races. If he could get his shit together, I wouldn't be the one worried about whether or not Sergei and Katya would have somewhere to live this month. I slowly breathed through my nose, willing myself to calm down.

"What was that back there?" Trey asked as he took a sip from the bottle.

I ran my hands through my hair and stared up at the sky, wishing I knew the answer. "I mean, you saw. Now I've got to figure out how the fuck to pay for—"

"No, not that part. I mean, what the fuck are both of you thinking? We agreed we were staying away from Ivy and then both of you lose your minds every time she is anywhere near you. Why do you care so much about Caleb Vance paying her attention? He's just a rich boy who will use her and then ignore her."

Cam shot him a warning look and snatched the bottle from his hand. "I don't give a fuck about Caleb. No one is supposed to be speaking to her. Not even Ros."

I laughed and pulled at my hair, letting the pain ground me for a moment. "Good luck telling Ros what to do. She couldn't care less about the Forsaken or any of that shit. Trey has a point, though. If you hate her so much because of her father, then why did it look like you were ready to beat Vance's ass?" I grabbed the bottle from Cam's hand and turned it up, letting the alcohol seep into my veins. It wouldn't solve my problems, but perhaps it could numb all of my feelings.

He stood up and crossed his arms over his chest. "I just don't want anyone else to touch her–or speak to her. If someone is going to break her, I want it to be me."

I smirked at him and took another swallow, ready to start a fight. "You know what I think, Cam? I think that you just love to hate her. You want her and don't want to admit it even to yourself. You claim you want to break her, but I'm willing to bet that she's the only thing you can think of when you're jerking off in the shower."

Trey stayed silent and pursed his lips, trying to hide his amusement when Cam rushed toward me and grabbed the collar of my shirt. His lips were inches from mine while he glared at me, the vein on the side of his neck pulsing from anger. "Fuck you, Niko."

I readied myself for the blow that I knew was coming and leaned closer, lowering my voice to a whisper. "Careful, Cam. Remember the last time our lips were this close? Tonight I won't stop you." I bit his ear, and he gasped before his fist landed on my stomach, knocking the breath out of me.

Trey raised his eyebrow and held his hands up. "On that note, I'm going to pass out. It looks like the two of you have things you need to work out. I'm not sure if it's fighting or fucking, though."

Cam glared at me and pushed me backward, the alcohol causing me to lose my balance as I stumbled. "Nah. I'm not putting up with his shit tonight. He's just being a prick."

Both of them disappeared into the house and Cam slammed the door behind him. *Whatever.* He could be pissed off.

I took off down the sidewalk with the bottle of cheap whiskey in my hand. At first, I wasn't sure where I was headed while I drank and thought of what I was going to do to fix my problems, but when Regina Spencer's house came into view, I knew. I tipped back the bottle and swallowed the remaining sip. Laying it down in the grass at the side of the house, I walked as quietly as I could so I didn't alert any of the neighbors. My limbs were sluggish from fatigue and the alcohol while I allowed my hands to trace the wooden siding.

The window I had been searching for was in front of me, and my vision doubled as I peered inside. Ivy was fast asleep laying on her side, her face pinched from whatever dream she was having. My fingers clumsily found the edge and pushed up, praying that she was foolish enough to leave it unlocked. It lifted easily, squeaking only the slightest bit as I opened it enough to fit through.

I hoisted myself up onto the open sill and swung inside, careful to catch myself before I hit the ground. *Reminder to self: don't drink before deciding to break into someone's house.* By some great miracle, Ivy didn't stir, and I closed the window before stepping close to her bed.

I stared down at her, admiring her sleeping form. She wore a black t-shirt and underwear. Her bare legs were tangled in the blankets and sweat beaded on her brow. Her long auburn locks fanned across her pillow and it took everything in me not to reach out to touch her. Any part of her. I took off my shoes and settled onto the edge of the bed, watching as her breathing picked up. Her hands clawed at the sheet beneath her like she was in pain. A sharp cry fell from her lips and I tilted my head to the side, curious about what she was dreaming.

I laid down beside her on the small bed, surprised that she didn't wake up at the mattress dipping beneath my weight. Putting my head on the edge of her pillow, I watched for a while, listening to her soft whines as the room spun around me. Tomorrow morning I would feel like hell.

A part of me, a very small part, wanted to wake her up and tell her everything would be fine. It would be a lie, though.

After Saturday night, she would know we were monsters.

Ivy

"Sure you'll be okay by yourself?" Frankie asked as she grabbed a messenger bag from the small office at the back of the shop.

I gave her a reassuring look and leaned against the counter. "Promise. Besides, we close in an hour. What could happen between now and then?"

She raised her eyebrows and drew her lips into a thin line while she studied me before nodding. "Call me if you need me. For anything."

As she left, I thought about how we'd fallen into such a comfortable schedule. Around eight every night she grabbed her things and checked in on me, ensuring that my day was going alright. I couldn't exactly tell her all the details about what had been happening for the past week, but it was nice to have someone in my corner.

Music streamed from my phone as I swept and straightened the racks, dancing and singing as I worked. The shop closed in less than an hour and no one came in this late. I actually wasn't sure why Frankie kept it open, but I wouldn't argue about working. It kept me from having to go home and face my aunt who had been suspiciously absent all week.

I grabbed a broom and let my mind wander to the night before. Caleb insisted that Ros and I come to watch him race. Racing didn't really appeal to me, and the week had already been exciting enough. Add in the fact that there was a football game on Saturday, and I really needed to finish some reading for classes. In typical fashion, I tried turning him down, but as always, Rosalyn dragged me along anyway stating, "College is about more than just classes, bestie."

Even to myself, I hated admitting that I had fun. The energy of the crowd was electric, and I was able to disappear in the sea of bodies, going completely unnoticed by everyone. Niko, Cam, and Trey were there, but none of them spotted me. At least not to my knowledge. If they had, they would have approached me, demanding that I leave or some other bullshit.

My biggest surprise was when Caleb kissed me, obviously caught up in the high of his win. I tried not to read anything into it, but I stopped and touched my fingers to my mouth remembering everything. His lips were soft but demanding, and his eyes held a question I wasn't sure how to answer. Rosalyn cheered at us wildly, grinning the whole time.

I went home alone and when I woke up, my sheets smelled like sandalwood reminding me of someone else. It had to be my subconscious reminding me of somebody I couldn't have. Not now.

The door chimed as someone entered the shop and I yelled out, "Be with you in one second," as I dumped the dustpan into the small can in the back. Brushing off my hands on my jeans, I stopped in my tracks as I took in the sight in front of me. Cam, Niko, and Trey hung around the front of the store, looking bored and sifting through things at the cash wrap.

Cam straightened up and stalked toward me slowly, almost like he knew that my heart raced in my chest and at any moment I might bolt out of the store. He clenched his jaw when he reached me and extended his arm, brushing his thumb over my bottom lip. I stood there frozen, wondering why they were here and hating the fact that part of me still enjoyed his touch. Trey cut the music that had been playing on my phone and I glared at him.

Coming to my senses, I placed my hands on his chest and pushed. He didn't move an inch, but it made me feel better. "Why are you here? Oh, maybe you need some surf wax."

Cam looked amused at my statement and grabbed a loop on my jeans, jerking me roughly toward him. He tipped his lips close to mine and hovered there for a moment. "What I need is for you to cooperate, but since that isn't going to happen, I wanted to extend an invitation to the party Saturday night."

My blood turned to ice. That was the party Rosalyn had convinced me to go to, telling me that the guys wouldn't even notice I was there. I cleared my throat and looked Cam in the eyes. "Thanks for the invitation, but I'll be busy."

His lips curled up before he leaned in to bite my lip. I gasped at the sting of pain and he chuckled. "It wasn't a request, Ivy. I'll see you there. We have a surprise for you, and I can't wait to see your face." My face obviously registered the horror I experienced at the idea of them surprising me. He hooked his fingers in Niko's direction. "Come here and show her who she belongs to."

Niko's eyes trailed up and down my body for a moment before he stalked forward and pulled me from Cam's grasp. He looked angry, but I couldn't understand why as he peered down. He grabbed my ponytail and tilted my head how he wanted before crashing his lips against mine. There was nothing gentle or reassuring by the motion. He was branding me from the inside out, marking me as he staked his claim.

Electricity shot through my veins at our contact, but I was mad. I couldn't believe the audacity of the three of them. Well, I guess Trey didn't count since he stood to the side looking bored while examining the handle of his knife. First Cam threatened me in front of a crowd, then he got me off in the library. Niko and Trey both tried intimidating Caleb. Now Niko's tongue was in my mouth and my traitorous body was enjoying every second of it.

They ran so hot and cold and it had been exactly a week since the beach. I was getting sick of whatever their game was.

I pulled back enough to raise my palm and strike Niko's cheek. "Fuck you." I faced Cam. "And you. You don't get to tell me who I belong to."

Niko swiped his tongue over his lip slowly while he gingerly rubbed his cheek, saying nothing, and Cam laughed. He winked at me before turning his back to me. "That's where you're wrong, little ghost. I'll see you tomorrow night at eight."

My mouth was dry, and I simply stood there while watching them file out and disappear into the night. I pulled out my phone and shot Rosalyn a text.

Me: Guess who just left Frankie's.

Ros: Caleb? After that kiss last night...

Me: No. The three douchebags.

Ros: You mean the three hot douchebags who can't seem to get their shit together? What did they want?

Me: For me to come to the party tomorrow night.

Ros: Oh shit.

Oh shit indeed. I shoved the phone back in my pocket and locked up the shop, lost in my thoughts. I wasn't ready to go home yet and see if my aunt was there, prepared to bombard me with questions about where I'd been or who I was spending time with. She hadn't been home lately to enforce the curfew she enacted, so I decided to trek to the beach. It was less than five minutes from the surf shop and the sound of the ocean waves would soothe my soul.

I climbed down the embankment separating the road from the beach and waded through the dune grasses as the sea came into view. The moon reflected on the water's surface and a sense of peace came over me. I took off my shoes, relishing the sensation of the cool sand beneath my feet and the scent of salt clinging to the air. strolling along the beach I almost felt free. Everything else faded, and I was just me.

Here, my father wasn't in prison for being a piece of shit. Here, I wasn't the rich girl who lost everything. Here, I wasn't hated for who I was related to or even desired for reasons I didn't understand. I didn't have to worry about what the future held or what would happen tomorrow. Or the next time I would manage to incur my aunt's wrath.

Suddenly, my throat felt thick as I stared down at my feet, sinking with every step. Who was I now after everything that had happened? I wasn't the same person from last year or even six months ago. After all the dust settled finally, who would I be? What pieces were still me? Did I still love to dance or read?

I stooped down to pick up a sand dollar that was partially concealed when I heard someone crying nearby. Between my thoughts and the roar of the water, I had somehow completely missed the small shadow sitting a few yards from me. I drew closer slowly, trying to see what was happening, but not wanting to startle the girl.

She was a little younger than me with brown hair and tear-stained cheeks. Her knees were drawn to her chest, and she held them tightly as she stared at the incoming waves. Apparently, she hadn't noticed me either.

Unsure of what to do, I sat next to her in silence and looked down at the sand dollar in my hand. She sniffled and stole a glance in my direction. Her voice was flat when she spoke. "It's supposed to be good luck if you find one."

I turned it over in my hand slowly. "Well, right now I need all the luck I can get."

She huffed out a stuttered breath and wiped her palms against her face. "Same. Want to talk about it?"

I shook my head. "I wouldn't know where to begin. What about you?"

She thought for a moment and then gave me a sad smile. "I wouldn't know either."

And that was how I spent the evening, sitting quietly with another sad girl on the shoreline, both of us lost in our thoughts. I didn't know who she was or why she was here, but the company was comforting in a way. When the moon was high in the sky, she dusted her pants off and declared that she'd better get home before her brother found out she was missing.

I didn't ask any questions because I knew I needed to do the same. The last thing I needed was to earn the displeasure of my aunt yet again.

Trey

Niko parked the car in front of the Lonely Sun and scanned the parking lot looking for the white Camry that Ashton Haney drove around town. He lifted his chin once he spotted it and grabbed for his door handle. "You guys remember the plan, right?"

The past forty-eight hours had been a shit show. All I wanted to do was hide in my apartment and work on my program, forgetting all about the Forsaken, Caleb Vance, and the green-eyed girl who was disrupting all of our lives.

Niko losing the race was a problem. The money he earned from the races was how he ensured his siblings had somewhere to live. Cam and Maya complicated matters. He'd never told us why he chose not to go home, or why Niko's father being high was better than his mother stumbling home drunk. Perhaps it had to do with the endless string of men that waltzed into the house unannounced and acted like they owned the place.

I could relate to that.

For the first time in my life, I almost wished that instead of an apartment, I'd bought a house. It would have solved at least a few of our problems.

I couldn't fix the tension that was brewing between Cam and Niko. It had been building for years, even if the two of them were oblivious to it. The other night I was almost certain it was going to finally come to a head. Who would have thought that the red-haired siren who appeared out of thin air would be the tipping point they needed?

Niko's assessment of the situation with Ivy was spot on. She'd caught Cam's eye, and he hated it. I was staying out of it for now. Did she intrigue me? Sure. Would I turn her down? No. Thoughts of her on her knees still kept me up at night. But I wouldn't stop Cam from exacting his own form of justice for Maya as twisted as it was. He'd almost lost her and what she'd been through…

Thomas Spencer deserved a bullet in the head, not a concrete cell to call home for a few years.

Part of me wished things were different. That Ivy was someone else. Cam's little ghost would have been perfect for the three of us. She wasn't scared by who we were or the demons that writhed under our skin, even though she should have been. She didn't back down from our demands and would tell us all exactly what she thought.

"Trey, you remember what we're doing tonight?" Cam asked, bringing me back to the present.

I stepped out of the car and placed my fingers on the blade sitting in my pocket, letting the smoothness of the handle soothe me before pushing up my glasses. "Yeah, I remember. We corner him in the bathroom, but don't kill him. Yet."

He got to live a little longer because we needed information from him. Ashton was higher up than we were in the gang's ranks, and Vincent confided in him more often than not. We hoped that he could tell us more about the dean's sudden interest in Ivy or how Vincent was tied to the whole mess.

The exterior of the Lonely Sun was nothing special–a flickering neon sun, a crumbling brick exterior, and prostitutes hoping to find someone willing to pay for a quick blowjob in the corner of a parking lot–but the interior was bleaker. The smell of body odor mingled with cheap perfume as our shoes stuck to the hardwood floor from the remnants of old beer and over-the-counter margarita mix that had been spilled by tipsy patrons.

We sat at the bar in front of one of the employees and ordered a round of drinks to blend in, gazing around the dimly lit space. A sad country song played from the jukebox in the corner and the singer crooned about how his wife left him and his dog ran away. It was fucking depressing, just like this place. Why did anyone come here to drink?

I wasn't even sure why I was here or involved with this side of the Forsaken. Vincent had told everyone that I was better suited to do different types of jobs for him.

Ashton sat in the corner at a table with a woman wearing a short red dress that rode up her thighs. Her hair was teased and heavy makeup accentuated the lines on her face. He came here every Friday night to drink and pick up whoever was interested. The neighborhood girls avoided him like the plague–they knew the kinds of things he liked after one of them left with a broken jaw.

This was the easiest place to find him, given that he'd supposedly fallen down on his luck since his last girl-friend kicked him out for cheating on her and stealing her painkillers. The final straw was wrecking her car one night. When the cops showed up and another woman was with him, it was over. Since then, Ashton crashed at various people's houses or in his car.

His greasy hair hung in his face while he leered at the woman across the table and she subtly pressed her breasts together. *We were doing her a favor, and she didn't even know it.* He licked his lips and stood, leaning over the table to tell her something. I watched as he disappeared down the dark hallway to the men's room to either piss or snort something up his nose.

"Showtime," Cam mumbled under his breath. The three of us slid from the stools and I threw forty dollars on the bar as I winked at the bartender. By tomorrow he would forget we were ever here, just another face in the crowd.

The back hallway's lone lightbulb flickered, casting the hallway in eerie shadow as Niko swung open the door. Inside, Ashton was bent over a urinal with his dick out, oblivious to his surroundings, and I sighed. I didn't know what Vincent saw in the people he surrounded himself with. To be career criminals, they weren't great at it. It was probably why half of them didn't last–either the cops arrested them or they ended up dead in an alley, their murders never investigated.

I pulled the knife out of my pocket, snapping it open with the motion of my wrist, and stalked behind him, pressing the blade to his throat. "Put your dick back in your pants and listen closely, or I'll gut you right here and leave your body on the bathroom floor."

His motions stilled and his throat bobbed as he swallowed. "What the fuck do you three want?"

For some reason, he still didn't realize that he wasn't in charge of the show, so I pressed the blade in slightly harder, allowing it to make a shallow cut. Blood beaded on his skin and I watched as it trickled down the column of his throat. "Here's what's going to happen. You're going to zip your pants up and we're going to walk through the backdoor to the car. After that, we're going for a ride and you're going to answer some questions.

I allowed the knife to slide across his skin, down to his abdomen.

Niko placed his hand on Cam's shoulder to gesture that it was time to move and opened the door to the hallway, which was thankfully empty. "Let's go."

The emergency exit alarm had been disabled long ago because of drunk patrons stumbling out with whatever warm body they'd found to spend the night with. The balmy night air cleared my senses and helped to wash away the grime of the bar's interior. Once we were outside, Ashton grabbed my wrist in an attempt to save himself, knowing that if he complied with my demands, his miserable life was over. I sank the blade through his shirt and into his skin a quarter of an inch, just enough for a warning.

I tried to swallow down how I was feeling. The violence, pain, and scarlet stains on his skin made me hard. I knew it was fucked up–some leftover shit from my past.

"Don't even fucking try it. If you get away from me, do you think you'll get away from both of them, too?"

"Let's put him in the trunk," Niko grumbled as he unlocked it. "I don't want blood on my seats." He pulled zip ties from the black bag he stored in the back. "And you owe me after this. I want my entire car detailed."

Cam stood casually, watching as Niko secured Ashton's wrists and I shuffled back, allowing them to wrangle him into the small space that would hold him for the next twenty minutes. He attempted to struggle until Niko pressed his fingers into the wound on his stomach, causing him to groan in pain. "If you think that we're bad, he could have sent Rhyker in our place."

Ashton's eyes went wide, and he stopped, his body turning compliant instantly. *I should have threatened him with that first.*

Everyone thought Rhyker was the happy-go-lucky Forsaken member who helped old ladies with their groceries and rescued cats from trees. And he did those things, but he was also the one that Vincent sent out whenever he needed to take someone out. Around the Forsaken, he was known as the Butcher.

Niko slammed down the trunk lid and glanced at Cam, who smirked. "Where the fuck are we taking him? Don't say your apartment because there are too many witnesses at this time of the night."

He had a point. Junkies and prostitutes hung around my street at all hours of the day. They were the last people that would talk to the cops, but better safe than sorry. A murder charge would keep me trapped in Clearhaven forever. "By the paper mill. There's that area covered by trees and people dump trash over there."

Tyburn Hill was secluded enough that no one would interrupt us. It was a common place to dispose of a body. The news reported someone was found there every week.

Niko nodded and got in, waiting for me to follow him. I crawled into the back and we took off, the breeze kissing my face. Niko turned up the radio, drowning out all the sounds of the city and the banging coming from the trunk. I spent the time going over my checklist of things to ask Ashton before I allowed him to die.

When we arrived at our destination, I glanced around, making sure that no one was there before tapping Cam's shoulder to signal that it was time. Ashton was suspiciously quiet, and the banging had stopped. I wondered if he'd resigned himself to his fate because the cuts weren't deep enough to kill him from blood loss. That would change soon.

Niko and Cam popped open the trunk and lifted the man we'd known for the past eight years, dragging him further into the tree line. I followed them, listening to the sound of leaves crunching under our feet. Once we were shrouded by darkness and the roadway was completely out of sight, we stopped and Niko turned him to face me.

"We've got some questions, and I know that you have answers." The man stared at me for a moment before spitting in my face. Niko wrapped his hand around Ashton's throat and squeezed while I readied the blade in my hand. "Disrespect is never tolerated."

I cut through the filthy shirt he was wearing, exposing his chest to the night air. "How are Vincent and Abraham Wells connected?" Ashton laughed, and I dug the tip in, allowing it to slide down his sternum. Even in the shadows, I could see darkness pooling on his skin.

"Fuck, put the knife down. You could have asked me that at the bar. My life isn't worth this shit," he gritted out. I raised an eyebrow at him while waiting for him to continue. "The dean's part of that secret society. Hell, everyone in power in this godforsaken town is. They're paying Vincent extra cash to distribute that new drug. One of their chemists came up with it."

We all knew that the dean was part of the Order, and I'd suspected that they were behind tease. "Why do they want Ivy Spencer on tea so badly?"

He lifted one shoulder, and I pressed the knife into the soft flesh of his stomach, allowing the blade to sink in. Cam's eyes narrowed when Ashton screamed. "I never knew you were such a bitch, Ashton," he muttered. "Answer the questions and, hypothetically, we'll let you go."

He hissed from the pain and gritted out, "Fuck, I don't know. Something about how the dean owned her."

Niko scoffed, and I smirked. She wasn't mine, but there was no way in hell that Ivy belonged to Wells. I'd make sure of it. It was Cam who responded first. "We own the new girl, not him. He can play his sick games with someone else."

I left the blade in place while I spoke. "Who else is involved in this business arrangement?"

A tear ran down his face. "Please, just let me go," he choked out. "I don't know shit."

I twisted the handle feeling resistance and chuckled. "Unlikely story. After all, you've been meeting with the police. What did you tell the detective down at the station?"

Ashton's eyes went wide with shock and Niko's grasp tightened, making him wheeze. "Why do you think Vincent wants you dead? What happens to snitches in our world?" I asked.

The man choked out a sob and struggled against Niko's restraint. "Just kill me. It's nothing you don't already know. The new guy on the force was on my ass, showing up everywhere and talking about how he could offer me protection." Niko let up on the pressure on his throat for a moment and he coughed before dragging in a deep breath. "No one's safe in this town. If they want you dead, that's what happens."

I yanked the blade from his stomach and held it to his throat. "What did you tell him?"

"Just that there's a new drug on the street and none of us really knows what it does."

Niko nodded to me, signaling that was enough. We'd planned this out ahead of time. I sliced open Ashton's throat and watched crimson run down his skin.

Niko let go of him, and Ashton fell to the ground, clutching at the wound. I could have made things easier for him with a single bullet, but he deserved everything he got. The tales I'd heard of him hitting women and kids stirred demons of my own from the past, reminding me of every "boyfriend" my mother brought home after my father went to prison. Shooting him would be too gentle of a death.

After pushing Ashton's body further down the hill into a ravine, we got into the car and I pretended like nothing had happened. We had learned nothing new other than that the dean thought he had some sort of claim on Ivy.

After tomorrow night, she'd know the truth. Even if Cam wanted to destroy her, she belonged to us.

Ivy

The stands were packed at the stadium, a sea of white and blue jerseys covering every inch of the bleachers. I scanned the crowd looking for Caleb, curious about where he was. He'd texted me earlier in the day under the guise of our project promising that he'd be here. Rosalyn yelled when someone from Clearhaven intercepted the ball from our opponents.

Groveton and Clearhaven apparently played each other yearly despite it being an out-of-conference game, each hoping for an easy win.

I stood quietly beside her and pulled out my phone noticing that around two, Caleb had gone silent. I shot him a quick text asking where he was and waited. And then waited some more. Ten minutes later, I shoved the phone back into my pocket, deciding not to let it ruin my night.

Ros grabbed my hand and squeezed. "Don't worry, he'll show up. In the meantime, we're here to have fun." I bobbed my head at her in agreement.

I was out of the house and away from my aunt on a Saturday. Rosalyn had purchased us sodas and candy for the game. Sports had never been my thing, but it was easy to get caught up in the excitement of the people that surrounded us. It was even easier to pretend that I was someone else. Someone whose life was normal and whose future was bright.

Last night, my aunt stumbled in after midnight, her words slurring slightly while she talked loudly on the phone to someone claiming that Jesus' first miracle was turning water into wine. I crept quietly to my door and pressed my ear against it, trying to listen to the conversation.

Regina had been acting suspiciously. First, she had a fit about me hanging around the Forsaken and imposed a curfew. Then she'd been absent for half the week. *Where had she been? Who was she talking to?*

The snippets I could overhear provided no answers, only more questions. Something about how "everything was going according to plan" and "she just needed a little more time."

I sipped the ice-cold soda in my hand, savoring the sweetness while I looked around the stands. Trey and Niko were also absent. Would they really miss their best friend's opening game?

The phone in my pocket never vibrated while people jumped up and down around me. It was fine. He probably had something better to do than hang out with Ros and me. It's not like we were anything special, just partners for a class project.

Finally, I settled into the game, watching as men in blue jerseys lined up. My eyes immediately caught on number thirty-eight. Even from this distance, I recognized exactly who it was. I wasn't sure if it was because of the aura of power he exuded or his gait, but there was no doubt in my mind that it was Camden Barrett.

The crowd around me exploded as the quarterback threw the ball down the field, number thirty-eight catching it easily. Watching him, I forgot about the laid-back guy who had an easy smile and gave no fucks about anything who was absent. Instead, I was enraptured by the man who was currently the center of my torment. It was almost too easy to ignore the cruel words he'd said to me as he glided down the field. Cam ran with the ball, gracefully bobbing and weaving through the other players until he reached the end zone, scoring a touchdown.

I grabbed Rosalyn and hugged her, letting myself get swept up in the game. When Cam took off his helmet and shook out his golden hair, the stadium lights glinted off of it. He looked nearly angelic, all the usual hardness gone from his features. This was what he excelled at, what made him thrive.

That was the way the rest of the evening went. We danced to the music of the band, cheered at every touchdown, and drank so much soda my bladder cried out for mercy. Occasionally, Ros would flip off one of the mean girls that shot me a look or narrowed their eyes, mumbling under her breath that they needed to get over themselves.

By the time we climbed into Black Betty, I was on cloud nine and looking forward to the party that Ros originally had to convince me to go to. Cam's "invitation" was the furthest thing from my mind as we grabbed tacos from the drive-through so that we had something to eat before drinking–Rosalyn's idea, not mine. We ate quickly as she drove to a house close to the beach, laughing the entire way. It was good, almost too good.

The driveway was full and the entire street was lined with cars by the time we arrived. No one had bothered to mention that the party was being held at a mansion. It was literally the biggest house I'd ever seen, and that was saying a lot. I'd grown up around wealth and decadence.

Music vibrated from inside, and people sat on the lawn in circles holding red plastic cups. I linked my arm with Ros as we drew closer to the door. "Who lives here?"

She grinned at me and lowered her voice. "Caleb's cousin Luthor. His parents are supposedly out for the month on a trip to Europe."

It was my turn to raise my eyebrows. Of course, they were in Europe. Until now, the only parts of Clearhaven I had seen were poverty-stricken or middle-class. Families doing the best they could to make it until payday; people living in modest houses and driving average cars. *Perhaps every city had a small group of the elite that ran everything.*

We walked inside and up the stairs, dodging couples who were making out and girls dancing in tiny skirts. Ros pulled me into the kitchen where bottles of liquor and mixer were lined up on the island cabinet. Rhyker, the Forsaken who played bartender last week, sidled up behind her and wrapped his arms around her waist, planting a kiss on the side of her neck.

Ros gave him a sheepish grin as she pushed at his face, but he clung to her and kissed her exposed shoulder. "Do you two want to party tonight?"

I lifted an eyebrow at his words, but Ros placed her hands on top of his. "Are you offering to share your weed with us?"

"I will if you want because I have a feeling that you," he stated quietly as he pointed at me, "are going to need to take the edge off before Cam sees you, but I've got something better."

His warning about Cam sent a chill through my body, but instead, I focused on the fact that he was offering to give us drugs. Ros let her head fall back against his chest. "Rhyker, if you're offering us some crazy shit like heroin, I still remember the time you–"

He quieted her objections by nipping at her ear and I asked myself not for the first time what their deal was. "Baby, I'm not giving you any of that shit. I've got some tablets of this new thing called tea if you want them. They're completely safe."

I turned back to the liquor on the island, deciding to mix myself a drink while I talked. "Listen, I really appreciate it, but I'm not into taking something new. Do you remember that news report a few years ago where that guy got high and bit someone's face? The last thing I need is to do some crazy shit like that and get arrested."

Rhyker's laughter filled the air, and his body quaked. I stared at him unsure of why he was so amused. Finally, he cleared his throat and pressed one last kiss to the top of Ros' head before releasing her. "New girl, you're hilarious.

The two of you already had it last week. Half the people here have. The punch at the beach was spiked with it and no one bit anyone's face or anything crazy."

His words crashed into me. I knew that alcohol had never affected me that way before. My skin itself was on fire and all of my problems melted into the background. And all of that was before Cam's shit this week. I held out my hand. "I want one."

He gave Ros a look, and she nodded her head, also holding her hand out. "I still want some of your weed later." She elbowed me in the side and lowered her voice into a mock whisper. "He has the good shit."

Long gone was the initial impression of Ros that I'd gotten when she sat at my kitchen table arguing with my aunt about religion. She was the person who was confident enough to bend the rules, didn't care what anyone thought, and had random guys who were smitten with her all while wearing floral dresses on Sunday morning.

Rhyker handed us each a small white tablet, and I stared at it for a moment, debating if I was really going to take it. *Fuck it.* If it made everything go away for the evening again, I was more than happy to try it.

We finished making drinks and Rhyker motioned for us to follow him onto the back deck that overlooked a gigantic pool. Thousands of fairy lights lit up the backyard, and I sipped my drink, waiting for the euphoria to kick in. He pulled out a joint from his pocket and lit it, taking a long drag before passing it to Ros. He gave me a strange look and pursed his lips. "Give the tea ten or fifteen minutes to kick in. In the meantime, enjoy the ride."

I stood there waiting for my turn while watching the people below push each other into the pool and flirt, thinking about how different things were. Not just about how my father had hidden a secret life, or that I had lost everything, but how different I was. I'd been to parties before and smoked weed, but knowingly taking a drug from someone who was a stranger? Me six months ago would never have considered that.

Ros handed me the joint and I took a drag, trying to remember to hold in the smoke and not look like a complete fool in front of my friend. My lungs burned and when I exhaled, I coughed. Ros grinned and patted my back, her eyes twinkling with amusement. Between the burn of the alcohol and the lightness of my head, I felt good. Really good.

And then the familiar fire started under my skin. Whatever punishment Cam had in store for me, I could live with as long as it didn't take away the bliss I was experiencing.

We finished smoking before Ros pulled both of us back inside, following the sound of the music and dancing. She snorted at something Rhyker whispered in her ear as we descended the stairs into a huge dimly lit living room. The furniture was pushed to the side, and I didn't pay attention to who else was in the room. All that mattered to me was the bass of the music.

I swayed my hips as we danced toward the crowd of people who were all writhing on the makeshift dance floor. One of the other women from the university was standing on top of a marble table, hands brushing up and down her sides to the beat. Rhyker stared at the corner of the room and that was when I saw it.

Trey, Niko, and Cam were sprawled out on a sectional sofa, dressed in jeans and t-shirts that accentuated every bit of muscle and put all of their tattoos on display. In Niko's lap sat the pretty dark-haired girl from the other day, the one that I knew he gave drugs to. Her arms were wound around his neck as she whispered something only he could hear. His eyes were closed and despite how things were, a brief flash of jealousy curled inside of me. He wasn't mine, and they had rules, even if Cam had already broken them.

Cam's gaze caught mine, and he hooked two fingers toward me, beckoning for me to come closer like he was a monarch holding court. I held my head back and laughed at the absurdity, deciding that he could go fuck himself. I tipped back the rest of the cup, letting the liquor burn my throat and the fire spread further in my veins.

I wrapped my arms around Ros' neck and pressed my forehead against hers. "Did I just see you ignore Camden Barrett? I can't wait to see how he reacts to that."

He probably wouldn't react at all. After all, they had the attention of the dark-haired nameless girl who seemed extremely comfortable sitting with Niko. The beat of the music drummed inside my veins as we moved together.

Suddenly, my hold on Ros was jerked away, and my body lifted off the ground. All I could see was a black t-shirt and the ground, a hard shoulder pressed against my stomach. I squealed at the weightless sensation and kicked my legs. The scent of the ocean bombarded me.

Cam. I watched Ros' eyes grow wide with disbelief and Rhyker shake his head before he looked away. Later, I would tell him he was a coward.

I glanced at the sectional sofa and noticed that the dark-haired girl sat by herself now; Trey and Niko were both absent. "Let me down," I hissed and hit his back. "There are rules."

Cam swatted my ass, his palm stinging me through the denim. "Which you are determined to break every chance you have. And since neither of us can seem to follow the rules, I want to show you a little surprise I've arranged for you."

His feet covered the ground quickly with me caught in his clutches as he climbed two sets of stairs. He stopped in front of a bedroom door and pushed it open before dropping me onto the ground. I landed with a thud as he flicked on the light switch, illuminating the office. A heavy wooden desk sat near huge windows, and book-cases lined all the walls.

My mouth fell open as I took in everything. Off to the left, a heavy chair sat in the corner and tied to it was Caleb. Ropes bound his torso and limbs, tethering him in place, and a black cloth was shoved in his mouth. His knuckles were busted and a new bruise was forming on his opposite cheek. Trey and Niko stood beside him, both looking entirely unbothered by the situation.

He hadn't stood me up. He'd been tied up here this entire time. That was why Trey and Niko had also been absent from the football game. "What the fuck is this?" I asked, my voice coming out quiet. Everything was slightly blurry between the alcohol, tea, and weed, and part of me wanted to believe that this was just another nightmare.

Cam gave me a cruel smile and leaned against the edge of the desk. "Little ghost, I think we have a problem. I seem to remember I told everyone you were an outcast and off limits." He turned his head to look at Caleb, who was openly glaring at him. "And Vance. You knew what we'd said, and yet the other night you kissed Ivy at the race. I hope it was worth it."

Cam straightened and strolled next to where I sat, crouching down so that he could meet my eyes. He traced along my jaw with his thumb, trailing it over my bottom lip. "Both of your actions can't go unpunished, so here's what's going to happen. After tonight, I want there to be no question that you're ours, Ivy. No one else is allowed to touch you without our permission."

He lifted his chin at Trey who sauntered toward me slowly, pulling a knife from his pocket. "Get on your knees, baby." I heard the flick of the knife behind me and a shiver skated down my spine. I should have been scared, but a part of me anticipated what was going to happen next.

"Fuck off, Cam. What will you do if I don't?" The edge of the knife tore through the back of my t-shirt and I rolled my eyes. "And you? Can you stop cutting off all of my clothes? Unlike some people, I actually have to work for my stuff."

Cam's lips twisted up at the corner, and he grabbed my chin with his hand. "The last thing you need to be worried about is your shirt, Ivy. Unless you want Prince Charming over there to know about why you're here in Clearhaven instead of at some posh Ivy League school, I suggest you get on your knees. I want him to see that you belong to the three of us."

I closed my eyes and positioned myself so that I was kneeling, the rest of the fight going out of me. My brain was muddled by all the conflicting emotions that raced through my veins alongside whatever I had taken tonight. I didn't want Caleb to learn about my past. Really, I didn't want anyone to know. The information was available with a simple internet search, but I'd hoped to simply blend into the shadows–just another anonymous body in town.

After tonight, I needed to distance myself from the handsome rebellious rich boy who was tied up in the corner. Other than this stupid project for class, we needed to stay away from one another. Hell, there was still time to drop the class.

I opened my eyes and looked up, watching as Cam slowly unzipped his pants, his hard cock springing free. I glanced at Caleb one more time, noticing that despite everything, a bulge tented the front of his pants. He was into this. He was just as fucked up as the three guys who had captured him and had me on my knees.

I wetted my lips and readied myself for whatever they were about to do to me, allowing the fire that was crawling across my skin to consume me completely. After tonight, all bets were off. Cam thought he could push me around and break me, but he was wrong. I would find a way to pay him back.

Caleb

E ven from a distance, I could tell that Ivy's pupils were the size of saucers. Her hair was wild and her cheeks were flushed pink and I was certain that I'd never seen anything more beautiful than her on her knees. *Anything more feral.* Despite the position they had her in, she still defied Cam at every turn.

I knew what her secret was. I had since she moved to Clearhaven after a discussion with my grandfather over Sunday morning brunch, but I kept my mouth shut. She didn't want anyone to know about her past, and I couldn't blame her.

After all, I had secrets of my own.

Initially, when I began talking to her, it started out as one more way to get underneath the Forsaken's skin, among other things. That was the reason that I showed up on Thursday night to race. Niko was undefeated, and I wanted to knock him down off of his pedestal. The three of them walked around like they were royalty, and everyone bowed to their demands.

But I quickly learned that I enjoyed being around Ivy. I liked her fight and the chaos that surrounded her. She drew me into her orbit with the anger that masked her sadness.

When Niko and Trey showed up as I was leaving for the football game this evening, I wasn't surprised. I got in a few punches of my own before Niko choked me, knocking me out.

And then I woke up here.

I stared at the red-haired girl whose face was lined with determination. Her chest heaved and I let my gaze travel down her body, noticing the white lace bra that barely contained her breasts. Her pink nipples were hard beneath the fabric, and she bit down on her lower lip before tracing it with her tongue. She was into this, just as fucked up as the rest of us.

I tried to shift in my seat to adjust myself and hide the fact that I was painfully hard, but it was to no avail. Ivy's lips parted and she grasped Cam's thighs, allowing him to sink inside her mouth. His hand cupped her jaw almost tenderly as he watched her, allowing her to set the pace. Their eyes were locked on one another and I would have done anything to trade places with Cam.

He could say what he wanted to, but I saw through all of his bullshit. Even though he wanted someone to pay for what happened to his sister, he was drawn to Ivy and he hated it. He was punishing both of them for crimes that neither had committed.

Cam's hips began moving slowly, rocking against Ivy's face, and she closed her eyes, letting herself get swept away in the moment. Her cheeks hollowed out as his pace increased with every thrust. One of his hands wound up into the back of Ivy's hair while the other stayed on her jaw. The muscles of his ass flexed with every stroke and her fingers dug into his skin.

Trey stood behind them, carefully tracing his knife in a pattern down Ivy's back, reverently never nicking her skin—something that surprised me given the cuts on my own torso from earlier. His motions stopped suddenly. He grabbed the clasp of her bra with one hand and undid the clasp, careful not to cut through the fabric. *I guess he listened to at least one thing she said.*

Her breasts spilled out, and I took in the contrast of her skin against Camden's thighs. Trey bit down on his bottom lip and freed himself, grasping his cock lightly. He slowly stroked himself while he traced the curve of her breast, occasionally flicking the flat side of the knife against her peaked nipples. A moan escaped from between Ivy's lips and her hand disappeared between her thighs. Niko, who had been standing off to the side and rubbing himself through his pants, darted closer and grabbed her wrist. "You won't get off unless we say so, and tonight isn't for your pleasure. It's to make a point."

I tried to free my wrists for the millionth time, not necessarily to stop what was happening, but to relieve the ache that was growing in my pants. To touch the wild creature that they had on her knees. Ivy wasn't the type of girl that could be owned or possessed by someone, even if the other men using her body didn't realize it yet.

Niko wrapped her hand around his cock and helped her find the rhythm he liked, the row of metal barbells shining beneath the office lights. Her hand moved fluidly up and down the length without hesitation while Cam's pace increased, brutally using her mouth. The tenderness from earlier was gone as he moved her head how he liked. Spit and tears dribbled down her face.

She was so fucking beautiful. Did she even realize that? All I could envision was her soft pink lips wrapped around my cock while I used her as I pleased. None of them deserved her. I would let her touch her clit while I did it, the moans from her mouth vibrating up my spine.

Cam's hand encased her neck and Niko licked a trail up her face, tasting the tears that had fallen. Finally, Trey carefully flicked the blade against the side of her ribs, blood tarnishing her perfect skin. His tongue brushed against the wound and he closed his eyes, a low groan slipping past his lips.

At the rate they were going, none of them would last much longer. Cam pulled his cock out of her mouth and rubbed the head against her lips. "Remember how I told you I was going to mark you so that everyone would see you were ours?" He jerked himself several times and his jaw tensed as white jets landed on Ivy's body.

"Open your mouth up, Ivy, and keep it open." She tried to defy him, but Cam grasped her jaw. When her lips parted, he leaned close and spit into her mouth. He moved out of the way, and Trey took his place. Ivy's tongue darted out to taste him, but he gave her a hard stare, stopping her in her tracks. Trey's cum joined Cam's on Ivy's breasts.

He ran his tongue along her bottom lip and nipped it before pulling away. "You're so pretty like this, new girl." Saliva fell into her mouth and her eyes closed.

It was degrading as shit but somehow still exciting. Niko leaned closer, running his tongue through the mess that had been made before grabbing Ivy's face. Cum and saliva dripped between her lips. He pulled her close and thrust his tongue inside, branding her as his.

Her motions faltered slightly, and he placed his hand over hers, helping her to finish him. He came on her stomach before he pulled away and gave her a kiss on the forehead. Ivy looked shocked as Cam bent down, snaking his hand into her pants. "Little ghost, you liked what we did to you," he smirked. "I think you like being treated like our whore. You look so perfect right now, your skin marked by us."

Her eyes fluttered closed as she rocked her hips against his hand. Cam pulled away when she moaned and yanked the gag from my mouth. "Open up," he commanded. I clenched my jaw in defiance, refusing to give in to whatever game he was playing. Rather than give up, he gripped my jaw and applied enough force that pain lanced through my face. I opened up, and he thrust his fingers inside my mouth. Ivy's arousal was still wet on his fingers and the taste bloomed on my tongue, salty and tangy.

She tasted good, but I would never tell them that. His fingers rubbed along my lips and he laid his forehead against mine, glaring. "That's the only taste you'll ever get of her." I spit in his face, but he simply laughed at me and rubbed his palm down his cheek, wiping it on his pants.

"Alright, Ivy. It's time to go. Grab your bra."

Her eyes widened and her eyebrows shot up. "What about my–"

Niko's chuckle rumbled through the room, and Trey shrugged. "Sorry, baby. Remember how we told you that everyone would know you were ours?" He handed her the thin white lace and waited. "Don't think about trying to clean up before you head downstairs. If you do, we'll just haul you back in here to do it again."

Her cheeks turned red, and she faced away from everyone while she fastened the bra and adjusted it. "Can I at least have my shirt?"

Trey smiled and picked it up off the floor, tucking it under his arm. "I don't think so."

"What about me? We're done here and I have shit to do," I grinned, determined not to let them get to me.

Cam rolled his eyes. "Not yet, lover boy. Can't have you trying to rush off and rescue the damsel in distress. Besides, who said we were done with you? You cost Niko the race and defied our orders."

Niko grabbed Ivy's hand and pulled her through the door. She cast one last glance at me before she disappeared and I wondered what in the fuck they were going to do next.

Tonight hadn't changed anything about me and Ivy. They just didn't know it yet. If they thought this was going to deter me from speaking to her, they were wrong.

Ivy

My entire body was engulfed in flames, and my mouth felt like cotton. I wasn't sure if it was from the tea I'd taken earlier, being turned on, being angry, or feeling humiliated. Niko's hand was placed on the small of my back, guiding me down the stairs. I thought he was just leading me outside to take me home, but I was wrong. Camden and Trey followed behind us silently as people stopped whatever they were doing to stare.

I was covered in semen, my lips were swollen, and whatever mascara Ros had put on me streaked down my cheeks. When we hit the bottom of the second set of stairs, I stopped in my tracks ready to fight them, but Cam simply leaned close and grabbed my wrist, dragging me forward through the crowd. "This wasn't part of the deal," I gritted out where only he could hear me.

"I told you that after tonight everyone would know who you belonged to," he smirked, hauling me to the edge of the room where a sound system stood. The whispers were growing and I kept my eyes on my feet. I didn't want to know who was seeing me in this state or what they were saying. Just a few more minutes of embarrassment and then I could hide.

Trey cut the sound and everything fell silent around us, suffocating me. Even the whispers stopped when Cam raised his voice. "In case you haven't heard, this is the new girl, Ivy. She defied our orders by talking to someone from campus. She's our property, our plaything to do with as we wish. No one else is to look at her, speak to her, or even think about her." He traced a finger through the cold cum sitting on my chest, smearing it further. He looked up, glaring at Rhyker. "And no one else is to give her anything to help her feel more comfortable during her stay here in Clearhaven, however short that may be."

Rosalyn glowered at him and gave him the middle finger before he shoved me back toward the crowd. "Now get out of here. If I find out that you go anywhere but home, next time will be twice as bad."

Flashes from people's phones went off in my periphery as I hurried toward the front door, the exit away from this hellhole. I grabbed the handle and ran outside, trying to pull myself together. I stared down at my shoes as my feet lead me away from the house. The ocean breeze chilled my skin despite the warm late summer temperature and I pondered how the hell I had ended up here.

Punishing me was one thing. I could accept that. Maybe I was a masochist because a part of me enjoyed how they treated me in the office. Fuck, I could even potentially accept how they'd treated Caleb. He had also dared to break the rules by trying to get close to me. Parading me around in front of the rest of the party, though?

Fuck them.

My legs were putty, and I zoned out, ignoring everything around me. Someone's hand grabbed my shoulder, but I shrugged it off. "Where do you think you're going?" Rosalyn's voice cut through the fog in my brain.

I didn't look up because I couldn't stand to see the pity in her eyes. "Home."

Rhyker jogged up to me and stood in my path, forcing me to raise my eyes. "For fuck's sake, Ivy, stop for a second. You can't walk home dressed like that. Someone else will see you and you'll end up on the evening news as another statistic."

The anger from early that had been extinguished returned with a vengeance. I jabbed my finger into his chest as I enunciated every word. "You fucking knew what they were going to do."

He opened his mouth and then shut it, choosing his words carefully. "I didn't know their whole plan, and I'm sorry. I couldn't have stopped Camden, anyway. At least let me or Ros take you home."

I crossed my arms over my body and stepped around him, looking back down. "No. You heard what they said. The last thing I need is for them to mess with anyone else because of me."

"If you won't let me help you, at least take this." Rosalyn shrugged off the thin jacket she was wearing and pressed it into my hand. Rhyker pulled a paper towel from his pocket and gave it to me, not meeting my eyes. "Don't you dare think that this is the end of our friendship, Ivy Spencer. I'll still be here when you're ready to stop being so stubborn. You better not let them win."

I wiped my chest and stomach off, throwing the paper towel on the ground, not caring if it was littering, before putting the jacket on over my bra. I buttoned as many buttons as I could, concealing at least some of my torso before sighing and gave her a weak smile. "Don't worry. They think they have the upper hand, but I'm not done fighting. I just don't want them…"

She simply patted my back. "Are you sure that you don't want a ride home? I can deal with those three."

I shoved my hands in my pockets. "No. You two go have fun."

Rhyker coughed and shifted on his feet. "It's not like that."

I turned my back to them and started walking. "Sure," I yelled over my shoulder.

After I was out of sight, I pulled my phone from my pocket, trying to decide on my best plan of attack and ignore the ache between my thighs. It was confusing. I was angry, but between the drugs and being denied an orgasm, I was left wanting.

I pulled up one of the social media apps to distract myself and briefly speculated about if it would be easier to just get into my car and disappear. Take the money from my bank account and try to start somewhere new. I'd never lived out of a car before, but I could figure it out.

I typed in Cam's name, dreading what I would find. Cars passed me on the roadway, but I ignored them as I scrolled through endless photos of the guys taking selfies together. Cam wearing his football uniform. The three of them taking shots. Girls clinging to each of them like they were the answer to all of their prayers. *Nothing I could use for blackmail.*

I pulled up the internet browser and typed in his name again, hoping that something I could actually use would pop up. There were a few news articles about his high school football days and how they were expecting him to attend one of the more prominent colleges several states away. I scrolled past several knowing that the reason he hadn't escaped was his younger sister. He stayed here for her.

And then I hit the jackpot. On the police blotter, Samantha Barrett had been arrested in Clearhaven for a DUI. I skimmed through the charges and court cases, taking in the information. From her mugshot, she was definitely his mother. The same crystal blue eyes and golden hair with pouty lips. In her younger days, she would have been attractive, but now her cheeks were ruddy from years of alcohol.

Out of curiosity, I typed in Trey and Niko's names. Earlier, my heart would have broken for them, but now I looked at it with clinical interest. All of their home lives were shit. Between alcoholism, drug abuse, prostitution, and prison, none of them had anyone. They only had each other.

Perhaps we weren't as different as I'd initially thought. No amount of sympathy could have stopped me from what I was planning, though. If they thought that I'd just fall in line, they were wrong.

Finally, my aunt's house came into view. My feet hurt from the trek here, and I was ready to crawl into the shower to scrub the night's events off of my skin. Unfortunately, the front porch light was on and her car was in the driveway. Silently, I hoped she was already asleep, but my heart raced in my chest. I glanced down at the time on my phone, noting that it was after midnight and I'd definitely broken curfew.

Slipping inside the dark house, I closed the door behind me carefully, hoping that it wouldn't give me away. It creaked and my aunt's voice traveled through the house. "Ivy, I was wondering when you would stumble in."

I plastered a smile on my face and ran my fingers through my hair, trying to tame some of the waves. "Sorry I'm late," I answered as I exited the small entryway into the light.

She lifted one eyebrow at me as she appraised my appearance. And when she opened her mouth, I knew that whatever she was going to say would piss me off. "Well, you're dressed like a common whore. I can see your bra, and I know your father taught you to dress better than that." Shock painted my features at the abruptness of her words. I knew I looked like hell, but she hadn't even asked if I was alright.

She sniffed as she pulled a cigarette out of a pack on the table and lit it. "I won't allow you to continue to break my rules, Ivy. I'll kick you out of my house before you tarnish my reputation here. You're turning into your mother and I can't have that."

My heart fell into my stomach and I suddenly felt nauseous. My mother. I didn't even remember her and had only ever seen one photograph of her in my entire life.

I was forbidden from asking questions about her. She was a dirty secret. As I had gotten older, I assumed that she'd abandoned me because she didn't want me. Perhaps becoming a mother was too much, or she couldn't handle my father's demands.

I cleared my throat, willing my tears to not fall while I straightened my shoulders. "Don't worry. This will be the last time I break curfew. You don't have to worry about me."

I didn't bother adding in that it was because I didn't have anyone as I trudged to the shower. Or that I was pushing Rosalyn and Caleb away to protect them.

I turned the shower on as hot as it would go and climbed in, thinking of what I would do first thing in the morning. Dropping world civilization as soon as possible seemed like the best choice and would keep Caleb at arm's length. I could exchange it for one of the general education classes I knew I needed to graduate. Something in the art or music department. I scrubbed my skin until it was raw and pink, almost like I could wash the events of the past few hours away.

Wrapping my towel around me, I tiptoed to my room, unwilling to speak to my aunt again. I pulled the lid off of the gray plastic box to find clean clothes and the first thing I saw was the t-shirt that Niko had dressed me in before carrying me home last week. His scent still clung to it and I pushed it aside while I dressed. Still, the shirt called to me. I grabbed it before heading to bed and lifted it to my nose.

The smell comforted me even though they'd shown me who they really were tonight. I guess they really had since the very beginning, but I had looked away. I pulled the shirt over my head and crawled beneath my blankets. The inside of my thighs were coated with arousal and the scent of sandalwood only intensified the throbbing between my legs.

I never had really touched myself before. The few times I had tried had only frustrated me further as I had fumbled, never able to get off on my own. Still, my hand trailed down my torso and slipped inside of the band of my underwear.

I closed my eyes and let myself imagine what tonight could have been like instead of the nightmare that it was. In my fantasy, Caleb wasn't tied to the chair and instead was behind me, squeezing my breasts while I straddled Niko's face. His fingers dug into my hips, forcing me flush with his mouth as his tongue explored inside of me.

I pulled up the hem of my shirt, exposing my breasts and pinched my nipples as my finger traced my clit, slowly getting faster as I thought of rough touches.

Trey would stand beside me, his thick cock pressed against my lips. My tongue would dart out to tease him, licking the bead of pre-cum off of his crown while Cam kissed my neck. His lips would latch on between whispered words where he told me I was such a good little slut for being able to take them all.

I needed more, and I pressed my middle two fingers inside, my palm grazing the sensitive bundle of nerves.

Electricity shot through my body and I gasped as I pistoned them inside of me and pulled on my nipples.

Niko's lips would find my clit and suck, allowing his teeth to brush along it, and Trey would grab my hair, encouraging me to put him in my mouth. He would rock his hips against my face and tell me how beautiful I looked. Instead of his usual indifference, he would look at me like I was the one who hung the stars in the sky.

I flipped onto my stomach, grinding against my palm while thinking of ocean blue eyes, wishing that instead of my fingers, it was one of their cocks. My muscles tensed as I writhed against my mattress and sweat beaded on my skin. Black spots appeared on the edges of my vision and everything ceased to exist as my body shuddered and my pussy clamped down on my fingers.

After I caught my breath and readjusted my clothes, relief was replaced by shame. I had just gotten off to thoughts of the three men who were determined to humiliate me. They had acted like monsters, casting me out of the house covered in come and yet I was imagining them bringing me pleasure.

I turned onto my side and pulled the blanket up to my chin, praying for sleep to come. In a few brief hours, I was going to be the one acting like a monster.

They just didn't know it yet.

Niko

The parking lot was full Monday morning by the time Cam and I had pulled up. I overslept and didn't want to get out of bed, the events of Saturday night playing through my head on repeat. Part of me wanted to regret what had happened, how harshly we'd treated Ivy, but I didn't. At least not completely.

I disagreed with parading her around in front of the people that had shown up for the party and disliked the fact that Cam kicked her out of the house afterward. I wasn't sure if he was trying to claim her or humiliate her with his actions. Maybe it was both. Pictures of her standing there in her bra were already all over social media by Sunday morning, and word had traveled around campus.

What I didn't regret was seeing her on her knees again, even if it was through coercion. The way her eyelids fluttered and her tongue darted out to taste whatever we gave her. She wasn't fragile and I would take her however I could get her, even if she hated me afterward.

Cam was so determined to break her, and all I wanted to do was possess her.

I exited the car and noticed that Trey was already waiting on us, leaning against a light pole, looking bored. As I ambled closer, he frowned and held up his phone. "Have you guys checked YouConnect this morning?"

I shook my head, curious why he was asking about the social media site that most of the university used. "No, why?"

Trey simply raised an eyebrow and typed something into his phone before passing it to Cam first. A string of expletives left his mouth, and he handed it to me so that I could see. A new account by the name of JustAGhost had posted screenshot after screenshot, targeting each of us. The user name alone told me who it was as I clutched the phone, the only person who dared to stand up to us. Evidently, Cam had finally gotten under her skin.

First was Cam, where there were mugshots of his mother who had been taken in for more DUIs than I could count and a charge of public indecency. What followed were pictures of him standing next to her at our high school graduation where it was evident from her glassy eyes she wasn't sober. There was nothing about his father because... no one knew who he was. Some drunken one-night stand that didn't bother staying in touch.

The next several posts were dedicated to Trey. Screenshots of the news report detailing his father's failed robbery attempt and the court case that followed appeared. Obviously, Ivy couldn't leave well enough alone and included mugshots of his mother as well. Years of prostitution charges were listed and my cheeks heated with anger. There were also the charges from where one of the

Johns had beaten Trey so badly, we'd carried him to the hospital.

Dread curled in my stomach knowing that I was next. What had she managed to pull up on my family?

My father's drug charges obviously showed up, but that didn't bother me. Hell, everyone in Clearhaven knew about the emergency phone calls whenever he OD'ed. What got me was the news articles about my mother's death. How she had been found overdosed in an alleyway not far from where hookers solicited potential customers. The jagged wound in my chest had never quite healed, and Ivy had managed to rip the bandage off.

The account already had 15,000 followers, and it had only started yesterday. Anger and shame mingled together and before I could stop myself. I threw the phone on the concrete sidewalk, the screen busting into a million pieces.

"Motherfucker," Trey cursed under his breath as he stared at the pieces of glass. "I should have known better than to hand the two of you anything of value."

I didn't need this right now. None of us did. The fact that I'd lost the race last Thursday still loomed over my head. I was already behind on rent and the next payment was coming up next week. Not that the information Ivy posted was some sort of big secret in Clearhaven. Everyone knew the background of the three broken boys who joined the Forsaken as soon as they were allowed. It was the fact that she threw things that were beyond our control back into our faces. Things that still broke us and we had never healed from.

My parents were always addicts, but losing my mother changed everything. We didn't have the money for a funeral and, seeing that the only thing left of her was a tiny box of ashes broke me. My sister and brother cried at night for months, asking when she would be back to kiss them goodnight. It was the final domino that pushed me into this life.

I flexed my fingers at my sides, trying to regain some semblance of composure."So what are going to do about it?"

Trey grinned at me and shoved his hands in his pockets. "I say turnabout is fair play. She should have known better than to fuck with us. It was a dumb move on her part."

As deep as my obsession with Ivy was, I had to agree with his statement. Her actions couldn't go unchecked. We couldn't look weak, especially not to Vincent or his associates.

Cam ran his hands through his hair. "I agree, but the two of you just chill. I'll take care of it. Unless she skips out, she has tutoring with me tomorrow."

"What are you going to do?" I asked, lifting my backpack higher on my shoulder.

When he grinned, a shiver skated down my spine. "Like Trey said, turnabout is fair play. Everyone here knows who our families are, but who knows about her history?"

I chewed on the inside of my cheek for a moment, mulling everything over. "Isn't that the only leverage we have?" I wasn't completely behind torturing her or making her an outcast like Cam, but if this was a chess game, sacrificing such a crucial piece made me unsettled.

Trey's eyes twinkled with amusement and he stood up straight, looking at the building behind us. "Don't worry about that. I set up a camera in the office the other night. I'm sure Ivy wouldn't want that getting out. Especially not with how her aunt is."

I should have expected nothing less from him. As outwardly cruel as Cam could be, Trey was cruel in different ways. He was logical and methodical, always thinking three steps ahead. Part of me wanted to see the tape of the four of us and relive the moment, but a voice in the back of my head reminded me that before everything was done, she'd hate us.

I took a deep breath and looked down at my phone. My class was starting in ten minutes. I gave them a fist bump before I left, trying to focus on other things. I had more important things to worry about, like how I was going to pay my rent and if I should ask Tyler to sign me up for a fight.

All day long, I'd thought about whether I should call Tyler. Instead of focusing on whatever the professor was saying in my economics class, I'd mulled over ways to make enough quick cash to satisfy my landlord. The guys were preoccupied with thoughts of how to pay back Ivy, and I didn't want to bother them with my problems. Cam and Trey both had enough shit on their plates.

I made a mental list of things that I could do. Stealing a car and offloading it at Mack's was one option. Breaking into a houses in the rich area of town was another. Hell, breaking into Caleb's house and stealing his grandmother's diamonds felt fitting, but something stopped me.

The only thing that was off limits at this point was selling my car. I'd poured my blood, sweat, and tears into it. Plus, it was our only reliable transportation. Trey's car could break down on the side of the road tomorrow.

Contacting Tyler would be the second safest option from a legal standpoint. The only thing I would need to worry about was winning. I wouldn't have the worry of searching for cameras or the police catching me lifting a car. I also wouldn't have to worry about pawning anything or the paper trail some shops kept.

As soon as my last class ended, I sat on the bench closest to the administrative building and pulled out my phone. Ivy had been absent around, which surprised me. After the stunt she pulled, I had expected to see her. I still couldn't believe that she had the nerve to use that as a handle. She knew we would realize who it was immediately.

After wasting some time on social media, seeing if JustAGhost had posted anything new, I closed out all the apps and opened my contacts. I allowed my finger to hover over the name while debating with myself. It was now or never and I didn't want Vincent or the guys to talk me out of what I was considering. Tyler picked up after one ring. "Yeah?"

I rolled my eyes at his greeting. He was all business, never one for easing into a conversation. "Look, I need you to hook me up with a fight as soon as possible."

He chuckled under his breath, and I heard the rustle of papers in the background. "The soonest I can do is October."

A heavy breath left my chest and my heart fell. "Any way you can do something sooner? I really need the money, man. After the last race…"

My heart raced as I waited for his next words and I chewed on the edge of my nail. "If you're willing to drive three hours, I can hook you up. You ever been to Strathmore?"

"Book me and text me the details. I'll be there."

My stomach coiled with nerves. I'd never really been outside of Clearhaven before–poverty tended to do that, anchoring people to a place–but this was my shot at trying to save the home I'd grown up in. It was the place my brother and sister went to sleep every night and where my mother's ghost haunted the halls.

I'd never fought inside of a ring before, even an illegal one, but I had been in plenty of fights. With shaky legs, I stood and gathered my things, taking a quick glance down at my phone as it buzzed in my hands, listing the information I needed. I would win my match because even without training, I had an edge few did–desperation.

Ivy

After the events of the party this weekend and then my decision to fight back against the guys, Monday I skipped classes. I wasn't ready to deal with the shame of being paraded in front of everyone at the party or confront the fact that I had to push Caleb away. I also wasn't ready to face the repercussions of posting what I had on social media. They deserved what I had done, but there would be consequences. For every action, there was an equal and opposite reaction.

Instead, I stopped by the small thrift store-swearing that I would look for one not affiliated with my aunt's church-and rummaged through the racks, looking for a few pieces that would make me feel more confident about myself. Other than the dress that Trey had cut off of me, it had been months since I'd worn anything that made me feel pretty.

I had decided that it was time to find myself again. It was time that I got back into a routine that didn't revolve around work, school, and studying. Even if I was pushing Ros and Caleb away, there was no reason I couldn't be happy, or at least appear that way on the outside. If anyone thought they could break me, they were wrong. I was already broken.

I pulled out several skirts and tops from the clothing racks and carefully checked the price tags before folding them over my arms. Several pairs of cotton athletic pants completed the list of items I was looking for. After paying for my purchase with the money Cam threw at me in the library, I stopped by the small shoe store next door and found knee-high black boots on clearance. They would be perfect to pair with the new to me clothes.

My last stop of the day was at a small dollar store at the end of the strip mall. Inside, I scoured through the budget makeup, determined to stretch the last of the money I had made "tutoring." Cam didn't learn anything, but I had earned every penny. Inside of the small yellow basket laid back eyeliner, mascara, and lip gloss.

After the three shops, I still had enough left over for a small latte. It was the break that I'd so desperately needed before reality crashed back in again.

The middle of my day was spent washing and hanging up my new purchases. My aunt was thankfully absent given that it was noon, and unable to criticize the purchases I'd made. I played music on my phone and sipped my coffee, trying to make it last as long as possible.

Tomorrow I would have to deal with Camden Barrett, but today I could pretend like I was the old Ivy Spencer who didn't have a care in the world. *At least for a little while.*

I still showed up at work that afternoon, pouring myself into what needed to be done. The summer was slowly coming to a close and soon the tourists who flocked to the beaches would be replaced by older couples who weathered each winter by moving south for the worst months. To get ready for the change, we added the new inventory she ordered of lightweight hoodies to the wall, the only addition she made to the shop.

Afterward, I swept the floors and carried out the trash while she watched me quietly. That evening before I left, her hand gently squeezed my shoulder, and a line formed between her brows. "Are you sure about what you're doing, Ivy?"

I gave her a once over, noticing that the lines around her eyes seemed a little deeper on her tan skin, and her mouth was set into a thin line. Frankie never worried and rarely talked about serious topics. She was a refuge for me in the middle of the storm, always quick to tell a joke or make me laugh.

I gave her a smile and swallowed. "I don't know what you're talking about, but if I did, my answer is yes. They need a reminder that they can't treat people like they are trash." Which was exactly what I felt like when they marched me downstairs in front of everyone.

She huffed out a breath and patted me. "I saw those posts. Just remember that you're playing a dangerous game. Be careful. The last thing you need to do is attract attention to yourself, and I'm not talking about those boys."

I didn't know how to respond, so I nodded and exited the shop, telling her I would be at work the next day. Unlocking the passenger side of the car, I crawled over the seats and mumbled to myself about finding the money to fix the door. The vehicle was great, but the daily ritual of climbing into the driver's side of the car was getting old. *That was probably what I should have done with the money I'd earned instead of buying new clothes,* a voice in the back of my head whispered, but I ignored it. Being practical only got you so far.

The campus gym was open until midnight during the week and I drove there without hesitation, knowing that at this hour, it would be empty. The guys would all be home or out doing whatever they did with the Forsaken and Ros would be busy. She'd texted me multiple times ensuring that I was okay, and I told her I was fine. I just needed space to deal with everything and didn't want her tangled up in whatever was happening.

Grabbing the bag I packed earlier and tucking my phone into the glove box, I headed inside the huge concrete building. I followed the signs on the wall while taking in the facility. The women's locker room sat on the left side of the building and I ducked inside to change my clothes.

Three girls stood to the side talking as they dried off and I kept my eyes cast down, careful not to draw any attention to myself. They spoke loudly to one another about the social media posts from last night, and it piqued my attention. My motions slowed as I listened in, glancing up briefly. "I don't know who posted any of that, but they need to watch their backs. It's old news to everyone that grew up here."

The dark-haired girl that hovered around Niko snorted to herself. "It's probably that whore who's been hanging around. None of them want her and she just keeps throwing herself at them. I bet that's why they had to show her a lesson the other night."

I was careful not to show any emotion even though blood rushed to my face and shoved my clothes inside a small brown locker. There weren't any locks on them, but considering how empty the building was at this time of the night, I wasn't concerned. A small gaggle of mean girls wouldn't deter me from my plans.

I kneeled down to tie my shoes while they kept talking. "They never treated me that way. Guess they just realize she's trash. Why else would they keep coming back to her?" She flipped her hair over her shoulder and adjusted her shirt.

They had no idea what was really happening, so I stood to make my escape and that was when they saw me. A cruel smile curled up on her face and I rolled my eyes, turning my back to them to leave. Suddenly my head was yanked back, pain lancing through my scalp from how tightly the person behind me pulled my hair.

I inhaled deeply and gritted my teeth. "Let me go, you dumb bitch. No one is supposed to touch me or speak to me. I'm pretty sure that includes petty things like pulling my hair."

She giggled at me and yanked again, passing me off. "I doubt that, sweetie." Her voice was saccharine and grated on me like nails on a chalkboard. "Stay away from the Forsaken. Niko is mine."

Despite her grasp on me, I laughed. My entire body vibrated as tears sprang to my eyes. "That's hilarious. Tell your boyfriend to stay away from me and keep his cock away from my mouth, then." Her grasp loosened on me slightly, the coarseness of my words shocking her, and I swung around to face her. Shoving her against the lockers, her head bounced against the metal, and I got in her face, grabbing her throat. "One last thing. What's your name?"

When she didn't answer, I squeezed enough that she knew I wasn't joking. The past few weeks around the guys brought out a side of me I wasn't quite comfortable with yet. I was sick of everything. "Arabella," she squeaked out, and I loosened my hold.

"Arabella." The name rolled off my tongue as I glared at her and she dropped her hand from my hair. Her two friends stood nearby with wide eyes and slack jaws. "Not only will I be telling Niko about tonight, but if you ever touch me again, I will gouge your eyes out." I let go of her and dusted off my hands on the black cotton pants I was wearing, acting like I was disgusted by her touch. If I had learned anything from my private prep school days, it was that you couldn't bow to mean girls. "Now, if you'll excuse me, some of us came here for a reason other than to gossip."

I found a treadmill out on the main floor and turned up the speed and incline, ready for my lungs to burn and muscles shake. A row of large televisions was mounted on the wall across from the cardio equipment, and I honed in on one playing a matchmaking reality show. Even though it was all fake, I hadn't watched anything in months and I quickly got lost in it as sweat poured down my back.

When the episode was over, I glanced at the clock on the wall and realized that my curfew was in less than an hour. Not wanting to argue with Regina more than I would in the morning when I dressed in my new clothes, I begrudgingly slowed the speed on the treadmill to cool down. When I finally jumped off, everything was shiny and my skin was hot from my workout. My heart still pounded in my chest and every muscle ached.

I felt good. Better than I had in a while.

Grabbing my towel from the small locker and a bottle of body wash, I quickly showered. Footsteps echoed against the tile in the room but I ignored them as I lathered up my body. Turning off the water and wrapping the towel around me, I exited the small stall. Opening the locker I used earlier, everything was missing except a note. I unfolded the paper, reading its contents in seconds. In scrawling loopy handwriting were two lines. "Payback's a bitch and so are you. Watch your back."

The missing items weren't in the trash or any of the shower stalls. I even looked inside of the toilets. Every time I found a single moment of peace in this town, someone had to fuck it up. Now I had to replace not only clothing but a pair of sneakers.

I closed my eyes, trying to center myself. Fucking Arabella. It was her or one of her friends. They were the only ones who knew which locker I had used earlier. All of my clothes were missing and so was the bag that contained my keys. I couldn't exactly show up at home in nothing but a towel. The look on Regina's face would be priceless.

In the corner of the room sat a small box labeled lost and found. I dug through the contents until I found a shirt and a pair of sweatpants. They smelled musty, but it was better than the alternative. I shrugged them on and then marched out to the desk barefoot. The student standing behind the computer gawked for a moment before speaking. "Can I help you?"

"Yeah, there were three girls who left here earlier. They have some things of mine. Do you know where they went?"

He continued staring for a few moments before smirking at me. "You're the new girl, aren't you? The one that was at the party—"

I cut him off, not in the mood to deal with whatever was going to come out of his mouth. "Listen, I just really need my car keys."

"My name's Jake." He leaned onto his elbows, leering, eating away at whatever personal space I had, and licking his lips. "I could help you get home. For a small price."

I held up my hand, done with the conversation. "Thanks, but no thanks." Super creep could go fuck himself.

Coming to the gym was the worst idea I'd had, apparently.

I walked outside and glanced around, trying to find the right object for what I had planned. A large stone with jagged edges sat in the landscaping in front of the building and I shook my head at what I was about to do.

I picked it up and winced as I stepped across the parking lot, the asphalt cutting into my feet.

My muscles felt like gelatin from my run, but if I could just throw the rock hard enough, I could bust my passenger side window and grab my phone. Even though I was trying to push Ros away, maybe she would do me one last favor by bringing me the spare key to the car.

A small black sedan pulled up beside me and honked the horn. I ignored it as I steadied myself, trying to figure out the best way to approach breaking out a car window. The window rolled down, and I froze when I heard his voice. "New girl, what the fuck are you doing? And what are you wearing?"

I turned to the car and Trey grinned at me, pushing his glasses up on the bridge of his nose.

I chewed on my lip, wondering whether I should bother telling him anything. He was part of the reason I was in this mess. If it weren't for their declarations and the show they put on Saturday night, I wouldn't be on Arabella's radar. "Can I use your phone? I need to call Ros."

He rubbed his bottom lip with his thumb and held my gaze. "If you tell me what happened."

I dropped the rock I was holding in my hand and leaned against the side of my car. "Nothing. Just a bunch of petty girls who are jealous of the three of you." I shoved the note in his direction. He took it from me and looked at it for several moments before placing it inside his center console, his expression never changing. "For the record, I just wanted to run. Now, can I please use your phone?"

His fingers swiftly moved over his screen and he placed it on speaker, waiting for Ros to answer. Her voice was groggy with sleep when she finally picked up. "What do you want, asshole?"

He tapped on the steering wheel and bit his lip. "Your girl seems to be in a bit of a predicament. Can you drop off her spare key?"

"Shit. Give me ten minutes. Text me where you are," she huffed before ending the call.

His fingers drifted across the phone's surface before he set the phone on his dash and looked back at me. I hated the fact that he was the one to help me, even though he disinterestedly stood by whenever Cam decided to punish me. I hated the fact that he always looked smug and, above it all, fidgeting with his stupid knife. Most of all, I hated the fact that I still found him attractive even though I was certain that beneath his exterior, he was worse than the others. "Come sit inside, new girl. Tell me about your day."

I shifted my weight onto my other foot. "I don't think that's a good idea," I muttered. "You'll probably cut off my shirt or something."

He held his head back and chuckled, his whiskey-colored eyes shining and locks of brown hair falling onto his forehead. "I promise to behave tonight. Don't tell me you would rather stand out there with no shoes." I debated with myself for a few moments before closing the gap. His car smelled faintly like weed and cigarettes, and I settled inside, pressing my body as close to the door as possible.

His amusement didn't fade at my posture. "Calm down, I won't bite. You seem like you've had a hell of a day."

He turned his body to face me completely and rested his back against the door. "Tell me something. How does revenge taste right now?"

My breath caught. With everything else that happened today, I forgot I had released the information almost twenty-four hours ago. "I don't... I mean," I stammered, unsure of what to say.

He pulled out a joint from his center console and lit the end, taking a long drag and passing it to me, his fingers brushing against mine. "Chill out. I'm calling a truce for tonight. Tomorrow is another story. You need to be ready for whatever Cam has in store. I don't know what game you're playing, but you can't win. Not against us."

I took a hit from what he offered me and closed my eyes, letting the smoke curl around me as I waited on Rosalyn to come rescue me. This would be the last time. The tears that always seemed to hover in the background were absent. Even if tomorrow was hell, releasing the information had felt good. It was worth it knowing that I'd gotten under their skin.

Niko

Even after Ivy had put everything on social media, I couldn't stay away from her. Later that night, I watched from the shadows on the porch of the vacant house across the street as she pulled in well after midnight. Her aunt was already home tonight, and I would have to be careful when I snuck in. I just wanted to see her again.

Waiting gave me too much time to think of everything going on in my life and what would happen if I couldn't come up with the money I needed soon. After I shattered Trey's phone screen, I offered to replace it, but he simply shook his head at me and said he had it covered. It was one more thing that I needed to pay for, and I wasn't sure how I would.

I had to keep my family together, minus my father. I didn't care what happened to him right now. He'd had every opportunity to get clean and hold down a normal job, but he was more concerned with getting his next fix.

Sergei and Katya were both still in high school, and I intended to keep it that way. Sergei had already been hanging around with some of the Forsaken in his class, hinting that he was ready to join. I'd forbidden it, but that didn't matter. He was seventeen and knew everything. Katya was a good kid, but now that she was getting older... There was no way that I could watch them twenty-four hours a day. The last thing that I needed was for us to lose our home and risk anyone else getting involved.

Add Cam and Maya into the mix, and I knew that everyone else was relying on me. They couldn't go home, especially not Cam. I knew what she did when she snuck in drunk in the middle of the night, and Maya... Well, after Thomas Spencer broke her last year, the last thing she needed was her mother's "boyfriends" being left unchecked. Us staying together was the best thing for everyone.

My phone buzzed in my pocket, and I sighed, rubbing my eyes. When I pulled it out of my pocket, I noticed it was Arabella. Again. I hit the power button, annoyed at the situation. She only had my number to buy drugs, but now she was clinging to me like she was something special. She wasn't.

I should have turned my phone off before I decided to stalk Ivy. I didn't exactly want Cam or Trey to know where I was. Visiting her went against whatever made-up rules were in place this week.

The yelling from inside of the house across the street drew my attention, and I crept across quickly to peer inside. Regina had a hand on her hips and a finger pointed in Ivy's direction. She yelled that Ivy had broken curfew again and thcrc wcrc rules to live there. Then she added in a scripture verse for good measure and said that she wouldn't allow her to run around town with the type of people she was.

Ivy stood like a statue in the middle of the kitchen barefoot wearing... what was she wearing? Her cheeks were rosy and eyes glassy as she stared into the distance, her aunt's words seeming not to impact her. She gave her a small smile and turned her back as Regina threw a cup at the wall and said something about how she was "ruining everything."

Ivy simply lifted her hand in a wave and disappeared. I waited for a few moments before I snuck around the side of the house to the window where Ivy's room lay. The light flickered on briefly and I watched as she locked the door behind her before leaning against it. She rubbed her cheeks and grabbed the hem of her shirt, pulling it over her head. I bit down on my lip; she wasn't wearing a bra and her pale skin was on full display as she removed her pants.

What I was doing was an invasion of her privacy, hell so was breaking into her house to watch her sleep, but I couldn't drag my eyes away. From this vantage point, I could see the curve of her ass and the gentle slope of her stomach, the cut on the side of her ribs that hadn't healed. How her nipples tightened from being exposed to the air. She opened a small container that contained clothing and pulled out black cotton underwear, stepping into them and dragging them up her legs. Her head tilted to the side, almost like she was lost in thought before she strode toward the bed and moved her pillow, pulling out a familiar t-shirt.

My already hard cock ached at the sight of her tugging on my shirt, it falling down her legs and covering her. She held the collar up to her nose and inhaled deeply, closing her eyes for a moment before turning off the lights. I bit down on my lip, copper and salt coating the tip of my tongue while I waited for the perfect moment. She pulled the quilt around her waist and in the moonlight I stood there, gazing at her.

After a while, her face went slack and her breathing slowed, her chest slowly rising and falling. I climbed in like I had several other times before and quietly slipped closer, laying next to her on the bed. Her body twisted in the covers again, exposing the patch of black cotton fabric between her legs, but this time, it wasn't in a nightmare. I was enraptured by the look on her face as a quiet moan slipped from her mouth. She was dreaming of someone and I could only hope that it was me. My fingers inched closer, brushing up her thigh as her hips rolled against the air.

Touching her lightly and watching her was torturous, and I struggled to keep my breathing quiet, not wanting to wake her. She needed the sleep, but she needed something else as well. I trailed my hands up her legs and traced along the edge of her underwear, dampness already coating them. Gently, so that I wouldn't wake her, I pushed aside the edge of the cloth and slipped two fingers between her folds. She was so fucking wet and hot already that I had to stifle a groan at the sensation.

Was what I was doing wrong? So fucking wrong, but it was worth it. Part of me was tempted to stroke myself to relieve the pressure, or at least unzip my pants, but I wouldn't. *At least not tonight.*

Her hips rocked against my hand, and her lips parted as I adjusted my position, sliding a finger inside of her. Leaning onto my elbow, I lifted the edge of the shirt she was wearing, my shirt, and exposed her breasts. Ducking my head down, I captured one nipple in my mouth, sucking on it gently. My tongue licked across the hardened peak while my thumb pressed down harder on her clit and her eyelashes fluttered. For a moment, I thought she would wake up and catch me in her room, but she didn't. I sped up the motion of my fingers and her pussy clamped down on them.

What I wouldn't give to chase her again in the woods, her heart beating in her chest as she looked for somewhere to hide.

Her breath caught as she trembled and her movements stopped as she trembled against the mattress softly whimpering. I pulled my fingers from her and put them in my mouth, licking away her arousal. Carefully, I adjusted the shirt to cover her body. Suddenly she rolled over and nestled into the crook of my shoulder, throwing her arm, over my chest. As she melted into me, I hesitantly brushed my fingers through the ends of her hair.

I closed my eyes, allowing myself to enjoy the sensation of her body against mine. It was both heaven and hell as I counted backward from one hundred, willing my erection to go down. For just a moment, everything was perfect in my life, but when the sun came up, things would go back to how they were.

When dawn came, she would be blissfully unaware of what had happened in the darkness and the weight of the world would crush all of us again.

Ivy

One would think that after the events of the previous week, I would have slept like a log, my body
and mind both exhausted. Of course, that wasn't exactly
how things worked. My nightmares were replaced by
something else entirely. When I did finally fall asleep, my
dreams were filled with four very familiar men touching
me and when I woke up, the clean panties I'd put on the
night before were drenched.

I was confused but relieved at the same time by the
turn of events. Every time I got high with one of the
guys, my nightmares vanished. It was a slippery slope,
but in the back of my mind I was contemplating finding
someone that sold tea. I would ask one of the three guys
who seemed like they wanted to break me, but I didn't
want them to have any more information on me than they
already had.

Determined to make the most of the day, I stripped out
of Niko's shirt. My sheets smelled like him every morning,
even though the shirt was slowly losing the traces of the
sandalwood and musk that were him.

After looking through my new clothes, I decided on my
black boots, a black skirt that skimmed mid thigh, and a

button-up shirt. At noon, I had a tutoring session with Cam, and I was determined to show him that Saturday night hadn't scared me off. I needed the hundred dollars, and he needed his grades to stay high enough to play football.

I applied my new makeup like a shield that would protect me. Heavy eyeliner and mascara covered my eyes, concealer hid the shadows from too many sleepless nights, and gloss coated my lips. Looking in the mirror, I could see traces of someone from the past, someone I almost didn't recognize anymore.

Grabbing my backpack which held my lit book and some paper, I hefted over my shoulder, dreading the fact that my aunt was still home. After last night's fight, I wasn't looking forward to seeing her this morning. Thankfully, she said nothing as I poured a cup of coffee from the carafe and added a heaping spoon of sugar.

She didn't have to say anything, though. Her eyes drift-ed across my clothing and she pursed her lips. It was obvious she didn't approve, but after the past few weeks, I didn't care. The worst thing she could do was kick me out because I was marring her perfect reputation.

If only the community knew the truth about her. My initial impression of her was completely off base. At one point, I thought she was just overbearing, but meant well. In truth, she was hateful and controlling. She tried to tear me down at every turn. It all changed the night that I went to the party on the beach.

That was the night that everything had changed and if I could go back, at this point I probably would. My plan of remaining just another anonymous face in a sea of people vanished, along with any hope that the next four years would be peaceful.

Once I was on campus, I was quick to make sure my mask was in place. No one here would see me crack. The heat wasn't as oppressive, leaving my eyeliner intact and I mulled over the fact that soon summer would ebb into fall. The distance to the library was short, and I lifted my chin, ignoring the looks of other students passing by.

I still had fifteen minutes before tutoring started with Cam, so I stopped at the computer near the entrance and logged into my email to ensure I had missed nothing in class the day before. I skimmed through announcements about several clubs. One from the Dean sat unread in my inbox and I clicked it, curious as to what it said.

Dear Ivy,

Your presence is requested at the home of Abraham Wells on Sunday, September 17th at 11 AM. The dress code is smart casual. Several members of Clearhaven University's Board of Directors will be in attendance, as well as other scholarship students.

Abraham Wells

Quickly I thought through a million scenarios, curious about how common it was to invite students to an event like this. Wells unnerved me even if he was one of my father's friends. I appreciated the scholarship that was given to me, but he was a bit too intense for me to feel comfortable in his presence. Was there any way to skip the brunch? I could fake a stomach virus or claim that I overslept. Pushing that aside, I logged out and climbed the stairs. I could only deal with one issue at a time.

Sitting on the third floor, at a table in the middle of the room, was Camden Barrett. When he spotted me, his eyes widened a fraction and I lifted an eyebrow. Silent communication passed between us as I closed the gap and sat next to him, unzipping my bag. Cutting through any niceties, I pulled out my book. "What are we working on?"

He opened his mouth and closed it when the Dean moved into my line of sight with several people dressed in business suits. My blood chilled, and I looked down, hoping he wouldn't notice me. "Ladies and gentlemen, if you'll excuse me for just a moment," he said, and a shadow hovered over me. "Ivy, what a surprise to see you here. Did you receive my email?"

I grabbed the edge of the table and gave him one of my best fake smiles. "I did, and I'm not really sure that I can make it. Between work and classes, my schedule is pretty hectic right now." So much for claiming that I had a stomach virus.

He grabbed one of my hands and squeezed. Cam's eyes narrowed at the gesture and I tried to pull away, but his grip tightened. "I'm sure you can find time. After all, certain benefactors will be present and they are curious who their money is going to this year." He glanced down at my clothes, his eyes lingering longer on my chest than I was comfortable with. "You look absolutely lovely today, Ivy, but I don't think that would be appropriate for a brunch. I'll send a package to your aunt later this week. Be sure to wear it."

It was my turn to be shocked as I froze, my hand trapped in his. "I don't think that's necessary, sir. I can find something for Sunday."

He squeezed again, and bile rose in my throat. "Nonsense. Think of it as a favor for your father." Finally he released me and breath rushed into my lungs. "See you Sunday."

He adjusted his tie as he sauntered back to the group of people who had sat at the table directly across from us. The world spun around me as I wondered what in the fuck was going on. Cam placed his hand on my thigh beneath the table, his fingers biting into the flesh hidden beneath my skirt. I hissed and glared at him. "What was that about, little ghost?"

I held his eyes. "Cam, I have no fucking clue."

His hand inched up my thigh, and his knuckles rubbed against my underwear. I kept my face as expressionless as possible, not wanting to cause a scene. "I have an idea."

The dean glanced up from the quiet conversation happening in his meeting and I looked back down, opening my book to a random page. "Here's what's going to happen, Ivy. You still need to be punished for the stunt that you pulled on Sunday night and I have a point to prove to Wells," Cam rumbled in my ear. His tone was laced with rage and possessiveness. His fingers pulled my underwear aside, and he cupped me.

"This pussy is ours. No one else's and it seems like Wells needs to understand that. You're ours to break... and ours to protect if we see fit."

Even as my face heated, his words shot anger through every inch of my being. It was his fault that last night Arabella stole my clothing. It was his fault that guys around campus leered at me.

"If I'm yours to protect, then call your bitches off, Cam," I mumbled. His fingers dipped through my folds and he plunged inside easily, a testament to how far gone that I already was.

His breath caressed my cheek, and he laid his chin on my shoulder. "What bitches? You're the only one I've touched in weeks, little ghost. When I'm in the shower, jerking off, it's to thoughts of you. Sometimes it's about burying myself in your sweet cunt, and other times it's about choking you with my cock."

His confession made me clutch the table a little harder. "I'm going to make you come on my fingers in front of him. My only question is, are you going to stay silent or will the whole library find out you're my dirty little whore?"

I bit the inside of my cheek, embarrassed by the sounds that his fingers moving in and out of me were making. Anyone who walked by would know exactly what was happening. The heel of his palm rubbed against my clit and I closed my eyes, trying to convince my body not to react. "To answer your question from before we were rudely interrupted, and because you missed class yesterday, we were reading *Sinners In The Hands Of An Angry God*. It would help both of us if you read it out loud."

I inhaled sharply, trying to ignore the sensation that was building inside of me, aware of the group of people sitting only a few feet away, and turned to the page where the excerpt began. The irony wasn't lost on me that Edward's sermon focused on hell as a real place and the judgment of God and I would be reading it while being fingered in public.

As quietly, my voice barely above a whisper, I read to Cam, his eyes never leaving my face. Every time he pressed against my clit, I stumbled over whatever I was saying. My heart raced in my chest and my knuckles turned white as Cam tortured me slowly. My thighs were coated in arousal, and as good as he felt, part of me was humiliated. He was proving to me and everyone else that his words were true: I was his whore.

Finally, I made it to the last paragraph, grateful that my body hadn't betrayed me yet. Out of my periphery, Abraham Wells stood. "Thank you so much for your time today."

Cam turned his head to look at them as his fingers sped up and my heart fell. I knew what he was doing. My fingers moved to his wrist and clamped down. "Please don't do this," I whispered. "Not right now."

He didn't stop though, even as the dean moved closer to our table after shaking several hands and patting someone on the back. Abraham Wells watched, a vein pulsing in his forehead and his jaw tight. That was when I came undone, closing my eyes and biting down on my lip, trying to stop my body from shaking under Cam's fingers. Cam pressed a gentle kiss to my neck. "Such a good girl, Ivy. I don't think that anyone but Wells even noticed what was happening. I didn't know that you could be so quiet."

As Cam removed his fingers, the squelch echoed in the library. Someone cleared their throat, and I looked up. "Is everything okay over here, Ms. Spencer?" the older man asked.

My mouth wouldn't move. Cam's fingers were still coated in my arousal and I watched in shock as he stuck them in his mouth and sucked. He winked at the dean before popping them out and placing his hand over mine. "Everything is perfect. Ivy was just helping me with something."

The dean's eyes narrowed at Cam. "The two of us have things we need to discuss, Ivy." He turned on his heel to step away and I let out a sigh of relief. Cam ran his nose along the column of my neck almost delicately. "Do you want to know what your reward is for being so good?" He shifted and pulled out his phone, typing something in before pulling me back against his chest. His arms wrapped around my waist as he positioned the screen in front of me. On it were news articles of my father and pictures of us uploaded to the YouConnect app. Before I could say anything, he pushed a button and it was released into the world.

A scream was caught in my chest, but I swallowed it down, refusing to let him see me while I shattered. "Do not fuck with me, Ivy. You won't win the game we're playing," he growled before releasing me.

My hands trembled as I shoved my book into the bag and zipped it up, scrambling to get away from him. "Fuck you, Cam," I managed to grit out even though behind my eyes stung. I thrust my hand in his face. "Give me my fucking money. I've earned it."

He smirked as he handed it to me, curling my fingers around the bills.

I adjusted my skirt and grabbed my bag, determined not to let him see how much he affected me.

Ivy

After tutoring with Cam, I took the money I "earned" and bought a new pair of running shoes and a lock from one of the local budget stores on the way to work. My next paycheck from Frankie would cover the payment I owed Ros' grandfather for my car.

The information about who I was and what my father had done was plastered all over the internet now for all of Clearhaven to see. There was no use hiding now, and I wouldn't allow anyone to control my life.

I struggled to figure out my emotions about what happened in the library. However, begrudgingly I felt about it, getting off in front of strangers was arousing. I was confused by both Cam's possessiveness and passion, but mostly I was angry. I was angry that he thought I was just a plaything he could use when he wanted, and then cast aside. Angry that he used me as a pawn in whatever game he was playing with Wells.

And now I absolutely dreaded going to the dean's house on Sunday morning. I didn't want to look him in the face knowing that he'd seen me fall apart.

I'd begun questioning whether a scholarship was worth the shit I was going through. At work, I was careful not to say much to Frankie. She had a radar for knowing something was wrong, and she shot me worried glances the entire night. Finally, she told me to get out of there, that I needed some time to myself. I gave her a hug and struggled not to cry when I left.

I did need some time to myself and space to sort through everything that happened. A moment to just breathe. I wasn't sure where I was going, but it wasn't "home." Everywhere I turned, someone was there. The gym wasn't safe, and neither was the beach. Driving down the road aimlessly and listening to music, I pulled down a small road and realized where I was–the cemetery where Ros and I had drank cheap vodka. It felt like an eternity ago, but that wasn't accurate. I missed the late-night texts we had, and our easy-going friendship, but my mind was made up. I wouldn't allow them to drag her into whatever they were doing.

Cutting my ignition, I crawled out of the car and shut the door quietly. It was peaceful here at night, the only sound was the crickets and owls calling to one another. I ambled aimlessly among the tombstones, reading the dates that were nearly worn away from age.

In the distance, faint music floated through the air and I followed the sound, tiptoeing so that I wouldn't make noise. The night blanketed me as I tried to find the source of the sound. Sweet-smelling smoke drifted along the breeze, but still, I didn't stop myself.

My boot caught on a vine and I stumbled, catching myself before I fell. The music paused, and I ducked down beneath the statue of the fallen angel, hoping that it would hide me from whoever was there. I was close enough to see the fire from a cherry in the darkness and a can being crushed underneath the phantom's hands.

"You can come out. I know you're there," a familiar voice murmured. Footsteps sounded near me and the flashlight from his phone shined down on me. "For fuck's sake, Ivy. Get up. Why are you hiding out here?"

Niko held out a hand and I took it, letting the warmth of his touch seep into my skin. "I just wanted some time to think," I stated quietly, afraid to shatter the moment. He turned off the light as I brushed the dirt off my knees. "Why are you out here?"

He shrugged his shoulders as he turned away from me and prowled back to a blanket a few yards away. Reaching into a bag, he pulled out two cans of beer and patted beside him. "I just wanted some time to think."

Hesitantly, I sat next to him and smoothed my skirt over my legs. The fact he echoed my words and offered nothing else made me curious, but I took the can from his hand. He leaned back against the grave marker and relit his joint, sucking in a lung full of smoke and holding it. I held out my hand, but he shook his head, motioning to me with two fingers. I edged slightly closer, and he caught my jaw between his hands, angling my head how he wanted. He pressed his lips against mine and understanding dawned on me. I opened for him and allowed the smoke to travel between us, dulling my sense and my thoughts. My skin heated, the telltale sign it was laced with tea.

After he pulled away from me, I rested my head against his shoulder and popped the tab on my beer. "What do you have to think about?" I asked as he inhaled more of the joint and I took a sip of the lukewarm liquid.

He raised his eyebrows and flicked out the cherry. "More than you know. What are you thinking about tonight?"

A comeback was on the tip of my tongue, but I decided to take another sip and just enjoy the way his body felt near mine. "Everything. Play a song for me?" My voice came out low in the darkness and he stalled before lifting the guitar into his lap. His fingers moved over the strings gracefully and I watched, mesmerized by the motion. Time evaporated as a mournful melody spilled from his soul and he occasionally hummed along. I let myself relax, feeling more calm than I had in days. He played, occasionally stopping to open a fresh drink or light a joint, but the two of us didn't speak. I didn't want to interrupt the moment, but I also wasn't really sure what to say.

His phone rang, breaking the magic of the moment. He cursed to himself as he answered the call, listening to whatever the person on the other end had to day. Finally, he hung up and sighed. "Show's over for tonight, baby. Duty calls."

I wasn't sure what he was rushing off to do, and I wasn't certain I wanted to know. "Hey, can I ask you for a favor?"

He stood up and started packing his things. "It depends on what it is."

"I want to buy whatever we were smoking. I've got the cash."

He ran his hands through his hair and sighed. "No. Not a chance in hell."

I wasn't expecting a flat-out rejection and for some reason, his words stung. I quickly adjusted my clothes and lifted the edge of the blanket, intent on folding it. "Right. Sorry, I just thought that after tonight…" My voice sounded hollow and I hated I was weak. I shouldn't have bothered.

As I folded the blanket in half, his hand landed on my wrist. "Why?"

His eyes were even darker in the moonlight, and his tone was sharp. I sucked in a deep breath. "It's to sleep. At night I have a hard time and I just wanted to escape."

He tapped on his thigh before dragging his hand through his hair. "Right." I worked silently as he zipped his guitar case and he slung it over his shoulder. "Follow me."

I wasn't sure why I listened to him when all I wanted to do was scream at him. He sold shit to Arabella; I had seen it. What was the difference between her and me? I carried the blanket clutched to my chest and tried not to let my emotions get the best of me.

The graveyard fell away as we walked and a small parking lot came into view. Niko opened the door of his car and shoved everything in the back seat before turning to me. I shoved the blanket in his direction, ready to run, but he caught me by the waist. "If I do this for you, you can't tell anyone, Ivy. And you have to promise me it's only to help you sleep."

I let his words sink in. He wasn't telling me no, he just wanted it to be a secret. I swallowed and bobbed my head as I reached into my bra for the money from Cam. I pulled out one bill, and he shook his head as he ducked inside his vehicle, opening the glove box. He handed me a small bag of pills. "Only to sleep."

I wrapped my arms around him and squeezed, hugging him tightly. "Thank you. I promise." His phone buzzed again, and he pulled away, staring up at the sky. "I guess I need to go anyway, before Regina has a heart attack. What time is it?"

He gave me a sad look before looking down at the illuminated screen. "Ten. Why?"

"Fuck. If she's home already, she's going to have a fit. I'm out past curfew."

He gave me a cheeky grin. "Just park down the street and use your window. It's how I visit you at night."

My eyes widened, but he simply lifted a shoulder. Was that why his scent lingered in my room and on my sheets long after it should have? He got in his car and started the engine, his cue that the conversation was over. I curled my fingers around the baggy in my palm and meandered back through the darkness, even more confused by my feelings than when I'd arrived.

The next morning, I was on campus after my classes started. A new bag was packed for the gym after my classes were over and a lock was carefully placed in the front pouch. I locked my car door and headed toward my lit class. The pills that Niko had given me had helped keep the nightmares away, but they also caused me to sleep past my alarm. I would drop civ later in the day and hopefully not have any run-ins with Caleb.

It was a big campus, so a girl could dream.

Caleb obviously had other plans. As I rushed down a hallway inside of one of the academic buildings, the heels of my boots clicking against the tile floors, muscular arms pulled me inside of a doorway. The only light in the space was a sliver under the door. Arms banded around my waist and I froze, unsure of who was touching me. I pushed against their chest, attempting to escape, but a quiet voice whispered in my ear. "Shh, princess, it's just me. Calm down, I've got you."

I eased into his embrace for a moment before remembering that I couldn't be here. He couldn't be here. "Caleb, you can't be in here. We can't be in here, especially not together. The guys..."

"Don't talk about them right now. This is just the two of us. Tell me where you've been."

I curled my hands into the bottom of his shirt. "After the other night, I just needed some space. I think that you need to find a new partner for class."

Warm palms engulfed my cheeks and soft lips met mine, barely there, like a butterfly's wings. "No."

I huffed out a breath, exasperated by the men that seemed drawn to me. First Niko told me no last night, and now Caleb. "It's for the best."

His mouth descended on mine again, swallowing my breaths, and he lifted my body pushing me against a wall.

My legs wrapped around him as items fell in the darkness, clattering to the floor.

Breathlessly, he pulled back and one hand cupped my jaw. "No. No one gets to dictate what is best for me, and you aren't allowed to pull away."

My hands traced along his broad shoulders. "I'm dropping Civ. Saturday night was insane. They kidnapped you." My words came out sharper than I intended. "What's the next step, Caleb?"

"The hell you are. Is that why you skipped Monday?" His thumb trailed my bottom lip. "They can't hurt me, Ivy, not really. I already knew who your father was and what he had done. They can't keep me away from you. Cam made a mistake letting me have a taste of you. He thought it would humiliate me by seeing you on your knees, but it only made me want you more."

He rocked his hips against me as he licked along my lip. His teeth grazed my jaw, and I was painfully aware of how little clothing we truly had between us. His hands gripped my ass, and my hands roamed his chest while his mouth explored my neck, sucking and biting the sensitive skin. My pulse raced and my resolve weakened with every passing second. His cock was hard beneath me, and every movement brushed against my clit.

"I don't just want you physically, princess. I want to know everything about you. What makes you tick?" He pressed a kiss behind my ear. "What do you love?" He nipped my earlobe and I shuddered. "What scares you the most?"

I grabbed for the button of his pants, wanting his words to stop. I could accept passion and desire, but his words were too much. What he wanted was more than I had ever given anyone. He stopped me, kissing my knuckles. "Not yet, and not here. I'm not fucking you in a closet. When I have you, it's going to be sprawled across my sheets."

I unwrapped myself from him and let myself slide down his body. "What do you really want from me, Caleb? Just be honest." That was something that I had learned quickly growing up. Everyone wanted something. It could be your body, or it might just be friendship, but nothing came without strings.

"You. You're what I want. But first, I want to taste you again." He dropped to his knees in front of me and his hands skated up my thighs to the edge of my panties. His fingers brushed across the cotton fabric and my cheeks heated knowing that he would find out they were already damp from making out. I held my breath as his nose grazed my pussy and inhaled deeply. "Fuck, you smell so good."

His fingers hooked into the waistband of my underwear and he slowly slid them down my legs, shoving them in his pocket. "I need those back," I tried to argue, but my complaints died as he hooked one leg over his shoulder and he licked me from the back to front.

His mouth latched onto my clit, sucking it hard. He pulled away briefly. "I don't think so. I think you need to walk around for the rest of the day and be reminded of how hard I'm about to make you come."

He nipped at the bundle of nerves before his tongue circled the sensitive flesh, soothing the bite. My hands wove into his hair and my head fell back against the wall behind me as he alternated between sucking and licking my clit. Every time I thought I was close to getting off, he would change what he was doing, intentionally denying me the orgasm I so desperately wanted.

My grip on his hair tightened, and I held his face where I wanted. His chuckle vibrated up my body and he pushed two fingers into me. Even though I was trying to be quiet so that no one would hear us, I whimpered as his fingers curled, hitting a spot I hadn't known existed until that moment. His lips wrapped around my clit as his fingers pumped in and out. I rolled my hips against his face, trying to find some type of relief.

When he sucked harder, a moan escaped from between my lips and shudders wracked my body. Wetness trickled down my thighs and his tongue lapped at it. Finally, he lowered my leg to the ground and grabbed my face. His mouth captured mine as he pressed his tongue inside. His lips were still coated with my arousal, and the salty taste made me groan. My hands reached for his zipper, wanting to return the favor, but he stopped me. "No. Today was all about you." He pressed his lips to my forehead before moving away.

I adjusted my skirt and messed with my hair, hoping to make it look less like I'd just been pushed against a wall and eaten out. "So, staying away from me isn't an option?"

There were so many other things I wanted to say. Caleb was funny and attractive. He was stubborn, and his no fucks given attitude appealed to me. He was willing to stand up to the guys, even if they tortured him. Why he felt they wouldn't take it too far was beyond me.

"You'll never escape me, princess. Not if I have anything to do with it." He grabbed my hand and opened the closet door. "But first, Civ. We still haven't discussed our project."

A smile spread across my face despite the weariness that I felt. He wanted me despite all the strings attached.

And then my heart fell as soon as I entered the hallway. Leaning against the wall was Niko, who, from the look on his face, had heard everything. "Vance, it's been what? Four days? You didn't get the message on Saturday night?"

Caleb winked and licked his lips, tugging me against his chest. "Get fucked, Stone."

Being stuck between the two of them was awkward, and I pried Caleb's fingers from my body. "I should go. See you in class."

I scurried down the hall away from them, my lips swollen and my cheeks red. Whatever pissing contest was about to happen, they could sort it out themselves. I never answered his question about what scared me the most. My answer wasn't the nightmares that plagued me or the fact my aunt could kick me out. It wasn't losing my scholarship. It was him.

Cam

I tugged on my jacket, the night air cooler than it had been. Mid-September in Clearhaven wasn't as warm as the balmy summers we were used to. Trey and Niko sat with me on the beach as we watched the waves roll in. "Tell me what happened Monday night," I said to Trey. "You mentioned something about having to rescue Ivy?"

He traced the bottle label with his finger, furrowing his brows in concentration. "All I know is I was running an errand for Vincent and was driving by the gym. Ivy was standing in the middle of the parking lot wearing sweatpants that were three sizes too big, no shoes, and holding a rock in her hand. She was going to break the window out of her car to call Ros." He reached into his pocket and handed me a small slip of paper. "And then she gave me this."

"Who was responsible?" Niko asked. "She didn't mention any of this to me when I saw her."

I reached out and grabbed the piece of paper, rolling my eyes at the message. "Let me guess. Some petty girl who thinks she has a claim on one of us."

Trey laughed. "Well, it wasn't me. I don't entertain women, even if it hurts their feelings. You should ask Niko about Arabella."

Niko scowled as he laid back on the sand, his face turned to the sky. "It might be her. She's been clingy ever since the night that she gave me the worst blowjob of my life. I had to imagine someone else to get off."

Until that moment, I had been unaware that Arabella had ever given Niko a blowjob. The night that we were going to share her, Trey scared her off before the fun had ever begun. Jealousy threatened to creep up, but it wasn't about the fact that he had been with Arabella. I pushed it aside, choosing to ignore the emotion. "Who did you think of?"

He didn't answer, instead turning his face to me and winking. I raised an eyebrow at him, but he stayed silent, staring at my lips. Finally, he cleared his throat. "On a serious note, Arabella uses the fact that I'm her dealer to her advantage. She blew up my phone that night."

I ran my hand through my hair. "What did she have to say?"

He scoffed at me before rolling onto his side in my direction. "I wouldn't fucking know considering the fact I turned my phone off. You should ask her yourself."

"I'll do better than ask her." Asking her meant that I would have to listen to her speak. "Trey, see if you can pull the camera feed from the gym that night. If it was her, she needs to learn her place."

Niko chewed on his bottom lip for a moment, and I was tempted to brush across the bruised skin with my thumb.

"I saw you released everything about Ivy's father on social media. How did that go, exactly?"

I smirked at him. "She took it better than I thought she would. Honestly, she just seemed a little pissed off."

Visions of Tuesday in the library played out in my mind, and I tried to stifle them. How her hands clutched the edge of the table and her knuckles turned white. How quietly she whimpered as I touched her, trying to keep the dean from seeing what I was doing to her. How softly her body shuddered next to mine. I was certain that she wanted to physically harm me after it was over, especially when she realized Wells had been watching everything. Fuck him. He needed to learn that he wasn't the one who had a claim on her. We were. Ever since that day in the church parking lot, I had been pissed at his and Vincent's words.

They weren't allowed to touch Ivy, and they needed to stay far away from Maya and Katya. They had an entire city full of delinquent youths to pick from for whatever they did behind closed doors.

"Anything else I need to know about regarding our girl?"

Niko raised an eyebrow at me, knowing that I was careful with what words I used. "Yeah. Caleb didn't exactly get the message we were trying to send to him. Apparently, being kidnapped and forced to watch the three of us with her didn't exactly scare him. Yesterday I saw him leaving the janitor's closet with her and I know for a fact they weren't just talking."

I leaned back on my elbows and stared at him for a moment. "Why didn't you tell me sooner?"

"Who the fuck knows? I have other things going on. I told Tyler I would fight in Strathmore because I need the cash." He shrugged. "Besides, I handled it. I don't know what else we can do. Short of killing him, which we can't, there's nothing else. Everyone knows who his family is and what they're involved in. We don't have any sex tapes to blackmail him with and even if we did, the fucker would just gloat about it. I mean, even if you forced him to suck your dick, he would smile the entire time." Niko's words rang true and I sighed.

Everyone knew exactly who his grandfather was. Fletcher Vance was the one who owned the paper mill outside of town, the major source of employment in the area. He was also connected to the Order of the Exalted. The same brand that was on Wells' forearm decorated his, pretentious fuck. People that crossed him ended up missing, never to be heard from again. His son and daughter-in-law had disappeared fifteen years ago, leaving behind Caleb. The rumor was that he had his own son killed, and honestly, it wouldn't surprise me. Men wearing suits guarded his property and no one could get in or out without an invitation. The whole thing was unsettling, and the fact that Vincent was connected to them bothered me.

Briefly, I wondered what would happen if I killed Caleb. He was a smug prick and needed to learn not to touch what wasn't his. Would they really know it was the three of us? "What do you mean, you handled it?"

"I roughed him up a bit and threatened him again. I don't know what you wanted me to do."

I turned toward him and grabbed his jaw, pressing my fingers into his skin. "I need you to tell me. That's what I want from you. I don't want to know this shit the next day." His hand grabbed my wrist, and he squeezed just enough to warn me he was getting sick of my shit.

"Don't take your frustration out on me, asshole. The two of us," his eyes darted in Trey's direction, who sat back looking amused at the two of us, "we're the ones who have always had your back."

I loosened my grip on him slightly before removing my hand completely and laying back on the cold sand. His hand fell away and rested between the two of us. "You're right. Is there anything else I missed? Ivy trying to break out her car window and Caleb ignores every warning we've sent him..."

Niko swallowed and chewed on his lip again, hesitating to answer me. "No, I think that covers it unless Trey knows anything else." There was more to his story, but I let it go. It would all come out in the wash eventually.

Trey tipped his bottle up and chugged the rest of what was left. "Not to my knowledge, but I think the two of you need to get laid or work off some of this pent-up aggression. If you want, I can make you a copy of the video I made the other night," he snorted before grabbing another beer from the bag next to him. "You want us to tell you everything, but you didn't exactly give us the details of how you took care of Ivy. All we know is that you released that shit on social media and told us to share it."

The three of us sat on the sand for a while, each of us keeping our secrets close to our chests. Not that I cared if they knew what I had done to Ivy or that I used her to piss off Wells. It was the fact that what happened was between the two of us for the moment. They would eventually find out everything, just not yet.

"Do me a favor. Can you hack into her email and social media accounts for me? I want to know who has been talking to her. The dean is still hanging around and I'm more than a little curious about why."

"Yeah, sure. That's easy enough. He's probably just being a creep like he usually is and thinks that she's a poor scholarship girl that would suck his dick for a little attention."

That might have been true, but I doubted it. There were easier targets on campus than Ivy and he had all the access to pussy he wanted through the Order.

Later that night, after drinking the rest of the beer we had brought and smoking more weed than was necessary, I decided to walk home. Niko questioned what I was doing and so did Trey, but I brushed them off, claiming that I just needed to let off some steam. It was only ten, and I just didn't want to be around anyone else. Frankie's shop was on the way, so I trekked down the empty road, kicking at pebbles as I went. Ivy's car was still in front and the lights were still on inside. I stopped for a moment and watched as she lifted boxes and carried them to the back room, probably taking care of something that had been delivered earlier in the day. Every once in a while, she would stop and wipe her hand across her forehead or brush stray hairs that had escaped from her face. Between tasks, she swayed her hips to a sound only she could hear, dancing with herself.

She was completely oblivious to what was happening on the other side of the glass and the fact that someone was watching her. If only she had been someone else, things could have been different. I admired the fact that even though we continued to torment her, she let it roll off of her back and gave shit back to us. There was no doubt in my mind that she would find a new way to pay me back for what happened in the library on Tuesday.

A car engine started across the street and the sound of it idling drew my attention. I looked in that direction and saw a black SUV parked across the street from the shop. The driver's identity was concealed by the darkness and something about the situation bothered me. I waited for several minutes for the driver of the SUV to leave, but he didn't. I was tempted to get closer and figure out who it was, but decided against it, choosing to watch them closely.

Finally, Ivy turned off the lights inside and exited the shop, turning the key in her hand. The driver of the vehicle also stepped outside, quietly stalking closer to her. I still couldn't tell who it was. They were dressed in a black beanie and long black trench coat. The shape seemed familiar, but I couldn't place it with the added bulk of the jacket. I kicked at the gravel to signal to them I was there and they froze, debating their next move.

Not wanting Ivy to realize I was there, I prowled closer to the shadow who took off in a run, crashing into the side of the car and pulling open the door. He drove off before I could reach him. I braced my hands on my legs and glanced in the direction of the fire-haired girl who was seemingly oblivious to the world. She unlocked her car door and when she removed something from her ears it hit me why. She was wearing earbuds.

The two of us would have a conversation about situational awareness later, but for tonight I needed to text Trey and Niko. I wanted to know who was watching Ivy and what they wanted. One of us needed to watch out for her when she was closing the shop by herself or have a conversation with Frankie about what had happened. The old woman was firmly anti-Forsaken, but she would do a favor for us if it dealt with Ivy. For some reason, the older woman was fond of her, and she wasn't fond of anyone else in this hellhole.

Clearhaven wasn't a safe place for young women who didn't have any family, and it seemed like Ivy had caught someone's eye. I just hoped it wasn't someone from the Order.

Ivy

The entire town was getting ready to watch the football game, whether they were attending in person or headed to a sports bar down near the water. I, on the other hand, had absolutely no desire to sit through another one of Camden Barrett's games. He could go fuck himself after the week I'd had. Between the after party last week, Arabella and her friends, and then the moment in the library.

The fact that tomorrow morning I had to sit through a brunch at the dean's house-made everything worse. The longer I thought about it, the more embarrassed I got. Abraham Wells knew exactly what had happened, judging from the color of his face and how tightly he pursed his lips. Hopefully, there would be enough people invited to the event that I wouldn't be left alone with him. I didn't want to know what he would say to me.

Instead of participating in whatever evening festivities most college students did on Saturday, I decided to study. Dressed in a pair of black athletic pants and one of my ratty t-shirts, I sprawled out across my bed on my stomach with my textbooks in front of me, determined to focus. My grades were important; I couldn't lose the scholarship that I had.

Someone knocked on my bedroom door, and I sighed, laying my head against my mattress. "Yes?"

With no further prompting, Regina opened the door. "This package came for you. Since when are you getting gifts from Abraham Wells?"

If I could suffocate myself with my pillow, I would. "I'm not."

She thrust the box in my direction and I sat up to open it, dread curling in my stomach. After the way, he insisted he would purchase something for me to wear, and how adamantly I didn't want to, this "surprise" was the last thing I wanted to deal with. I opened the lid on the white box and moved the tissue paper. Inside was a navy blue tea-length dress with three-quarter-length sleeves and a lace overlay. It was something I wouldn't have chosen for myself in a million years and reminded me of the dresses that the women surrounding my father wore. I grimaced when I saw the cream-colored flats that matched the lace and put the lid back on the box, pushing it toward her. "I don't want it."

She gave me a tight smile and placed her hands on her hips. "Of course you do, honey. You should have told me you were seeing him. A man like that can offer you a lot more than the three you have been running around with."

The temptation to stab her with the pencil laying beside me was strong, but I ignored it. Instead, I wrinkled my nose and shook my head. "First of all, that would be gross. He's the same age as Dad and they're friends. You have everything completely wrong. This is for a brunch tomorrow, Regina."

Her smile stayed in place. "No, I don't think I have anything wrong at all. You just don't realize it yet. Speaking of your father, what's the meaning of that social media post?"

Camden's actions from Tuesday still managed to bite me in the ass, even though I chose to ignore the whispers in the hallway and the glares from people at Frankie's. "I don't know what you're talking about. I haven't been on social media this week."

She huffed out a fake laugh. "Don't play coy, Ivy. It doesn't suit you. The post was shared all over Clearhaven. I have people sending it to me in private messages. It was started by Camden, the thug I told you to keep your legs closed around. I think you wanted to pay me back for trying to keep the two of you apart."

I hid my face between my hands, wishing that the conversation was over. "You have everything wrong. The last thing I want to do was be around Cam right now. I just want to study by myself—and for everyone to leave me alone. Why would I want anyone to know that my father is in prison? Not everything is about you."

She closed the gap between us, and her palm landed on my cheek with a loud slap. I was too stunned to feel the sting of pain that should be present. Out of all the bad things my father had done, and the torture the guys had put me through, none of them had ever hit me. Instead of being sad, all I felt was rage. "Reputation is everything in this town, something you haven't figured out yet. If you were going to sleep around, it should at least be with someone who won't be dead in the next six months. It's funny, I told your father he should have never..."

She trailed off and backed away, brushing her hands on her skirt like there was dirt on them. "He shouldn't have what?"

She ignored me and closed the door behind her as she stomped away. I threw the box against the wall. It wouldn't leave a hole and it wouldn't damage the contents, but it would make me feel better. My phone chimed next to me and I saw I had a text message.

Caleb: What are you doing? Watching Cam tonight?

Me: No, I was trying to study, but I need to get the hell out of here.

Caleb: Perfect. I'll be there in five.

How did he know where I lived? I touched the warm spot on my cheek before responding.

Me: Meet me at the bus stop. I'll be right there.

The last thing that I needed was for my aunt to see a fourth guy hanging around me. She would immediately assume that I was sleeping with him too. Wednesday he'd made it clear that my plan to stay away from him wouldn't work and somehow he also knew what my father had done before it was released on social media. He still liked me despite knowing who I was and where I came from.

After debating with myself for a moment, I popped one of the pills I'd gotten earlier in the week into my mouth. If anyone deserved an escape, it was me. By the time I got back home, the tea would be in full swing and I could pass out until I needed to get ready for the dean's "mandatory" brunch. I changed into a nicer t-shirt and slipped on my new running shoes before grabbing my ID and phone. Listening for a moment to make sure that my aunt wasn't still hiding in the hallway, I locked my bedroom door and crawled out of the window, making sure to close it all the way. If Niko could sneak in this way, I could sneak out.

I glanced at the house, paranoid that my aunt would be standing at the window, and snuck around before breaking into a light jog, ready to put distance between myself and whatever in the hell had just happened.

True to his word, Caleb sat inside his bright yellow sports car at the bus stop. He grinned when he saw me and pulled open the door handle. His face fell as I slid in next to him, his thumb touching my cheek. "What happened?"

I shrugged, not wanting to talk about it. "Just a misunderstanding. Tell me where we're going."

His eyes were dark and I could briefly see beneath the easy-going façade that he usually wore. Just like the three other men in my life, a monster lurked under his skin, enraged about whatever he was imagining. As quickly as it had appeared, it vanished, and he gave me a cocky grin. "I was just thinking that my princess might enjoy pizza. Have you been to Master Pieces on the Strip?"

A brief pang shot through my chest remembering the last time I had been there, back when things seemed impossible, but they were infinitely easier than they were now. Back when I first met Ros and Cam just seemed like another college fuck boy. "Yeah, I've been. The food is pretty good."

He placed a chaste kiss on my lips and waited for me to fasten my seat belt. "After that, we can do whatever you want to. It's close to the beach and we can walk over."

I didn't tell him that walking along the beach at this time of the night was the last thing I wanted to do. He was trying to cheer me up, rescuing me from the house that felt less like a home every day. I tucked a piece of hair behind my ear. "That sounds nice."

He turned up the music while he drove and I laid my head back against the seat. The tea was beginning to kick in and the stress of the evening melted away, leaving behind fire in my veins. Even the bass from the music left goosebumps on my skin. It was a feeling I wasn't sure if I would ever get enough of. Nothing seemed to matter except sensation itself.

The ride was too short, and he opened my door, giving me a curious look. I climbed out of the car and wrapped my arms around him, burying my head in his chest. He smelled so good at the moment and all I wanted to do was hide inside his scent. He chuckled as he ran his hand through the ends of my ponytail. When he pulled away, he gave me a curious look and reached for my hand. "You're okay, right?"

I nodded and felt my mouth pulling up. "Never better."

He watched my face for a brief second before tugging me inside the restaurant. A young woman with bright blond hair was the hostess, and he whispered something to her before pulling me through the crowded space. Televisions playing the game were mounted to a wall near the bar, and music from a band filtered through the air.

It was complete chaos between all the noise in the space, but it was comforting. It was the kind of place you could hide in plain sight. Maybe Cam was right; maybe I was a ghost.

To the right side of the restaurant, a thick glass door stood and slowly we made our way toward it. When we finally emerged from the other side, a wooden patio came into view. It was covered with small metal tables and speakers streamed music from inside. Compared to the inside, it was less cramped. Caleb led me to a table at the edge that overlooked part of the beach and pulled a chair out for me to sit on. "I thought you might like it out here better tonight. Saturdays can be a little crazy, but the music is good, and the food is even better."

I folded my hands in my lap and just watched him as he scanned the menu, trying to decide what he wanted. "What are you having?"

I scooted my chair closer to him and let my chin rest on his shoulder, not really caring what I ate. A small voice inside of my head wanted me to tell him that all I wanted was him, but I stopped myself. Caleb's sincerity scared me and it was the drugs talking. Still, part of me wanted to know what it would be like to have his mouth on me or his cock inside of me. "What's good?"

He smirked at me. "Practically everything."

When the waitress arrived to take our order, I told her I would have the same thing as Caleb. We ate in comfortable silence while I danced in my seat to the band playing through the speaker.

"What's their name?" I asked as I shoved a piece of crust into my mouth.

"Hmm? Oh, Dissension Stars. I went to high school with the guys. Supposedly, they have a record deal and are flying out to LA next month."

I had to admit that they were good, and internally, their success made me happy. At least someone had escaped Clearhaven. A group of girls strolled through the patio door giggling and I grimaced, recognizing one of the voices. It had to be my luck that Arabella would be here out of all the places in town. I turned my body away from them, hoping that they wouldn't see me in the dim light. For a while I thought my plan worked. Caleb asked me questions about my classes and the two of us talked about our projects.

My luck eventually ran out. After the waitress disappeared and their drinks were delivered, I heard a snarky sounding, "Watch this."

I assumed she was simply going to walk over to the table and threaten me to stay away from Niko some more. In the state I was in, I was ready to tell her he was crawling into my bedroom window, not hers. Instead, the icy liquid was poured over my head, freezing my skin and drenching my clothes. I was in too much shock to react. Caleb shot out of his chair and grabbed her by her upper arm. "What the fuck, Arabella? What is your problem?"

She simply gave him a saccharine smile. "Caleb, I don't know what you're talking about. Get your hands off of me or I'll tell Granddaddy you've been spending time with her. You know better than to hang around with trash. It looks bad for all the Vances."

Instead of letting go of her, his grip tightened, and she winced as he leaned in close. "Politely fuck off, Bella. Grandfather knows exactly who I hang around with. Touch her again and see what happens. I would hate for your car to blow up next week with you inside of it."

She rolled her eyes and dug her nails into his hand, blood welling on his skin. "You wouldn't dare. Besides, why would you want her, anyway? If three men aren't enough for her, why would you think a fourth would be? You saw her at the party."

He let go, and she sauntered back to the table, her bottom lip sticking out in a ridiculous pout. The words and the ice in my lap were enough to sober me up some. Who was his grandfather? We hadn't known each other long and things like family connections mattered little to me anymore. How were Arabella and he related? He handed me napkins from the dispenser and I tried to dry myself off, but it was no use. Sticky sugar stuck to my skin and dripped from my hair. "Let's just go," I told him, disappointed that no matter where I went, someone was there to bother me.

I picked up my glass and as we passed by, I poured it over Arabella and kept walking. Fucking bitch.

The ride home was awkward. I was worried about Caleb's leather seats and the fact I was drenched in soda. Whatever plans I had died before they began. A part of me had wanted to convince him to kiss me and straddle him in his car despite his words of wanting to lay me out on the bed. Instead, I awkwardly sat in the passenger seat and asked him questions about how he knew Arabella. It turned out that she was his cousin. Even Caleb seemed tense after the confrontation at the restaurant. He dropped me off a block from my aunt's house after a single kiss.

I snuck inside through the window, my newfound source of freedom, and gathered clothes for a quick shower. While I was in there, I hoped Niko would visit me, even if I was asleep. Something about the fact that he snuck in made me feel a little less alone, even if I wasn't awake.

Caleb

E arly Sunday morning after my workout, I showered and dressed in black slacks and a white button-up. My grandfather expected my presence this morning. A brunch at the dean's house was the last thing on my mind, especially after Arabella's behavior last night.

Her showing up at Master Pieces was unexpected and the two girls who she surrounded herself with only condoned her behavior. Emmaline and Violet were harmless enough, but when the three of them were together, their behavior took on a life of its own. Mob mentality exhausted me at the best of times, but the motivation behind their actions angered me. Arabella deciding to call me out in front of Ivy for "tarnishing" the Vance name was too much. Pouring her drink on Ivy? Completely uncalled for.

I knew everything about Ivy's background, including what her father was in prison for. What started as a simple favor for my grandfather turned into something else. Approaching her to be my project partner wasn't altruistic, but it quickly morphed into something different. The fact that it got under Camden's skin only sweetened the deal.

The dean's house was located directly off campus, a gigantic two-story brick colonial with white columns and black shutters. Why a single man would need so much space was beyond me, but I adjusted my tie and got out of the car, ready to deal with whatever bullshit was about to happen.

From the edge of my vision, a Honda Civic drove slowly down the road and I held my breath, praying that it wasn't who I thought it was. When I saw the smashed door, I hoped maybe it was a mistake. She would keep driving and pass by the house.

And because life is a bitch, none of that happened.

Instead, Ivy pulled down the long driveway and parked along the curb. As she crawled from the passenger side of her car, I noticed what she was dressed in and my heart raced. Whether it was an act of defiance or she genuinely didn't know the dress code of the event we were walking into, I wasn't sure. Plump pale thighs were showcased in all of their glory, accentuated by a red plaid skirt and tall black boots. The shirt she was wearing stretched taut over her breasts and I wanted to cover her with my jacket to hide her from the predators inside. She was wearing more makeup than usual, the dark black eyeliner accentuating her bright green eyes which were dilated again today.

I thought last night had been a one-off when I realized she was high, nuzzling her face against my skin–a way she was blowing off steam. Now I was a little more worried, but until I knew more, I'd keep my mouth shut. We both had other things to worry about. I plastered my typical arrogant expression on my face and leaned against the car, waiting for recognition to dawn on her. Her face lit up when she saw it was me. "What are you doing here?" she rushed out. Her cheeks were flushed and her hair curled wildly around her face.

I gave her a quick peck on the cheek and held out my arm to her. I leaned in and lowered my voice so that only she could hear me. "The better question is, what are you doing here, princess? I thought you had work today."

She quirked up an eyebrow as she laced her arm through mine. "How do you know that? I never mentio ned..."

We started drifting toward the door. "Well, I needed to know where you were so that I could see you when Cam was busy, so I decided to do some research." I left out the part about how my grandfather had encouraged the behavior. Eventually, I would have to confess that information, but for now, I didn't want her to second guess my motivations. What had started out as a way to keep tabs on Thomas Spencer's daughter had turned into something different. Now I would do what I could to shield her from the powers that be in this town.

There was nothing I could do about her presence today or the outfit that she was wearing, but after this, I would have to keep a closer eye on her. She didn't know what she was getting into. Being tangled up with the Forsaken was bad enough, but they weren't the actual issue.

The corners of her lips turned up at me. "It's creepy that you know so much about me, but kind of sweet. Are you proposing a hidden love affair, Caleb Vance?"

I wanted nothing more than to correct her. To tell her that there was nothing secretive about how I wanted her, but kept my mouth shut. If the dean or my grandfather caught wind of what I wanted to do to Ivy...

I pressed the doorbell beside the massive black wooden doors and waited for a moment before it opened. Emilia, the housekeeper, squealed with excitement when she saw me. "Caleb, look at you. Just as handsome as ever." She wiped her hands on the apron attached to her waist before squeezing me tightly.

She was the mother figure that I needed after my parents vanished. My memories of my mother and father had dimmed throughout the years, but the ones with Emilia were bright spots from my bleak childhood. She taught me to bake chocolate chip cookies and how to read. When I was sick with the flu in third grade, she was the one who sat at the edge of my bed and read me stories about dragons and knights. My grandfather was always too preoccupied to spend time with me and felt that I needed to toughen up because the world was a cruel place. I was destined to rule and rulers couldn't be weak.

Perhaps that was the real issue between me and Cam. It wasn't the curvy red-headed girl that haunted my dreams, but that we were the future kings of two kingdoms that held only a tentative peace, poised to go to war at a predetermined time.

Finally, Emilia let me go and sniffed. "I've missed you."

My throat felt tight. My grandfather had let her go when I was a senior in high school, replacing her with a young girl half her age named Claire. There was no way in hell he had hired Claire for her cooking skills given the fact that she could burn water. At the time, it had devastated me. The fight that ensued resulted in a broken nose and scars that I hid beneath my clothes. At least he helped Emilia find a new job.

Unfortunately, it was with Wells. The only comfort I had in the situation was the fact that at least I still got to see her around holidays. It was no different from the arrangement many of my "friends" parents had when their parents divorced and their father upgraded his wife to a new model.

"I've missed you too. I'm assuming that Fletcher is already here?"

She gave me a tight nod and then looked at Ivy with something that could only be labeled as a mixture of worry and pity. "Be careful with this one. They collect pretty girls." Ivy's eyes widened, but I didn't address what she said. They did collect pretty girls, especially ones who had no money. "You'd better go say hello."

I patted her shoulder one last time before heading further into the house. Ivy stepped beside me, staring at the side of my face expectantly. "What was that about?"

I rolled up the cuffs of my sleeves to avoid her gaze. "Which part?"

"They collect pretty girls?"

"She meant every word she said. Try to avoid being cornered by any of the men here, Ivy. I can't protect you if you're caught in their web."

Her face paled. This was the most serious I had ever been in front of her. "Why do you know so much about me, but I know nothing about you or your world?"

Her question stopped me in my tracks. We were feet away from the dining room where I knew a dozen "well respected" men would be seated around a table acting like this was just another Sunday morning. I wanted to touch her, reassure her that everything was going to be alright, but I couldn't. Not right now. Someone could be watching us. "We'll have to talk about all of this later. This world is something that you don't want to be a part of. You were once and you have a chance to escape it. That's like saying you crawled out of hell and want to return."

Her features hardened at my words and I knew they were probably taken out of context, but I let her turn away from me. It was probably better if she was angry, especially heading into the den of wolves.

As soon as we set foot inside the massive dining room, all eyes were on us. My grandfather gave me a handshake, but from his posture, I knew he would have questions for me later. He wasn't pleased with the fact that we had shown up around the same time, and there would be no convincing him it was just a coincidence. His gaze trailed down Ivy's body and he pressed his lips together in a thin line. Disapproval. Other members were busy staring at her, specifically the creamy skin of her thighs that I wanted wrapped around my face. It took everything in me not to hide her behind me, but an action like that would be seen as a weakness.

In this world, women were simply another thing you surrounded yourself with to show off your success or a hole to stick your dick in when the need arose. The men here wouldn't understand me wanting to hide her away from them. Abraham Wells stood from the head of the table, the look of displeasure clear on his face. "Ivy and Caleb. I wasn't aware the two of you were close. Come have a seat and I can introduce you to everyone."

I didn't need to be introduced to anyone here. I had known them since I was small.

Ivy made small talk while holding her chin high and sipping on the mimosa that Emilia sat in front of her place. My appetite had vanished as soon as I saw the Civic pull into the driveway, so I sat there, completely checked out of everything around me until a firm hand landed on my back. "A word, son." I gently touched the scar on my chest hidden beneath my clothes. It was the same one that each of them had on their bodies.

I was careful not to give away how I was feeling as I stood. Apprehensive. I didn't want to leave Ivy alone, but couldn't defy my grandfather in front of the other men at the table. We walked down a long hallway into a small office and he shut the door behind him, blocking my only exit. "What's the meaning of this, Caleb?" His face was amused, but his tone was clipped with anger. "I told you to get close to her, not fuck her."

I grinned at him and sat in the chair next to the bookcase. "Who said I've fucked her? You didn't say that I couldn't taste her pussy."

He closed the gap between us quickly, his hands pressing down on the bruises he knew were underneath my shirt. "She's not yours. I've told you that since the beginning. If you need to get your dick wet, there are a thousand other girls in this town. At least a hundred within the Order would fall on their knees for you. Your job was to make her comfortable and give her a false sense of security. Take her out to dinner or see a movie." He rubbed across his chin and glared. "One day you'll be given someone by the Order, but it will never be her. Any idea you have of saving Ivy ends today."

The pain searing through my bicep made my eyes water, but I wouldn't show him how much it hurt. How much his words hurt. I knew who they had chosen for me, but neither of us wanted the other. When we'd found out, we had both agreed to pretend like it wasn't real. The older men might change their minds and realize how ill fitted we were for one another. I gritted my teeth, trying to decide how to proceed with the conversation. "And what if I choose not to fall in line?"

His fingers loosened and he clenched his jaw. "It would be a shame. There are other people I can bestow my favor on, son. Never forget that. You're simply one tool that is at my disposal. After all, what if I gave your assignment to your cousin? What would he think of Ivy? It's a miracle she hasn't drawn his attention yet."

Everything was too much, and I stood, clearing my throat. "I get it."

I had to play my part to keep her safe, at least until the time came that I would be forced to let her go. Part of me wanted to march into the dining room and yell at her to run, take everything she owned, and leave the town. I wouldn't though. I was selfish enough to believe that saving her from the men in the dining room was possible.

Ivy

After Caleb was whisked away by his grandfather, I tried to focus on the juice and muffin that Emilia had placed in front of me before she disappeared. My appetite was completely gone, and the men sitting around the table stared at me too intensely. It wasn't just that I was a scholarship student that was under the microscope. That much was evident from their lingering glances and the fact that all conversation had died the moment I had walked in. I cleared my throat and pushed my chair back away from the edge of the table. "If you'll excuse me."

I rushed out of the room and pushed into the hallway in search of a restroom. There was something too familiar about the men who were leering at me and panic clawed at my throat, attempting to break free. I needed a moment to breathe away from everything. A stiff hand grabbed my wrist and tightened, squeezing the bones to the point of pain. "Where do you think you're going, Ivy?"

A shiver ran down my spine as I turned to face Abraham Wells. "The restroom. I needed to freshen up."

His hand darted out and cupped the side of my cheek. "You just got here and your makeup looks like it's still intact to me. Tell me, why aren't you wearing the dress I sent you?"

I swallowed and shook my head. "It's not exactly my style."

The corner of his lip lifted. "I'm sure it's not, but you'll grow used to my gifts." His hand dropped and his index finger traced my collarbone. I tried to jerk away, but the pain in my wrist grew, spreading up my arm. "Did you like your little game with Mr. Barrett in the library?"

My voice faltered and my face grew hot with his words. I had known that the dean was aware of what Cam was doing, but the affirmation made me uncomfortable for reasons I couldn't pinpoint. "You're hurting me," I whispered. "Please let me go or I'll scream."

A malicious smile spread across his face. "Even if you did, the men in the dining room wouldn't save you. I could strip you down and fuck you in front of the table in front of them, and do you know what they would do? Ask if they could have a turn."

Something about his words made bile rise into my throat. My stomach churned, and the world spun around me. "Stay away from Camden. He thinks he owns you, but he has no claim."

Suddenly he stalked closer, forcing me backward and caging me in. My heart galloped in my chest as his papery lips brushed against mine. He let me go finally, and I fled down the hall into a random room, slamming the door behind me. I slid down the wall as tears streamed down my face, not understanding how I attracted the attention of Wells.

After Caleb's grandfather spoke to him at brunch, his entire demeanor changed toward me. He gave me an occasional tense smile and escorted me to my car, but he seemed strangely distant, preoccupied with whatever had happened between the two of them. After I'd made it back home, I tried to send him several texts, but he was silent on his end. He didn't even bother to look at them. For some reason, I had assumed that we were growing closer between dinner and what happened in the closet.

The longer I sat in my room, wasting time before I headed to work, the more frustrated I got with everything. I headed down to the local fish market near the Strip and used some of the leftover cash from my tutoring session to buy fresh shrimp. I didn't have time to enact my plan before work, and I wasn't thrilled about my car smelling like seafood, but it was fine. Everything I needed was stored in a small bag, ready for later.

I parked in front of my aunt's and bided my time after my shift. When midnight struck, I started jogging with my satchel full of goodies, dressed in dark denim and a black t-shirt, deciding that it was time to enact a small amount of petty revenge. I didn't have any leverage over the members of the Forsaken, but I did have pettiness on my side. Between the time of night and the color of my clothes, I hoped no one would notice me.

Nikos's house was only a few blocks away and from the rumors that I had heard, the two of them lived together. I didn't know exactly where Trey lived, but he wasn't the one I wanted to pay back. Not really. He helped me call Rosalyn when I needed it and that cleared at least some of his debts. Earlier at work, I searched for Niko's name on the internet and discovered he lived a few blocks from my aunt. As I strolled, I scanned the house numbers, trying to ensure that I broke into the right one. I stopped underneath an oak tree and pulled out my phone, triple checking for the last time that the house I was standing in front of was the correct one, and then took a deep breath. It was now or never.

Nikos's car was absent from the small driveway and wasn't parked along the side of the street, which was perfect. It would make what I was planning easier. All the lights in the house were off except the kitchen, and I peered into the window. No one was up and everything was silent. I crept around, glancing inside and praying that the neighbors wouldn't call the cops. In this neighborhood, it was unlikely, but with my luck lately...

Finally, I found the back door. There wasn't a welcome mat in front of it, but there was a large rock sitting to the side. Lifting it, I discovered a small silver key and struggled not to laugh. To supposedly be hardened criminals, the guys thought it was secure to put a key under a rock.

My heart beat in my chest as I slid the key into the lock and opened the door as quietly as possible. It creaked softly, and I darted inside. My entire body vibrated with nerves as I unzipped my pack and pulled out the shrimp from earlier. After a quick once over, I realized that all the air vents in the house were located along the baseboards. I pulled out my screwdriver and got to work, moving as quickly as possible. The adrenaline flowing through my veins was heady as I shoved handfuls of shrimp into every vent I could see and replaced the screws. Eventually, they would figure out why the house smelled, but there would be no way to trace it back to me.

Softly, I snuck through the back hallway, seeing that there were three bedroom doors. I had saved the last little bit and wanted to ensure that I was punishing the right person. One wrong move and my games were over. I stared at each of the doors, pressing my ear against them to see if I could hear any noises from inside. The closest one had soft snores, and I shook my head knowing that wasn't the room I wanted. Shuffling to the next door, I held my breath. No sound was coming from inside, but that meant little. I turned the knob as fast as I dared and glanced inside. Pushed against the wall was a queen-size bed that had a navy comforter strewn across the top. I struggled to remove the vent from near the baseboard just inside of the room. Old paint covered the edges of it and I chewed the inside of my cheek as I used the tool in my hand to pry it open.

After depositing the last bit of seafood, I closed the door behind me and moved to the door at the end of the hallway. Only one more thing and then I could get out of this house, away from the possibility of getting caught.

I located the bottle of shampoo and grinned to myself. I pulled out the tub of blue dye, opened the shampoo cap, and poured what I could inside. With a small piece of toilet paper, I wiped down the exterior of the bottle before throwing it in my bag.

It felt good to take back another piece of my life, even if it was temporary and childish. With halting hands, I zipped up my bag and slung it over my shoulder, ready to make my escape. The rush of everything was heady, something else that would be easy to get addicted to. Everything was bright, and my entire body vibrated from the thrill.

A car door slammed outside and loud voices that were all too familiar shouted at one another. I ran into the hallway, hoping that I would have enough time to make it to the back door. Suddenly, large hands caught me and a firm body pulled me into the third bedroom. A scream left my mouth, but a hand clamped over it. "Unless you want to get caught by them, shut up. I'm trying to help you."

I pulled away and a guy a few years younger stared down at me. He placed a finger over his lips, telling me to be silent. I observed him while listening to someone slam the front door, noting that he shared the same eyes as Niko. He had broad shoulders and a tattoo that peeked out from the collar of his t-shirt. "So you're what all the fuss is over. I can see why they both want you."

"I don't know what you're talking about," I hissed under my breath. "The only thing they want is to be complete, utter assholes. I've decided it's their primary goal in life."

He tilted his head to the side and smirked. "Keep telling yourself that."

"Why are you helping me? You could have let them catch me."

He tenderly touched the side of my cheek and then moved to sit on the edge of the bed. "Maybe I just like chaos."

We stayed like that until the bedroom door closed in the hallway. A smug look spread across his face and he closed his eyes. "If you want to run, now's your chance. The two of them are fighting and at any moment, one of them will storm out of the room to go smoke in the backyard. Your other option is that you can stay the night with me, but something tells me that my brother will be even more pissed knowing that I stole his girl and my dick game is stronger."

My mouth fell open to argue with him, but he started counting backward. "Ten, nine–"

I didn't want to see what happened when he finished and took his advice to run. As I reached the back door, I heard the bedroom slam again and Cam mumbling under his breath. My ears roared as I ran out into the night. I didn't stop until I was outside of my bedroom window, my lungs burning and every muscle shaking. I slid down the side of the house and laughed to myself.

The next day Cam showed up on campus, his normally sunshine-colored hair lightly tinted shades of greens. I hated that it didn't make him less attractive, but I still had a smug sense of satisfaction that I had gotten away with it.

Trey

I sat in front of my computer with an energy drink open, staring at the monitor. Ivy's university email was boring for the most part, except for two emails from the dean. One requested she meet him in his office and the second was an invitation to a brunch at his house. I noted Ivy hadn't responded to either, but that didn't necessarily mean anything.

My phone rang next to me and I silenced the call, trying to focus on everything I needed to do. Finding proof of Arabella's involvement with harassing Ivy was next on my list, and whoever wanted to talk could wait until later. It rang again and picked up the phone, not bothering to see who it was on the other line. "What the fuck do you want?"

"Is that how you greet your mother after all this time, Trey? I taught you better than that." It took everything in me not to tell her that the only thing she taught me was that she was a bitch that allowed her boyfriends to use me as a punching bag, but I held my tongue. It was better not to give her the energy that I could use elsewhere.

"Okay, I'll try again. What the fuck do you want, mother? Why are you calling me? I thought that when I made it clear, whatever relationship we had was severed." It wasn't on the advice of a therapist or anything like that. Cutting ties with her was the best thing I had done. That and getting a place far away from her.

There was sniffling on the other end of the phone. There was no doubt in my mind that her tears were as fake as her acrylic nails. Even if there wasn't food in the house, her nails were always done and her hair was perfect. She claimed it was to help lure in clients and provide us with a better life, but I knew better. It was really to help her party. "Trey, baby, please. I wouldn't call if I didn't need you. I need some money. Ricky, you remember him, right? I owe him a little cash, and I was wondering if maybe you could let me borrow it."

I lifted my glasses to my forehead and rubbed my eyes. It was the same thing that I had heard a million times before. Let me borrow money or I need to pawn the television. Whatever she needed to do to keep the party going and get her next fix. "Of course, I remember Ricky. He's the dealer who broke my arm when I was in seventh grade. After that, you swore you wouldn't bring him around anymore, but that only lasted a week," I spit out. I didn't bother mentioning the other dozen times he'd done terrible things to me or how every time was the last time. "The answer's no."

"But, baby," she wailed and I rolled my eyes. "If I don't have the money by next week—"

I hung up the phone, not wanting to hear anything else she had to say. I had other things I needed to do, like pull the footage from the gym last week. My phone rang beside me again and I cut the power. If Cam or Niko needed me, they could find a different way to contact me or wait until the morning. After the last errand I ran for Vincent, he could go fuck himself.

I sat back in my chair and watched the grainy footage from my monitor. On it, Ivy went inside the gym with a small black bag. Less than an hour later, three women came out carrying a very similar black bag. My bet was Arabella and her two cronies, Emmaline and Violet. I tapped my foot and thought of the best way to get through to her. She was obsessed with us. Well, maybe Niko the most. She clung to him every chance she got, but we couldn't kill her. It was the same problem we had with Caleb. Her grandfather secretly ran the entire town and people that pissed him off suddenly disappeared.

In the end, I decided to leave it up to the guys how we would threaten her and decided that I needed a break away from everything. My favorite new video clip was simply a click away. I opened the folder on my desktop and hit play.

Ivy had no idea that we had filmed the night in the office where Caleb had been tied to the chair. If Cam was intent on destroying her, then he had to have things to hold over her head. I unzipped my pants and palmed my dick, wrapping my fingers around it.

In the video, Cam traced along Ivy's jaw and then I moved forward. Her cheeks were flushed and her pupils blown, giving her a wild look as she dropped to her knees. The knife shredded the back of the t-shirt, exposing her bare back, and blood rushed away from my brain straight to my cock. "Can you stop cutting off all of my clothes?"

I had wanted to tell her there wasn't a chance in hell. I would buy her whatever she needed, but her clothes were the least of her problems. As the cloth fell away from her body on the screen, her rosy nipples were on full display beneath the thin lace of her bra and her mouth fell open as she grabbed Cam's thighs.

Slowly I glided my fist up and down, taking my time to enjoy every sensation and imagine it was her pillowy lips wrapped around me. Her tongue would swirl along my crown as I gripped her hair. Slowly I squeezed as I watched the red-haired girl deep throat Cam's cock, imagining that it was me instead of him. Her cheeks would hollow out around me as I hit the back of her throat, urging her to relax enough to let me slide down her throat.

Even as I worked my hand up and down my shaft, I needed more. On the monitor, I glided a blade along Ivy's skin before I unclasped her bra. Her tits were perfect and her nipples were hard as I traced my knife along it, teasing her.

I pumped my hand faster and rocked my hips upward, trying to imagine that instead of my fist, it was her tight pussy.

My eyes were glued to the monitor as Ivy's hand disappeared between her thick creamy thighs and Niko grabbed her wrist. If it had been up to me, I would have let her get herself off while I was down her throat, my hand wrapped around it so I could feel her screams.

I needed more and pulled my knife out of my pocket, slicing it across my palm. Crimson ribbons of blood trailed down my skin and I gripped my cock again, watching as blood stained my skin. Each up and down motion stung the cut, and I hissed. My eyes darted between the girl on the screen and my cock.

Ivy's hand was now wrapped around Niko while Cam used her face, and I groaned. We had gotten to the part of the film where my self-control slipped. Carefully, I had cut along her ribs, allowing droplets of blood to decorate her skin. I had licked and sucked along the wound while Ivy moaned.

I moved my hand faster, feeling my balls tighten and the base of my spine tingle. I fantasized about what it would feel like with my dick deep inside of her, her pussy strangling me as she came.

And when I came on her chest, I closed my eyes and bit my bottom lip. Every muscle in my body tensed as hot jets of cum spilled onto my fingers, mingling with the blood that was already there.

I stood and headed to the restroom, looking for a towel to clean up, feeling more frustrated than I had. *Fuck, I needed to get laid.*

***

The next night, Cam, Niko, and I waited in the gym parking lot around nine. Arabella liked to visit every day around this time with her friends. I hopped on the hood of her fancy luxury car and fidgeted with my knife while we waited for her to make her grand appearance. Niko stood nearby smoking a joint while Cam crossed his arms over his chest, glaring in the gym's direction. There was no use telling him to calm down when he felt like this.

When Arabella did finally appear, her friends followed behind her, and they were giggling at something. Arabella pulled out her phone and took a selfie of the three of them that would appear on YouConnect in the next hour after she doctored it. When she saw the three of us, she grinned and ran toward Niko, wrapping her arms around his waist. He took one last puff of the joint he was holding before placing his palm on her forehead and pushing her face back. "Why the fuck are you touching me again? I've told you a million times that this, us, it's never going to happen. You're just too fucking stupid to realize it."

Arabella pouted at him but shuffled back. "But you're out here waiting for me."

Cam prowled forward and grabbed her hand, his eyes wild in the moonlight. "We are. It's because I have a surprise for you." He placed his arm around her shoulder and motioned for her to follow him. When he opened the back door of her car, her mouth fell open. "That was locked."

I scratched across the finish of the hood with my knife, watching her expression as the screech of metal filled the air. "You're going to–"

Cam interrupted her by pulling a black bag from the car. "We're going to what, baby? Pay for a fresh coat of paint? I don't think so. Why is Ivy's shit in your car?"

Her mouth opened to speak, but Violet was the one who finally answered. "We don't know how that got in there."

Cam laughed and pulled Arabella closer, squeezing her tightly to him. "Oh, the three of you know exactly how that got in there. Didn't I tell you she was off limits?"

Arabella's face turned red, and she tried to struggle against him. "You're hurting me, Cam," she whined.

"Not nearly as much as I want to. If it were up to me, you'd be in an unmarked grave." He nodded to me as Niko moved in front of her friends, isolating them from saving her. I grabbed the ponytail that swung nearly to her waist as Cam held her still and sawed through her hair with the blade in my hand, watching as the dark locks fell to the ground. Arabella screamed, but no one came to save her. They wouldn't—not on campus.

I allowed the edge of the knife to nick her neck, and blood trailed across her skin. Cam let go of her and pushed her toward her friends. "Good luck having your hairdresser fix that. Next time, it will be more than your hair. Stay the fuck away from Ivy."

Niko spit at her foot, and the three of us loaded back into his car. As we drove away, I watched Arabella cover her face with her hands. "Do you think she learned her lesson?" Niko asked.

I scoffed at him. "I seriously doubt it. We kidnapped her cousin and jacked off on the girl that he was trying to impress. The whole family is fucking crazy." She deserved more than just a bad haircut, but our hands were tied. Somehow I doubted Arabella had learned her lesson, but I was weary to escalate the situation any further. The last thing I wanted to deal with this week was Fletcher Vance. Between Niko's debut fight, everything with Ivy, Cam playing football, the program I was designing, and all of our classes, the week was already pretty full.

Ivy

Frankie had closed the shop early Wednesday night, so I decided to take advantage of the free time that I suddenly had. After seeing Niko in the graveyard, I didn't want to head back there. I would rather have dealt with a crying stranger on the beach than run into anyone I knew. The town was too damn small, and I didn't know of enough places where I could hide in plain sight.

The last thing I wanted to do was deal with any of the guys who had surrounded me since my arrival in Clearhaven. They seemed to hide around every corner. Caleb had been silent, only sending me texts to let me know he had started his end of our class project. Ros had sent me a text to check on me last night and I reassured her that everything was fine and we would have to get together for coffee or pizza when my aunt was away at work. I missed our constant camaraderie, but I really didn't want to drag her into any of the mess I was caught up in.

After locking up, I headed to the beach, my black hoodie zipped up. The wind at night in Clearhaven was cool, but I refused to stay inside or go home to hide. That was the last place I wanted to be.

I unzipped the boots that I had worn every day since buying them and replaced them with my athletic shoes before jogging across the street to where the ocean waited for me. A storm brewed off the coast and I watched as lightning struck the water, mesmerized by the perfection of it all. Maybe once I left Clearhaven, I would find somewhere near the ocean to settle doing something that I loved.

"Hey, Ivy. What are you doing out this late?" an unfamiliar deep voice called from down the beach. I wrapped my arms around myself, unsettled by the fact that I was no longer alone. Standing about fifteen feet away were two large men, their features shrouded by the darkness. It was one thing to stumble on a lonely crying teenager and another by a man this time of the night, especially after everything that had happened. I'd had to deal with men winking at me and making enough lewd gestures for a lifetime.

I took a step backward, trying to put more distance between them and me, but I backed into a broad chest and broad arms banded around me like a vise. "Let me down," I told whoever it was, but their hold tightened.

"Not a chance in hell, beautiful. Everyone else in town has had a turn with you. Why shouldn't we?" His hot breath made my stomach churn. My cheeks heated at his words from anger and embarrassment. Sure, I had been seen with a lot of men since I had shown up in Clearhaven, but that was my choice—most of the time. Even if I had sucked off a hundred men since I had been here, that was my business and no one else's.

I dug my short nails into the skin on his arm and he cursed, loosening his hold enough for me to scramble away. "Fucking bitch," he yelled, but I didn't waste any time as I took off across the beach, my feet sinking into the sand with every movement. I shouted, hoping that someone would hear me and scare off the three men that were behind me. The air rushed from my lungs as someone collided with my back, tackling me onto the cool sand. The grains bit into the skin of my legs, but I fought to stand. Anything to escape. It was one thing for me to give my body away and another for someone to take what wasn't theirs. "Help me with her. I wish I had known she was a fighter before tonight. Tonight would have happened a lot sooner," someone else said. "Hold her ankles, John."

His weight was crushing me and I couldn't get enough breath, couldn't fill up my lungs. I couldn't get my knees underneath me to stand. Hot, sweaty hands gripped my ankles, and fingers pressed against the bones. The man at my back shifted, one hand circling my neck and the other pulling up the edge of my skirt. Every time I fought, he squeezed harder, the edges of my vision spotting with black. The third man moved in front of me and fell to his knees. I distinctly heard his zipper being released even as I fought, everything slowly dimming around me. "Open your mouth up, whore." I clenched my jaw in refusal. A fist hit the side of my head, pain lancing through my face as my underwear was ripped down my legs. "You can have a turn with her when I'm done," one of them said.

Fingers branded my thighs, prying them apart. I coughed, trying to get just one more breath so that I could continue fighting. A gunshot echoed through the air nearby, but I couldn't hold on. Everything went black around me.

When I came to, Frankie sat beside me on the back-seat of a car, my head cradled in her lap. Behind my eyes pounded and my throat felt raw, either from being choked or from screaming. The skin on my legs didn't feel much better. The gentle motion of a car driving vaguely registered in my mind as Frankie stroked my hair, looking at me with a mixture of pity and relief. "Were they able–?"

"Shh, don't say anything, girl. I was able to get there before…" Her voice broke and she looked off to the side so that she didn't betray her emotions. I wasn't as lucky as hot tears fell down my cheeks. No matter what, they wouldn't stop, even as she murmured reassurances to me. I curled onto my side and let myself feel, even if just for a moment. By the time the car stopped, we were in front of Regina's house. I wiped at my nose and winced at the pain I felt as I touched it. The pain I felt everywhere.

Someone cleared their throat from the front seat and I looked up to see who my second savior was. Rhyker was staring at me from the rearview mirror. "Baby girl, let me help you into the house."

Frankie shook her head at him. "I've got this. You stay here. It will take more than a young punk to shut Regina Spencer's fat mouth." She ran her fingers across my cheeks gingerly. "You ready to do this, Ivy?"

I turned my face away. "Not yet, please." I didn't want to hear what my aunt would say. Even though I couldn't be certain, I knew it wouldn't be pleasant.

Frankie carefully cradled my face in her hands, forcing me to look at her. "You won't hide, Ivy. Not now and not ever. Don't let them break you. You remind me so much of someone that I used to know."

And with that, she opened the car door so that the two of us could face the world—or at least my aunt—together.

I trudged into the house with my face hidden, my head hung low. As expected, Regina was sitting at the kitchen table with a coffee cup of wine. "Where the hell have you been, Ivy?"

Frankie wrapped an arm around my shoulder, holding me up as the tears started again. "Shut the fuck up, Gina, and leave the girl alone tonight."

My aunt stood and I tried to move, but Frankie held me firmly in place. "How dare you talk to me like that in my house?"

"I'll say a lot worse, you hypocrite. Sit back down and enjoy your wine while I make sure your niece is taken care of." My aunt stood there with her mouth open as Frankie helped me into my room. "She's always been a bitch," Frankie mumbled so that only I could hear. A small laugh escaped me despite the tears that were still in my eyes. Blame it on hysteria, but it was good to see someone stand up to her. "You've got it from here, right?"

I nodded to her, and my throat felt tight. I gave her a quick hug. "Thank you for everything tonight," I whispered as I wrapped my arms around my chest.

She gently patted me before she turned away. "Anytime. I was just glad that I was there."

After she had driven off, I snuck into the bathroom and stood beneath the shower spray, scrubbing my skin until my body was raw and the water turned cold. I popped some pain relievers and one of the pills Niko had given me, ready for the oblivion it would give me. My head was cloudy and my heart heavy as I locked my bedroom door and put on the shirt that Niko had dressed me in. I rolled onto my side and curled my legs up to my chest while I held the shirt close to my face, trying desperately not to think of what almost happened. If Frankie hadn't found me in time.

My chest heaved as I cried and I held my pillow over it to muffle the sound. I didn't want Regina busting into my room. My window creaked as it was lifted and I turned to face the wall. I didn't want anyone, especially not one of the guys, to see me like this. His fingers trailed down the injured skin of my legs softly. "What happened tonight?"

I said nothing because I didn't know how to respond. He pulled me into his chest and held me while I cried silently into his shirt. "I should bring you something different to sleep in," he said gruffly, his voice thick with emotion. "You probably need to wash this one."

My breath stuttered when I tried to speak. "I can't be-cause then it won't smell like you," I whispered so quietly I prayed he didn't hear my confession.

We lay there until a dreamless sleep overtook me and when I woke up, he was gone like always.

Cam

When I woke Thursday morning, Niko was still gone and his side of the bed was cold. For the past two weeks, he had been sneaking out at night, especially when we argued, but usually, he was back before sunrise. I didn't know what he was doing, whether it was escaping to the cemetery or if he had a girl that he was secretly seeing, but I'd let him keep his secrets. The three of us had plenty of them and one more wouldn't hurt. He needed to blow off some steam, especially because Friday evening he had a fight in Strathmore. None of us had been there, and I was the only one that had ever left Clearhaven for even a brief amount of time—and that was only because of football. None of us were really looking forward to the fight, though. Too much was riding on it.

I staggered to the kitchen, ready to make a cup of coffee before my classes, and Niko sat at the small table with his head in his hands. When we looked up at me, his eyes were bloodshot from not enough sleep and his mouth was set into a firm line. "You look like shit. What's going on with you?"

He shifted in his seat and ran a hand through his hair, pulling lightly at the roots. "Someone attacked Ivy last night. She wouldn't tell me what happened, but she has bruises on her throat and face and her legs are scraped up. We need to fix this shit."

I laid my coffee cup on the cabinet top without saying a word. "Give me five minutes and send a text to Trey." I threw on a t-shirt and my sneakers. No one got to touch her except for us, and the people in this town were about to get that message. I didn't ask when he had seen Ivy or how he knew what had happened, but part of me questioned if maybe that was where he had been escaping to every night.

We drove to Trey's apartment in silence. Niko looked worried, but all I could feel was pissed. Trey didn't ask questions, and Niko didn't turn on any music. The tension was suffocating inside of the car. When the three of us finally arrived at Regina Spencer's house, I got out and didn't bother knocking on the front door, instead taking it upon myself to rush inside. Regina was making some-thing in the kitchen and opened her mouth, but with one glare, she stopped whatever she was going to say. I didn't have the patience to deal with her holier-than-thou crap this morning or her idle threats about how we all needed to stay away.

I opened the small bedroom door that belonged to Ivy and found her curled up on her mattress facing away from me. Her legs were exposed from beneath the blan-ket and abrasions covered her calves. Gently, I touched her shoulder, trying to convince her to face me. Trey stood in the doorway observing us curiously and Niko lingered in the hallway, holding something in his arms. "Little ghost, I need you to look at me."

She stayed completely still until Niko crossed the threshold in the room and sat down beside her. "Ivy, I brought you something." Finally, she turned her head, and I swallowed when I saw the swelling on her face and the bruises lining her skin. Around her neck, someone's handprints circled it. I sat back watching the two of them and jealousy flared inside of me at how tenderly he touched her. She scooted up against her pillows into a sitting position and crossed her legs. Her eyes were swollen from crying and her skin was paler than usual. She tugged the blanket up around her chest, and I waited patiently for Niko to coax the information I needed out of her.

He placed a pile of t-shirts into her lap and grabbed her hand, brushing his thumb across her palm. "You need to tell us who did this to you. I can't protect you if I don't know."

A fire raged behind her eyes briefly, removing the morose expression she had been wearing. "Protect me?" A wry laugh bubbled up in her throat. "All of you are the reason I'm in this situation."

My patience snapped. "How about this, then? I need to know who the fuck attacked you so they can never lay their hands on you again. Even if we torture you, no one else is allowed to."

Even I was beginning to slowly question my motivations with the red-haired woman who fought me at every turn. I wanted revenge for what had happened to Maya and the fact that I had almost lost her. She was one of the few things I had left in this world. Ivy haunted my thoughts, though. I wanted to punish her and break her, possess her, but no one else could touch what was mine.

Her fingers caressed the clothing laying in her lap. "I have no idea. Frankie and Rhyker are the ones who stopped them."

I lifted my eyebrows at her words and balled my fists at my sides. My voice had a hard edge when the next words came out. "What do you mean, stop them? Ivy, what did they do?"

She closed her eyes. "Nothing happened, Cam. Just let it go."

But I wouldn't let it go. She had to know that. She said nothing else, and I gestured for the guys to follow me. We left her sitting on the bed, clinging to Niko's shirts for comfort. If he brought her a feeling of safety right now, even if it was false, I wouldn't destroy it. Not yet. She needed something and so did he, something that I couldn't give either of them.

As we were trying to leave, Regina blocked our path to the doorway. She held a cup of coffee in one hand while she lifted her chin in defiance. "The three of you know better than to come to my house."

I sighed because I had more important things to deal with than her shitty attitude. "We were just leaving. I needed to check on your niece after last night."

She shrugged at me. "What happened to Ivy was her fault. If she had dressed differently or maybe kept her legs closed, then she would have been safe. She has a curfew for a reason, and she broke it."

It was Trey who got to her first, not giving me a chance to react. He shoved her into the plaster wall and her head bounced against it. Before I could stop him, his knife was pressed against her throat. "Is that so, Regina? So if I decided to end your life right now, would it be your fault and not mine? Because I think you're asking for it." The usual calm demeanor had faded away, leaving only cold anger. "Who she fucks or not is her business. I think that you're just jealous of her because no one wants you and they never have." Slowly, he trailed the blade down her neck. "I wonder if Ivy knows your secrets?" He pulled away and adjusted her shirt, ignoring the horror-stricken look that was plastered on her face. "Stay the fuck out of our way."

I pushed past the woman who clung to the wall beside us, hitting her with my shoulder as I left. If Ivy was mine, really mine, I would make sure she never set foot in this house again.

But she wasn't mine.

The drive to Frankie and Rhyker's was short and the entire time I chewed on the corner of my nail, ignoring whatever Niko and Trey were saying. They lived on the outskirts of the same neighborhood, but the houses here were nicer. Even the air felt cleaner. Rain began falling around us and thunder boomed in the distance, setting the mood for how the rest of the day would go.

My mother had stumbled into the house earlier, waking me up from a dead sleep. A man screamed at her and glass shattered somewhere in the house.

I just prayed that they wouldn't wake up Maya. Well, and then I prayed to a god I wasn't sure existed that whoever had come home with my mother wouldn't hit either of us... or worse. I'd made sure that Maya had finished her homework and gone to bed hours ago while Mom was out on what she called a date. Even in eighth grade, I knew what that meant. As I showered earlier, I knew she would come in drunk or high with someone that she had picked up. My only hope was that they would stay away from me and my sister.

The door to my room creaked open, and I held my breath, hoping that it wasn't one of her boyfriends. I laid completely still, not wanting to move a muscle. Relief flooded my veins, and I relaxed as the smell of roses filled the air. It was just my mother coming to check on me. The mattress dipped as she lay behind me, her hands landing on my hips. She sniffled to herself and her fingers trailed the edge of my shirt.

I quickly shook myself out of the memory as Niko cut the engine in front of Frankie's house. That was the night that I had learned that even if God existed, he had forsaken me completely. Even if I wanted to punish Ivy, I wouldn't allow others to touch her.

I knocked at the front door, not daring to barge into Frankie's house like I had Regina's. She would shoot me and not think twice about it, even if we were friends with

Rhyker. The short older woman answered the door and moved aside. "What do you three want?"

"We need to ask you or your grandson some questions if we can." I was careful not to overstep my boundaries or she would shut down and kick us out. Frankie was the one person in this town who didn't care about the Forsaken or the Order, even if she technically played by the rules. I was surprised that she still allowed Rhyker to live here with what he did. We could ask him what happened later in the day, but I wanted to take care of everything now.

She impatiently gestured for us to enter the house and waited. "I suppose you've seen what happened to the girl?" She waltzed past the three of us and yelled for Rhyker to get up, not bothering with the niceties most people would have. When she sat down, she picked up her knitting needles and began working, not bothering to say anything until Rhyker stumbled into the room. "Tell them about last night."

Rhyker leaned against the door frame and yawned. "Ma, you could have told them. I'm not even awake yet."

She leveled him a look over the top of her knitting needles. "Well, if you weren't out at all hours of the night torturing people, you'd probably have had some coffee by now." Every time she opened her mouth, she surprised me. She knew what we did and even though all four of us had at least a foot on her, she didn't care.

"Fine. You're probably right." He motioned for the three of us to follow him to the kitchen and spoke while he filled a carafe with water. "What did she tell you?"

Niko pulled a chipped cup from the cabinet. "Nothing."

He scooped coffee into the basket and hit the power button without looking at her. "You know how I try to take her out to dinner twice a month." He gestured toward the living room. "She claims she isn't lonely since my granddad died, but I know better. Anyway, we were driving past. I needed to get her home before I went to work, and we noticed Ivy's car was still in front of the shop. Ma told me to park, and that something wasn't right. I thought she was overreacting and figured Ivy was with Ros. We heard screams and by the time we got there, three guys had her held down on the beach. Ma had a shotgun and scared them off, but if we had gotten there a minute later..."

The rage I was trying to keep concealed threatened to boil over. "Who was it?"

"Peter Bell and Jake Fox. The third one ran off before I could see who it was."

Niko clapped a hand on Rhyker's shoulder in thanks and I tipped my head in Frankie's direction. She raised an eyebrow at me before we turned on our heels and headed for the front door. Frankie was one of the only people in Clearhaven that didn't put up with our shit and I didn't want to piss her off. Ever.

After all, she was the one that had raised Rhyker. He had inherited his crazy from somewhere.

The rest of the day we spent in classes trying to act like everything was normal when it was anything but. This week we didn't have the luxury of waiting until Friday night to take care of what needed to be done because of Niko's fight and Saturday I had a game. Trey had already promised that he would look for camera feeds in the area to figure out who the third mystery assailant was, but Peter and Jake were dead. They just didn't know it yet.

We had given Ivy some space for a few days, but I doubted Niko would keep his word. When we passed her on campus earlier, she was back to wearing baggy jeans and t-shirts, either to conceal some of her injuries or to hide her body. A piece of me wanted to reassure her that the words her aunt had spoken weren't true. It wasn't her fault the same way that it wasn't Maya's, but I shoved it down.

That night, we headed to a party at Phi Delta. Peter and Jake were brothers of the fraternity and every Thursday they partied before stumbling into class Friday morning looking dazed. Our presence wouldn't alarm anyone considering that we added to the entertainment. There was an unspoken agreement that every Thursday night we would be there to give the pretty polished rich kids what they wanted. It was another one of Vincent's orders that I hated. In the past, I hadn't minded as much because there was always a gaggle of girls who were ready to spend the night with guys from the wrong side of the tracks that their father wouldn't approve of, but tonight, it just annoyed me. I bided my time, waiting in the corner and sipping a soda.

Once Peter disappeared outside onto the back deck, I made my move. Niko and Trey already had Jake waiting in the car. I pressed the gun into the small of his back when I stepped up behind him. "Let's go, rich boy. We're going to walk around the house and you aren't going to make any noise or I'll blow your brains out."

He whimpered a little and his gait faltered as we made our way over to Niko's car. To the untrained eye, it looked like we were just two guys having a conversation, which is exactly what they would tell the police when they investigated their disappearance. This murder wasn't sanctioned by the Forsaken, and we wouldn't have the cops on our side. I shoved my victim into the back seat with my weapon trained on him and Niko took off. Usually, I would feel regret or remorse for what I was going to do, but tonight all I felt was icy rage. Even though five people were crammed into Niko's car, only three would be returning.

I wasn't sure how we would find the third man who attacked Ivy on the beach, but we would. They would expose themselves. Eventually.

Caleb

My fingers hovered over my phone, begging me to text the auburn-haired girl that had been on my mind. I sighed and pocketed it, choosing to stay away to keep her safe instead. If my grandfather or any of his associates thought we were getting too close, it would spell disaster for both of us. I wasn't sure why they were so preoccupied with Ivy considering the fact that she seemed to be unaware of the fact her father had promised her to Abraham Wells.

Seeing Ivy with Cam and Niko was bad enough most days, but the idea of her being with Wells infuriated me. I flexed my fingers around the highball glass I was holding and tried to push the thoughts out of my head. I couldn't think about it right now, especially given who else was gathered around the mahogany conference table. Fletcher Vance, Abraham Wells, Andrew Jensen, Gervais Fouquet, and Zachary Dixon sat around with cigars lit, casually talking business. I ignored most of it and kept my mask carefully in place.

"Caleb, how is Rosalyn doing?" Fouquet asked me, pulling me from the chaos in my head.

I tilted my head to the side and stared at Andrew. "You should ask the deacon. It's his granddaughter, after all."

My grandfather clenched his jaw and took a long puff of his cigar, blowing smoke into the air before leaning back further into his seat. "Caleb, we've talked about this. You are being asked because she is who we have matched you with. Neither of you have taken that seriously. Ms. Jensen has taken it upon herself to run around with gangsters, and you seem to be too caught up in Ivy Spencer, even after our last conversation."

Wells spoke up. "Not that I can blame you. If I were your age and had been asked to befriend a girl like Ivy, I would have taken advantage of the fact as well. I just want you to remember that all of your actions will have repercussions for her. She will be punished how we see fit."

Ivy had already been punished enough even if the drugs they plied her with distorted her memories. I'd heard the whispers behind closed doors. As bad as Andrew Jensen was, at least he protected his granddaughter.

I glared at the dean and took a sip of the liquid in my glass, not wanting to fuel the fire further. "For everyone's information, I have only contacted Ivy since our talk to discuss an assignment for class."

I wanted to add that the last thing I wanted was for Ivy to draw the attention of Luthor or for Ivy to be punished more than she already would be. Being betrothed to Wells would already be her own personal hell. I had seen how he treated the girls at parties, and I knew what happened when they were summoned to his office. I also knew that I couldn't live with myself if Ivy actually married him.

"That also wasn't the arrangement, Caleb. How can you make her feel safe if you've distanced yourself from her? She needs to remain unassuming until all the pieces fall into place."

I stayed silent and stared into the distance, hoping that the conversation would end. "Now on to other topics." I zoned back out, not really caring about zoning regulations or political topics. Everything in Clearhaven was run by the men sitting around the table. They decided who became mayor and who sat on the city council seats. The police were in their pockets and paid well for their part. The Order chose which businesses received permits, which laws were passed... and which girls would either learn to serve them or disappear.

Conversation slowed as several young women entered the room carrying glasses of champagne. At least they were local women that I knew were over the age of eighteen, but I wanted no part of what was about to happen. I inhaled sharply and tried to stand, but a heavy hand pushed me back into my seat. "You can't leave before the festivities are over, son," my grandfather whispered in my ear. "Remember my promises. If you don't start playing your part, I will let your cousin have the girl that you're so preoccupied with. What was it that happened to Leyla that night? My memory seems to have failed me a bit."

I didn't bother looking at him and turned up my cup, refusing to allow my emotions to show on my face. The night before Leyla disappeared, she had been paid to spend the night with Luthor. I wasn't in the room, but I heard the screams that echoed down the hall and her pleas for someone to save her. My grandfather simply laughed with the men standing near him as they joked about how she knew what it was like to be used by a real man now.

The morning after, I saw the mangled bedsheets covered in scarlet stains being stripped by whatever housekeeper he had at the time. She disappeared the next week. No one ever asked what had happened to either of them. That was something the Order was good at: finding people that no one would miss.

Fletcher Vance's grip tightened on my shoulder. "You're a part of this, whether or not you like it. Now you're going to sit back and let one of our whores unzip your pants and do her job. Any more resistance and you know what will happen," he threatened in a low tone.

He let go of me finally and gave one of the girls a charming smile, motioning for her to come closer. His arm banded around her waist as I poured more alcohol, hating myself and the life I was born into. If I had known that tonight was one of those meetings, I would have tried to find an excuse to get out of it.

"Make sure you take good care of him tonight, Clarissa. He's been under a lot of pressure lately," my grandfather murmured against her neck.

I closed my eyes and sipped on my scotch while Clarissa kneeled in front of me, wishing I was someone else. While she unbuttoned my pants, I tried to come up with some sort of plan to save Ivy. Hell, to even save Ros. There had to be some way out of the hellscape we were stuck in.

Niko

The metal warehouse looked like it had seen better days. Pieces of paint flaked off of it and spots of rust showed through. Concrete stairs and double doors lay twenty feet to my left, but instead, I lit a cigarette and inhaled deeply, hoping that the act would calm my nerves. Cam and Trey stood by waiting patiently for me to finish before I went to find Tyler inside.

Strathmore was nothing like I expected. The news always painted it as a place where politicians and businessmen hung out in fancy restaurants, but there was a film that seemed to cling to the city. There was poverty in Clearhaven, but this was different.

I crushed the cigarette under my heel before taking one last look at the parking lot. It was filled with cars and motorcycles, which meant that the inside would be crowded, hot, and loud. Even from outside, I could hear the dull roar of people talking and yelling inside. My fight was in less than an hour, the second to last of the night. I took a deep breath before climbing up the steps.

My knuckles were already busted open from the night before. So were Trey's and Cam's. Peter and Jake had gotten what they deserved. My only regrets were that

I wasn't able to hurt them more than I had. Ivy hadn't spoken to me and when I tried to check in on her after I was finished, her window was locked, a signal that she wasn't ready to see me yet. If she ever was.

Opening the door, the sound intensified to a deafening level. I pushed past the bodies in front of me, trying to catch sight of either Tyler or the person running the fight. In the center ring, two men were hashing it out, sweat and blood covering their bodies. Cash exchanged hands, and the air smelled like musk, beer, and smoke.

Finally, I saw them. An older man sat against the far wall at a table with Tyler across from him. Their heads were bowed close, no doubt in order to hear what the other had to say.

I hated everything about the place and the fact I was fighting. Racing was one thing, but at least outside the sea of people didn't feel as suffocating. Once I reached the table, I took another deep breath and tapped on Tyler's shoulder to get his attention. He looked at me and grinned, holding out his fist for a quick bump. "My boy! The man of the hour. Niko, this is Maurice. He runs stuff up here. I was just telling him you were going to make us a lot of money."

He glanced over what I was wearing with approval: Jeans, a black shirt, and the steel-toed boots I wore when I was out on certain types of errands for Vincent. Maurice didn't stand, but he extended his hand for a shake. "A fighter with no frills. We'll see how well you do tonight, and maybe we can make this a regular thing." I kept my mouth shut, choosing not to tell him that the last thing

I wanted to do was make this a regular thing. Between the drive and gas money, it wasn't really how I wanted to spend my Friday nights. Getting my face beaten to a pulp wasn't really my scene.

A blond-haired guy holding a leather jacket jogged up to Maurice and planted a kiss on his cheek. "Maurice, baby, tell me you saved me a spot tonight."

The older man rolled his eyes and wiped his hand across his face. "Dammit, Ethan, you always do this to me. Where the hell is Ignacio? He was supposed to keep an eye on you. Aren't you supposed to be laying low? If you get arrested, I don't want to hear anything from Dominic this week."

The man he called Ethan, who looked more like a tattooed surfer than someone I expected to fight in a place like this, gave me a wink. He was at least a decade older than me, but his arrogance made me chuckle. "No one knows I'm here but you. Help me out."

I gave Tyler a wave goodbye to let him know I would see him after my fight and pushed back through the sea of people, closer to the makeshift ring. Anxiety churned in my stomach and crawled beneath my skin. I was ready for the fight if for no other reason than to burn off the excess adrenaline that made my heart pound.

When Ethan prowled into the ring, I grinned to myself. Somehow, he had managed to talk his way into a spot. Ethan wasn't a small guy. He was about my height but made like a swimmer with broad shoulders and a tapered waist. When he stripped off his shirt and threw it at a guy near the ring who glared at him, I could see just

how much ink covered every inch of his skin. As tall as
Ethan was, his opponent was taller and bulkier. I watched
mesmerized as the two of them exchanged blows. Ethan
bounced around easily on his feet, dodging and ducking
out of reach. He was completely at ease in front of the
crowd and when he emerged victorious, the other man
unconscious on the concrete floor, I cheered.

And then the announcer called my name, cringing me
back to reality. I was here to participate, not simply
watch. Cam gave me a tight hug. "You've got this, man."
Trey lightly punched my shoulder, and I exhaled, steady-
ing myself as I walked to the metal fencing rounding the
ring. I hopped over and a hand caught my bicep. Ethan
stared at me for a moment and his features softened as he
leaned close so that only I could hear what he wanted to
say. "You're about the same age that I was when I started,
and I can tell this is your first time."

"How?" I mouthed at him, certain that the noise from
the surrounding people would wash out my words.

His eyes twinkled with amusement. "You're a little too
pale and you're covered in sweat. Right now, you need to
push out everything else that is going on inside of your
head. Don't let him land too many punches." he tipped
his chin toward the person I was paired against. We were
evenly matched as far as height, but he outweighed me by
at least fifty pounds of muscle. "He's fucking brutal; don't
let him corner you. Remember that the only rule here is
not to murder the other person." He slapped my back. "I
put my money on you."

"Thanks," I told him and moved away, ready to get the fight over with.

The other guy started toward me fast as soon as I was inside, obviously also ready. He was faster than I would have thought considering his sheer size and I had made the mistake of thinking that I would have time to acclimate. His fist caught my jaw, momentarily stunning me before I realized I needed to move. Ethan was right. This guy was brutal. I had been in plenty of fights, but none of them were like this. I careened to the left to avoid another blow to the face. His foot almost caught my knees, but I managed to step out of the way just in time and landed a punch against his ribs. We danced like that for what could have been seconds or an eternity. The only thing I could think about was that I needed to win. My brother and sister were relying on me. As soon as my palm collided with his nose, a crunch I felt under my touch, and blood trickled down his face. Even over the crowd, I could hear sirens in the background.

The anxiety that had slowly been disappearing returned, amplified by the knowledge that I couldn't get caught here. None of us had bail money. The demeanor of the other man changed swiftly. He thrust his hand toward me and patted me on the back. "Maybe next time we can actually finish. Get the fuck out of here. You don't want to get caught by Strathmore PD."

I gave him a quick nod. Cam and Trey waited beside Ethan as I jumped over the metal fencing, the four of us pushing with the rest of the crowd to escape out of the exit before the entire thing was busted up. As soon as we were outside, Ethan vanished into the night and the three of us raced toward my car. Cam jumped in the driver's side, peeling out of the parking lot and speeding in the opposite direction of the red and blue lights. As they vanished in the rearview mirror, a wave of nausea washed over me.

Whatever chance I had to get the money I needed had just vanished.

I pulled out my phone and sent a text to Tyler asking him if there was another fight or a race scheduled for the next week. The response I got back was exactly what I had been expecting: no. I sent a second text to the slumlord that owned the house and asked for just a little more time. His response was better than I expected. He said he could give me until mid-October. Instead of making me feel better, like there was hope, all I felt was my throat tighten. I laid my head against the car window and stayed there for the rest of the drive. Once we were outside of Strathmore's city limits, Cam slowed down. He grabbed my hand with his, lacing his fingers with mine and squeezing gently. I knew Trey saw it, but I didn't pull away from him. The last time I'd seen the hurt wash over his face and tonight I didn't think I could handle it.

I didn't know what the fuck I was going to do, but I couldn't give up. Too many people were relying on me.

After Cam dropped Trey off, I asked him to drop me off a few blocks from the house. The corner of his mouth tipped up, but he said nothing. I wasn't sure if he knew where I was going, but I didn't want to argue.

I walked to Regina Spencer's house, hoping that just maybe I could see the girl who preoccupied too many of my thoughts. My heart fell when I tried her window and it was locked. She was shutting me out still. My finger ran over the scar on my hip where she had marked me.

It wasn't like I could blame her, but it hurt. Just a little bit.

Ivy

It had been two weeks since my attack, and things had been fairly quiet. Well, quiet as far as Clearhaven went. There had been a few minor incidents of bullying, but they didn't even bother me. Trash had been shoved into my car and the word 'whore' was spray painted on the sidewalk in front of my house. The side of the Honda had been keyed, as if that would bother me. Had they seen the driver's side door? Despite my physical appearance, a few guys propositioned me for money.

Mostly, I felt nothing. Not about any of that.

The Forsaken left me alone for the most part. We were all choosing to ignore each other, which suited me fine even though sometimes I still wore Niko's shirts to bed, even if I locked my window at night. The bruises from the unknown men had mostly faded, the remnants easily covered by foundation and concealer, and life continued on as usual, with me praying that the next four years would go by quickly.

Rosalyn had texted me earlier that day asking if I wanted to grab a cup of coffee on campus before I holed up inside my room for the weekend and I agreed. Since I was off the Forsaken's radar for the moment, seeing the one person who I could call my friend was a risk I was willing to take. As soon as she entered the small dining hall, she wrapped her arms around my neck and squeezed tightly. The hug made my body hurt, but I relished it. I missed human contact and the small display of affection made me feel happy for the first time in days.

"How are you feeling?" she asked me, worry creasing her brow.

While we waited in line for the barista, I messed with the edge of my t-shirt and tried giving her a reassuring look. "I'm fine. I've just been busy between work and school."

She raised her eyebrows and put a hand on her hip. "You're fine? Even after what happened on the beach?"

I didn't want her to worry about me and I didn't want to talk about how I was really feeling. The pills that I had gotten from Niko weren't working as well as they had in the beginning, and the supply I'd gotten was dwindling. The nightmares had returned, making me dread the idea of sleeping. Being held down while phantom hands clawed at me reminded me too much of what happened at the beach. Even now, the thought made me feel sick. "Yeah, I'm just trying to focus on the positives. Now that I've started focusing on school, Regina's laid off some."

We gave the barista our order and stepped outside to the campus greenway where the sun was already setting. Frankie had given me the day off, and I wasn't really sure what to do with my time. All of my homework and half of the project with Caleb were complete. I didn't have a clue how I had time to accomplish all of that while high and half the time drunk. I briefly considered running again at the gym, but the thought of being out by myself that late didn't appeal to me.

"What are your plans for the evening? The guys are all busy with some big meeting involving the gang so we could go to dinner and they would never know. Just the two of us."

I hesitated for a moment before giving her a small smile. "Yeah, that sounds good. Let me grab my car so that when we're done, I can head home. The last thing I want to do is invoke Regina's wrath again."

Lately, our relationship had been less volatile. Between the fact that I was a homebody who never broke curfew and me wearing jeans and t-shirts to conceal the bruises on my body, she'd left me alone. Occasionally, she asked if I had spoken to the dean, but I avoided her questions by quickly changing the subject. He had sent me an email to which I didn't respond asking for me to stop by his office, but after the brunch where he cornered me, I would have swallowed rusty nails rather than be alone with him.

She grabbed my arm, stopping me in my tracks. "Don't worry about your car right now. I'll just drop you off later."

"I really should go get my car," I insisted. "Just in case. What if Rhyker is done early or something?"

"No, it's really not a problem. Besides, I miss you playing DJ while I drive."

I narrowed my eyes at her and pulled her along to the parking lot. "Ros, what are you hiding?" She looked guilty while my gaze swept the parking lot. "Where the fuck is my car?"

She cleared her throat and gave me a sheepish grin. "It was supposed to be a surprise, but I'm having your door fixed. It should be done by the time I drop you off tonight. After what happened at the beach, I wanted you to have an easy way to escape if you needed it."

I turned my face away from her so that I wouldn't cry again. I had given her grandfather his payment for the car last week and squirreled away the rest of my paycheck to replace the smashed in door. Crawling over the seats was fine when I thought Clearhaven was safe, but now? "I can't pay you back this week, but between the hours I am working at Frankie's–"

She grabbed my hand and pulled me over to Black Betty. "You don't owe me anything, Ivy. Well, just one thing, but it isn't money. After today, stop shutting me out of your life. I know why you have been avoiding me, but the guys won't mess with me. We grew up together and right now I am doing Niko several favors. They'll get over themselves at some point. Cam just needs to work through his shit."

And in the meantime, I was caught in the crossfire.

I simply grabbed her hand and squeezed. Ros always made me feel a little less alone. "Thank you for everything."

"Whatever, bitch. Now get in the truck so I can kidnap you."

Despite the tightness in my throat, I snorted. "The last thing you need is kidnapping charges, so I guess I'll go."

We hopped in the truck and headed to a small diner that wasn't on the Strip, hoping to avoid at least some of the crowd. Everyone would be getting ready for parties and the game this weekend. As Ros drove, she peered at me from the corner of her eye. "Did you hear about the two guys that are missing from campus?"

I shook my head while watching the buildings pass by. The leaves had begun to change colors and spots of red, orange, and gold decorated the trees. "Who is it? Do the police have any leads yet?"

"Peter Bell and Jake Fox, two of the frat boys from campus. What I heard was that they showed up at a party and then vanished sometime that night. One of them left a note saying that they both wanted a fresh start and that they couldn't get that in Clearhaven. The parents argue that there is no way either of them would have done that. Peter was dating Arabella's friend Violet, and she is claiming that he wouldn't have left her behind."

In the back of my mind, a voice told me that there was something weird about the entire situation. Maybe the two men had run off to escape Clearhaven. God knew that was what I wanted to do, but I had to ask. "When did they go missing?"

Ros turned off the main drag and parked in front of Waffles and Scoops. "About two weeks ago." Right around the same time that three men attempted to rape me on the beach. I couldn't say for certain what had happened to Peter and Jake, but I didn't think that they had left town either, and the only people who knew for certain were currently avoiding me. I clutched the door handle, ready to get out and change the subject.

I didn't feel sad that the two of them were dead. If they were the ones who attacked me, they deserved whatever happened to them. The only thing that I felt was a trace of fear. One guy was still out there and they could come back.

Ros and I ate patty melts and drank milkshakes at a booth inside. The interior was exactly like what you would expect and transported you to a different era. Red stools and checkered tile with pin-up girl posters plastered on the walls. Even though I wasn't overly hungry, I forced myself to eat. I hadn't been interested in food lately–I hadn't really been interested in anything–but Rosalyn was watching me carefully as she shoved cheese fries into her mouth. We took our time eating and talking as the sun disappeared and the sky faded to black.

A bell over the door rang and the high school girl who was waitressing told whoever it was to sit wherever they liked. The diner wasn't super busy yet and there were plenty of open booths. Drunk college students wouldn't stumble in until after midnight. I glanced over my shoulder when people sat in the booth directly behind me, annoyed that our bubble of privacy had been broken.

Arabella sat there staring with her two friends, a smirk plastered on her face. "Who would have imagined that we would have run into you here, Ivy?"

I didn't respond and turned away, choosing to grab one of Ros' fries. "Just ignore them," she said under her breath. "Bella is a bitch because she wants Niko, but she can't have him.'

I scoffed and grabbed another fry, even though I was ready to leave. One of the other girls, the one with bleach blond hair, spoke up. "You know, I heard that they all dumped you now. Guess they found out about what a piece of trash you really are."

I stood up and leaned over the girl, whose eyes widened. "Here's the problem with that rumor. I would have to date one of them for them to dump me." The girl's eyes widened and behind me, I heard a soft laugh. "I'll be back. I just need to get some fresh air. Something in here smells bad."

Rosalyn grinned at me as she scooted out of the booth. "Yeah, let me pay and we can get the hell out of here. I'll be out in just a minute."

The night air cooled my face when I exited the building. Tonight had been damn near perfect before Arabella showed up and I wondered why she was so obsessed with me. I had left her alone and Niko wasn't speaking to me—I locked my window every night.

Leaning against the tailgate of Rosalyn's truck, I stared up at the sky and took a deep breath. Gravel crunched nearby, and I looked up. A man stood a few feet away, and I straightened up, ready to run if I needed to. Something about him was familiar, but I couldn't place it. "There you are. I was wondering where you had gone to."

His smile was stiff and didn't reach his eyes. I took a step back, but he was fast, grabbing me by the arm and yanking me close to him. "Not this time. No one's here to save you, and I think my sister has plans for you." I suddenly felt a sharp prick in my neck and a wave of nausea hit me, even as my limbs began relaxing.

My vision went dark as a scratchy hood was placed over my head. "Let me go," I managed to slur out, my fists weakly pounding against my assailant. I can't believe this is happening again. At least Ros knows where I am. If she hurries, she'll see him and call the cops, or maybe Niko. Would he save me even after everything that had happened?

A car door opened nearby and my body was shoved inside. I fought to keep my eyes open and my breathing even, although I thought my heart would burst out of my chest. What was going to happen to me? My eyelids were as heavy as my limbs and something inside of me was terrified of letting go and giving into the grogginess overtaking me. My legs and arms were no longer my own. I didn't know what he would do to me, what he wanted, or if I would ever wake up again. I was torn between trying to fight and just giving in.

Flashes of the monsters that visited me night after night played behind my eyes. The hands that grabbed at me while I couldn't fight back and the sense of hopeless-ness that accompanied the dreams. The thought intensi-

fied the nausea that threatened me. Throwing up in the
hood was the last thing that I needed to do.

Eventually, the need to sleep, even if for just a moment,
won.

When I finally woke, it was to icy liquid being poured over
my body, shocking me awake. My head pounded from
whatever they had given me, and the shivers wracking
my body only intensified the pain. The hood was still in
place and I couldn't see anything. A cold, hard surface
was beneath me and my ankles and wrists were tethered
together behind my back, contorting my body into an
uncomfortable position. "How much did you even give
her?" a shrill feminine voice asked. Fucking Arabella. I
should have known that she was involved with whatever
bullshit was happening to me.

A masculine laugh echoed in the space, and I wiggled
my fingers, trying to regain sensation. "I gave her enough
to get her in the car. She should be waking up now. Let
me know when the three of you are done with her and I'll
take care of it. Remember not to kill her. You know who
she belongs to."

My breath felt too hot inside the hood, the scratchy
fabric clinging to my skin. I tried to stay calm, knowing
that if I hyperventilated right now, it wouldn't do any
good. When something heavy hit the center of my stom-

ach, I screamed. That wasn't a punch. Each successive blow caused more pain to lance through my body. Again and again, they hit me with something heavy, and my throat grew hoarse from the screams that they elicited.

And then the taunts started. Whore. Trash. Slut. Between each blow to my body, the three of them chanted things. Words like those could be ignored, but they morphed into something else entirely. "Everyone knew why you showed up here. The poor fallen rich girl living in poverty. From what I heard, daddy never really loved you. That's why you were sold off to the highest bidder." Someone drove their foot into my ribs and I groaned despite not wanting them to know that I was even conscious. I reminded myself that the man from earlier said they couldn't kill me, but when someone kicked me in the head, that thought faded away. Even if they didn't kill me, they were trying their damnedest. Breathing became difficult as the pain overtook me and tears trailed down my face.

Eventually, I closed my eyes, realizing that there was no escape from whatever hellscape I found myself in. I faded in and out of consciousness, allowing the pain and fatigue to pull me under, blanketing me from whatever happened. If they killed me, at least the pain would end. I briefly questioned what would happen if I died. Would the nightmares that haunted me also cease to exist, or would we be trapped together for the rest of eternity? The last thing I heard before the darkness took me was, "Let's see if they still want you after this. No one will," as pain seared through my cheek.

Trey

My eyes were blurry from staring at the screen in front of me, the lines of code fading into one another. Every time I attempted to compile it, there was an error message. Somewhere, there was a typo, and I just needed to find it. My phone had been vibrating beside me for the last hour, but I had ignored it. My mother had called earlier in the day and I didn't want to deal with her again so soon. Whatever mess she was in between her drug dealers and Johns, she could work out. Once I left home, I swore I wouldn't help her out of any more situations or give her money to feed her addictions.

I grabbed my keys and headed out, making sure that I locked the door behind me. If my mother discovered where I was living, she would steal anything she felt was worthwhile to pawn. I learned that when I was a teenager. And if her dealer found out where I lived and she really owed him that much money... I didn't want to think about it.

What I really needed was to grab more energy drinks. Niko and Cam were no doubt asleep by this time of the night, especially with the game tomorrow. We'd been lying low and focusing on school and shit with the Forsaken since the night Peter and Jake disappeared. Someone at the party had snitched and claimed that they saw Cam with one of the guys. The police had shown up on campus and asked us a few questions, but the three of us played it cool. They didn't have any evidence we actually knew anything and were grasping at straws. They needed someone to point a finger at or give a reason for what happened.

If Peter and Jake had been kids from our side of town, no one would have lifted a finger. The authorities only cared if they were rich white kids who had their entire future in front of them. No one was surprised when someone from the wrong side of town disappeared. They were declared runaways if they were under the age of eighteen and if they were older... Their mothers cried themselves to sleep with the help of a bottle. Dozens of missing posters littered the outside of the tienda on the corner and the gas station near the highway, faded and tattered from the weather and time.

Cam was still playing football and stealing time for photography when he had a chance. Niko was... who knew? He was quieter than usual and disappearing or making excuses for reasons he couldn't go out with us at night. I had tried to talk to him, but ever since the fight was broken up, he had been avoiding conversation. As far as what I had been doing, it was just more of the same shit on a different day. Running errands for Vincent in the middle of the night and focusing on my programming while trying to keep my head down.

I tried to start my car, and the engine sputtered for a moment before finally turning over. My phone rang again, and I sighed before looking at the screen. Vincent. "Sup?" I answered, not really in the mood for whatever he wanted.

"Where the fuck are you and why haven't you been answering my calls?" Shit.

"Sorry man, I didn't hear it ring." It was a lie, but completely believable. Music played in the background and a woman squealed. "What do you need?"

"Sam has a package for me, and I want you to bring it over. I can trust you'll keep your mouth shut."

I knew the drill, but I didn't understand why shit like this couldn't wait until morning. "Yeah, I got you."

Sam lived behind the gas station, so the stop was easy enough, but it meant that I would be out longer than I cared for. I pulled into his driveway and he opened my backdoor, depositing a tote bag of whatever. The two of us never spoke and this pick up was no exception. I could have been transporting black market organs and I would be none the wiser. Occasionally curiosity almost got to me, but it was better if I didn't know. The only thing I really cared about was the money I earned doing bullshit like this. It meant that after I graduated, I could get the fuck out of here and drag the guys with me.

When I pulled up at Vincent's house, Angel was outside waiting for me like usual. He gave me a cocky grin when he opened the back door and removed the bag, hoisting it over his shoulder. "Catch you after the game tomorrow night?" he asked, making small talk. I always wondered why Angel hung around this town and how he had ended up in the Forsaken. If you observed him long enough, you quickly came to the conclusion that he was smart. He watched everything going on around him and was careful with what he said.

I bumped knuckles with him through the driver's side window. "We'll have to see. You know how Cam gets if he loses a game."

"I hear that." He turned his back to me and disappeared inside the front door.

On the way back to the gas station to finally pick up a source of caffeine, my phone vibrated again, but I ignored it. Whatever Vincent wanted could wait until morning. Between his neighborhood and mine, there was a long stretch of road that was completely empty late at night and thick clusters of trees grew on both sides of the road. In the early fall, I loved rolling down my windows and turning up my music, letting myself go for just a moment. I could almost taste freedom, even if I still had seven more months until I could leave Clearhaven behind.

On the side of the road, a pale shape lay in the ditch. It wasn't a bag of trash and it wasn't an injured animal. Typically, I would ignore shit like that, especially as late as it was, but something about it stole my breath. I hit the brakes so hard that my car swerved to the right as it skidded to a stop. I opened my door and jogged over to the mass in the ditch. It was a woman and from the shirt she was wearing, I knew exactly who it was. A note was pinned to the front of her shirt, but I didn't look at it yet. Her wrists and ankles were tied together behind her back, and a black sack concealed her identity.

Niko was going to be devastated. I wasn't sure what Cam would feel, but he was going to fly off the handle.

I reached for her wrist and pressed down with my thumb, checking for a pulse. At least she was still alive, even if after this she didn't want to be. I worked quickly, untying the black sack tied around her neck and lifting it. My fingers gingerly traced her pale face and examined the injuries that I could see. Blood was caked around her nose and the side of her head, but her face looked better than I had expected. They had avoided hitting her in the face for the most part. The long red tresses that I'd grown accustomed to seeing were gone; inches of her hair had been hacked off, and I knew exactly who was to blame without ever looking at the note. I undid the knots on the rope and lifted her carefully. Her face tensed in pain even though she wasn't conscious. "New girl, I need you to wake up."

My mind raced through all the possibilities of what I could do with her. The hospital wasn't an option, not in this town, and neither were the cops. Her aunt could go fuck herself. Gently I placed her on the backseat and slid inside the car, knowing that I really only had one option—Niko's house.

I took off looking down at my speedometer occasionally, careful to keep it under the speed limit. The last thing that I needed was for the sheriff to pull me over at this time of the night with Ivy in the condition she was in. Ivy whimpered softly, the pain and the motion of the vehicle rousing her slightly from whatever state she was in.

Some foreign emotion clung to me as I glanced in the rearview mirror at the girl laying there and mingled with the anger I felt. It had been years since I had been afraid. I wanted to chalk it all up to fatigue, but that wasn't accurate. If Cam wanted to punish her, I'd allow it, but no one else was supposed to touch her.

I skidded to a stop in front of Niko's house and got her out, cradling her against my chest while I jogged down the sidewalk toward the front door. In my arms, she felt small and fragile, vulnerable and breakable. So unlike the hellcat that I knew she really was inside. No one else could ever put up with the bullshit she had lived through. I shifted her weight and tried the knob, which surprisingly wasn't locked. "Niko!" I called out, not caring if his father was home. Even if he was, he would be too high to be of any help.

Niko and Cam appeared from the kitchen, with Ros and Rhyker directly behind them. Niko's hair was disheveled like he had been running his hands through it and Ros' eyes were red. "Where the fuck have you been? Why haven't you answered the phone, asshole?" Cam gritted out. Every part of him was tense when he saw who I was holding in my arms.

"Shit," Niko muttered under his breath as he took Ivy from me. She quietly groaned and Ros started crying again, hiding in the crook of Rhyker's shoulder.

"Guys, I didn't know you had been trying to call me. I thought it was my mom. She's been calling again," I mumbled, hoping to defuse the tension that rolled off Cam in waves. "What's going on?"

Ros rubbed her hands across her cheeks. "We went to the diner and Arabella showed up. Ivy walked outside while I was paying, and by the time I was done, she was gone. I called Niko to see if he had heard from her or knew anything. We drove around for hours trying to find her. The cops won't do anything unless she's missing for twenty-four hours. You remember what happened when my uncle was missing..."

She trailed off while she watched Niko. He touched Ivy's hair, what was left of it, clenching his jaw before he pulled the note from the front of her shirt. "They cut off her hair in retribution. The bitch is dead."

"It was an eye for an eye." I'd heard Niko pissed before, but this was different. I looked at him and shook my head. "If she was anyone else, I'd agree. We need to be smart about our next steps. Right now, we need to focus on Ivy. We need to undress her and see how bad she really is. I didn't take her to the hospital because..."

Ros' eyes went wide. "You can't," she hissed at me. "The last thing she needs is to get any more attention from anyone within the Order. She already has Wells sending her emails."

I pushed my glasses to the top of my head and leaned back against the wall. "I know that."

Rhyker pulled Ros to his chest and met my eyes. "Call Angel. He was a medic in the Army before all of this bullshit. Tell him I told you to call and not to tell Vincent. He owes me a favor."

I wanted to ask why, but instead dialed the number. "Didn't expect to hear from you again tonight."

"Yeah, me neither. Listen." I relayed the message from Rhyker and asked him to meet us at Niko's house. He swore under his breath but told me he would see me in fifteen.

The moments while we waited were some of the longest in my life. When I heard his motorcycle pull up outside, I breathed a sigh of relief. She needed more than a simple once-over from a gang member, but it was better than nothing. I regretted the fact that none of us had majored in something dealing with health care. With a little more knowledge, we wouldn't have had to bring someone else into this shit.

Angel strolled through the door and paled when he saw the girl Niko had laid on the couch. "What the fuck is going on, you guys?" he muttered before sitting on the edge of the sofa.

Cam started toward him, but Niko pushed a hand into the center of his chest, holding him back. "He has to examine her, Cam," he whispered. Angel lifted the shirt covering her torso and Cam tried to move again, but Niko caught him around the shoulders with both arms and blocked his vision. "He has to."

Ivy groaned beneath Angel's touch and her eyelids fluttered as he pressed on her ribs and stomach. Black and red streaks marred her skin. Whatever had happened to her, this wasn't just punches and kicks. Rope burns adorned her wrists. His fingers stopped at her neck and he tilted his head to the side as he examined something. He pulled out a small penlight and lifted her eyelid, staring at her pupils. "I wish she was awake. She definitely has a concussion and I think they drugged her. I'm going to stitch up her cheek the best that I can but... Just keep an eye on her. I'll be back in the morning. She might be awake by then."

"What do we need to do until then?" Rosalyn asked.

Angel pressed his lips into a thin line as he shoved the penlight into his pants. "Nothing. Now you wait and keep her comfortable. Give her something for the pain." He looked between Cam, Niko, Rhyker, and me. "I'm sure between the four of you, someone has something. And, Rhyker, you need to take Ros home before her grandfather has a fit. My debt to you is paid after tonight."

Rhyker extended his hand, and the two of them shook, unspoken communication occurring between them.

Angel went outside and pulled a small bag from his saddlebag. He kneeled beside the couch, and I watched in amazement at how quickly he worked stitching her cheek. "It's probably going to scar," he muttered to himself as he worked. "I'm sorry, baby girl."

He shoved the dental floss back into his bag and stood, passing me the needle. "Throw that shit away. I'm headed out, but try to keep it clean. I'll come by to check on it again tomorrow."

After he finally left, Ros pressed a quick kiss to Ivy's forehead and Rhyker took her home. "Should we try to clean her up?" I asked.

Niko shook his head and bit the inside of his cheek. "Let's just get her comfortable. When she wakes up, we'll do it."

Cam lifted Ivy from the couch and headed toward the bedroom that he and Niko shared. The three of us worked on removing her shoes and the jeans she was wearing before adjusting her on a pillow in the center of the bed. Cam lay on one side and Niko on the other while I made a pallet on the floor.

"They can't be allowed to get away with this," Cam muttered. He was on his side, propped up on his elbow and staring down at the girl I'd found on the side of the road while Niko watched them both carefully.

Niko reached out and brushed the hair from Cam's eyes before resting his hand next to Ivy. "We will, but first, let's worry about tomorrow."

Ivy

Every part of my body ached. Behind my eyes, both arms, my wrists, my cheeks. It even hurt to breathe. It felt like my head was heavy and full of water I couldn't clear. My eyes were glued shut, and I struggled to open them. When I finally did, I regretted it. The light streaming into the room was blinding and made me want to vomit. My throat was dry as I swallowed down the bile that tried to escape.

I tried to figure out where I was, but the bedding surrounding me was unfamiliar. Then it dawned on me. The scent of the ocean and sandalwood tinged with musk didn't reassure me as it might have a few weeks ago. Sure, Arabella was behind the attack, but I was quickly learning to trust no one. I just needed to figure out how to get up so I could walk home and lay in my own bed.

And then there was the vague scent of rotten seafood that someone had tried to mask with air fresheners. No amount of odor eliminator could get rid of that smell. It just added to the nausea. I really hadn't thought through my plan for revenge and I regretted it.

The pain was blinding as I tried to sit up. Every breath was a struggle from the pain in my sides. Still, I fought,

my fingers digging into the mattress as I inched my way
into an upright position. The world spun around me and
I waited for it to stop, closing my eyes for a moment.

"Look who's finally awake," a deep voice stated, and I
looked up. Trey leaned against the doorframe, shirtless in
low-slung basketball shorts. Ink that was typically hidden
by his shirt covered his ribs and chest. "How are you
feeling, new girl?"

"It hurts," was all I managed to get out. Even talking
hurt.

He closed the gap between us and sat on the edge of
the bed. His finger traced the marks on my wrist and I
winced. "I bet. Let's get you some water for your throat
and I'll get you something to help you feel better. I'll be
right back."

I closed my eyes again, resting my head against the
headboard behind me. Voices drifted inside from the
hallway, and I snorted when I overheard what they were
saying. "Quit spraying that shit. It isn't helping!"

"Yeah, well, maybe you need to clean your gear or you
left food somewhere weird again. Open the windows up
because I can't live like this."

"Do you think someone spilled shit on the carpet?"

"After we check on Ivy, we'll see how much it costs to
rent a machine because this is fucked."

I laughed slightly and instantly regretted it. Apparently,
laughing also made me hurt. They got everything they
deserved, but unfortunately, I was also going to be punished by the smell—at least until I could figure out how to
get the fuck out of there.

Niko popped his head into the room and frowned when he saw me sitting up. In his hands, he had a bottle of water and some pills. He approached the bed carefully, like I was a wounded animal. "How are you feeling?"

It was only the second time someone had asked me, but I held out my hand, determined to do things on my own. He uncapped the bottle and handed it to me. The water made my throat feel a little better. Swallowing the pills was another story. Each one felt like a shard of glass, but I didn't dare to say that out loud. I also didn't bother asking what he gave me. After what had happened to me since I ended up in Clearhaven, maybe death would be a mercy.

The irony wasn't lost on me that the boys who torment-ed me were now my caretakers as Cam entered the room. His shoulders were tense and his jaw was clenched as he looked me over. A mixture of anger and sadness was plas-tered on his face. I wanted to hide beneath the blankets from the world and the guys who were all treating me as if they were actually concerned. I didn't know how they were connected to my latest attack, but I knew they were. All roads led back to them.

I didn't want to feel anything for any of them, especially not Cam. My body was already broken and my heart, no matter how bruised, was all I had left.

Trey finally returned holding a pile of clothes. "I think we should get you cleaned up, new girl. You've been in those clothes since Friday morning. "

I wanted to ask them how long I had been out, but chose to keep my mouth shut. Whatever Niko had given me was slowly taking effect, helping to at least dull the pain. Slowly, I scooted to the edge of the bed. Niko offered me his hand, but I ignored it, determined to do everything by myself. He ignored me, pulling the blankets back and moving them out of the way while Cam ran a hand through his hair. "This is fucking ridiculous," he muttered before scooping me into his arms.

Even being picked up hurt, despite whatever drugs were coursing through my system. He held me against his body like I was something precious and not something he was determined to destroy. Tears pricked at the back of my eyes again, a feeling that I was becoming all too familiar with. I didn't get Camden Barrett. He was hot and cold, busy telling me he would break me and then treating me like porcelain. He walked down the hallway and deposited me on the toilet while he turned on the water. I stared at the mirror in front of me for a moment, not recognizing the woman who looked back. The red mass of waves that had once hung to my waist were gone. Three-inch curls that were haphazardly cut were left in their place. Dried blood clung to the side of my head and under my nose. My face was a little swollen, but it wasn't as bad as I expected.

My body was another story, and I looked down at the bathroom tile to avoid seeing anything else.

Niko appeared a moment later, holding a pair of basketball shorts and a cotton shirt, but Cam scowled at him. "She's not wearing that. Go get some of my clothes." Niko opened his mouth to argue but Cam simply said, "Don't test me today."

Niko disappeared as Camden adjusted the temperature and then turned to me, wordlessly reaching for the hem of my shirt. I closed my eyes and pretended I was somewhere else as he helped me remove my clothes and his eyes took in the bruises that marked my torso. Gently, he took my chin and lifted it. It was a contrast to how he usually treated me. "The people responsible for this will pay, little ghost. I promise you. No one is allowed to break you but me, and I would never hurt you like this."

Cam stalked out of the bathroom, leaving me sitting there by myself. A moment later, Niko reappeared holding a different set of clothing. I didn't know why it mattered what I wore. As soon as I could, I would fall back asleep. Being awake was exhausting and at least I could hide from reality in my dreams, no matter how shitty they were. Taking in a deep breath, I tried to stand, but my knees buckled beneath me from a sharp stab of pain. Warm hands caught me and held me, holding me up. "Come on. Let's get you into the shower and then back into bed."

As much as I didn't want Niko worming his way into my heart, when he said things like that, I could feel where he had worked his way through the cracks. He knew me and what I wanted. He stripped down quickly, and I tried to look away. The three men who were looking after me while I was broken looked like they were crafted by Renaissance sculptors. Their muscles were hard lines carved into their flesh and then adorned by tattoos. Anyone else would be happy to be surrounded by them, but I just wanted to be left alone.

Maybe Cam was right. I was a ghost, clinging to the shadows and unnoticed by most. Forgotten by nearly everyone.

Niko helped me into the shower and held me up from behind. The warm spray of water hit my skin, and I hissed from the sting. Slowly, he soaped up a cloth and rubbed it over my body, gently washing every part of me. Afterward, while I leaned on the wall, he shampooed my hair. Well, what was left of it. His fingers massaged my scalp and let myself enjoy his touch. He turned off the water and toweled me off before dressing me in the clothes he had brought in before turning away.

Instead of picking me up like Cam had, Niko waited patiently for me to stand and walk back to his room. Every step was torture, and I knew my original goal of trying to go home on my own was unattainable. Out of the corner of my eye, I saw the girl from the beach watching me. She said nothing and ducked back around the corner.

By the time I was tucked back into bed, my eyes were heavy again and I was ready to sleep. Any questions that they had could wait.

By Wednesday, I was ready to go back home, or at least to Regina's house. The headache that had plagued me since I woke up was long gone, but the smell in the house had intensified. Stick-on air fresheners were scattered across the house, but it didn't help. It just smelled like flowers mixed with dead fish. Who would have known that my trying to get back at them would backfire? Rotting shrimp permeated every surface of the house, but no one had figured out the source–which was every vent I had found. I had missed every class this week and Rosalyn sent me assignments when she could, but I was determined that by Friday I would be back on campus, bruises and all.

From the whisperings I had heard from the guys late at night, they were planning on paying back Arabella and her friends. It gave me a smug sense of joy to know that they wouldn't go unpunished for what happened to me, but was it enough? Could I keep them from targeting me again? The line she had said about my father selling me off to the highest bidder played in my head on repeat and I pondered if there was any truth to it.

I spent the daytime catching up on what I had missed earlier. Niko or Trey brought me food and tried to convince me to eat. I nibbled at whatever they offered, but my appetite was gone. I was confused about why they were taking care of me when three weeks ago, Cam had made it clear he wanted to tear me down.

Despite my absence, my aunt hadn't written to me, which made me feel sick.

Niko helped me to wrap my ribs, and every night they made a small fire in the backyard. He pulled me into his lap and gave me bottles of beer to take with my pills. My pain was present but dulled in those moments. I listened as they talked about sports or things with the Forsaken while Niko slowly stroked my back.

Every night I lay wedged between Niko's and Cam's bodies, and one of their hands laid on my hip possessively. Their presence reassured me and terrified me at the same time. No one had mentioned the terrible haircut I had that I knew I needed to fix, or the bruises that were slowly turning greener.

Still, I knew I couldn't get comfortable with them. Even though it seemed like things were changing, there was a false sense of security clinging to them.

Thursday morning, when Trey and Cam were both absent, Niko sat on the edge of the bed to check on me. He handed me the pills he usually did and a fresh bottle of water. "What are your plans for the day?"

"I'm going home today after the three of you leave for school." My voice sounded surer than it had for a while. I couldn't cling to them. Once I was feeling better, things would go back to how they had been, no matter what I wanted. Despite the pain, the past several days had been something out of a fantasy novel. Three guys who waited on you hand and foot and cared about how you were feeling? It wasn't reality, especially given the three guys. I'd begun questioning if the kick to the head I received last Friday night had given me mild brain damage.

He swallowed, and I watched his Adam's apple bob. "Are you going to push me away again?" I shrugged at him and stayed silent. "You need allies and I could be that. I could convince Cam to lay off, at least until you feel better."

"We'll see." That was all I could offer him. He pulled my clothes from his dresser, placing them in a neat pile. They had been washed and folded. My heart was shattering into a million pieces, but I couldn't show him. I couldn't let anyone know. A small part of me wanted to stay forever, but it would never last. Cam had made it obvious that no matter what, he would break me eventually. What he didn't realize was I was already broken and now I didn't know if I could put myself back together again.

Niko pulled a small baggy of pills from his pocket and laid them beside it. "Remember, these are only to help you sleep."

I just nodded at him, letting him blindly believe that was what would happen. A small part of me speculated that if I took them all at once, I might fall asleep and never wake up again.

Ivy

When I arrived at Regina's house, my car was sitting out front next to the curb and hers was gone, hopefully to work. My eyes widened when I saw the door was fixed and there was a bow on it. After sending Ros a quick text message thanking her for my car and letting her know I was back home, I hid the baggy of pills inside a hole in the underside of my mattress. There they were out of sight. I tried to tell myself that I would only take them when I was going to sleep and that I could live with the pain. My ribs still ached and my bruises were still tender, but it was fine. More and more, I was wondering if I should pack my things in the car and try to start over somewhere else.

I messaged Frankie to let her know I would be at work later that afternoon. Rhyker had spoken to her for me when I was staying with the guys. She tried to convince me to take more time off to recover and that my pay-checks would be fine, but I couldn't. I needed out of my head and away from the house. Staying busy would keep me from thinking too much and reliving everything. If I could just stay busy...

I found a pair of scissors in the kitchen and stepped into the bathroom, examining what was left of my hair. Carefully, I trimmed some pieces to even them out. No one had said anything about it yet, and I was grateful. I knew it was just hair and that it would grow back, but the angry red wound on my cheek was another story. I could hope that it wouldn't scar, but the stitches told another story. If Arabella thought that cutting my hair off while I was tied up would break me, she was wrong. Nothing she did could be as bad as what the guys had done or Caleb pushing me away. I wiped away the hair that was left laying on the sink and started the shower to get ready for work.

After I dressed in a pair of jeans and a shirt, I applied eyeliner and mascara before deciding to style my hair. My aunt had a bottle of gel on the shelf and I squirted some in my palm, determined to make the most of the situation. I ran my hands through my hair, dispersing the product evenly before scrunching it some. Between the new haircut and the eyeliner, I looked like I belonged in a '90s punk band. I could live with that.

The pills hidden under my bed called my name and impulsively I popped one into my mouth before I left. If I was stuck in hell, I might as well make it more tolerable.

Friday morning, I was on campus early. Caleb had sent me three texts asking me to talk while I was at work last night. I finally caved and agreed to meet him before classes to get it over with. As much as I didn't want to admit it to myself, I missed him, even though he had been ignoring me.

Niko, Cam, and Trey were waiting beside the building where my first class was held and I rolled my eyes at them as I tried to rush past. Caleb was supposed to meet me inside in five minutes, and I didn't have time to deal with whatever they wanted. Sure, they had taken care of me, but they were ultimately the reason I was incapacitated in the first place. As I opened the door, someone's arm banded around my torso and pulled me back against a hard chest. "Where do you think you're going without even saying hello?" Niko murmured against my neck before biting a spot below my ear. I elbowed him, but he simply chuckled. "I really like your hair like this."

I huffed out a breath and turned to face him. "Since when do you want me to say hello?"

He raised an eyebrow up at me. "It's obvious that we were waiting for you." He held up a small paper bag. "I brought you breakfast."

I stared at him for a moment. "Why would you do that?"

He lifted a shoulder in response. Cam watched the situation with curiosity and ran his thumb over his bottom lip, lost in thought. "Little ghost, you left without saying goodbye. Why are you here so early?"

I grabbed the bag from Niko before shifting away. I wasn't sure if I should trust them not to poison me, but the food smelled good and they hadn't killed me. Yet. "If you must know, I'm meeting Caleb in a few minutes."

The muscle along his jaw ticked, and he stalked closer, touching my uninjured cheek. "The fuck you are. After last weekend, everything you do is our business. Everything."

I glared at him and tried removing his hand, but it didn't budge. "Why shouldn't I meet him, Cam? Give me a good reason and I'll think about it."

"I could give you a million, but I'll just tell you one. You shouldn't trust Caleb. His grandfather and your father are friends. In fact, his grandfather and Abraham Wells are also good friends. Don't you find it suspicious that Caleb didn't try to contact you the entire time that you were staying with us, but now suddenly he wants to talk?"

My heart fell, and I clutched the paper bag tighter. Any hope that I had managed to gain regarding Caleb died a little with every word Cam spoke. "Are you trying to insinuate something?" I asked quietly.

Footsteps sounded behind me and Cam leaned forward, brushing his lips against mine in an almost kiss. "You're a smart girl. I'm sure you can put the puzzle pieces together." He drifted away and looked over my shoulder. "You're a slow learner, Vance. So is your cousin."

When I turned my head toward him, his eyes widened for a moment, but he was quick to wipe the shock off his face. Instead, he focused on Cam and smiled. "Well, good morning to you, too. Here I was thinking that we were making friends after our run-in at the party where you shoved your fingers in my mouth. Guess I misjudged the situation." He put his hand on the small of my back and winked. "The same way you misjudged the fact that I would only get to taste Ivy one time."

My cheeks heated as I stood there caught between the four of them. I cleared my throat and opened the door. "If you want to talk, let's talk."

I headed inside to a small sitting area designed for students to study in between classes and pulled out an orange chair on the far side. Caleb followed me inside a moment later. He pulled a chair up next to me and reached for my hand. I pulled it away and crossed my arms over my chest. "What did you need to say since it had to be in person?"

"First, I want to know what in the fuck happened, Ivy? I saw you last week and you wouldn't talk to me. Your cheek..."

"Is the least of my problems right now."

He chewed on his lip for a moment. "I'm sorry for pushing you away. I thought it would be better. My grandfather and his friends... they're..." He struggled to find the words to say, and I grew more aggravated with the conversation by the moment. "I think you need to leave Clearhaven. Pack your bags, change your number, and never look back. I pulled some money out of my trust fund. The two of us can go together. We'll ditch my car at the state line and buy something with cash. Hell, we can get new identities even. I overheard–"

I cut him off by standing up. "I can't just run away with you. This is crazy! We barely know each other. When were you going to tell me your grandfather was friends with the dean and my father?" He paled a bit and stood up, trying to reach for me, but I stumbled back. "How do I know I can trust you? What else have you decided to hide from me, Caleb?"

"Then just take the money I withdrew and run, princess. I'll make sure that enough time has passed and then I'll find you."

I shook my head in disbelief. "No. I'm not taking your money. When I decide to run, it will be on my terms, and I'll make sure that no one from Clearhaven will ever find me. First, you don't talk to me for nearly three weeks and then you try to convince me to run away. What's really going on?"

He worried his lip between his teeth again, the skin raw. "I can't tell you."

His words tasted bitter, and I turned my back. "Let me know when you can," I shouted over my shoulder.

On the outside I was strong, but inside, everything hurt. I had hoped that he would clarify things for me, but he was quick to tell me he couldn't. The same way that I couldn't just take his money. In a different lifetime, maybe we could have run away together and had a happily ever after. I could have pretended to be completely oblivious to his current connections.

But this wasn't a fairy tale, and everyone had secrets, including me. I bolted inside the bathroom to splash water on my cheeks and take something that would dull my feelings again.

Cam

I sat in the passenger seat of Niko's car on Saturday evening waiting for Arabella and her friends to come out of the house. Thankfully, this week was a bye week. I had too much shit to do, and even though I loved the game, I needed a moment to breathe. I also had something that I needed to take care of. Ivy was safely tucked away at Frankie's, out of harm's reach, and Rosalyn was under direct orders not to allow her to come to the Forsaken party that was happening tonight. Rhyker knew what we were doing and agreed, stating that Ivy had already been through enough shit.

Arabella, Violet, and whatever the third girl's name finally sauntered out of Luthor's beach home fifteen minutes after she said she would. Punctuality wasn't her strong suit, and she didn't even try to make an excuse, unlike Ivy. The three of them were dressed in skirts that barely covered their asses and tank tops that plunged to their waist. It was perfect for what I had planned. She looked at the seats in the car and grinned at me. "There are three of us and only—"

I gave her my best fake smile and pulled her into my lap, tucking a strand of hair behind her ear. She had gone to the hairdresser shortly after her little incident in the parking lot at the gym and now her hair was neatly trimmed into a chin-length bob. Her actions against Ivy were completely unnecessary. She didn't even the score, but women rarely did. Which is why I invited her and her friends out tonight. I had told her to stay away, and that Ivy was off limits, but Arabella refused to listen. "That's because I wanted to keep you close to me tonight," I whispered in her ear.

She was an idiot for trusting me after everything that I had said to her. All three of them were. All it had taken for them to agree to come with us was a small phone call stating that we missed her and the Forsaken were throwing a party. She squealed with joy and told me she knew we would get tired of Ivy at some point. I laughed to myself about that. I wasn't done with Ivy yet. Not by a long shot.

Niko pulled a joint out from the glove box and lit it up, taking a long drag. "Aren't you going to share with us?" Arabella asked in her nasal voice. That was the thing about Arabella and other girls like her. She rarely went off script. I knew that as soon as Niko lit up, she would demand to share.

I wondered what her grandfather's reaction would be if he knew she followed the three of us around like a lost puppy, begging for dick. In seven months' time, she would graduate and leave all of this behind. We were simply something to do while she bided her time and, later on, have stories to tell her friends at the country club. She probably already had a loveless engagement on the horizon brokered by elderly men to strengthen "family ties." Whatever that meant. When she became a lonely housewife whose husband was cheating on her with his secretary, we would be the ones she fantasized about at night as she got off.

I brushed my fingers along the exposed skin of her arms. "Don't worry, baby. I have something for you and your girls and once we get to the party, there will be more where that came from." I pulled the new strain of tea we were supposed to distribute from my pocket. The new strain hit harder and hadn't been tested by the three of us yet, but I had seen what happened when one of Vincent's girls took it. It was perfect for what I wanted.

She held out her hand, but I clicked my tongue. "Open up." And like the good little slut she was, she complied, allowing me to place the pill inside her mouth. I brushed my thumb along her lower lip and watched her eyes dilate before giving the other two to Trey. He smiled at the girls who were sitting on either side of him, leaning against him. If they thought they were safe with him, they were wrong.

By the time we pulled up in front of Vincent's, their pupils were blown and they swayed on their feet once they got out of the car. Arabella wrapped her arms around my waist to hold herself up and I allowed it, considering it a necessary evil. We strolled up the sidewalk with her clinging to me, smelling my shirt. I rubbed a circle on the exposed skin of her back to reassure her. "Once we're inside, I'll get you a drink and drop you off in the game room. You should make some new friends while you're here, baby. I've got something to take care of, but I'll be back as soon as I can."

She stuck out her bottom lip and pouted. "But I thought we were going to hang out."

I gave her another fake smile and poked her bottom lip. "Don't worry. You're going to have a great time."

The music from inside was deafening, and people were everywhere. The lights inside were dim, but in the corner, I saw several of the guys look Arabella over from head to toe. They were another group of people that would never go off script. The predictability was boring but perfect. I pushed into the kitchen and grabbed a red plastic cup. "What would you like to drink?"

She nuzzled into my chest again, rubbing her body against me. "Something with fruit." Her voice was husky, and I tried not to laugh at her. This was her version of being seductive, and it was pathetic.

I poured some pineapple juice, coconut rum, and melon liqueur into the cup and stirred it. "Try this and see what you think."

She tipped the cup back and swallowed. And swallowed. And swallowed some more. I raised my eyebrows when she handed it back to me. "I need another." As I fixed her a second drink, Trey and Niko came into the room with Violet and... whatever her name was in tow. "Guys, you've got to try this drink," she told her friends as she rubbed my chest.

I gave them a tight smile. I wasn't supposed to be bartender tonight, and my patience was already wearing thin with Arabella touching me so much. Niko's eyes crinkled at the corner as he watched me. He knew how much I hated her and he was amused by the whole thing. I handed them each a drink. Arabella fisted the front of my shirt and brought me down closer to her mouth. "You promised there would be more of the pills when we got here, Cam."

That was off-script for the evening, but I was prepared for it all the same. "Are you sure you need another one? You seem like you're already feeling pretty good."

She licked her lips and batted her eyelashes. "Please?"

I handed her the three remaining pills from my pocket and they each took one. "Alright ladies, time to get you settled in while we talk about something important." I placed my arm around Arabella's shoulder and led her down a set of stairs into a finished basement. Along the walls, there were couches and loveseats where people were making out. The lights had been replaced with colored bulbs, casting the space in a red light. Speakers played the music from upstairs. A few people were playing darts on the far side of the room and a game of pool was happening in the middle.

Angel and Rhyker watched me from the bar that was set up along the left side, and I lifted my hand to point to them. "If the three of you need any more drinks, just ask them and they'll take care of you tonight," I said loud enough for Arabella to hear me over the bass. "Do you like pool?" She nodded her head at me as she took everything in, and I led her toward the table. Vincent walked toward us with Justice a step behind him.

"Boys, who have you brought with you tonight? You rarely introduce us to your friends."

I grinned at him and gave him a fist bump. "Hey man. This is Arabella, Violet, and..."

"Emmaline," Trey supplied as he stared at me.

"Yeah, Emmaline." I gave the brunette a cheeky grin. "I promised to show the three of them a good time tonight and maybe the guys could help me."

Vincent narrowed his eyes for a moment at me, but then smirked. "Yeah, I bet we can." His fingers traced along Arabella's chest and her lips parted at his touch.

I squeezed her fingers and leaned in close. "Give me fifteen minutes and I'll be back to check on you."

Her eyes were fixated on Vincent as he kissed her knuckles and I was long forgotten. I guess bagging him would be the ultimate fuck you to her family. The five of them gathered around the pool table and I snuck outside to give time for my plan to work.

Niko pulled out another joint and lit it, letting his body rest against the side of the house. "Are you sure about this?"

Trey rubbed his eyes. "She gets what she deserves, Niko. Don't forget about what she did to Ivy. Besides, she's getting exactly what she wanted, just not with us."

When we were done smoking, we snuck back inside and took our time heading back to the basement. It was a shame that I had to take the pictures I needed with a phone and not my camera. When we finally found our way back to the girls inside, even I was surprised. I expected to get a few photos of her with her skirt hiked up, but the scene in front of me exceeded my wildest expectations.

Violet was lying on top of the pool table with her skirt around her waist and her tits hanging out. Arabella was bent over with her face between Violet's thighs and Vincent plowing into her from behind. His palm held her down against the green felt. In the corner, Emmaline was riding Justice like her life depended on it. I opened the camera on the phone in my hand and snapped a few quick photos.

The scene almost would have been hot if the three of them weren't such cunts. I sent the photos to Trey so he could do his thing with them and laughed at the entire situation. All of their parents would receive an email shortly, and so would Fletcher Vance, Arabella's grandfather. I almost wished that I could see the look on his face when he realized Vincent had railed his granddaughter.

We were also posting it on social media for the rest of the campus to see. I wasn't allowed to kill Arabella, which was exactly what she deserved, but no one said that I couldn't make her life hell.

Niko

Later that night, after most of the partygoers had left, I grabbed one last drink before heading to the deck. Vincent was sitting outside by himself, and I needed a chance to talk to him without the guys around. They meant well, but they would stop me from what I was planning. Cam and Trey had headed home earlier in the night. They were sending out photos of Arabella, Violet, and Emmaline for everyone to see. I had argued that they deserved to be killed no matter what the consequences were, but Cam reminded me I needed to have patience. This was just a warning. No one in this town was un-touchable, even if they thought they were.

Arabella and the others were... somewhere. Holed up in one of the rooms or on a couch. Their hangovers tomorrow would be the kind that would make them wish they were dead, especially when they found out what we had done.

Vincent lit a cigarette in the darkness and gave me a long look as I approached him. "The girls that you brought with you tonight are wild as hell. I like them."

I wasn't sure how to respond. He was going to lose his shit when he found out that Arabella was Fletcher's granddaughter. There were just some things he didn't like messing with. "Yeah, they are something else." I shoved my hands in my pockets and rocked back on my heels. "I need a favor, and I was hoping that maybe you could help me out."

He studied the cherry on the end of the cigarette for a moment. "What kind of favor do you need, Niko?"

The conversation was going better than I anticipated but I was weary. Favors came with a price tag. "I need to make some quick cash. The rent's behind and it's due next week. I've tried everything, but the next race isn't for a few weeks and..."

He gave me a smug look. "That's all? I expected something worse. I know exactly what you can do. There's a party tomorrow night at Gervais Fouquet's house and I think that they'd appreciate you. It would add to the entertainment."

I took a large sip of my drink and nodded to him in acknowledgment. "What's the pay?"

"A thousand cash. Just treat them right and do what they ask. Take some tea before you head over there. They'll like that. A good-looking guy like you shouldn't have any problems making money at a party."

I felt sick to my stomach but chugged the drink in my hand and crushed the cup. "Thanks, man. I really appreciate it."

I lay in bed that night and felt like I was drowning. Cam snored softly beside me and I watched him while I struggled to breathe, wondering how in the hell I was going to keep what I was doing a secret. Whatever may have happened between us in the future vanished into thin air. If he or Ivy found out, neither of them would want me.

Gervais was a part of the Order, just like every other rich person in this town. Just like every person who had power. I knew exactly what I was walking into tomorrow night, but I had to. I needed to make sure that Katya and Sergei stayed in school and that the three of us stayed together, no matter what. They were all I had.

The next night, I parked in front of the brick mansion and popped some tea, just like Vincent suggested. I'd worn a pair of dark-wash denim jeans and a black button-up shirt, not knowing the dress code for an event like this. What did you wear when you were going to suck a rich dude's dick?

Even though I'd considered it with Cam, I didn't have any experience, and the entire situation put me on edge. After I felt my muscles relax, I knocked on the front door. Gervais answered the door and he smiled at me. "Oh, you're the young man that Vincent texted me about. Come in and get a drink. Do you like wine?" His words were colored by his accent, making me feel more at ease even as he let his eyes linger longer than might be polite.

The truth was I hated wine. It was too bitter and dry for my tastes and gave me a terrible hangover, but I still politely responded, "I'd love a glass."

He gestured for me to come in and once I was inside, his hand landed on my back, urging me to continue forward. He made small talk about just relaxing tonight and how it was a small party, but I was too busy looking around to pay any attention. The difference between how I lived, and he did was staggering. Crystal chandeliers hung from the ceilings and the marble floor was so clean, light reflected off of it. Large oil paintings hung on the walls and piano music floated through the air.

The apprehension that I had felt when I arrived faded away as I looked at the other occupants of the room. The party wasn't what I had expected it to be. Everyone was glassy-eyed and rosy-cheeked from the alcohol, but it wasn't the orgy I had expected. Everyone was still clothed. A few women sat around the room talking to the men beside them, laughing.

Gervais brought me a glass of scarlet-colored liquid and I took a sip, allowing the bitter fruitiness to coat my tongue. "Thank you."

He gave me a small smile. "You're welcome. I have a few friends that would love to meet you."

I drank the wine as we sauntered around the room making small talk with all of his guests. Every time that my drink was half empty, someone would refill it casually. My body and head felt light, almost like a balloon that would float away. After a while, I put my glass down, knowing that I had more than enough to drink. Everything was too hot, and I unfastened the top button of my shirt, hoping that it would cool me some. I couldn't quite hold on to the conversation that the men surrounding me were having about the stock market. I heard the words, but they seemed almost distant.

I mumbled an excuse about needing to find the restroom, and someone offered to help me find it.

That was the last thing that I actually remembered with complete clarity about that night. Everything went dark afterward. Later, I would recall that my legs and arms wouldn't work. It was like they didn't belong to me. Tea had never affected me that way, and neither did alcohol. I remember in the middle of the night laying on my stomach, my clothes stripped away. Someone whispered in my ear something about being a wolf in sheep's clothing. The voice was so familiar, but I couldn't place it and didn't know if my mind was playing tricks on me. The only other thing that I remembered was blinding pain as someone shoved themselves inside of me. What I didn't know was how many of them there were or if there were photos taken of me like that. Vincent hadn't warned me they would drug me.

The next morning, I woke up feeling sore. My head felt like I had been hit by a freight train, and so did my ass. I ignored the droplets of blood on the sheet as I dressed quickly, ready to get the hell away from Gervais. On the bedside table were five one hundred-dollar bills and a note.

Niko,

I had a great time last night. I hope to see you around.

Gervais

I shoved the money into my pocket and dialed Vincent. When he answered, I didn't let him speak. "I thought you said it was a thousand."

"Calm down and be thankful you got the job. It was a thousand, but I had to take my cut. You know I get fifty percent, whether it's drugs or ass."

I hung up and peeled away, driving aimlessly. Of course Vincent got a cut. Nothing that he did was for free. I beat on my steering wheel and allowed tears of frustration to stream down my face. I had been so close to having a solution to my problems. Instead, I just had one more secret to keep.

Ivy

None of the guys had spoken to me since our run-in on Friday morning. Well, except Caleb. He texted me once a day to ask me if I had considered his offer. I didn't bother responding to him because the answer was still the same. I couldn't run away with someone I didn't really know or trust. Angel stopped by to remove my stitches at Frankie's shop. He awkwardly handed me a bottle of vitamin e oil and told me to apply it to the scar. It supposedly helped it heal.

I was curious what his story was and how he had gotten tangled up in the Forsaken. He was quiet and intense but looked like the god Thor come to life with his long blond hair and bright blue eyes. When he stared at you, it was like he was prying pieces of your very soul from you.

I saw Rosalyn flirt with him as he was leaving, but decided not to question her about it. She'd already said that Rhyker and her weren't a thing, even if he hadn't gotten the message yet. If she wanted to tell me something, she would.

The project for Civ was due the next Friday and Caleb already had my half. The project was worth thirty percent of my grade and my scholarship depended on my doing well. He said that he would send me the finished paper in my email if I wouldn't meet him. Even if I refused to run, he would still submit the assignment for us.

Monday night I popped two of the tablets that were left in the bag after my shower, hoping that by doubling the dose I would actually sleep and praying that my nightmares would stay away. They were bad enough over the summer, but after the attacks... somehow things had gotten worse. It was no longer faceless men that were vaguely familiar. They had morphed into something else entirely. Men who held me down while I struggled against them and people kicking me while they taunted me were added. Every spiteful thing that had been said was uttered back by the phantoms.

I was also beginning to wonder if the recurrent dreams–the ones where I watched the girl being used by the older men–had any basis in reality. Some parts seemed so familiar, but if something had happened to me, wouldn't I remember it?

The air in the house was stifling, so I lifted the window to let in the fall breeze hoping that the mosquitoes would stay outside where they belonged. My aunt was gone again. When she saw the scar on my face, she shook her head and told me that no one would want me now. It was a slap in the face, a mirror to what Arabella had said to me before she cut me. Maybe they were right. The only four guys who ever had any interest in me either wanted to punish me, keep secrets from me, or lie to me. Maybe I was defective even before my face was scarred.

I shrugged off the pants I was wearing and changed into one of Niko's t-shirts, letting the scent that lingered on the cloth soothe me before I crawled beneath the sheets. I closed my eyes and drifted off.

A while later, the creak of the springs on the bed woke me. I was still groggy, but I pried my eyes open to look at the man who had snuck in again. He was lying on his back, and the scent of sandalwood enveloped me as he traced along my jaw. "You left the window open for me tonight," he murmured quietly in my ear.

I managed to roll over toward him, letting my fingertips play in the dark strands of hair that had fallen into his face. "I didn't mean to."

There was tension between us that had never been present before, but I chalked it up to the drugs that were still racing through my veins, setting my body on fire. Even his breath against my neck was torture as I stared into his eyes, which were as dark as the night. My fingers traced his lips and along his jaw, memorizing how each feature felt.

"I know you didn't mean to, but I decided to take advantage of the fact that you did." He caught my wrist and pressed a feather-light kiss on my pulse. Even the simple action made me clench my thighs together. His being this close to me was a bad idea.

"You should go," I whispered.

He pressed another kiss to the inside of my forearm. "I should, but I'm not going to. I guess that's something you'll have to live with."

I thought of how effortless Rosalyn made it seem to have casual situationships with her string of men that seemed to worship her and how much I admired that. She was bold and maybe it was time for me to be bold as well. Even if I couldn't have him in the light, I could still have him with no strings attached in the darkness. I straddled his waist and his hands grabbed my hips. "What are you doing, beautiful?"

"What I want." My lips crashed down on his as my hands slid under his shirt, touching the taut muscles that hid beneath his clothes. My fingernails scratched at his skin as his mouth parted for me, allowing my tongue to explore his. The kiss was passion and desperation intertwined with sorrow. It was everything that I felt but couldn't say. He seemed hesitant to kiss me back, allowing me to do all the work. I rolled my hips against him, grinding my pussy against his cock through the material between us, trying to goad him on. I wanted him to lose control with me. Even in the grove of trees with Cam and Trey, his actions had been measured.

He flipped me onto my back and nestled his body between my open thighs, giving in to temptation. My legs wrapped around him to hold him close as I rocked against him, needing more. Our tongues battled before he broke away, breathing heavily. He groaned and laid his head against my shoulder. "Ivy, we really shouldn't. There are things you don't know."

I nipped along his jaw and untied the sweatpants he was wearing, slipping my hand inside. His cock was hard, and I circled my hand around it, relishing how thick it was. I moved up and down its length, mindful of the row of barbells that decorated it. The only one who had ever been inside of me was Cam, and I wondered what it would feel like as he thrust deep inside of me, taking me hard and fast. He groaned as I moved my hand faster. "And there are things you don't know about me. This entire town is full of secrets."

His mouth latched onto the skin on my neck, sucking it hard enough to leave a mark behind. His teeth grazed along the skin before his tongue swirled over it, soothing the discomfort. My heels dug into his back while his mouth and tongue worked my body into a frenzy. My back arched off of the bed as he pulled up my shirt, exposing my breasts to him. He pinched one nipple as he sucked the other into his mouth. All I wanted was him, even if I would regret it when I woke up.

I pulled my underwear to the side and rubbed the head of his cock through the wetness, trying to show him what he was doing to me. Every pass of his head against my clit brought me closer to where I wanted to be. "Fuck it," he muttered to himself, pulling away from me.

Immediately, I missed the heat from his body, and a hollowness formed in my chest. He was going to leave. I had thrown myself at him and for some reason, he didn't want me even though he was lying in my bed. I rolled onto my side so that I could avoid looking at his face. He ripped something open and a second later, he rolled me onto my back before yanking my underwear down my legs. He pushed my thighs apart and slammed inside. "Where did you think you were going?" he pulled nearly all the way out before slamming inside again, the force taking my breath away. "Isn't this what you wanted, Ivy? Even after I said that we shouldn't, you still wanted me." Thrust. "Or at least my cock." Thrust. "Or you just want to punish yourself."

There was a harshness present in his tone that wasn't usually there, but I let myself get lost in his body, my nails biting at his skin and my heels digging into his ass. Every pass of his cock and the piercings lining it hit a spot inside of me I didn't know existed. The sound of our skin slapping together filled the air, and I could only hope that my aunt was passed out. He grabbed the edge of the mattress with one hand and reached between us with the other, rubbing my clit. His touch wasn't gentle, and I bit his shoulder to hide the scream that was attempting to break loose from my throat. His thrusts grew harder, nearly violent, and I felt like I was going to split in half before I ever got off. "How does it feel for me to be filling up that tight pussy, baby? Tomorrow, when you're rushing around on campus or working in Frankie's shop, you'll still be able to feel me inside of you. Even when you sit down tomorrow, you'll know I was there."

It hurt, but felt good when he pinched my clit, sending me over the edge. The world around me spun as my body shuddered beneath his and wetness flooded the sheets from between my legs. Even as my muscles trembled, he didn't slow down. Instead, he threw my legs over my shoulders as he continued to ram into me, his mouth set in a cruel smirk.

I wasn't sure what had flipped the switch inside of him, or what had happened, but this wasn't the Niko that I had grown so used to. The one who I never thought would hurt me. It was nothing like what I had imagined it would be. For some reason, I thought that after he came, he would lie beside me and hold me to his chest while he played with my hair. Instead, he pulled out before he filled the condom and tucked himself away, not bothering to look at me as he walked away. He climbed back outside into the night and closed the window, slamming it shut. He didn't even bother to say goodbye.

Another piece of my heart shattered, and I wondered what in the fuck just happened.

Trey

Cam was sitting on my couch, glaring down at his literature book like it had killed his best friend. He was never exactly happy, but all day he had been more of an asshole than usual. Arabella and her friends hadn't been on campus since I emailed their parents using a throwaway account, so it seemed like Cam's plans to get back at them had worked. That alone would have usually lifted his spirits.

I tried to ignore his sighs as I looked through the dean's private email account. His university email account hadn't given us any new information. Most of it was correspondence about financial documents and events going on around campus. There were a few to Ivy that made me raise my eyebrows. Several were sent recently that she hadn't bothered to respond to. He wanted to speak to her in person about her scholarship for the spring semester, but even that went unanswered.

Abraham Well's private email was a different story. Nothing was specifically detailed inside the messages, but there were certain ones that stood out. They were vague enough to mention new merchandise being brought in, but I knew what it was talking about. A party had occurred Sunday night and a man only labeled as X stated that there was a unique product that would be passed around. Wells replied he wouldn't miss the opportunity to sample fresh goods and asked if pictures would be uploaded to the usual site afterward.

Cam slammed his book down on the coffee table in front of him, and I rubbed my eyes. "What is going on with you today?"

He leaned forward, resting his elbows. "Where the hell is Niko at? Ever since the party with Arabella, he's been missing." He shifted on the couch and looked up at me. "Ivy didn't show up today."

I stared at him blankly, not knowing what to say. "Maybe she decided she didn't need the money from tutoring you anymore. She hasn't shown up since those guys attacked her on the beach. Why would today be any different?"

He shrugged at me and I decided to drop it, not knowing where his mind was at. Of course, Ivy hadn't shown up today. He was so hot and cold with her, she probably had no clue how he felt. The intensity of his supposed hatred was only equal to how much he wanted her, but couldn't have her. The real issue wasn't that Ivy hadn't shown up again. It was the fact that Niko had also been absent. The two of them had lived together since we were in high school. They ate together, rode to school together, slept in the same bed, and fucked the same women.

I'd seen how both of them looked at each other when they thought no one else was watching. Cam didn't like the fact that Niko was shutting him out. I didn't know what in the hell was up with him, but I figured he would talk to me if he felt like it.

My phone rang next to me and I didn't look at the screen, instead just answering and assuming it was Vincent needing a favor. That was a huge mistake. "Hello?"

"Hey, baby. I know you said we could talk about me borrowing some money later, but..." I most certainly hadn't said anything of the sort, but her drug-addled brain probably couldn't remember that. I put the phone on speaker and placed it on the desk while she rambled. "So he told me I gotta have the money to him by Saturday. You've got to help me, Trey."

"You know I can't do that, Mom. I have to pay my rent and electricity. I'm sure that there is someone's dick you can suck for money, just like you did while I was growing up."

She wailed on the other end of the line, trying to elicit some sort of emotional response from me. "Everything that I ever did, I did for you. You just don't understand the sacrifices–"

I hung up the phone, unwilling to hear what else she had to say. It was always the same old shit painted with differing degrees of guilt. I doubted that her drug dealer would actually kill her, but if he did, the world would be a better place.

Cam stood up and stretched before he headed into the kitchen. "How long has that shit been going on?"

I grabbed the energy drink sitting on my desk and frowned when I realized it was empty. "A couple of weeks I guess. She just hasn't gotten the hint yet."

"Be glad she doesn't know where you live."

I grabbed my keys. "No shit. Let's get out of here. I need caffeine and you look like you could use a beer. Plus, I have an idea where lover boy is at." Cam scowled but followed me out the door.

I stopped by the convenience store so that we could both grab caffeine and alcohol for later, but that wasn't the real purpose of the trip. I had been suspicious of Niko for a while. Sometimes he would disappear to be by himself in the middle of the night, but the frequency lately was higher than usual.

When I turned down the street Regina Spencer lived on and killed the engine a block from her house, Cam raised an eyebrow at me. "Why are we here?"

I smirked at him as I grabbed my energy drink and exited the vehicle. "You'll see." I shoved one hand in my pocket as I chugged the icy beverage and we strode toward Ivy's house. Rather than going up to the front door and knocking, I cut into the yard, clinging to the shadows.

The curtains in front of Ivy's window were drawn and on her bed, Niko was lying on his back with Ivy straddling him. Cam's eyes grew wide and his jaw tensed as he watched the scene unfolding in front of him. Whatever anger he felt took a backseat when Niko flipped her onto her back and her legs wrapped around his waist. He groaned beside me and laid his head against the siding. "You knew this was going on?"

My eyes were fixated on the two bodies grinding on the bed and Ivy's hand disappearing beneath Niko's pants.

"Not this exactly. I wasn't aware that we were going to get to watch them fuck."

Ivy's back arched off of the bed toward Niko and he pulled up her shirt, exposing her perfect tits. All I could imagine was that I was the one who was sucking on her nipples, trailing my knife across her gorgeous pale skin, leaving trails of crimson behind. Blood rushed to my cock, and I laid my can on the grass beside the house. Even through the panes of glass, I could hear Ivy's soft moans. My cock ached from seeing the two of them and my fantasy, begging me to touch it and find relief. It had been too long since I had fucked anyone. Hell, I only got to jack off on Ivy. Right now, I would sell my soul for her pouty lips to be wrapped around me while I used her.

Cam's eyes were dark and hooded, and his hand shoved inside of the athletic shorts he'd shrugged on after practice. Every muscle in his body was tense as he watched Ivy roll away from Niko while he rolled a condom on. His face was stormy as he ripped her panties off and roughly forced her thighs apart. When he thrust inside of her, I had to suppress a groan of my own. I wasn't sure what was going on but from where I was standing, it looked like he was hate fucking her.

"Fuck it," I muttered to myself, unzipping my pants and freeing my dick. I spit into my palm and wrapped my hand around my cock tightly, letting myself get lost in the feeling. I could almost imagine that it was Ivy's tight pussy clenching around me as I listened to the violent slap of skin coming from inside of the bedroom. Ivy's whimpers were music to my ears as I jerked myself faster. I wanted to get off as fast as possible knowing that we needed to vanish before Niko was done.

Cam's breaths were ragged standing next to me as his hand moved up and down his shaft. Niko's back was lined with deep red scratches, and I wanted more than anything for Ivy to inflict the same level of pain on me. When Niko threw Ivy's legs over his shoulder giving me a look at her beautiful cunt, I knew I wouldn't last much longer. That we were watching them and they had no idea—that we could be caught at any moment—turned me on.

Ivy screamed and her body trembled, her nails cutting into Niko's back as her face twisted with pleasure, and that was all it took. Cam closed his eyes and groaned beside me, every muscle in his body tense. I leaned my forehead against the windowsill as thick ropes of cum shot onto the side of the house and my heart pounded in my chest. I gave myself a moment to recover before tucking myself away.

When I glanced back in, I noticed Niko had pulled out of Ivy and I grabbed Cam's arm. "We need to vanish or he's going to know."

Cam gritted his teeth and I could hear it where I stood. It was a miracle he hadn't chipped any of them. "Maybe I should let him catch me and then make him clean up the mess I made."

I grinned at him and pulled slightly. "With the mood he's in... I might wait until morning."

We jogged back to my car, and I laughed to myself. Maybe that was exactly what the two of them needed: an honest conversation and a hate fuck to clear their heads.

The next morning, I hung near the administrative office and watched as Ivy headed inside. She had finally responded to an email from the dean and stated that she would stop by on her lunch break. The blinds in the dean's office were open, and I snuck around the side of the building so that I could stay concealed but still had a good vantage point to watch what happened.

Ivy seemed nervous as she walked in holding her backpack close to her chest. The dean crowded her space, touching her every chance he got as he backed her up against a wall. I popped the tab on my energy drink as I watched him say something to her and the color drained from her cheeks. A look of resignation passed over her, and she turned her face away. He leaned closer to her, his hands landing on her hips as he pulled her against his body. Ivy didn't seem happy about whatever was happening, but she wasn't fighting him, either. What did he have on her that we didn't? Why was he so obsessed with her?

I raised an eyebrow, questioning if Cam knew about this. It didn't take long for me to find out what he thought. "What the fuck are you doing over here?" he whispered. I held a finger up to my lips and pointed in the window's direction. The dean's hands had traveled further up Ivy's torso and they were resting beneath her rib cage. "Do you think..."

I shook my head at him. "If you don't want him touching her, you probably need to go interrupt this, Romeo. I don't know what I think right now, but he's holding something over her head the same way that he does with us. You, of all people, know how this works. What we really need to do is find time to break into his office and figure out what's going on. While we're in there, we can find out what evidence he has on our shit and steal it back."

Cam turned red when he saw Wells' hand drift further north and trace the swell of Ivy's breast. "I'll be right back."

In less than sixty seconds, I had a front-row seat to Cam busting into the office. The wooden door bounced against the wall and the dean stumbled back like he had been burned. Cam grabbed Ivy's wrist and dragged her outside with him. Once they were away from the building, he nodded at me. "What the fuck is going on between the two of you?"

Ivy took a deep breath and jerked her arm away from Cam. "Fuck you, Cam. Why would you think that anything is going on with us? He just wanted to talk to me about my scholarship."

"Yeah, well, that didn't look like it dealt with any scholarship I've ever seen. Tell me what's really going on. Are you actually fucking him?"

Ivy didn't answer, choosing instead to glare in response. The two of them were drawing more attention than they needed, so I stepped between them. "Cam, go cool off. The two of you can talk later when there are fewer witnesses."

He was gritting his teeth so hard that I could hear them from where I was standing. It was a miracle that he didn't break a tooth. After looking between me and Ivy, he stalked away muttering under his breath. I stared as his form slowly disappeared across the campus greenway before I took another sip of my drink. "You alright?"

"Yeah, I'm fine."

I didn't turn to face her, but I knew she was lying. Even her tone sounded dejected. "New girl, let's go get some lunch. I know he was talking to you about more than a scholarship, but unlike him, I'm going to let it slide. You'll talk when you're ready."

She rolled her eyes at me. "Do you think that I'm sleeping with him?"

I swallowed the last bit of liquid in the can and smiled. "It doesn't matter what I think. I'm just along for the ride."

Cam

The water in the pot on the stove rippled while I listened to Niko and Trey talk at the kitchen table. Niko was actually around for once, and even though something was going on with him, he was enraged when he heard about Wells and Ivy. "He had his hands on her? In his office?"

Trey stayed silent for a moment. "I think that there is more to the situation than meets the eye, guys. I get it. The two of you want her, but what do we really know about her? Her background?"

I picked up the box of spaghetti noodles and opened it. Everyone still had to eat, no matter what was going on in our lives. "Exactly," I bit out. "What do we really know about her? For all we know, she's just as bad as her father. Wells could be using her to find out more about us. Between him and Vincent, potentially they worked out some sort of deal to keep us in line. She could have been playing us the entire time."

The water finally bubbled, and I broke the noodles in half to fit them all inside the pot. "I really don't think that's what was going on, asshole. Did you see her body language? She looked like she was just getting it over with."

Niko tapped his foot and rubbed his hands on his pants. "Are you sure that's what the two of you saw?"

"Positive," I snapped, over the conversation. "I still don't trust her. If she is working with Wells to collect evidence on the three of us, we could be fucked over. She's seen us dealing drugs and knows that we're associated with Peter and Jake going missing. If the cops ask her, will she keep quiet?"

Trey traced the edge of his energy drink with his finger. "We never told her anything, Cam. She's smart enough to put the pieces together, but we didn't give her any details. As far as the drugs, she won't say anything. Have you really taken a good look at her lately? She's strung out half the time. Her eyes..."

Niko's motions stopped, and he paled. I narrowed my eyes at him. "What?"

He shook his head. "I didn't say anything."

Maya and Katya sauntered into the kitchen, holding their backpacks. My sister was the one who spoke, digging through the back of the refrigerator. "What are you guys talking about?"

"Don't worry about it. Dinner should be done in a little while."

Maya popped her head out and clutched the refrigerator door. "You don't have to lie to me, dickhead. You're so loud that we could hear you outside. Lay off her. She really isn't that bad. You're worse than the boy who pulls little girls' pigtails to let them know he likes them." She flipped me off and started digging through the refrigerator again, dismissing me.

With the exception of plastic bags rattling, everyone was silent. Katya's eyes had gone wide as Sergei stepped into the room and leaned against the doorframe. "How would you know she isn't that bad, Maya?"

Maya slammed the door shut and huffed out. "She talked to me on the beach, alright? One night, I snuck out when I was upset. Plus, I saw the three of you taking care of her. The house is too small and there aren't any secrets here. Every time the two of you fight," she pointed between me and Niko, "we hear it. We can hear everything."

I gave her a hard look. "You spoke to her."

Sergei grinned at me and patted me on the shoulder. "I have, too. Completely agree with Maya on this. I offered to let her ride this dick, but she ran." He laughed at his joke and it took everything inside of me not to choke him.

"You did what?" Niko sputtered before standing up and closing the distance between the two. He fisted the front of Sergei's shirt in his hand.

Sergei's smile widened, and he leaned closer. "Don't worry, nothing happened. I think she was scared of what my abilities were, but I need to tell you a secret." I expected him to say something ridiculous, but his next words made me see red. "You should check the vents."

Niko let go of him and grabbed a screwdriver from the junk drawer before kneeling on the floor. He carefully removed the screws and pulled the plate out before gagging. "What in the literal fuck?" he managed to get out between heaves.

Ivy thought that she could fuck with me, but she was wrong. My sister was completely off-limits to her. Her family had done enough damage and Maya was still fragile. Her therapist had such as much. The icing on the cake was that she was responsible for how the house smelled. And to top it off, she was responsible for my hair turning green before I realized there was dye in the shampoo. It had mostly faded now, but still.

All of it was Ivy's fault, and she had sealed her fate. After her attack, I had allowed myself to think that maybe there could be something between the two of us, but now?

She had made me look like a fool. I wouldn't allow anyone else to touch her, but she was mine to torment.

That night, after we finished cleaning rotten shrimp from every vent in the house, I went to Trey's. Niko had disappeared into his room and told me he needed to catch up on some things. He was lying, and Maya was right. You could hear everything in this fucking house. As he strummed on the guitar, the mournful tune drifted through the walls. I left him alone, giving him time to think about whatever was bothering him.

Even though I had made spaghetti, no one had the appetite to eat. We scrubbed every surface in the house afterward and left the windows open, but it didn't matter. The longer I thought about everything, the angrier I got.

Trey and Niko had convinced me not to drive to Frankie's shop to confront Ivy. The more that I scrubbed, rage blinded me. Fuck her.

I mulled over the best way to get back at her. She was already avoiding Caleb. All it took was me telling her who his grandfather was. If I couldn't have her, then neither could he. There was nothing I could do about Rosalyn–she was ride or die. She'd proven that to the three of us more times than I could count. Even with all of our shit, she still stood by our side. Her aunt already made her life miserable. Regina Spencer had a tendency to do that. We had found nothing about her mother and her father was in prison. It was hard to break someone when they didn't have anything left.

There was only one thing that she cared about, and that was her scholarship. Trey sat in front of his computer with a knife in his hand, pressing the tip into the pads of his index finger. "You're sure about this? If I do it, there's no going back. It might finally send her over the edge."

I twisted the top off the bottle of beer in my hand. "Good."

"And if she leaves? There's nothing holding her here."

I shrugged at him. Ivy leaving would be the best thing for Maya. It would be one less reminder of what Thomas Spencer had done to her. It would be the best thing for all of us.

The cracks that had formed in our close-knit group hadn't appeared until after her.

Trey turned back to the monitor and placed the knife beside him before he began typing. I watched him while he worked and ten minutes later, he sat back in his chair. "It's done."

I smiled to myself and finished my beer. The reaction from Ivy was going to be priceless.

The phone rang again, and I rubbed my eyes. Thursdays were the day that I could sleep in. The only thing I had to do was show up at work, but someone was insistent that they needed to speak to me. My finger drifted across the screen to answer the call. "Yeah?" I answered, sounding half-dead.

The positives of taking tea were that everything was a little duller and the nightmares that kept me up all night were missing. The downside was that when they wore off, I was exhausted. No amount of caffeine could shake the weariness I felt in my body. I wasn't sure if that was the drugs or a small touch of depression. The pills that I had gotten from Niko were nearly gone, and I would have to replace them soon. There was no way in hell I could ask any of the guys for them, not now that Niko wasn't speaking to me, and Rhyker would tell Ros.

"Have you checked the grades for the project yet?" Caleb asked on the other end of the line. His voice held a sharp edge to it, and I wondered why he was pissed off.

Other than the texts telling me I should run away, we hadn't communicated. Hearing his voice was a shock to my system. "What?" It's not that I didn't hear him, it was that in my brain the words didn't make sense.

He lowered his voice and spoke slowly. "Check. The. Portal. Our grade was posted last night after eleven."

"I don't have a computer at home, Caleb, and my phone is too slow to pull it up. Everything crashes. Just tell me what is going on."

The sound of keys clicking angrily filled the background. "Well, according to this, we made a twenty-five on the assignment."

Panic filled my veins, turning my blood to ice. My heart skipped a beat, and I clutched the sheet beneath me. "That's impossible. I saw what you wrote and... there has to be some kind of mistake. I'm getting dressed and heading to the school to talk to the professor. Maybe it's a typo."

An eighty-five I could accept. Hell, even a seventy-five. But a twenty-five? That was the kind of grade that gave you no room for mistakes, especially since it was worth thirty percent of my grade. A grade like that would put my scholarship in jeopardy.

It would change my future yet again.

I stood outside Professor Hurst's office by ten waiting for her lecture to be over. I scanned the bulletin board attached to her door that had a large sign that read "No appointments outside of office hours. No exceptions." Foolishly, I hoped she would make one, just today. Time ticked on as I examined every flier taped to the cinderblock walls waiting for the professor to arrive.

When she did, I knew I was out of luck. The look on her face when she took me in sitting on the floor beside the door was one of frustration. "Can I help you?"

I stood and adjusted my clothes. "Actually yes. I was looking at the grades from the project and—"

"I'm sorry, but all grades are final and not up for debate. If you want, I can set up an appointment for the two of us to sit down and discuss why I graded it like that."

I balled my fists at my side. "I was just wondering if there was a typo. With the information we presented, I just can't imagine getting a low grade." I was grasping at straws, trying to find a way to get through to her.

Her face hardened. "I highly doubt that, miss. After all, this isn't high school anymore. The work that may have passed there won't here. Clearhaven has expectations for their students."

I inhaled deeply trying to keep my temper. You would have thought that Clearhaven was Ivy League or prestigious from the way she was speaking. "Professor, I understand what you are saying, but I am positive that there has been a mistake."

She rolled her eyes at me as she unlocked her office. "I've heard that many times over the years, and I reassure you that there has never been a mistake. However, if you are insistent," she pulled a clipboard from her desk, "then feel free to make an appointment."

I scanned over the paper and the rage inside of me nearly boiled over. The next appointment was in mid-November. That was a long time to wait in limbo, stressing whether or not I would be here next semester or if I could even pass the class. The other seventy percent were divided equally into two chunks: the mid-term and final. Both had essay portions, and if she didn't like my project, a quickly scrawled essay question could be my downfall. The midterm was scheduled for Monday morning and my heart sank further into my stomach.

I jotted down my name on the empty line in November and left without a word, headed to the campus green. Standing near the fountain was the target who would absorb my wrath. He was six foot three with golden hair and a smug smile plastered on his beautiful face. Without thinking, I walked up to him, balled up my fist, and hit him as hard as I could. Any conversation that was going on stopped as everyone watched to see what I would do next.

He didn't drop the smug look. Instead, his tongue darted out to lick the drop of blood from the corner of his mouth. "Why'd you do that, little ghost? What's the matter?" he taunted.

I went to hit him again, but he caught my wrist and pulled me against his body. "I love it when you lose it like this, Ivy, but you're causing a scene. If you wanted my dick again, all you had to do was ask, baby,"

I growled in frustration and kicked his knee. Rage was the only thing holding me together. "I don't know how you did it, but I know you're responsible for my fucking grade, jackass. I know it's you."

His lips traced the shell of my ear, and he chuckled. "How I did it is a secret. Let me list your sins so that you can understand why. We won't even start at the beginning. You were the one who messed with my shampoo. You were the reason the house smelled like death for weeks on end. Do you know how long it took to clean that up? You allowed the dean to touch you, even after I said that no one else could. But your biggest sin, Ivy, was speaking to my sister." A tear fell down my cheek as I listened to him list everything that supposedly I had done.

The girl that peered at me from around the corner was his sister. The one that my father hurt.

"I didn't know," I whispered. Trey and Niko stood off to the side wordlessly. Trey's face had the same bored expression it did the day that Cam threatened to tell everyone about my father. For some reason, I had thought that the two of us were growing closer, or at least had an understanding of some sort.

His thumb caught one of the tears, and he licked it off. "You have the sweetest tears I've ever tasted. I warned you that you should leave, but you chose to stay, so now you have to suffer the consequences. Poor little rich girl that no one loves. How does it feel to be utterly alone?" His words were a dagger to the heart. "Who do you really have, Ivy? A best friend that you've known for two months? What do you really know about her? You have no one and nothing. Even the piece of shit car you drive isn't yours yet."

I pulled away from him and ran to the parking lot as fast as I could. While I was speaking to the Professor and confronting Cam, someone had sprayed shaving cream on my car and taped photos of my father's mugshot to the exterior. I looked at the parking lot and saw that fliers were tucked beneath every windshield wiper in sight. Fuck this. It was the least of my problems. The entire universe could know who my father was and what he had done. It wouldn't change anything.

Cam's words rang in my ears on repeat as I drove to the one place I had. At least at work, Frankie wouldn't pry. I could spend hours losing myself in whatever she needed to have done at the shop.

I had thought that after they had taken care of me, things would be different, that maybe we had some sort of unspoken truce. The bruises on my body had faded, but they still weren't gone, and somehow things were worse than ever. I hated that what he said to me was accurate, and I hated that I was crying yet again.

For the first time in my entire life, I felt completely alone and like there was no hope left.

Niko

I vy ran away, and I just watched her as her figure disappeared around the corner. Part of me wanted to run
after her, but after how I had left things Monday night,
I let her go. It was better this way. Leaving Clearhaven
behind would be good for her, even if she didn't see it yet.
She would be out of the gaze of the Order, out of harm's
reach, and somewhere that I couldn't hurt her anymore.

I'd spent the week feeling like a complete failure. The
letter from my landlord would be in the mail either today
or tomorrow, telling me I needed to vacate the premises
within ninety days. I wouldn't waste his time like that.
I'd find somewhere new before Christmas so he could
make the repairs that were needed and move a new set
of tenants into the house. He'd given me the extra time
I asked for but despite pawning everything that I had
of worth, I was still short $500. I had to buy groceries
and pay the power bill. Cam had chipped in his half of
the expenses, but it just wasn't enough after my father
had "borrowed" some of the cash without my knowledge.
After all, drugs were more important than the children he
had helped bring into this world.

The other feeling I couldn't shake was one of disgust. What I had done over the weekend ate at me. I was tainted inside now by what had happened. I shouldn't have treated Ivy the way I did. When I crawled through her window, I wanted nothing more than to watch her sleep. She didn't know what I had done and if she did, she wouldn't have practically begged me to fuck her. I lost my temper with her and the world and treated her like trash.

I somehow fucked up everything that I touched.

After the crowd around us dispersed, I glared at Cam. "Was that really fucking necessary? Her grades? The stupid scholarship is the only thing she has left." I shoved Trey, who stood there watching the two of us. "I know you were involved. What did she do to you?" He didn't respond, and I rushed past Cam, ramming my shoulder into his to make a point. Heavy footsteps followed me to the parking lot, but I ignored him. He needed to know that I was pissed. When I saw the flier beneath the blade of my wiper, I exploded. I kicked the tire of my car and started walking, ripping every one that I found from their place. "The damage was already done, and you got the response you wanted. Was this fucking necessary?" I shouted at him.

His jaw clenched and he picked one up. "This wasn't me. I wouldn't bother with something so childish. Everyone already knows who her father is." My heart hurt for Ivy seeing this shit so soon after Cam fucked with her. Cam, Trey, and I stepped from car to car, collecting the fliers in silence. It didn't fix anything, and it didn't solve my problems, but at least Ivy wouldn't be forced to see them again.

Once we were done, I got into the car and waited for the two guys that I called my best friends. The look on Cam's face made me want to murder him, so I chose not to speak while I drove home. The air itself was thick from the tension between the two of us. I wasn't really angry at Trey for what happened; he was just following orders like he always did. But Cam? I was enraged at him.

She had planted shrimp in the air vents, but that was well deserved for all the shit we had put her through. Her speaking to Maya, though? That was the catalyst for ruining any chance of a future? I thought that he would have chilled out about it by today, but that wasn't the case. Ivy speaking to Maya wasn't out of malice or to hurt her. I didn't know the story, but I knew Ivy, even if she thought no one did.

I got out of the car and slammed my door to make a point once I was home. He wasn't getting off as easily as he always did when the two of us would argue and then, after we slept, everything was better. I stopped by the mailbox on the way inside, knowing that the letter I was waiting for could be in the stack. I stalked into the kitchen, pulling out a bottle of cheap whiskey I'd hidden in the back of the cabinet. Not bothering to grab a glass, I took a sip and let it slide down my throat as I threw the envelopes on the table.

Cam grabbed my shirt collar and pulled me close enough that his lips were only an inch from mine. I stared at them for a moment before turning my head and taking another drink. "Let go of me."

He grabbed the bottle from my hand and turned it up. I watched as the bottle bubbled once before he slammed it down on the table. "Not a chance in hell." His grip on me tightened, pulling me closer into his orbit so that I couldn't escape. All I could see was the rage in his ocean-colored eyes being reflected on me.

I bit my lip hard enough that I tasted blood. "I don't want to do this with you right now."

"And I don't give a fuck. What's going on with you? Is this really about Ivy, or is there something else you want to tell me? You've been sneaking out of the house for weeks and then this week you've been in a weird mood."

He walked us back several steps and the back of my legs hit the lower cabinets with a thud, throwing off my balance. "Fuck you. You don't know what you're talking about," I gritted out. He used his weight to push me backward, bending my body as he hovered close. My hands clutched the countertop so that I wouldn't do something stupid like hit him.

"That's just it, Niko. I do know what I'm talking about. You not coming to Trey's last night? Me waking up every morning and your side of the bed is cold? You crying in the shower? Quit fucking around and talk to me." He kicked my legs apart and dissolved any distance between us. My body reacted to being so close to him, despite my anger at him and the world. I prayed he wouldn't notice that I was hard, but the chance was slim. His hands let go of my shirt and gripped my jaw, his fingers biting into my skin.

His lips crashed against mine and his teeth bit down on my lower lip, aggravating the bleeding skin. I hissed as his tongue lapped at the wound before he plunged his tongue inside my mouth. Everything dissolved around us except the anger simmering beneath both of our skin as he punished me with his hands and mouth. We were still fighting, just speaking a different language. I grabbed at his hair and pulled, hoping to inflict on him the pain that I felt inside, and groaned, rocking his hips against me to show that he was into this. I shoved him hard to right myself and turned us, slamming him into the wall behind us.

Tension and frustration had been building between the two of us for a while. The long stares and the jealousy. The bickering. We were both broken and our souls called to each other even though they shouldn't. Whatever was happening between us would change things, and potentially not for the better. I pushed all the jumbled thoughts out of my head as I allowed my hands to skim beneath his shirt and enjoy the feeling of his muscles tensing beneath my touch. He tasted like copper and whiskey and I wanted more.

Slow clapping brought me back to the moment, bursting the bubble we had been shrouded in. I pushed him one last time as I stumbled away and wiped my mouth with the back of my hand. "Well, it's about fucking time. I'm happy that Mommy and Daddy are making up now,"

Trey grinned from the doorway. "I take one phone call and miss all the fun."

My cheeks heated at the fact Trey had seen me in a momentary lapse of insanity. The anger and passion between us dissipated as I righted my clothes. Cam ignored him as he stared at me with hooded eyes. "I'm still looking for an answer from you, asshole."

I couldn't tell him I'd been sneaking around to see Ivy or that I'd been the one giving her drugs. I couldn't tell him what had happened on Sunday night. There was no way in hell I would tell him what had transpired on Monday night in the shadows of her room. Instead, I sifted through the mail on the table and handed him an envelope addressed to Mr. Nikolai Stone. There was no junior attached to the name. It was meant for my father who would never open the envelope. I didn't bother opening the letter. I knew what the contents contained.

His eyes scanned the words, and he muttered under his breath before crumbling the paper in his fist. "Why didn't you tell me? I could have given you the money."

I scoffed at him. "What money? From selling photographs? The money you use to help me buy gas? None of us have anything."

He closed his eyes. "The money I've been saving to buy a car, you douchebag. I would have given it to you and not thought twice."

I buried my face in my hands. "I couldn't ask you for that, Cam."

"Yeah, but you would have put his dick in your mouth a few minutes ago," Trey mumbled to himself as he stared down at the letter in his hands.

I didn't bother to tell them that was just the tip of the iceberg and that there were more secrets that I had been hiding. I didn't tell them I felt like I was drowning. Instead, I grabbed the whiskey from the table and swallowed the poison inside the bottle.

"We always have a backup plan," Cam said to himself. "Just come stay at my mom's."

I glared at him and sat in the chair closest to me, feeling too heavy to stand any longer. "Why? You don't even want to stay there."

His voice was barely above a whisper, and I wondered if Trey could hear what he said. "I just don't want to stay there alone."

That night when I passed out from everything that I had drank, Cam's body lay closer to mine than usual. His breath ghosted along my skin and I considered when the fuck I would come clean to him. What would his reaction be when he discovered everything that I had been hiding? Would he still want me? More than anything, I wanted him to put his arm around me or to hold my hand and tell me everything would be alright. But he didn't. Nothing would be alright because this was Clearhaven, where the rich got richer and the poor suffocated under the weight of the world.

Caleb

Ivy had been ignoring the texts that I had sent her since I confronted her on campus. Instead of just leaving me on read, she no longer even opened the messages. I had meant every word that I'd said about giving her the money to run, but she didn't trust me—with good reason. She needed to get out of Clearhaven, but she was stubborn.

I sat at the table in front of my grandfather, pushing food around my plate. Eggs were another dish that Claire couldn't cook. He had requested that we eat breakfast together last night, citing that he needed to speak to me alone about Order business. He looked completely relaxed with a national newspaper spread out in front of him, staring at an article on stock market trends. I'd tried telling him when I was in high school that no one read physical newspapers anymore, but he was set in his ways and stuck in the past. Claire refilled the black coffee in his mug and he absentmindedly grabbed a handful of her ass. She giggled, oblivious to the fact that she was just one of many women that my grandfather employed in one fashion or another.

After she left the room, I cleared my throat, hoping to grab his attention. He held up one finger. "Don't worry, I haven't forgotten you're still there, Caleb."

He continued to read, and I pushed the plate away, no longer caring about appearances. "Yes, but you're forgetting that some of us have other things to do today. I have class in less than an hour."

He neatly folded the paper and pushed his reading glasses to the top of his head. "Fine. Let's get to business, shall we? It's been a while since you've done any jobs for the Order with the exception of Ivy Spencer." He reached down into the briefcase sitting beside his chair and pulled out a manilla envelope, passing it to me. "As you know, we all have sacrifices we make for the greater good."

Carefully, I unsealed the envelope and pulled out the documents. I bit the inside of my cheek as I scanned the photograph, instantly recognizing the subject and then looked at the accompanying information. "What's this?"

My grandfather tapped his finger along the top of the table. "You know what it is. Don't play dumb, son. She needs to be taken care of."

I closed my eyes, trying to find the best way to ask the question that was on the tip of my tongue. A way that wouldn't invoke his wrath. Fletcher Vance was not known for his patience, especially behind closed doors. He didn't like anyone to question him, expecting everyone to act as soon as he told them to. "What did Clarissa do except suck my dick? Last time I checked, that didn't put the Order in danger."

He chuckled to himself before rubbing between his eyebrows with two fingers. "No, the blowjob isn't the problem. If it was, half of Clearhaven would be dead right now. The issue is that she opened her mouth about what happens behind closed doors and we can't have that. She was also caught speaking to the new police detective. You know what you have to do."

I shoved everything back into the envelope and stood up to leave the room. Before I reached the exit, his voice stopped me. "Make sure that it's taken care of in the next week, Caleb. I shouldn't have to remind you what's at stake if you don't."

I had made a mistake in him discovering that I cared about Ivy Spencer, and now he would hold it over my head. Him making me disappear the same way my parents had was the least of my concerns. I wasn't ready to die yet, but him hurting Ivy because of me? I wouldn't be able to live with myself.

This was why I had tried to distance myself from her. Why I had tried to convince her she should take my money and leave. If the Order was willing to kill Clarissa for spreading rumors, what would they do when Ivy began remembering everything that had happened to her?

Trey

Before classes on Friday morning, someone knocked on the door to my apartment and I staggered out of bed, unsure of what was going on. It was too early to deal with whatever fuckery was happening. After a quick glance outside, I realized the sun wasn't even up. I managed to put on clothes before stumbling to the door, lamenting the fact that I had only been asleep for three hours.

The blow-up between Niko and Cam the night before had been coming, but not even I had expected to walk in on the culmination of it. Seeing the two of them didn't surprise me, not really. The two of them somehow fit together, even if no one else saw it. I'd excused myself shortly after to give them some space. Things would either work themselves out or they wouldn't, but there was no way in hell I was getting caught in the crossfire.

Niko losing his house though... that I hadn't expected. Since we had been in high school, he'd always made sure that every bill was paid and that his younger siblings had everything provided for them. It was funny how one thing could change the course of everything else. Maybe chaos theory was correct and a butterfly's wings could change the trajectory of someone's entire life. Or potentially it was just fate.

Still, as I answered the door, I never expected to see my mother there. I had never given her my home address, and her presence was anything but welcome. "What do you want?"

"Not even a good morning, or it's nice to see you?" The lines on her face were deeper than the last time I had seen her and her skin seemed dull, probably from whatever drugs she was taking. Her clothes were clean, which was surprising given the circumstances.

"It's five in the morning. What did you really expect?" I bit out. There was an edge to my words that my mother didn't seem to notice.

She peered around my body, looking into the space beyond my shoulder. "You wouldn't answer my text messages, so I thought maybe I could talk to you in person," she whispered. Seeing her in person almost made me cave. At one point, I adored her. She was the person who gave birth to me. She was who had bandaged my knees when she wasn't too high to know what was going on around her.

"Right. I thought that when I moved out, we agreed that we'd never speak again." It was hard to be angry at her this time of the morning. All I could feel was indifference and mistrust. The number of lies that she had fed me over the years made it difficult to look her in the eyes.

Her red-rimmed eyes became glassy, probably to garner my sympathy. "Trey, when I said that I needed your help, I meant it. They'll kill me if I don't have the money by Sunday."

That was all it took for me to close the door on her. It was always about money, something I didn't have a lot of. Everything that I had saved was to help move me and the guys away from a place that God had forgotten about long ago. She pounded at the door as the deadbolt clicked into place, and I turned on music to drown out the sound. It was too early.

Later in the morning when I left for classes, my mother was gone. I knew she would grow tired of waiting by the door and expecting me to cave. As I popped the tab on my energy drink and got into my car, a thought hit me. How did she know where to find me?

When I moved out to escape her and the string of men that she brought home, I never gave her an address. I had always been careful not to disclose where I lived to anyone other than the guys to prevent her from following. In fact, with everything that had been going on, I hadn't considered how in the hell she had gotten my phone number either. I'd been so caught up in the Forsaken and Ivy that when she called, I had just accepted it at face value.

When I got home late that night, the door to my apartment was standing wide open. I sighed and pulled the knife from my pocket before stepping inside, questioning what in the hell was going on. As long as I had lived in this building, no one had ever tried breaking in. In fact, that was the thing about living in this part of town: no one had anything worth stealing, so there was very little property crime.

Papers were scattered across the floor, and furniture was turned over. A new hole decorated the wall next to the door. The entire place was trashed, but that wasn't the worst of it. The computer that I had spent so long building and upgrading was missing.

It was really the only thing of value in the entire place. It was the only thing that was truly mine other than the shitty car I drove and the clothes on my back. The programs and files on it were backed up on the cloud, but that wasn't the point. It was mine and yet again, something else was taken from me.

Immediately, I knew who was responsible, even if they weren't the ones who had broken in. It was my mother, or at least one of her friends. Someone had followed me home and decided to take my things in order to pay for her debts. I was lucky that my car wasn't outside. They would have stolen that too and stripped it for parts.

Not bothering to close the door, I straightened up one of the overturned chairs and sat down in it, resting my head in my hands. I had worked so hard to get away from her and now she thought she could come back into my life, picking up where we had left off. Sitting in the chair gave me time to think and figure out what my options were.

Grabbing the baseball bat I kept in my closet, I stood and closed the door behind me as I left the apartment. There was no point in attempting to lock it given the wood that was splintered along the frame. Locks only kept honest people out. Slowly, I drove to Niko's, sipping on the flat energy drink from earlier in the day and rehearsing what I wanted to say to my friends.

Niko needed somewhere to stay with his sister and brother, Cam hated going home, and now I needed to move. The timing was shitty, and we all had enough going on, but perhaps there was a solution that could benefit all of us.

I pulled up in front of Niko's house and they were both sitting on the stairs, speaking in low tones. When Niko saw me, he raised his eyebrows, surprised that I had shown up. Earlier, I had told them I was headed home to work on homework and a new app that I was designing. Now I was swinging a bat in my left hand, waiting for them to wrap up their conversation. "What are you two talking about?" I asked casually.

"Just what the hell I'm going to do about everything." The circles under his eyes told me he hadn't been sleeping well. Join the club.

I sat on the step below them, leaning against the bat, and held out my hand, gesturing for them to pass me whatever they were drinking. "That's actually why I'm here. My mother found my apartment. This morning I just thought she would get bored and leave me alone but... Someone broke in and stole my computer."

Cam's eyes widened, and he handed me a can of beer from the bag beside him. "What else did they take?"

I rubbed my eyes and stared into the distance. "No clue. I didn't even bother checking. Want to come with me to get it back?"

Cam smirked at me. "Fuck yes. Let's do it. Does she still live over on Bradford?"

"Last I heard." As we drove, I tried to find the right way to approach the other topic that had been on my mind. I hesitated for a moment because I wasn't sure how either of them would react. The three of us were proud and didn't like relying on anyone else. "Listen, I've been thinking. What if we buy a house together? Y'all need somewhere safe to crash and I need to move somewhere new. If my mother or her dealer have broken in once, they'll do it again."

Niko looked in the rearview mirror. "Trey, it's a great idea, but where are we going to get the money to do something like that? I couldn't even pay the rent this month."

I rolled my eyes and didn't bother looking in his direction, instead focusing on a single star in the sky outside my window. "That's because you didn't let us know you were that far behind. I've been saving money since I got the apartment so that when we graduated, we could all get the hell out of Clearhaven and get a fresh start. Maybe we need one now."

"And I've got the money I was saving to buy a car." Cam sat up straighter and put his hand on Niko's knee cautiously. "How much do we need?"

"The two of you can't just—"

I cut Niko off. "We can. The three of us have been through hell together. I have no idea how much money it's going to take, but we'll figure it out. It's going to take some time to find something, but we can start this weekend."

Niko groaned and rubbed a hand through his hair as we pulled up in front of my mom's trailer. "You should stay with us tonight after we get your computer back. Tomorrow you need to change your number."

I tipped my chin up in acknowledgment as I crawled out of the cramped back seat. The three of us sauntered to the front door, which was cracked open. I kicked it in, not bothering to check who was inside. "Surprise, Mom! I'm home!" I yelled as I swung the bat at the pictures lining the living room wall. Glass shattered and wood cracked as I smashed everything in sight.

Cam just grinned at me and I rolled my eyes. "Are you sure she's even here? She—"

His words faltered as my mother stumbled into the living room. "Trey, baby," she slurred. Track marks lined her arms and her dirty satin nightgown hung off of her body. "You didn't tell me you were coming for a visit."

I slammed the bat into the television sitting on the floor in the corner. "Oh, Mom! You know how much I love to see you. Especially when you steal all of my shit! The same way you have my entire life. Give it back."

After destroying half of my mother's house, she finally confessed where she had taken my computer. After a quick trip to Rick's Pawn Shop, it was back in my possession.

I wasn't sure if moving or changing my number would solve the family issues I had, but it was better than dealing with them late at night. Ignoring them had worked so far and at that moment, I didn't have a better solution.

We sat around drinking in silence until Cam stood up and stretched. "Monday there's a mandatory assembly on campus."

I stared at him, wondering what that had to do with anything and how it was going to solve our problems. "And?"

He tucked his hands into his pockets and shrugged. "I was just thinking. What if we were to break into Wells' office then? We can dig up some dirt on him. He'd be willing to pay us to keep quiet. Right now, we need every penny that we can get."

Niko tapped on his bottle, thinking. "It's dangerous to fuck with him too much."

I mulled it over for a moment. "What the hell? Let's do it. If nothing else, we might find the information that he has on us and destroy it." After a freshman overdosed on campus, we called Vincent to figure out a way to cover it up. Unfortunately, Wells showed up instead. The cops stayed out of it, but ever since that moment, he had held evidence of the crime over our heads at every turn.

I smiled to myself. "This weekend presents us with another opportunity, gentlemen."

Saturday night after the football game, the annual Forsaken Halloween party was being held at the graveyard and I knew how I wanted to celebrate. Rosalyn would be there with Rhyker, and if I dared to make a wager, she would insist on Ivy tagging along. I detailed my plan to the guys, and they were in agreement. We were going to give Ivy an evening to remember before she tried to disappear from Clearhaven.

Ivy

Saturday evening when I got home from work, a small white box sat on my pillow and I stared at it for a while in confusion. The front door had been locked when I arrived home and my windows had been locked all week. Still, I went through the house double checking every lock to ensure that there wasn't a way for someone to get inside. Finally, after eyeing the box with apprehension, I opened it. Inside was a baggy of pills and a note. *For you.* It had to be from Niko.

Even though things had been awkward, maybe he was worried about me, especially after how he'd left things the last time he was in my room. It didn't help that he refused to stand up to Cam. Or that he went along with changing my grades and printing out fliers of my father.

Throughout the week, I had been cutting back on what I was taking, but the withdrawal was brutal. Word on the street was that tea didn't have any side effects and wasn't addictive, but that was bullshit, at least for the amount I was taking. In the morning my head hurt and my hands trembled and at night I woke up in a pile of sweat, but I wasn't sure if that was from the nightmares or weaning myself off. I'd felt empty all week and sometimes I was certain that the hollowness would consume me.

The temptation to take one of the pills nagged at the back of my mind when the phone in my bag rang. I pulled it out and saw that it was Rosalyn. She had been trying to call me all week, especially after news of my confrontation with Cam spread on campus and pictures of the fliers circulated on social media. I hadn't answered because I wasn't sure what to say and pretending to be fine was too difficult. I looked at the phone for several moments before silencing it telling myself that I would talk to her first thing in the morning. She'd understand if I just changed into my pajamas and lay in bed, especially if I brought her coffee.

Ten minutes later, someone knocked on the front door and my heart beat against my ribs, the fear reminding me I was actually alive. Who would knock on the door at this time of the night? I looked out the front window with a sigh of relief. Rosalyn.

I unlocked the deadbolt and opened the door. "What are you doing here? Shouldn't you be in bed or visiting one of the men that are chasing you around?"

She laughed at me as she walked inside. "Perhaps, but we're going out."

I shook my head, not wanting to disappoint her because we hadn't spent a lot of time together lately, but also not wanting to leave the house. I had been miserable company lately with everything that has been going on. Cam and the guys had basically stripped everything that I still had away. Caleb, my optimism, and potentially my scholarship. Add in attempted rape, being assaulted, and my hair being forcefully cut. Really, I just wanted to sleep. "I don't think so. Not tonight."

She laced her fingers with mine and dragged me toward my bedroom. "Yes, tonight. I heard a rumor from a source that the Forsaken are holding their annual Halloween party tonight. I told you when you first arrived, it was the event that you absolutely couldn't miss. I would be a terrible best friend if I didn't convince you to go with me."

Despite not wanting to leave the house, her words made me grin. "Right. Let me guess. The source was Rhyker because he wanted to see you."

She sifted through the gray tote, throwing a skirt and low cut top on the bed. "I would never reveal my sources, Ivy. Get dressed because you're going, even if I have to throw you over my shoulder and carry you out of the house."

I snorted at the vision of her trying to tote me anywhere. I wasn't exactly slender, but Rosalyn would find a way if she could. "Fine, give me fifteen minutes and I'll go. No promises on if I'll have a good time." The three members of the Forsaken who had taken up entirely too many of my thoughts would be there, probably looking for a quick lay or someone to torment. The thought made the party sound infinitely less fun.

"Oh, you'll have a good time. We'll just hang out on the outskirts. Apparently, Dissension Stars are playing tonight."

I did really like Dissension Stars the time that they played at Master Pieces. Picking up the skirt laying on my quilt, I tried to remember everything that Rosalyn had told me about the party the first time she mentioned it. "Wait. They have a band playing in the cemetery?"

"A band and a bonfire. No second thought. Just get dressed."

Rosalyn was being a little pushy, but that was just her and I knew she had my best interests in mind. Still, I shooed her out of the room so that I could get dressed. She waited in the hallway while I tugged on my clothes. After a moment's hesitation, I popped one of the pills that had been left on the box on my pillow. If I was going to a party, I might as well be comfortably numb, just like everyone else who was there.

The party was amazing, and Rosalyn was right, at least for a while. No one even noticed we were there except Rhyker. He was drawn to her like a moth to a flame as the band played. The bonfire that someone had set cast everyone in an eerie light as people danced and cheered, begging for them to play a cover of their favorite song. The alcohol warmed my veins and made me feel hazy while I swayed to the beat. Everything was perfect. For a bit.

Strong hands grabbed my hips, and I jumped, unsure of who was behind me. "Little ghost, I didn't expect to find you here, especially after this week."

I groaned to myself, the noise lost from the volume of the music. There was only one person who called me a ghost no matter how much I felt like one, and I wasn't in the mood to deal with him. "What do you want, Cam?"

I glanced behind me, seeing that he had face paint on in honor of the upcoming holiday. His tan was painted white and black accents were added around his eyes and mouth, making him look like a skeleton. His lips latched onto the sensitive skin of my neck before he traced his nose up the length of my neck. "We need to have a conversation. Alone."

Ros side-eyed him and rolled her eyes. "I don't think so. Whenever the two of you are alone together, something bad happens."

I held up my hand to stop her. "It's fine. I mean, really, what else could they do to me this week?"

The corner of Cam's lips curled up in amusement. "Besides, it won't just be me and her. Trey and Niko are here also."

"Like that makes things any better, asshole," Ros muttered.

I gave her a look that I hoped would be reassuring. "I'll be back."

Cam grabbed my elbow and dragged me across the graveyard. As we walked, the tombstones fell away and the music dimmed. A small part of my brain screamed at me to turn back around and save myself. I might have if

I had any self-preservation left, but instead I stumbled over roots numbly. When Niko and Trey came into view, we stopped and Cam shoved me forward. Both were wearing face paint similar to Cam's and a chill ran down my spine. Niko leaned against an ancient oak tree, the cherry from his joint the only illumination.

"What are you doing here, new girl?" Trey asked. His voice was dark and there was an edge to it that wasn't normally there. "This is a Forsaken party. I would have thought that after everything that we had done to you, you would have stayed away."

We were all cast in shadows, and it was the first time that fear grabbed me. Blood rushed in my ears and my heart hammered rapidly in my chest. Even if I were to yell for help, no one would hear me. Even if they could, no one could save me. Still, I tried to act brave, and I threw my shoulders back. "I was invited to come by Rosalyn. Besides, it's not like there is anything left you can take away from me. What are you going to do, humiliate me further?"

Cam's hands landed on my hips, and he laid his head on my shoulder. "That's where you're wrong, Ivy. People always have something left to lose, and it's clear from your attitude we haven't broken you yet."

My nails bit into the top of his hands, and I shifted to face him in the darkness. "What do you mean that there is always something left to lose?" A wry laugh escaped from me against my will. "You already used all the information you had about me to try to get me to submit, and it didn't work. My dad being a criminal is old news now."

In the darkness, Cam's blue eyes looked nearly black, and I swallowed hard as he leaned closer. "You really think that you have nothing? Baby, I promise you that you will always have something left to lose. Did you really think that we would release the information about your father without having something else to hold over your head? You remember that night in the office where I had my cock down your throat and you left covered in cum? There's a tape of that. Unless you want your aunt to see how eagerly you stuck your tongue out and practically begged for more, don't go there."

Niko stepped up behind me, wedging me between his body and Cam's. The heat radiating off the two of them was suffocating. Niko's hands rested on my ribs and his lips brushed against my jawline. Despite the fear coursing through my body and the malice in their tone, my body shivered with anticipation, wondering what he would say. "How do you think your aunt would react to seeing you like that? After all, she's a pillar of the community. Do you really think that she'll let you live at her house after a video like that gets out? Especially given her standing in the church."

Trey stalked toward me and caressed my jaw before turning my face toward his. "No, I don't think that her aunt would let her stay there after that. Poor rich girl. How does it feel to have everything stripped away, piece by piece?" He traced his bottom lip with his tongue. "There is that assembly on Monday that the entire campus has to go to. It would be a shame if that videotape were accidentally played."

"Why?" My question came out barely above a whisper and any false bravado I had faded. The knowledge that there was a videotape of that night slowly sank in. They were right. Regina would kick me out without a second thought if she saw what they had done. Forget the fact that they had blackmailed me into it. She wouldn't care. She had already made comments about "keeping my legs closed." Having actual verification would just fan the fire.

Trey's fingers dug into my skin and all traces of the apathy that were usually present dissolved. "Why not?"

My mind reeled as I tried to come up with some way to convince them not to release the information. There was still a chance that my professor would see that the grade had been tampered with. Or I could potentially somehow convince the guys to change it back. "What do you want from me?"

Cam took a step back. "Just because I want to break you doesn't mean that I don't want to play with you still, little ghost. Remember that you're ours."

Niko bit my earlobe and I could feel how hard he was against my ass. "I suggest that you run."

He shoved me, and I froze before finally turning on my heel and running.

The last thing that I wanted was for them to release the tape that would strip the last thing I had left from me. I didn't really enjoy living with Regina and I didn't exactly trust her, but I didn't have a lot of choices.

My shoes caught on roots and brambles as I ran in the darkness, further and further from the party that was happening somewhere in the distance. The light from the bonfire was long gone, as was any illumination from streetlights or houses. My eyes struggled to adjust in the shadows, everything cast in tones of gray. The muscles in my legs screamed at me as my feet padded along the silty dirt. Thunder rumbled in the distance, ratcheting up my heart rate further, and sweat trickled down my back. The skin on my thighs burned, as did my lungs from running.

Every part of me felt like flames as I slowed my approach. Between the adrenaline and tea, I almost wanted them to catch me. The trees that dotted the ancient cemetery were thick in this part, their limbs barren and black against the night sky. I rested against the trunk of one close to me, trying to catch my breath and listen for the sound of footsteps or snapping twigs. It was completely silent save for an owl in the distance. The heavy beat of the band was completely lost. A branch snapped somewhere nearby, and I pressed my hand over my mouth, hoping to stifle the sound of my uneven breaths. Slowly, I backed away with my heart galloping against my ribs.

Walking backward was a mistake. I stumbled, falling onto my ass. A laugh echoed among the trees and I scrambled backward, trying to regain my footing. I spun around, running blindly. Hands grabbed me around the waist and pushed me to the ground. Burning pain seared the skin of my legs as the earth cut into me while the weight of one of the guys pressed me further into the dirt. "I think that you're just as fucked up as us," a deep voice whispered in my ear.

I hadn't expected Trey to be the one to catch me. He was always the one who seemed completely indifferent to my existence. I mean, he had helped me a few times when I needed it like with my car, but other than that. Still, as I lay beneath him, my cheek pressed against old leaves, my skin heated as I inhaled his musky amber scent. A tear trickled down my cheek against my will, a reminder of the adrenaline that was coursing through every inch of my body. "What are you going to do to me?"

His tongue flicked out, licking the tear. "Don't worry, pretty girl. Only what you truly want me to." His teeth nipped at my ear and he rustled behind me. A click sounded near my ear and a sharp point kissed the exposed skin of my back. "Are you going to be a good girl who stays still when I release you, or am I going to chase you again?"

I didn't reply as I tried to slow my breathing. I was going to run again, but I didn't want him to know that. His weight eased off of me and he kneeled beside me, his hands slowly brushing up my legs. The point of the knife traveled along the inside of my thighs before slicing through the fabric of my underwear. "Every time," I muttered to myself, and his palm landed against my ass.

"If it were up to me, you wouldn't ever wear underwear," he murmured and pressed a kiss to the stinging skin. He shifted behind me and I took it as my chance to escape. I wasn't running because I was scared of him, even though I probably should have been. It was the idea of resistance. Just because I agreed to it didn't mean that I shouldn't fight back. There was nowhere else in my life that I could, no one else I could fight with.

I scrambled to my feet and took off running, the cool night air brushing against every intimate part of my body while the scrapes on my skin screamed at me. I looked behind me out of habit, trying to gauge whether Trey was catching up to me. The breath was knocked out of me when I ran into a hard wall of muscle and arms banded around me. "I knew you were going to run again. You like this as much as I do," Niko whispered, darkness lining his tone. One hand grabbed the ass cheek that still throbbed from Trey and I moaned against him as electricity shot through my skin.

He was right, and so was Trey. I did like it and I was just as fucked up as they were, if not more. Despite everything they had done, I was attracted to them and I hated myself for it. Niko's mouth was punishing as it sought entrance to mine. His teeth bit at my lips and tongue. Frustration at my life bled through as I gripped his biceps and dug my nails in. I caught his lower lip between my teeth and bit down hard until copper flooded my mouth.

He groaned against me and grabbed my hair, pulling my face away from him. "I like that you try to play rough, Ivy. I think it turns you on." He spun me around and shoved me against a tree, my face pushed against the rough bark and his body pressed into my back. Two sets of footsteps approached as Niko reached beneath my skirt, running his fingers through my folds. "Your cunt is always so wet and greedy for us."

Cam cleared his throat and leaned casually against the tree, his head propped against his elbow. "That's because her body knows who owns it." His hand joined Niko's beneath my skirt as he plunged two fingers inside of me. Niko circled my clit as Cam pumped in and out. I gasped and laid my head against Niko's shoulder, using his body as an anchor to the world.

"Here's what I think should happen. The other night, when the two of you were fucking, we didn't get a good view of Ivy," Cam stated, his tone cold even as he curled his fingers inside of me. Niko's motions faltered and his body tensed behind me. Cam chuckled to himself. "Don't worry, Niko. You didn't think that you could keep it a secret from me, did you?"

Cam's other hand squeezed my breast through the fabric before he grabbed Niko's shirt, pulling him closer. His lips ghosted over Niko's. They were both so close that I could feel their breaths against my skin. "But both you and me have had a turn with our little ghost. I think it's time that Trey had a turn, don't you think?" He turned his face toward me slightly and licked along the wounded skin of my bottom lip, his eyes dancing with amusement. "Do you think you deserve to come?"

I closed my eyes, choosing not to answer that as Niko's fingers circled the sensitive nub. My walls clenched around Cam's fingers and my muscles tightened. Just when I thought I was going to get off, Cam removed his hand and gripped Niko's wrist. "Not until she's earned it."

My body slumped against the tree trunk, every inch an inferno of lust and anger. He had just denied me an orgasm after chasing me through the woods. After tormenting me since the beginning of the semester. I raised my hand to hit him, but he caught it and pulled me against his body. "Don't you dare, little ghost. I'll let you get off if you're a good girl." He tugged the hem of my shirt and pulled it over my head before pushing me toward Trey, who was sitting against the base of a tree five feet away, his pants pushed around his thighs. Cam's arm was thrown around Niko's torso, holding him in place.

I wasn't sure what I was doing as I straddled Trey. With more gentleness than I thought was possible from the three of them, Trey's hands gripped my hips and guided me, slowly sinking me onto his cock. "Just move your hips, new girl," he whispered in my ear. "This is as much about punishing Niko as it is about you. Just focus on me and I'll make sure you feel good."

And I did. It was easy to get lost as the edges of reality faded as I rolled my hips against him while his lips traced along my collarbones. "Why is Niko being punished?" I whispered to where only he could hear.

"Because Cam is in love with him... and you. They've never had secrets before and you're destroying the three of us." He thrust his hips up into me, his pelvis hitting my clit.

"Fuck, just like that," I whimpered.

His arm wrapped around my waist, tethering me to him, and he picked up the knife laying on the ground beside him, placing the handle in his mouth for a moment. He pulled it out with a pop. "Do you trust me?"

"Not a chance in hell."

He smirked at me as the handle of the knife disappeared from sight. "Close your eyes then and just feel."

My head fell onto his shoulder as he slowed his motions momentarily. Something warm and wet dripped down my back and across my ass. The tight ring of muscle that no one had ever touched before was being circled by something cold and hard. I gasped at him and tensed, but slowly it eased inside, burning and stretching me. The sensation of fullness was painful, yet somehow amazing. "Tell me you just didn't–"

His mouth captured mine as he roughly rammed upward, stealing my words. Every thrust hit my clit. When he finally pulled his mouth away, he grinned. "Don't overthink it, new girl." My fingers wove into his hair as he pushed the handle to the knife further in. The hand that had been gripping my hip cupped my cheek, and he turned my face as his hips rolled beneath me.

Standing fifteen feet away, Niko was on his knees with his eyes closed and Cam's cock in his mouth. Cam's eyes locked on mine in the dim light and Trey brushed his nose up the column of my neck. "There are worse punishments out there, Ivy. Remember that."

By the time the Forsaken were done with me, Rosalyn had left the party and the band was long gone. The guys said nothing as we trudged through the cemetery. Dirt was caked on my skin, and every muscle in my body screamed at me. I picked leaves out of my hair as I wondered why my skin felt so sticky. As we neared the parking lot, I glanced down, realizing what the warm, wet feeling had been. Blood. I looked like I had been an extra for a horror movie. My mouth fell open, and I punched Trey's shoulder. "You've got to be shitting me."

"That's not what you said fifteen minutes ago. In fact, it was something like 'Oh, God, Trey. Don't stop.'" He fake moaned and then winked at me. "Let me know if you ever need a repeat, new girl."

Cam

All weekend, we discussed what we were going to do during the assembly. The timing, what exactly we were looking for, and how we were going to break in. The administrative offices were closing early that day and it would give us ample time to look through Wells' files without getting caught. We would still have to be careful, but a few hours of uninterrupted time in the dean's office. Usually, there was at least one person working until late in the evening or people milling around campus that would see us. Not this time.

Niko stood at the heavy double doors and picked the lock while Trey and I kept lookout. It was unlikely that anyone would venture this far from the auditorium, but it was a precautionary measure. The days were getting shorter now and by the time we left, the night would help to conceal our exit.

Adrenaline pumped through my veins, setting me on edge, and when Niko disappeared inside the building, it was time to get to work. Looking for something to blackmail the dean with was infinitely more interesting than sitting through a presentation about a collegiate honor society, especially one that we had sat through for the past three years. With Ivy's actual grades, she should have received a letter from the college, but not now.

We walked into Wells' office and flipped on a flashlight, heading to his desk. Inside the top three drawers were literally nothing but office supplies and old sticky notes. Niko dug through a set of filing cabinets, looking for anything that could be of use to us. Trey turned on his computer while I sifted through the contents, finding nothing of use.

We worked quietly in the dim light. The only noise was the click of keys from the computer or the rustle of papers. We moved methodically as we sifted through the contents of the office. Finally, I caught a break. The bottom right drawer was locked, and I tried to wiggle it, hoping the lock would magically pop. Niko sighed at me. "Move over, asshole."

I watched as he inserted a small lock pick, his fingers carefully twisting until he heard a click. He stepped aside, and I kneeled down, curious about what the locked drawer would hold. Two manilla envelopes laid in the bottom of the drawer and I held my breath as I carefully opened the first. Inside were photos of the guys and me digging a hole deep in the middle of the woods. Beside us lay a blue tarp with sneakers that peeked out at the end. That was the last time I had trusted Vincent and how Abraham Wells managed to weasel his way into our lives.

I stared down at my phone, trying to decide what to do. Fucking experimental drugs and fucking David Hyde. The guy had always been the life of the party and pushed too much too fast. He was the guy who stood on top of tables wearing his stupid cowboy hat, singing old country and western songs at the top of his lungs. Women loved him and everyone laughed at his jokes, but he had one problem.

David loved cocaine more than he loved life itself.

When he'd heard that we had new shit, he swore he would take it easy. None of us had any idea how it would impact anyone. After the party cleared, he came to me sweaty and pale. I knew something wasn't right.

And then he collapsed.

Niko had checked him for a pulse, but there was nothing and there was no way in hell I was calling the cops. They would find all the drugs on David and us and my life would be over. I wouldn't take the fall for whatever dumb shit had happened tonight.

Finally, I settled on calling Vincent. I put the phone on speakerphone and waited for him to answer. "What do you want?"

What a way for him to answer the phone. "We've got a problem. Someone took the new shit you're pushing and now I'm staring at a dead body."

Vincent huffed out an audible breath. "Fine. Load it up in your trunk and I'll meet you over near Tyburn Hill."

After wrapping David in a blue tarp that Niko kept in his trunk, we drove toward Tyburn Hill and waited for Vincent to tell us what in the fuck he wanted us to do. Headlights blinded me from behind and I stepped out of the vehicle, waiting.

Abraham Wells exited from the passenger side of the car, a gun in one hand and his phone in the other. "It looks like you three are in a bit of a predicament." He motioned to *us with the gun. "Mr. Stone, I believe you should grab the shovel from my trunk. Move slowly and I might let you live."*

Vincent finally turned off the car and slammed his door shut. "Abraham, we've talked about this before. You can't shoot my guys just because you feel like it."

He scoffed at the younger man, his weapon trained on Niko the entire time. "Who would really miss the three of them, Vinnie? No one."

Vincent shrugged, and his lips quirked with amusement. "Yeah, but they're loyal. It's hard to train young guys." I balled my hands into fists, trying to let their words roll over me. "Isn't that right, Camden? Blood in and blood out."

I passed it to Trey before turning my attention to the second envelope.

Niko's eyes widened as the sound of heavy doors slamming echoed outside of the office. He shoved my shoulder and mouthed, "what the fuck?" Trey clicked on the keyboard until I tugged on his shirt. The three of us dropped to the floor behind the desk and I scrambled to shove myself underneath it.

My heart pounded in my ears as steps grew closer to the door. It opened and light spread across the office space. I swallowed, getting ready to spring into action. "They must have forgotten to lock up," a deep male voice muttered. Keys jingled as the door closed again and I relaxed, laying my head back against the wood of the desk.

"Well, that was close," Niko mumbled, taking the envelope from my hands. He slowly opened it and pulled out its contents. His face paled as he examined each one and I wondered what in the fuck it was he was seeing.

Niko

Time stopped as the photos tumbled from the envelope. Every one of them was of Ivy. They started out innocently enough. Her at parties with her father, holding a crystal glass in between well-manicured fingers. Slowly, they morphed into something else. Men stood around a poker table, but instead of cards, Ivy lay in the middle. She wasn't present at the moment it was taken; the vacant look on her face said she had checked out before then. Her eyes were glassy and limp hands fell off the edge of the table. The dress she had been wearing in earlier photos was pushed up past her waist and the straps pulled down below her breasts, exposing her to the men in the photos. Her legs were spread wide. Each of the photos showed a different old man with a potbelly and shriveled up dick using her like she was nothing more than a rag doll.

I stared at the photos in my hands, trying to quell the wave of nausea that threatened me. She had been passed around at one of their parties, the same way I was.

It was difficult to see the identity of the men in the pictures, but they all had one thing in common. Each had a scar on their forearm. They were all members of the

Order. My breaths had grown ragged. "What the fuck?" I muttered before gagging.

I turned the picture over. On the back, in neat cursive, someone had written, "My little lamb. Age sixteen." I still didn't know all the details, but this was why Abraham Wells was obsessed with her. This was why he wanted her to take tea and why he wanted me to steer clear.

I ground my teeth as I stared at them, wondering if Ivy had any clue about what had happened to her. She had thought she was a virgin when she met us, but they had used her like she was a piece of trash to pass around. Suddenly I wanted to talk to her and ask her questions about what she remembered, but doing so would out my own secrets.

Maybe one day.

I shoved the pictures back in the envelope and handed them to Cam before standing. Sweat beaded on my brow as I leaned against the wall for support. A heavy hand landed on my back and rubbed gentle circles. "Let's get the fuck out of here. We got what we came for."

"Don't use those to blackmail Wells, Cam. We've done enough to her."

Cam nodded as he took my keys from me and I settled into the backseat of the car. The entire ride home, the images that I had seen haunted me. Even the cool glass beneath my cheek did nothing to stop the thoughts that tumbled through my head. Whatever vendetta Cam had against Ivy had to stop. She had suffered enough under our hands.

When we got home, Maya was sitting on the couch, her lips pursed. She stood and shoved against Cam's chest. "You're an asshole."

Cam looked confused as he stumbled back. "What?"

"I saw what you posted on YouConnect."

Apprehension clawed at my heart as I sat in the auditorium. I had taken the last of the pills in the box that had been left on my pillow in the restroom before walking inside. Saturday night, the guys claimed they would keep the recording of me to themselves as long as I did what I was told, but now I was worried they had changed the terms of the agreement. It wouldn't be the first time something like that had happened. After all, Cam had initially wanted me to vanish from Clearhaven, but instead, things twisted into something else entirely.

My muscles still ached and my skin stung from the abrasions I'd gotten on Saturday night. That evening, I'd managed to sneak past Regina into the bathroom without her saying a word. The jets from the shower burned my skin as I scrubbed it raw, trying to clean the debris, dirt, and blood from my body. I swore to myself that I would never allow Ros to convince me to go to another party every again. Every time, something seemed to happen.

I should have hated the three of them with their perfect smiles and how they tormented me, but I didn't, at least not entirely. I was attracted to them and something inside of my mind was stuck on the idea of what could have been. They weren't entirely bad. I saw that in small glimpses, like when they took care of me. Niko who played guitar quietly in a graveyard and Trey, who had found me on the side of the road. Hell, even with Cam's fierce loyalty to his sister.

But as I sat there clutching the arms of my seat, I realized I didn't trust them.

Rosalyn was absent, and I texted her, hoping that she was just running late. The dean took the stage and tapped the microphone, ensuring that it was on. "I'd like to thank you all for coming. As you know, academics are a vital portion of..." I zoned him out and stared down at my feet, counting down the seconds until I could leave. "And now, without further ado, I'd like to play a short film about the history of Clearhaven University."

The lights dimmed around us and I settled in, thinking anything was better than listening to Abraham Wells drone on. I was clearly wrong. The first minute was full of clips of smiling students and flowers that grew on campus, but then it changed. Gasps lit up the entire auditorium as I watched with horror at the film playing on the screen. They had done it even after telling me they wouldn't. My face was feverish with embarrassment. From the angle of the camera, you couldn't see Caleb tied to a chair, but it was obvious that it was me kneeling as Cam thrust into my mouth. I sat there horrified as people turned to face me. Low murmuring started and people nudged the people next to them, pointing in my direction. None of the faculty moved to stop the film. "Remember how I told you I was going to mark you so that everyone would see you were ours?"

Before I knew what I was doing, I leaped out of my chair and bolted to the door. My life in Clearhaven was over. My aunt would see the video and kick me out if someone hadn't already texted her. I raced to the parking lot, my hands shaking as I fumbled to pull out my keys.

I didn't know where I would go, but anywhere would be better than here. I peeled out of the parking lot and headed north, pushing the speed limit. The sun was already setting, but that was fine. Who needed sleep?

Tears trickled down my cheeks as the film played on repeat in my mind, along with the whispers and looks. They had broken their word and betrayed me. As I recalled Cam's words from Saturday, a sob erupted from deep inside of me, crushing whatever had been left of my heart. "I promise you that you will always have something left to lose."

Fuck them.

Blue and red lights flashed behind me as I approached the city limit and I gaze at my speedometer. Eighty-one. I slowed the car and pulled over on the shoulder, praying that the cop would take mercy on me. He approached the vehicle with a hand on his weapon and I wiped my cheeks on my sleeve as I rolled down the window.

"Miss, I need you to step out of the car for me." I raised my eyebrows at him in confusion. Typically, with a routine traffic stop, he would ask to see my license and registration. "Now."

Hesitantly, I unbuckled my seat belt and removed myself from the car. "Turn around and put your hands behind your back." My brain was screaming at me that this wasn't right. Something was off, but I ignored it. I was just on edge from everything that had happened. Surely, after he searched the car and found nothing in it, he'd let me go with a ticket.

Metal clicked around my wrists, securing my hands behind my back, and he led me to his unmarked car. His partner that I hadn't seen until that moment opened the trunk and that was when I realized I needed to fight. Something about the whole situation was wrong. I thrashed against the hands holding me, trying to force me closer to the trunk, but the partner prowled closer and I saw it. In his hand was a needle. "Please, don't do this," I cried. They ignored me as he stabbed me in the neck and depressed the plunger. He tossed it to the side of the road before lifting my feet.

The officer behind me lifted my torso. "You really should save your energy. You're going to need it."

I kicked at him, hoping that they would drop me, but it didn't do any good. They deposited me inside the cramped trunk and slammed the hood. The last thing I heard before losing consciousness was, "Don't worry, Mr. Vance. We got her."

Caleb

F lames crackled in the stone fireplace in front of the leather settee, and embers flew into the air. Casually, I brushed my fingers through dark brown curls, allowing them to linger for a moment. My grandfather was busy in his study meeting with Abraham Wells and Deacon Jensen about god knows what while I nursed the scotch in my glass, waiting for a text message.

Rosalyn's head lay on my lap, entranced by the fire. "Any word yet?" she asked, not bothering to turn toward me.

My fingers stalled as my phone notified me I had a text message.

Q: I've taken care of it.

I took a drink of the smoky liquid before responding. "Yeah, it's done."

She sighed and pulled her knees closer to her chest. "Do you think that she'll know it was us?"

Ivy Spencer was a complication that I had never imagined appearing in my life. Despite knowing that I should push her away, she occupied more of my waking thoughts than I cared to admit. I picked up one of Rosalyn's curls between my thumb and forefinger, examining it absentmindedly. "Let's hope not."

Acknowledgments

I don't really know where to begin with this... time to awkwardly bumble through again. First and foremost, I'd like to thank my family bc ... you guys have eaten straight trash since I started this project. I disappear for days on end into my office AKA the cave never to be seen again. I truly am a possum.

Jess: Thanks for letting me spitball with you and yelling at me through my self-doubt with this book, because there was a ton of it. AND thank you for helping me run a Tiktok and street team!!!

Jacci: Thanks for helping me with my Facebook group and hops... Also for trying to get me organized even though I am a dumpster fire most days and super impulsive.

Next up, I would like to thank everyone who alpha read for me: Jenna, Val, Martha, Chelsea, Danielle, and Amanda. All of you helped me to polish this story, shape it, and mold it into what it is. I made you laugh, cry, and yell at me a few times. You tolerated my what-ifs, ramblings, and the days I dropped six chapters out of nowhere. You guys are the best.

My TikTok and street team: You guys rock. Between NSFW gifs, jokes, and just hyping me up even on my bad days. Thank you so much for sharing #allofthethings!

Nixxie: Thanks for being there for this, even on the darkest of days when the weight of the world was crushing me. Who knew a bad joke about parallel lines would become a friendship?

AND finally, thank you, dear reader. Somehow people continue to read the crazy plots I weave.

Other Works

By Celeste Night

Promises Series

Queen of Clubs

Promise of Embers

Promise of Flames

Promise of Hellfire
Forsaken Series

Flawed Hearts

Foolish Hearts
Standalones

Ties That Bind

Deviant Devotion
Anthologies

Personal Demons

About Celeste Night

Celeste Night detests writing in third person , so....

I am a romance author living somewhere outside of Birmingham, AL with my husband, two children, two dogs, three cats, and a partridge in a pear tree. I studied psychology in undergrad and thought I was going to be a therapist. Even when I was young, I would weave crazy stories and as I grew older dabbled in fan fiction. I never imagined that I would write a novel, much less publish it, so the journey has been amazing!

My relationship with the infamous Mr. Night was ripped straight out of the pages of a book (complete with angst and drama) and one day I might fictionalize that. I love morally gray (sometimes morally black) men and memes. When I'm not plotting imaginary murders or dreaming up my next favorite book boyfriend, I enjoy reading and playing video games (looking at you Stardew Valley). My favorite holiday is Halloween and my favorite color is black. I love possums because I also wake up screaming each morning.

Follow me on social media to stay up to date on my latest projects! Find the links at www.celestenight.com !

Printed in Great Britain
by Amazon